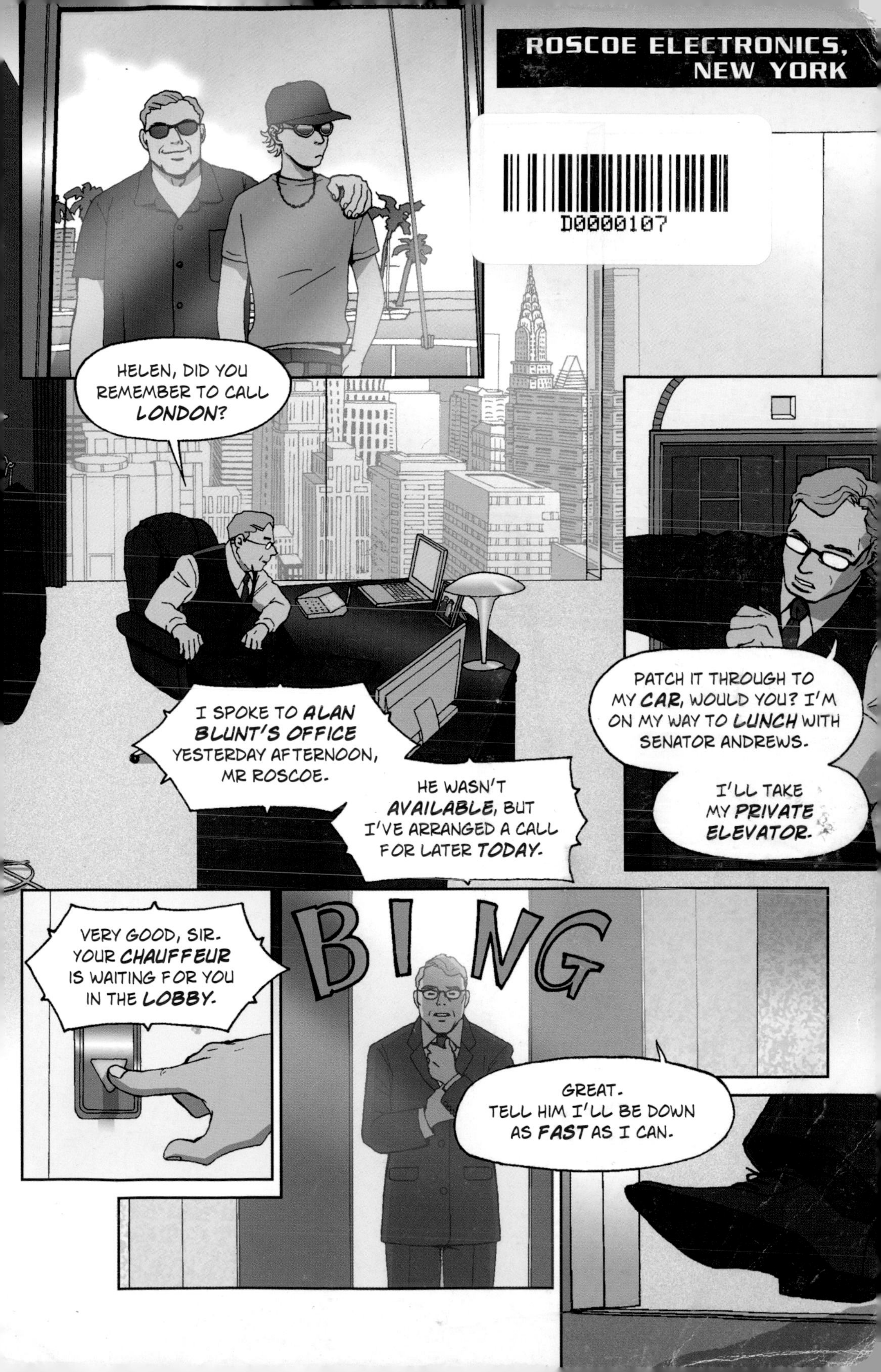
ROSCOE ELECTRONICS, NEW YORK
HELEN, DID YOU REMEMBER TO CALL LONDON?
I SPOKE TO ALAN BLUNT'S OFFICE YESTERDAY AFTERNOON, MR ROSCOE.
HE WASN'T AVAILABLE, BUT I'VE ARRANGED A CALL FOR LATER TODAY.
PATCH IT THROUGH TO MY CAR, WOULD YOU? I'M ON MY WAY TO LUNCH WITH SENATOR ANDREWS.
I'LL TAKE MY PRIVATE ELEVATOR.
VERY GOOD, SIR. YOUR CHAUFFEUR IS WAITING FOR YOU IN THE LOBBY.
BING
GREAT. TELL HIM I'LL BE DOWN AS FAST AS I CAN.

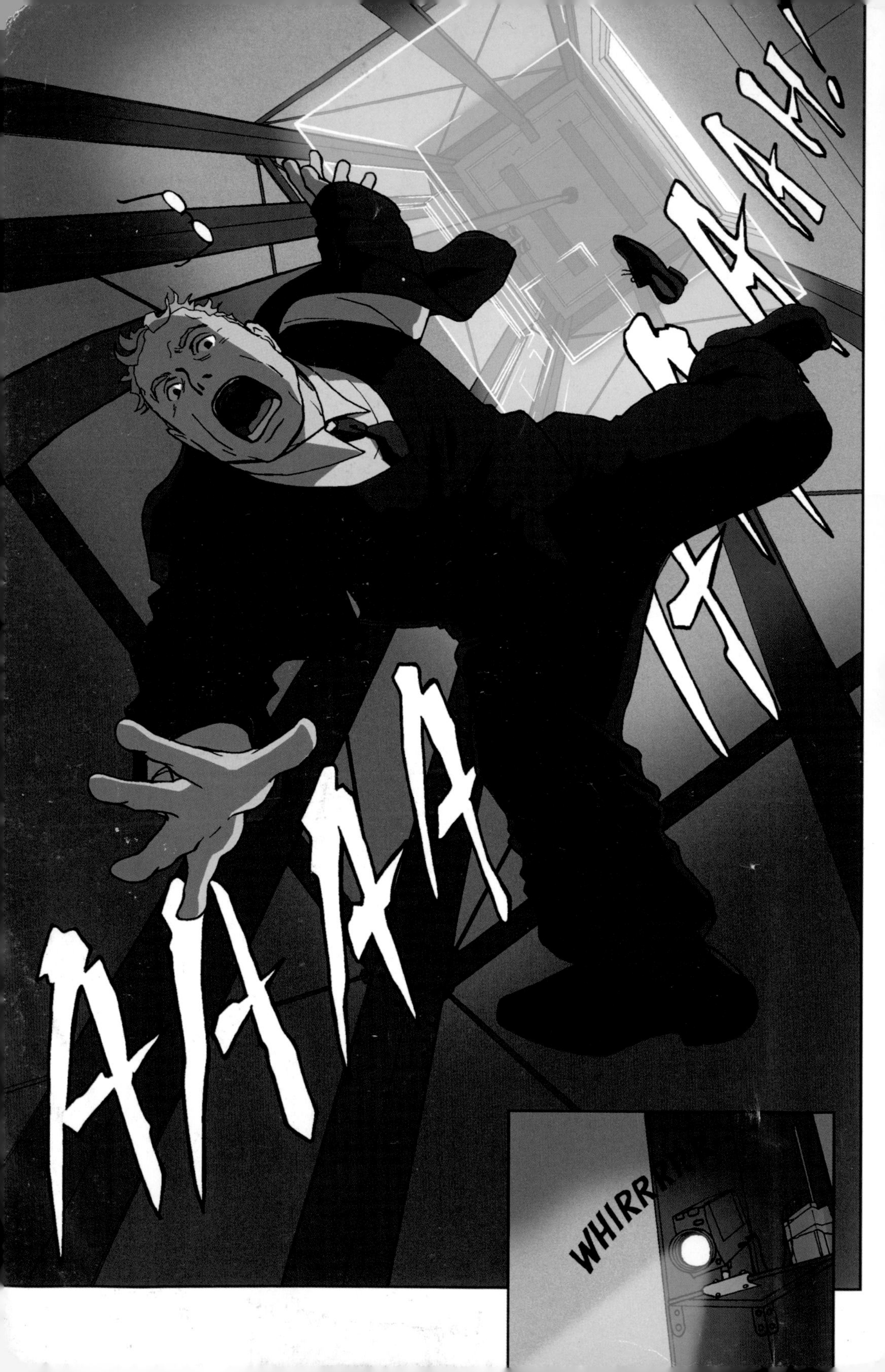
AAAAAAAAH!
WHIRRR

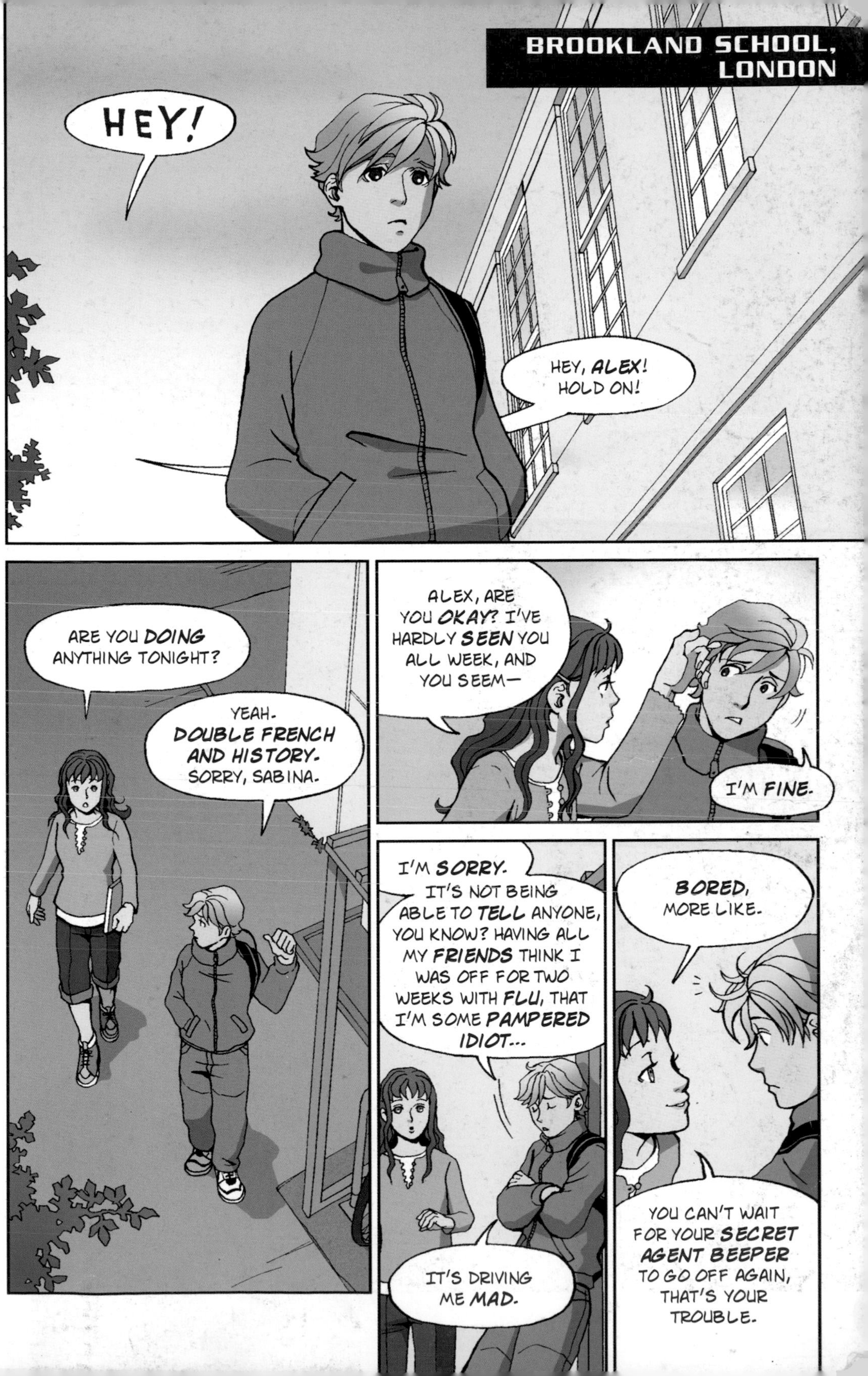
BROOKLAND SCHOOL, LONDON
HEY!
HEY, ALEX! HOLD ON!
ARE YOU DOING ANYTHING TONIGHT?
YEAH. DOUBLE FRENCH AND HISTORY. SORRY, SABINA.
ALEX, ARE YOU OKAY? I'VE HARDLY SEEN YOU ALL WEEK, AND YOU SEEM—
I'M FINE.
I'M SORRY. IT'S NOT BEING ABLE TO TELL ANYONE, YOU KNOW? HAVING ALL MY FRIENDS THINK I WAS OFF FOR TWO WEEKS WITH FLU, THAT I'M SOME PAMPERED IDIOT...
IT'S DRIVING ME MAD.
BORED, MORE LIKE.
YOU CAN'T WAIT FOR YOUR SECRET AGENT BEEPER TO GO OFF AGAIN, THAT'S YOUR TROUBLE.

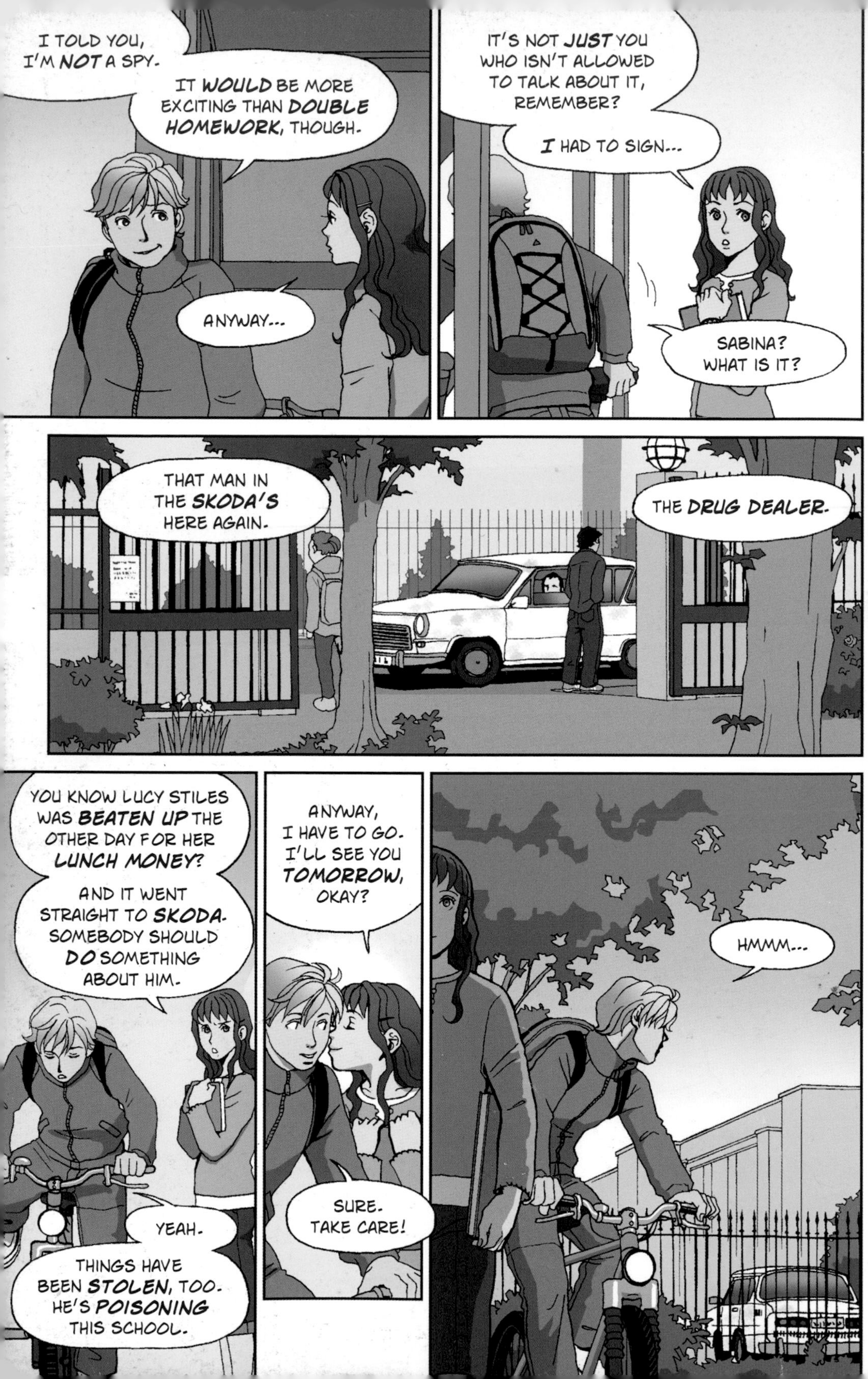
I TOLD YOU, I'M NOT A SPY.
IT WOULD BE MORE EXCITING THAN DOUBLE HOMEWORK, THOUGH.
ANYWAY...
IT'S NOT JUST YOU WHO ISN'T ALLOWED TO TALK ABOUT IT, REMEMBER?
I HAD TO SIGN...
SABINA? WHAT IS IT?
THAT MAN IN THE SKODA'S HERE AGAIN.
THE DRUG DEALER.
YOU KNOW LUCY STILES WAS BEATEN UP THE OTHER DAY FOR HER LUNCH MONEY?
AND IT WENT STRAIGHT TO SKODA. SOMEBODY SHOULD DO SOMETHING ABOUT HIM.
YEAH.
THINGS HAVE BEEN STOLEN, TOO. HE'S POISONING THIS SCHOOL.
ANYWAY, I HAVE TO GO. I'LL SEE YOU TOMORROW, OKAY?
SURE. TAKE CARE!
HMMM...

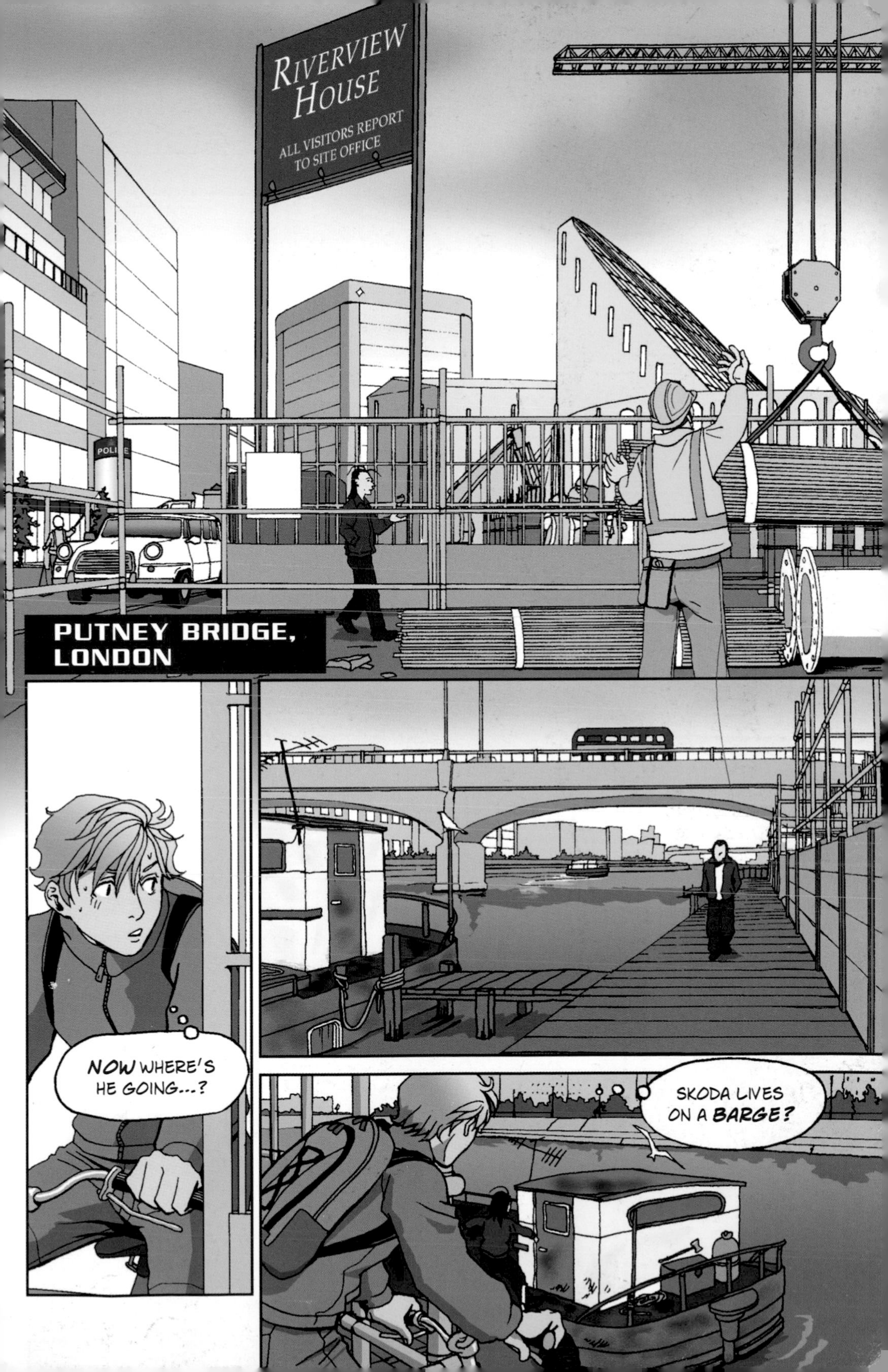
RIVERVIEW HOUSE
ALL VISITORS REPORT TO SITE OFFICE
POLICE
PUTNEY BRIDGE, LONDON
NOW WHERE'S HE GOING...?
SKODA LIVES ON A BARGE?

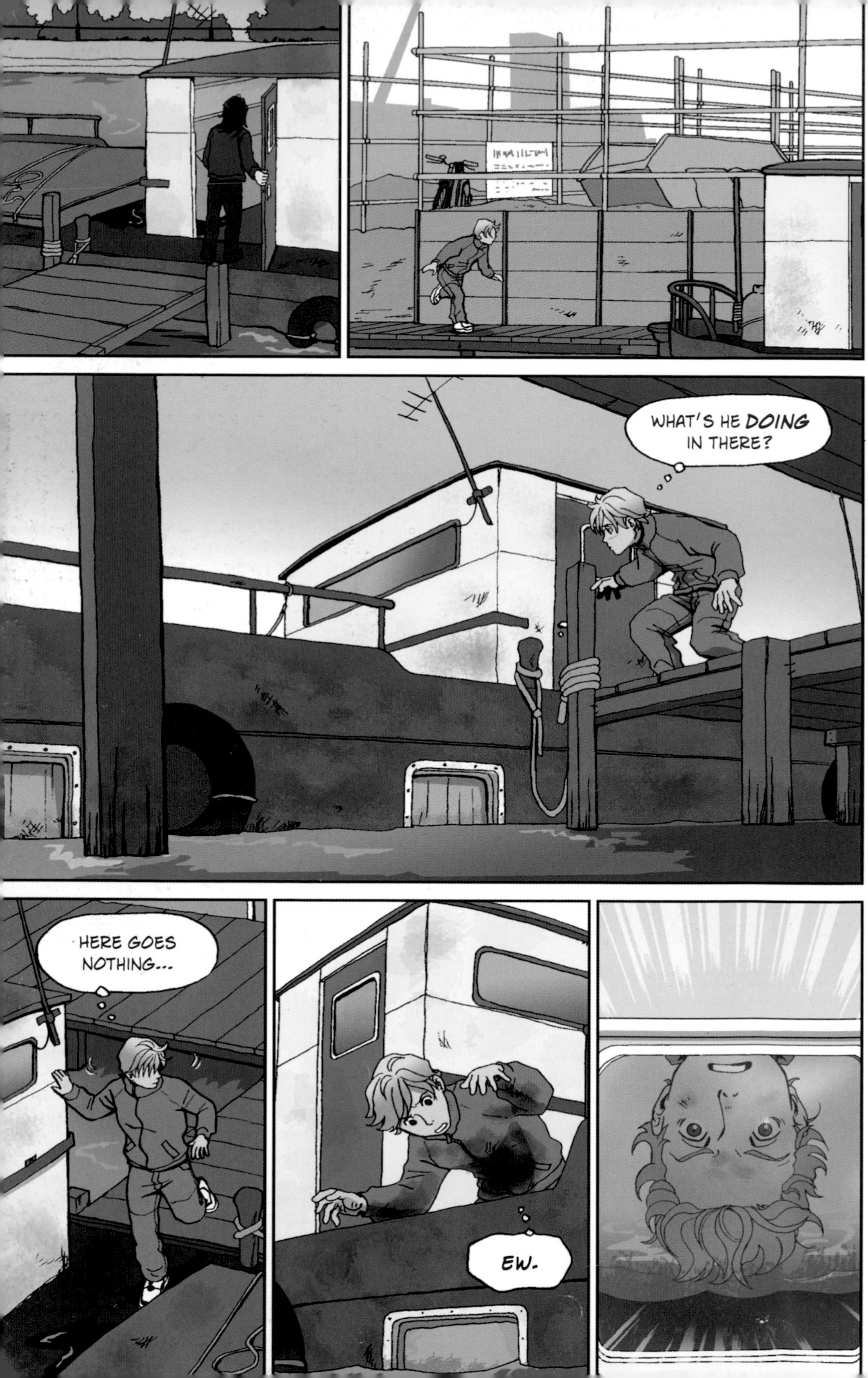
WHAT'S HE DOING IN THERE?
HERE GOES NOTHING...
EW.

SOMEBODY SHOULD *DO* SOMETHING ABOUT HIM.

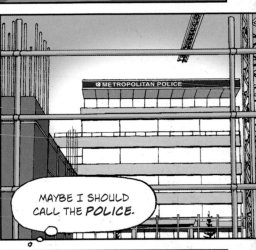

IT'S A FLOATING *DRUGS* FACTORY...!

MAYBE I SHOULD CALL THE *POLICE.*

...

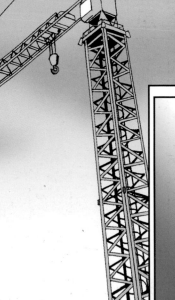

OR BETTER *YET...*

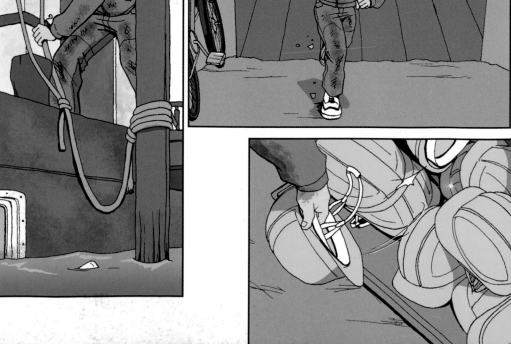

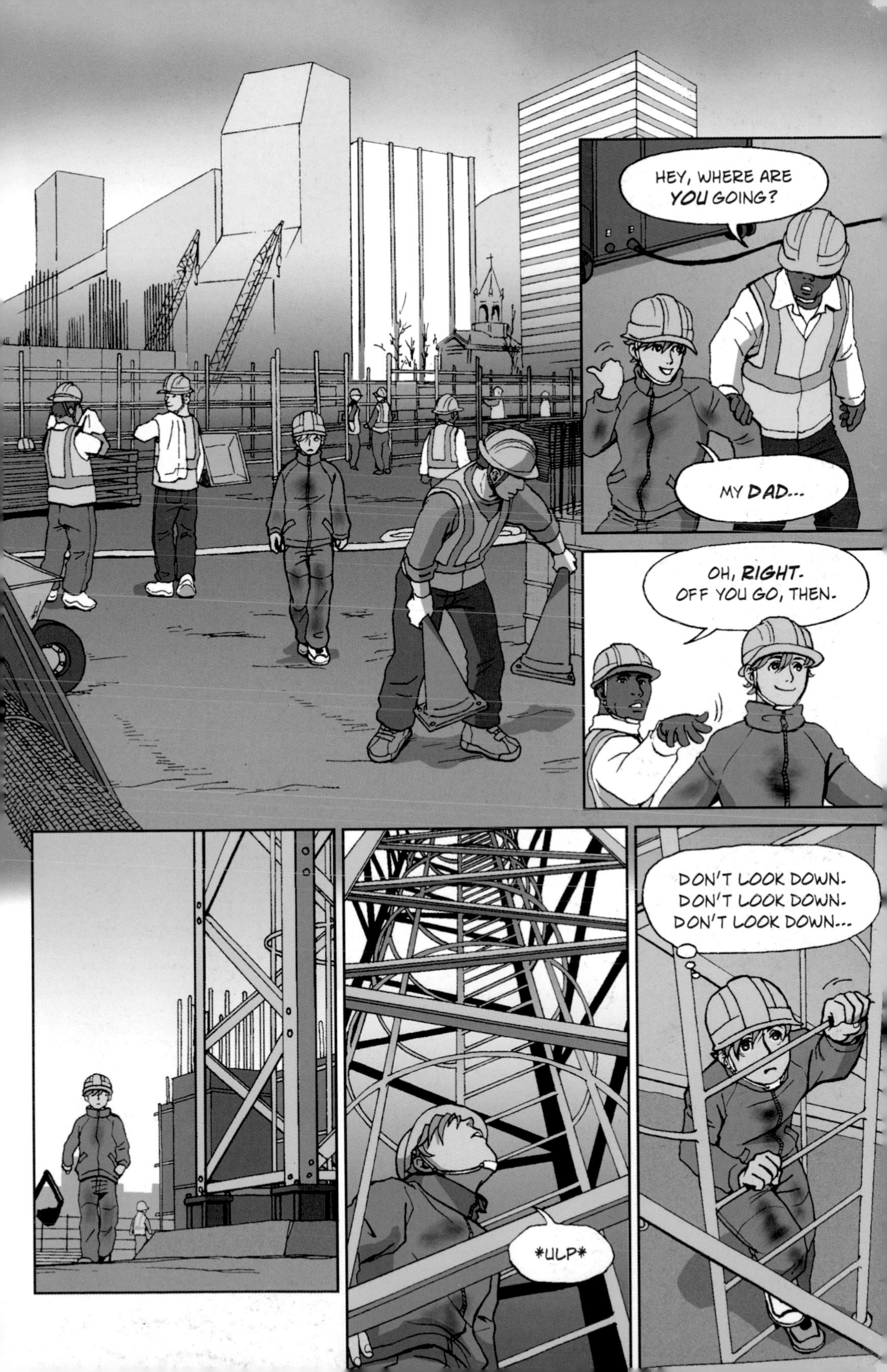
HEY, WHERE ARE YOU GOING?
MY DAD...
OH, RIGHT. OFF YOU GO, THEN.
DON'T LOOK DOWN. DON'T LOOK DOWN. DON'T LOOK DOWN...
ULP

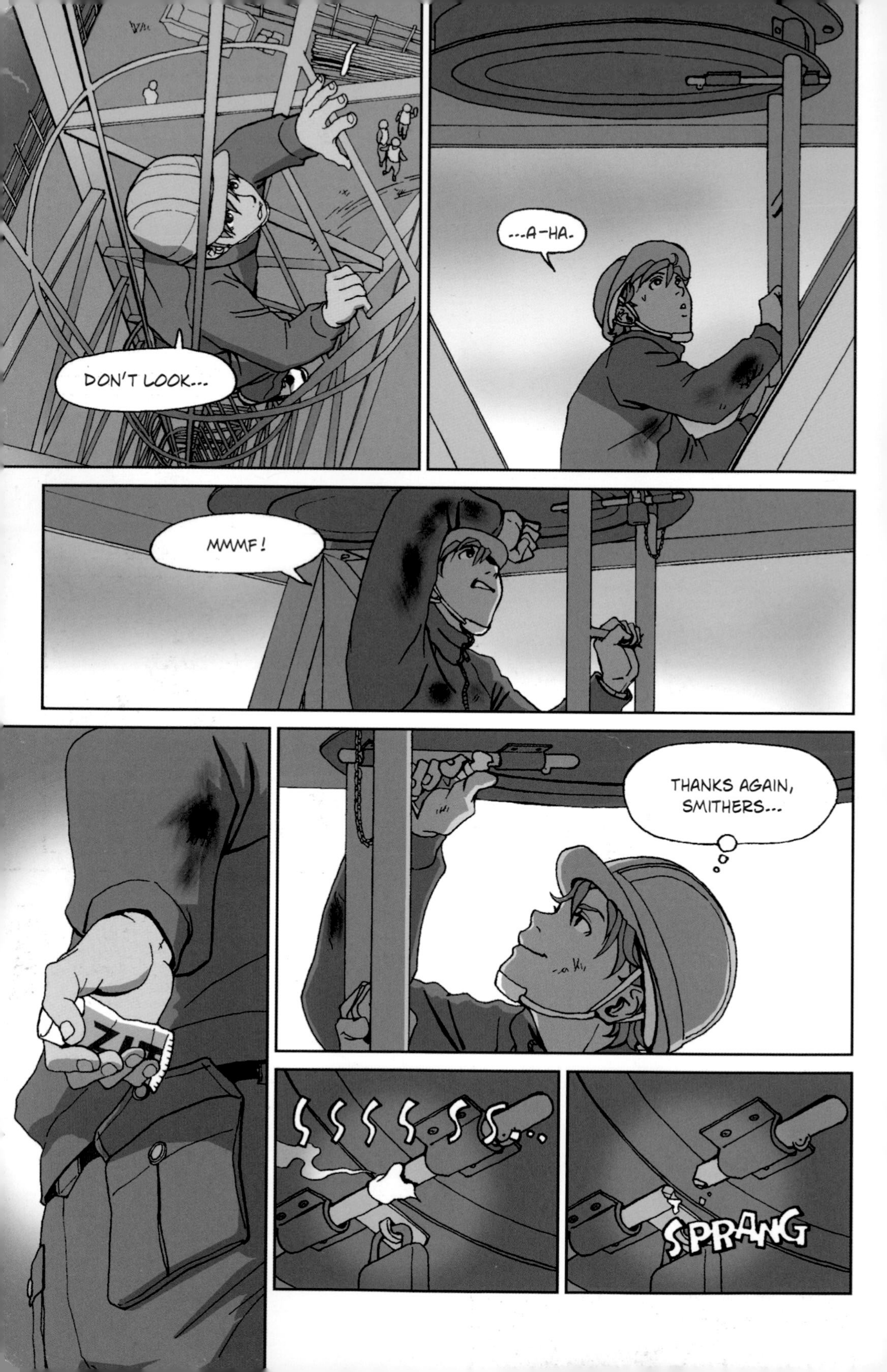
DON'T LOOK...
...A-HA.
MMMF!
THANKS AGAIN, SMITHERS...
ZIT
SPRANG

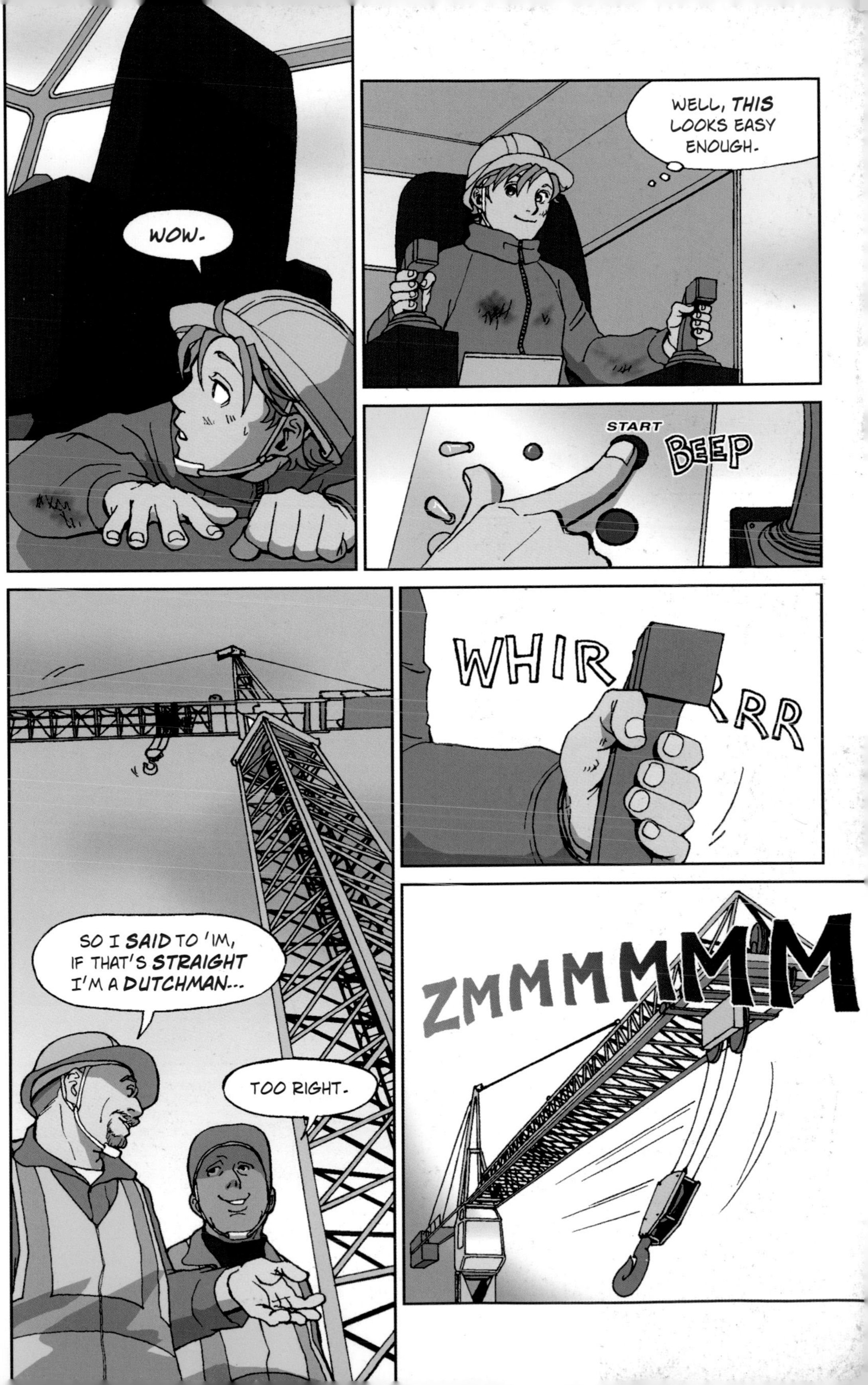
WOW.
WELL, THIS LOOKS EASY ENOUGH.
START
BEEP
WHIRRRR
SO I SAID TO 'IM, IF THAT'S STRAIGHT I'M A DUTCHMAN...
TOO RIGHT.
ZMMMMMMM

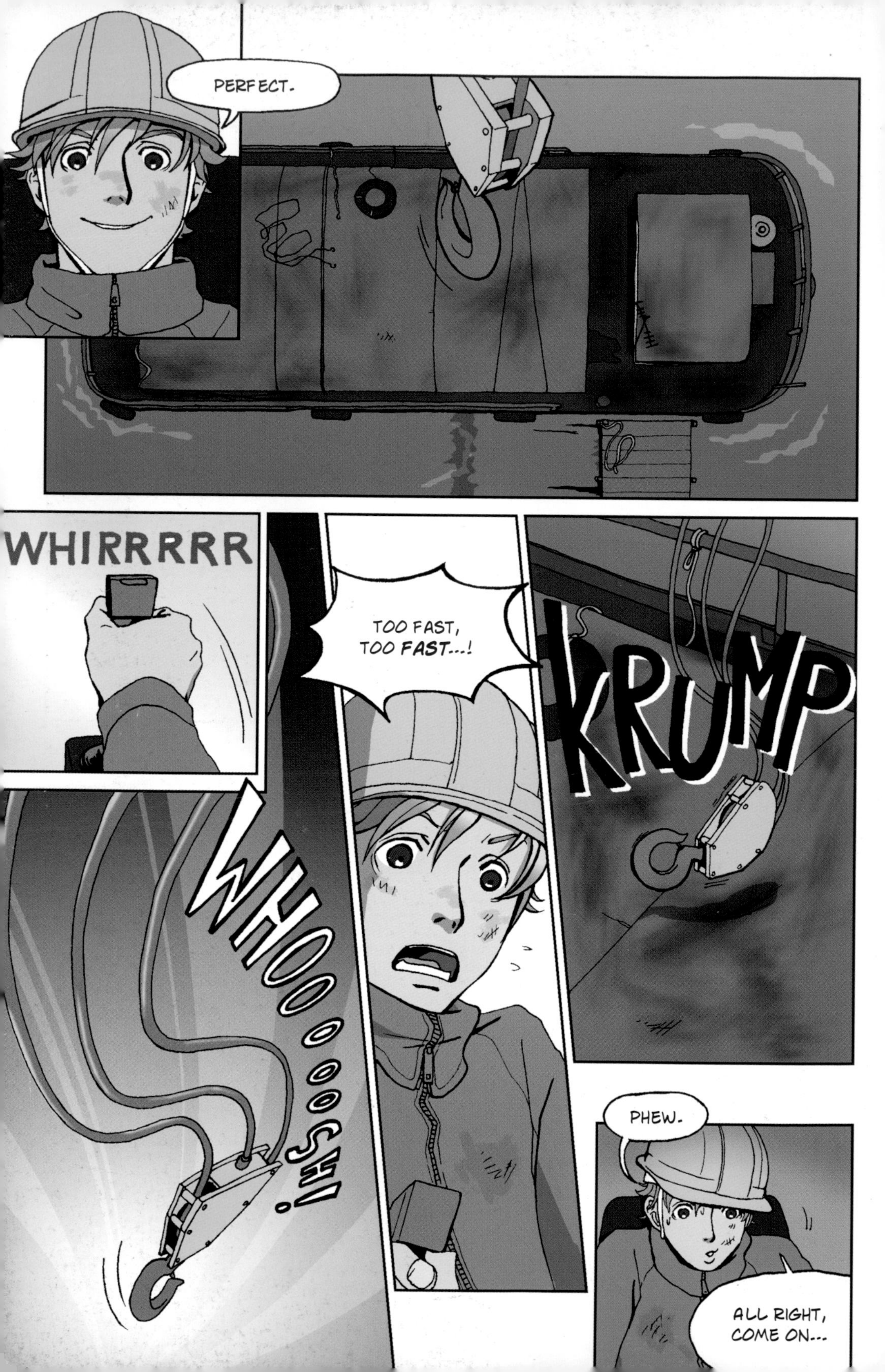
PERFECT.
WHIRRRRR
TOO FAST, TOO FAST...!
KRUMP
WHOOOOOOSH!
PHEW.
ALL RIGHT, COME ON...

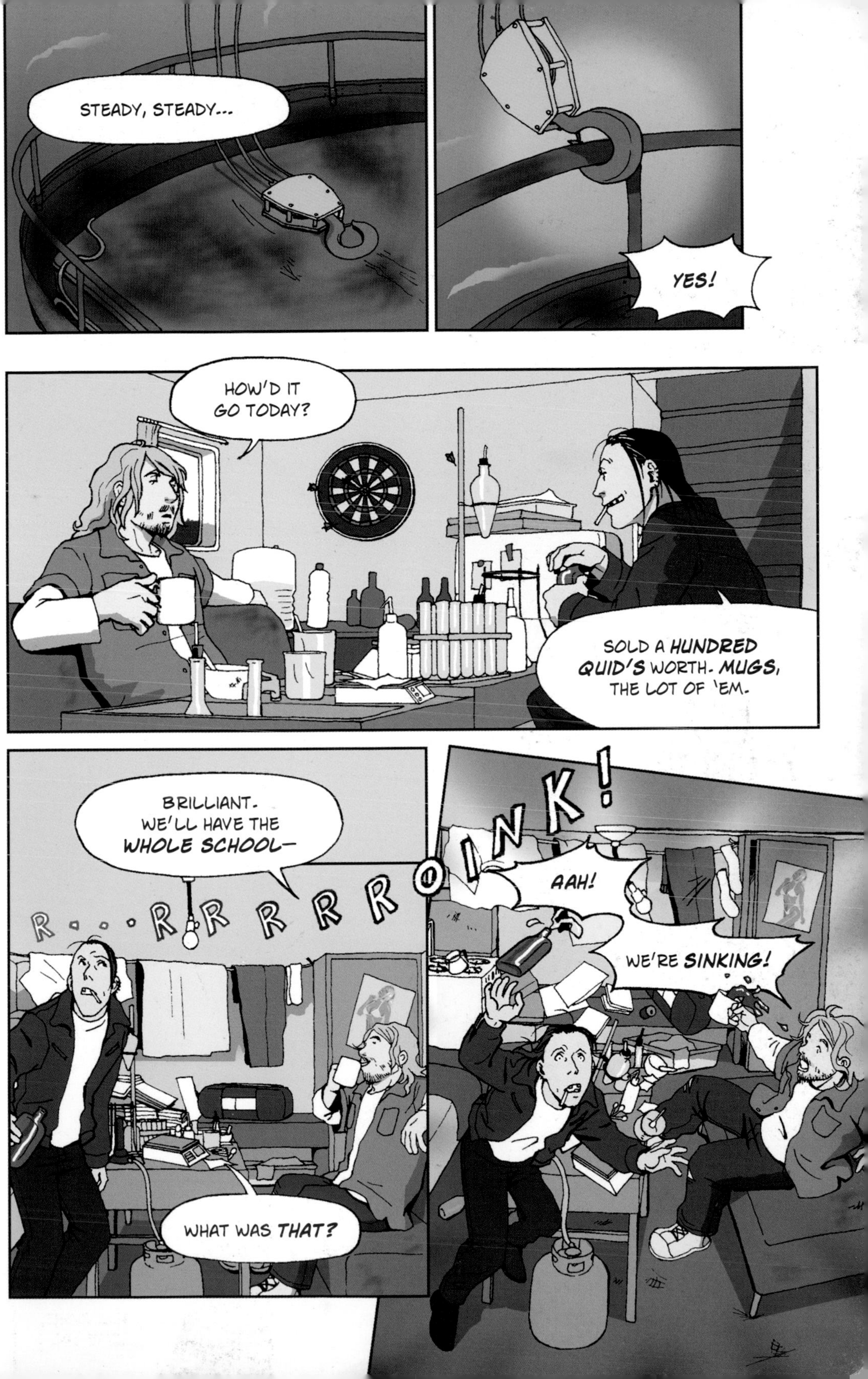
STEADY, STEADY...
YES!
HOW'D IT GO TODAY?
SOLD A HUNDRED QUID'S WORTH. MUGS, THE LOT OF 'EM.
BRILLIANT. WE'LL HAVE THE WHOLE SCHOOL—
R...RRRRROINK!
WHAT WAS THAT?
AAH!
WE'RE SINKING!

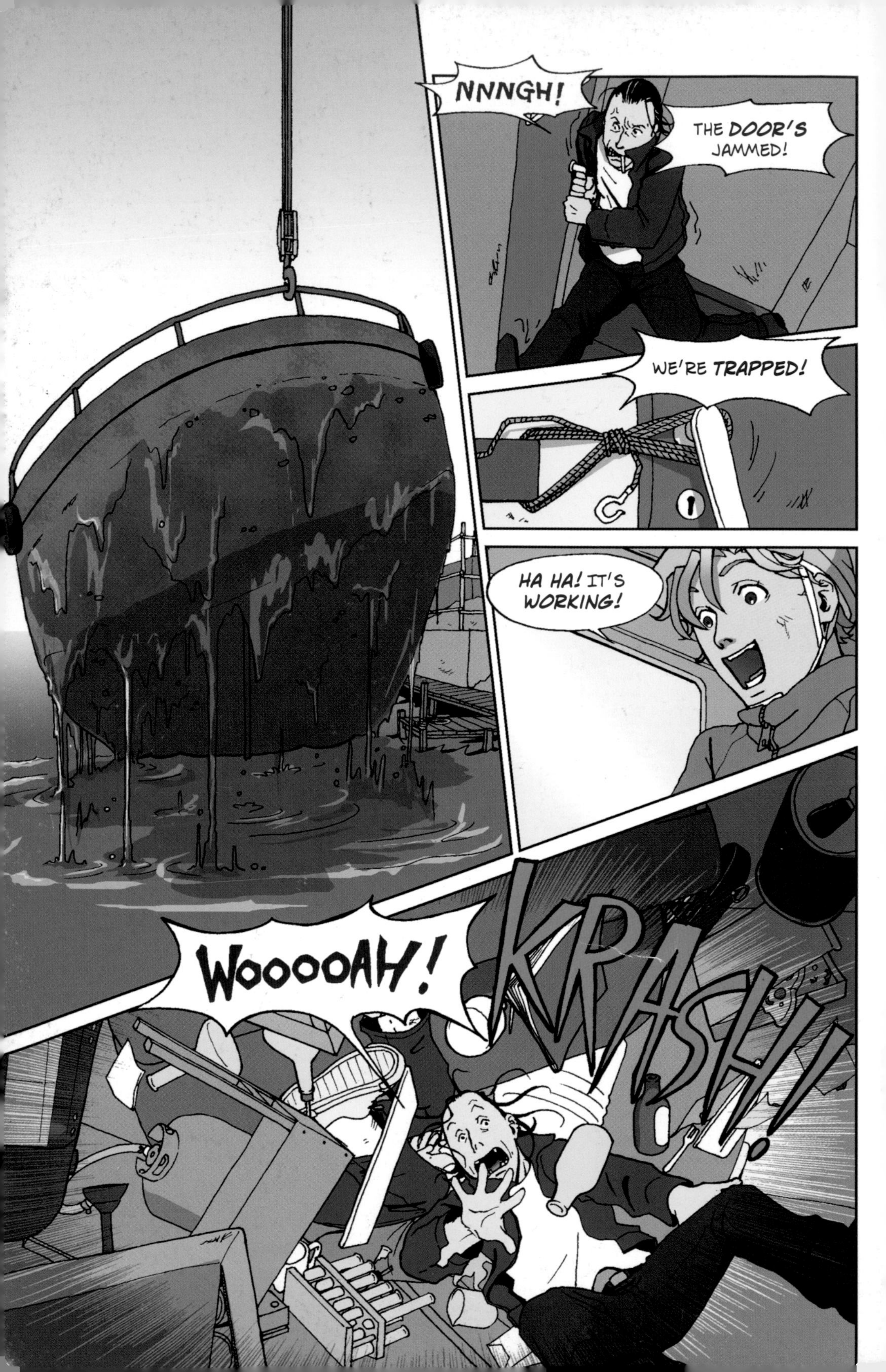
NNNGH!
THE DOOR'S JAMMED!
WE'RE TRAPPED!
HA HA! IT'S WORKING!
WOOOOAH!
KRASH!!

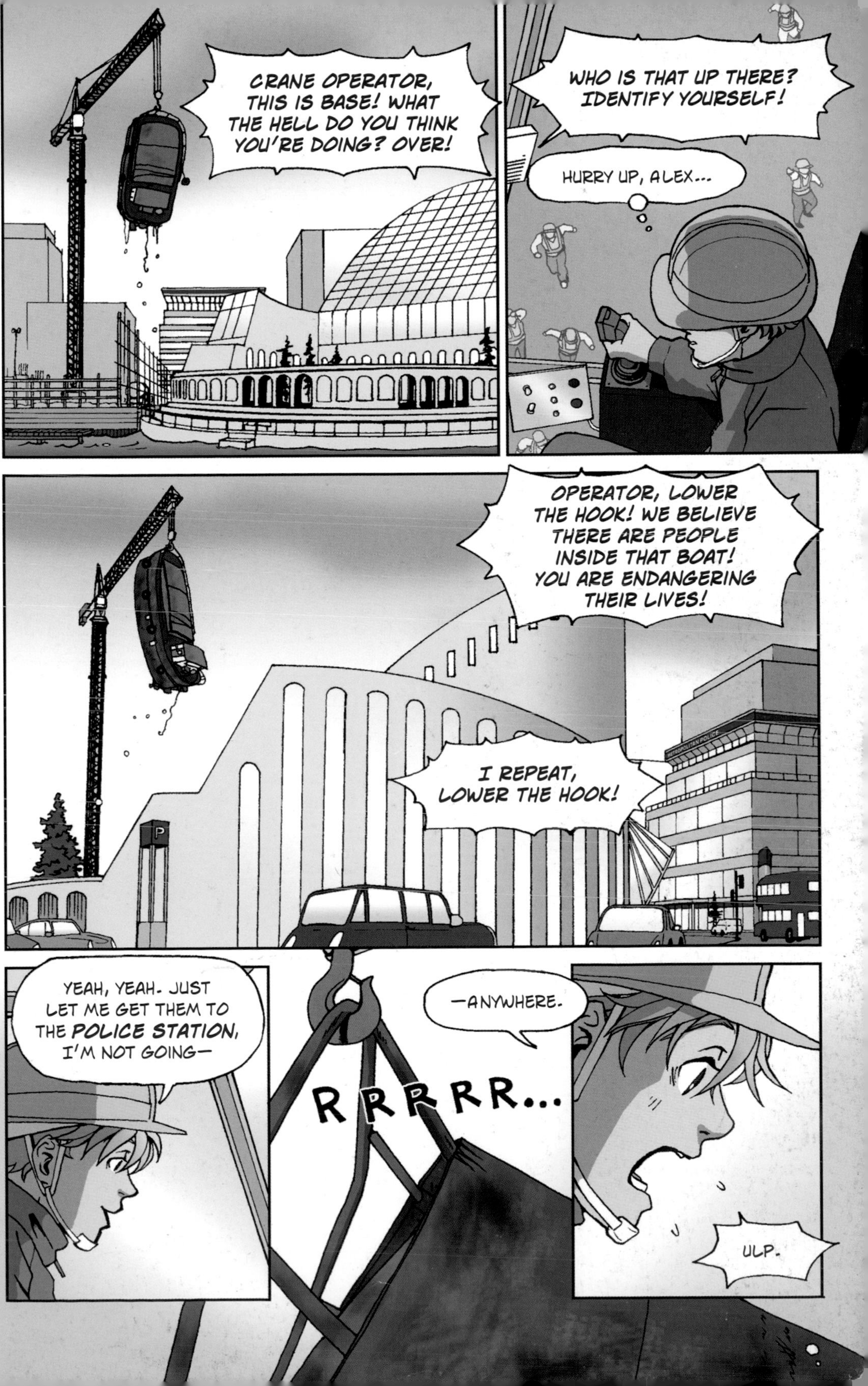
CRANE OPERATOR, THIS IS BASE! WHAT THE HELL DO YOU THINK YOU'RE DOING? OVER!
WHO IS THAT UP THERE? IDENTIFY YOURSELF!
HURRY UP, ALEX...
OPERATOR, LOWER THE HOOK! WE BELIEVE THERE ARE PEOPLE INSIDE THAT BOAT! YOU ARE ENDANGERING THEIR LIVES!
I REPEAT, LOWER THE HOOK!
P
YEAH, YEAH. JUST LET ME GET THEM TO THE POLICE STATION, I'M NOT GOING—
—ANYWHERE.
RRRRR...
ULP.

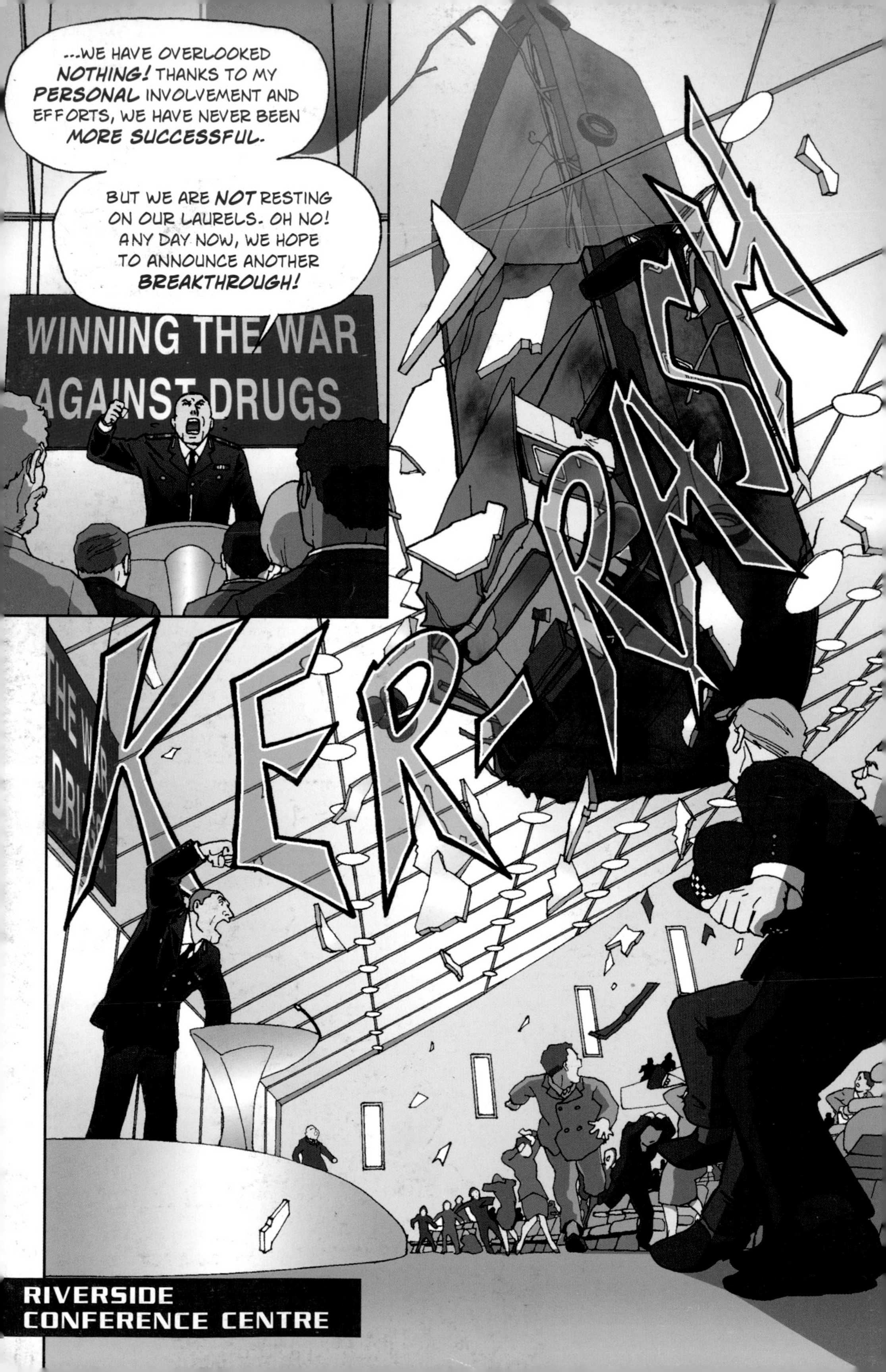

...WE HAVE OVERLOOKED NOTHING! THANKS TO MY PERSONAL INVOLVEMENT AND EFFORTS, WE HAVE NEVER BEEN MORE SUCCESSFUL.
BUT WE ARE NOT RESTING ON OUR LAURELS. OH NO! ANY DAY NOW, WE HOPE TO ANNOUNCE ANOTHER BREAKTHROUGH!
WINNING THE WAR AGAINST DRUGS
KER-RASH
RIVERSIDE CONFERENCE CENTRE

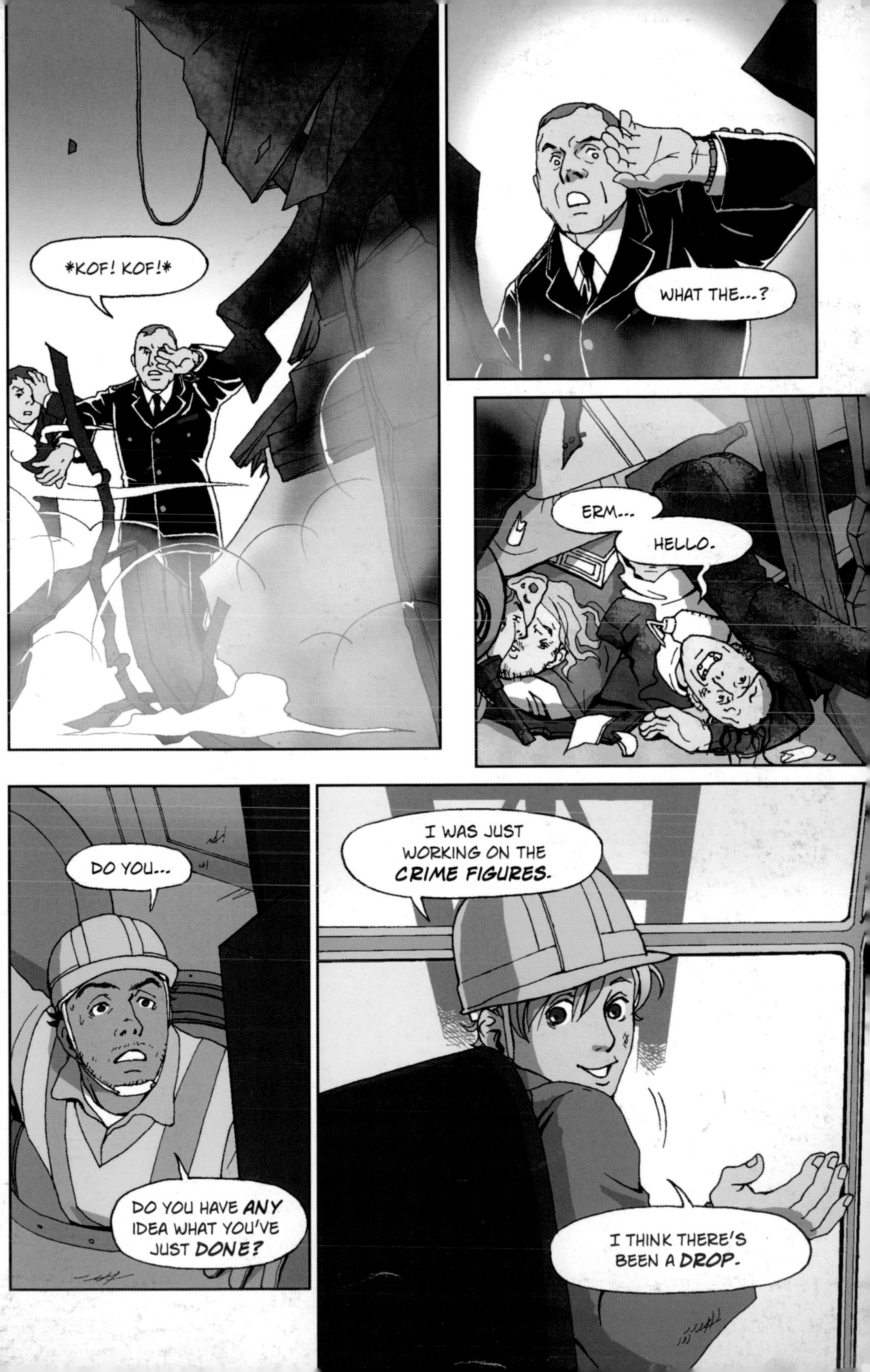
KOF! KOF!
WHAT THE...?
ERM...
HELLO.
DO YOU...
DO YOU HAVE ANY IDEA WHAT YOU'VE JUST DONE?
I WAS JUST WORKING ON THE CRIME FIGURES.
I THINK THERE'S BEEN A DROP.

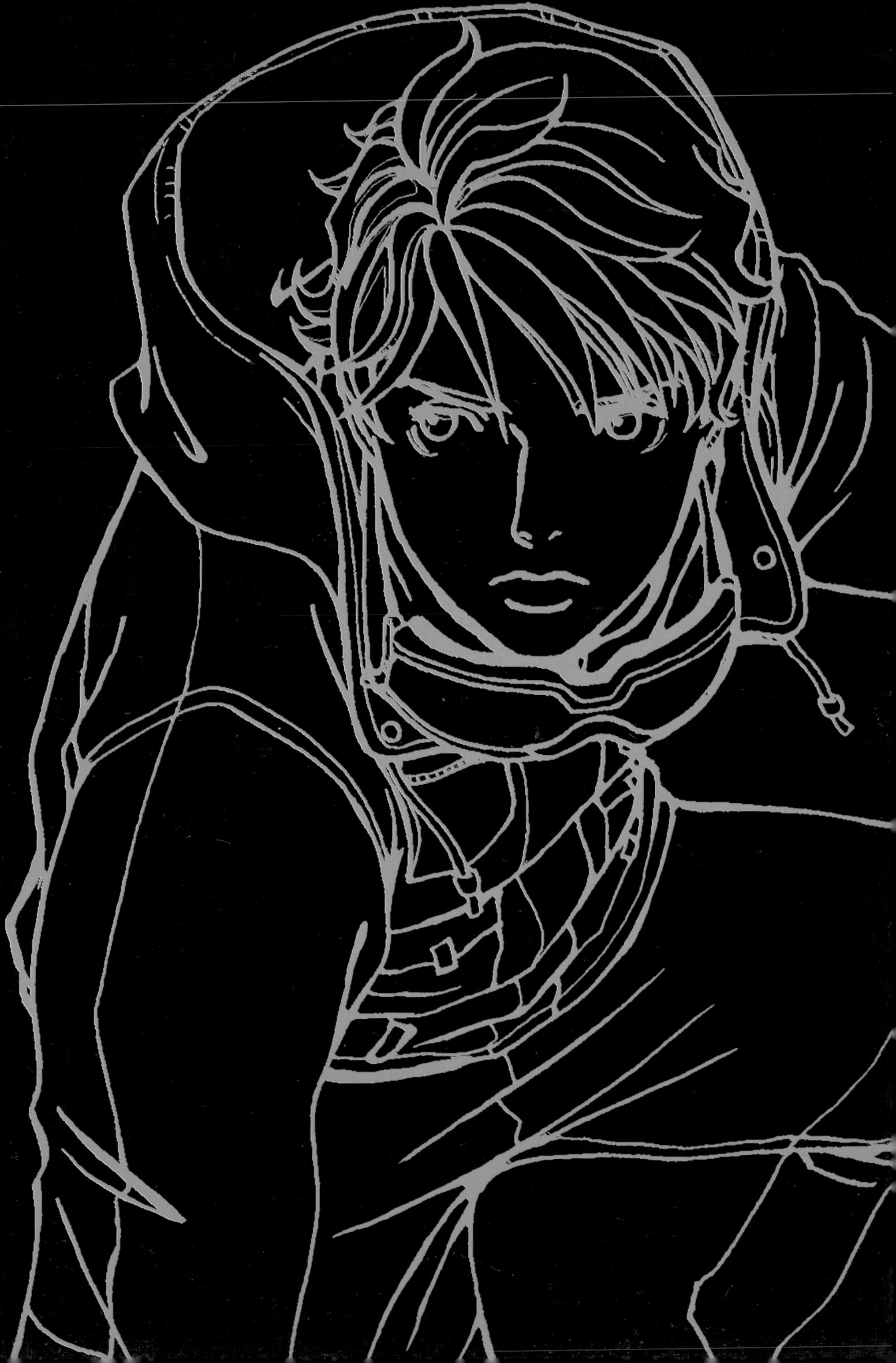

POINT BLANK
ANTHONY HOROWITZ

Adapted by
Antony Johnston

Illustrated by
Kanako Damerum
& Yuzuru Takasaki

PHILOMEL BOOKS

PHILOMEL BOOKS

A division of Penguin Young Readers Group.
Published by The Penguin Group.

Penguin Group (USA) Inc., 375 Hudson Street, New York, NY 10014, U.S.A.
Penguin Group (Canada), 90 Eglinton Avenue East, Suite 700, Toronto, Ontario M4P 2Y3,
Canada (a division of Pearson Penguin Canada Inc.). Penguin Books Ltd, 80 Strand, London
WC2R 0RL, England. Penguin Ireland, 25 St. Stephen's Green, Dublin 2, Ireland (a division of
Penguin Books Ltd). Penguin Group (Australia), 250 Camberwell Road, Camberwell, Victoria 3124,
Australia (a division of Pearson Australia Group Pty Ltd). Penguin Books India Pvt Ltd, 11 Community
Centre, Panchsheel Park, New Delhi - 110 017, India. Penguin Group (NZ), 67 Apollo Drive, Rosedale, North
Shore 0745, Auckland, New Zealand (a division of Pearson New Zealand Ltd.) Penguin Books (South Africa)
(Pty) Ltd, 24 Sturdee Avenue, Rosebank, Johannesburg 2196, South Africa. Penguin Books Ltd, Registered Offices:
80 Strand, London WC2R 0RL, England.

This is a work of fiction. Names, characters, places and incidents are either
the product of the author's imagination or, if real, are used fictitiously.

This book has been typeset in Lint McCree and Serpentine Bold.
Published simultaneously in Canada. Printed in China.

ISBN: 978-0-399-25026-2
5 7 9 10 8 6 4

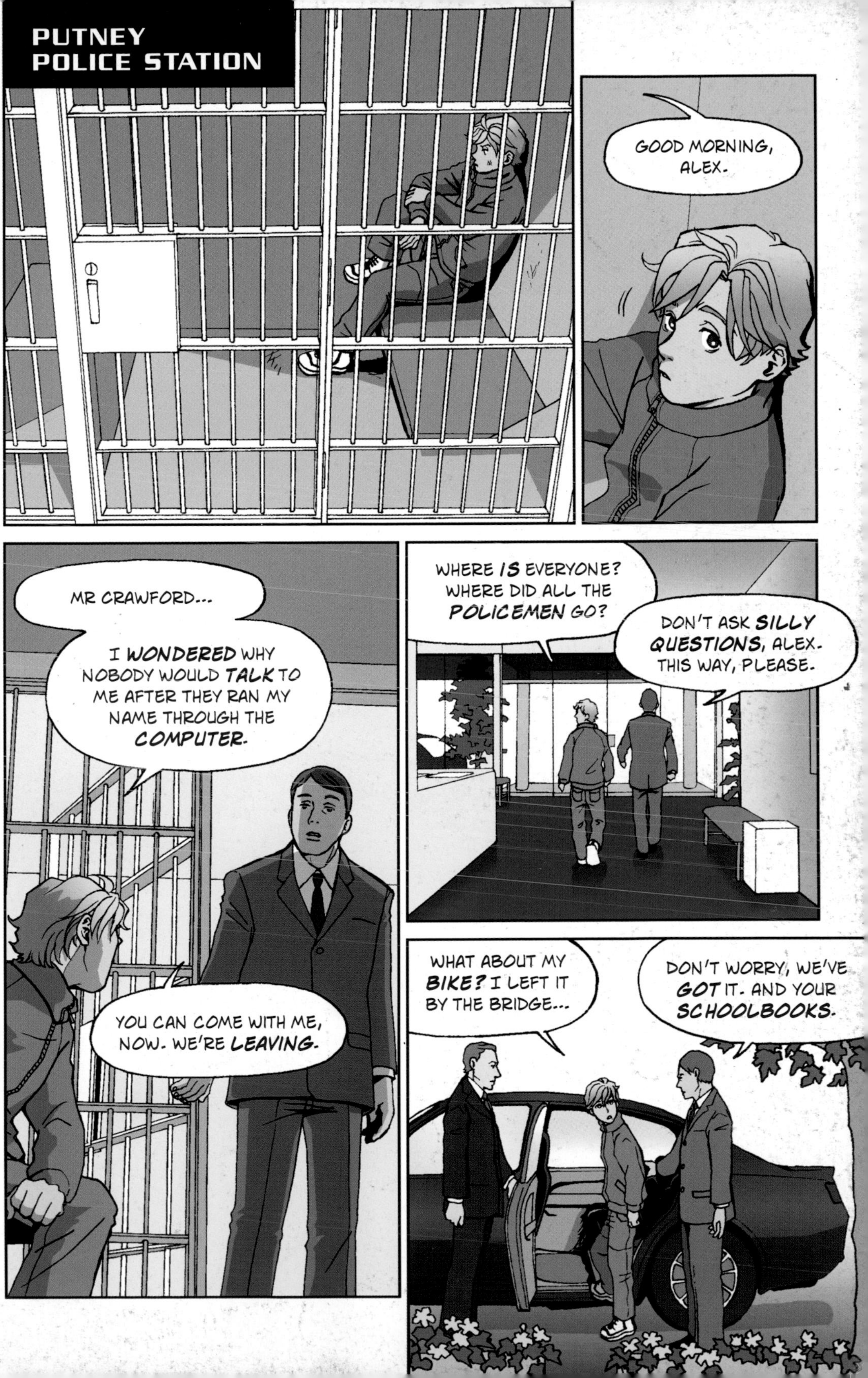
PUTNEY POLICE STATION
GOOD MORNING, ALEX.
MR CRAWFORD...
I WONDERED WHY NOBODY WOULD TALK TO ME AFTER THEY RAN MY NAME THROUGH THE COMPUTER.
YOU CAN COME WITH ME, NOW. WE'RE LEAVING.
WHERE IS EVERYONE? WHERE DID ALL THE POLICEMEN GO?
DON'T ASK SILLY QUESTIONS, ALEX. THIS WAY, PLEASE.
WHAT ABOUT MY BIKE? I LEFT IT BY THE BRIDGE...
DON'T WORRY, WE'VE GOT IT. AND YOUR SCHOOLBOOKS.

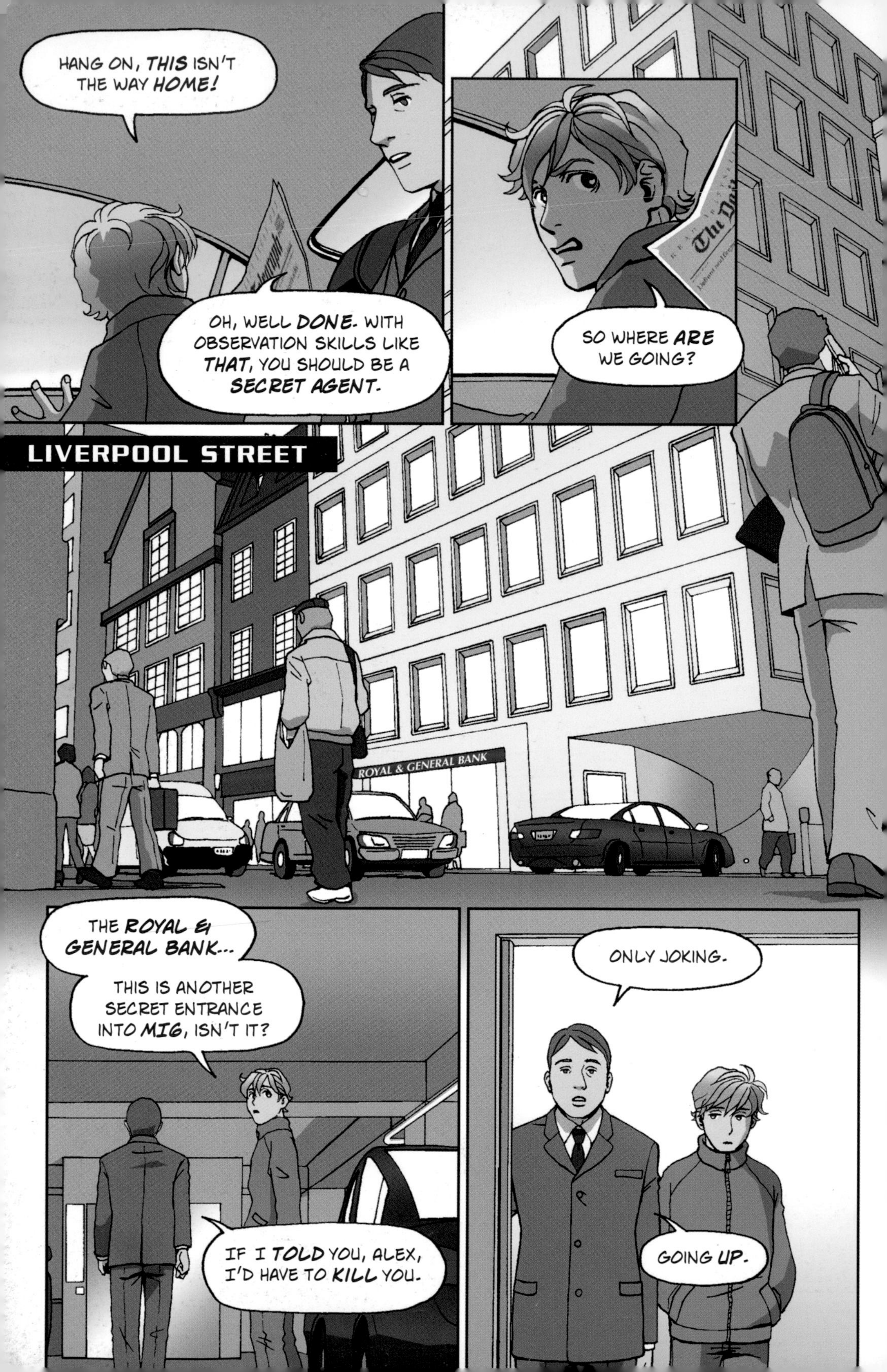
HANG ON, THIS ISN'T THE WAY HOME!
OH, WELL DONE. WITH OBSERVATION SKILLS LIKE THAT, YOU SHOULD BE A SECRET AGENT.
SO WHERE ARE WE GOING?
LIVERPOOL STREET
ROYAL & GENERAL BANK
THE ROYAL & GENERAL BANK...
THIS IS ANOTHER SECRET ENTRANCE INTO MI6, ISN'T IT?
IF I TOLD YOU, ALEX, I'D HAVE TO KILL YOU.
ONLY JOKING.
GOING UP.

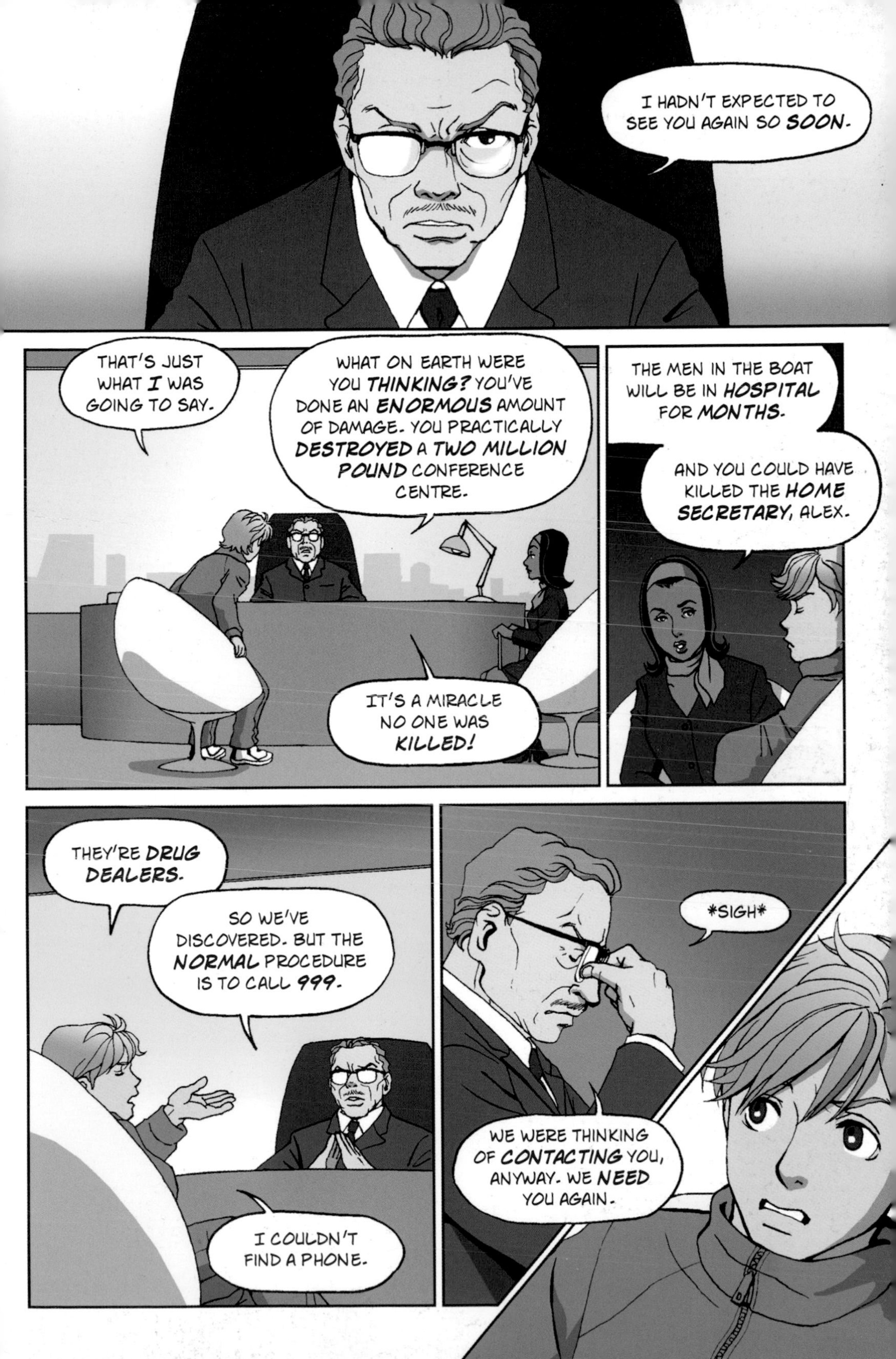
I HADN'T EXPECTED TO SEE YOU AGAIN SO SOON.
THAT'S JUST WHAT I WAS GOING TO SAY.
WHAT ON EARTH WERE YOU THINKING? YOU'VE DONE AN ENORMOUS AMOUNT OF DAMAGE. YOU PRACTICALLY DESTROYED A TWO MILLION POUND CONFERENCE CENTRE.
IT'S A MIRACLE NO ONE WAS KILLED!
THE MEN IN THE BOAT WILL BE IN HOSPITAL FOR MONTHS.
AND YOU COULD HAVE KILLED THE HOME SECRETARY, ALEX.
THEY'RE DRUG DEALERS.
SO WE'VE DISCOVERED. BUT THE NORMAL PROCEDURE IS TO CALL 999.
I COULDN'T FIND A PHONE.
SIGH
WE WERE THINKING OF CONTACTING YOU, ANYWAY. WE NEED YOU AGAIN.

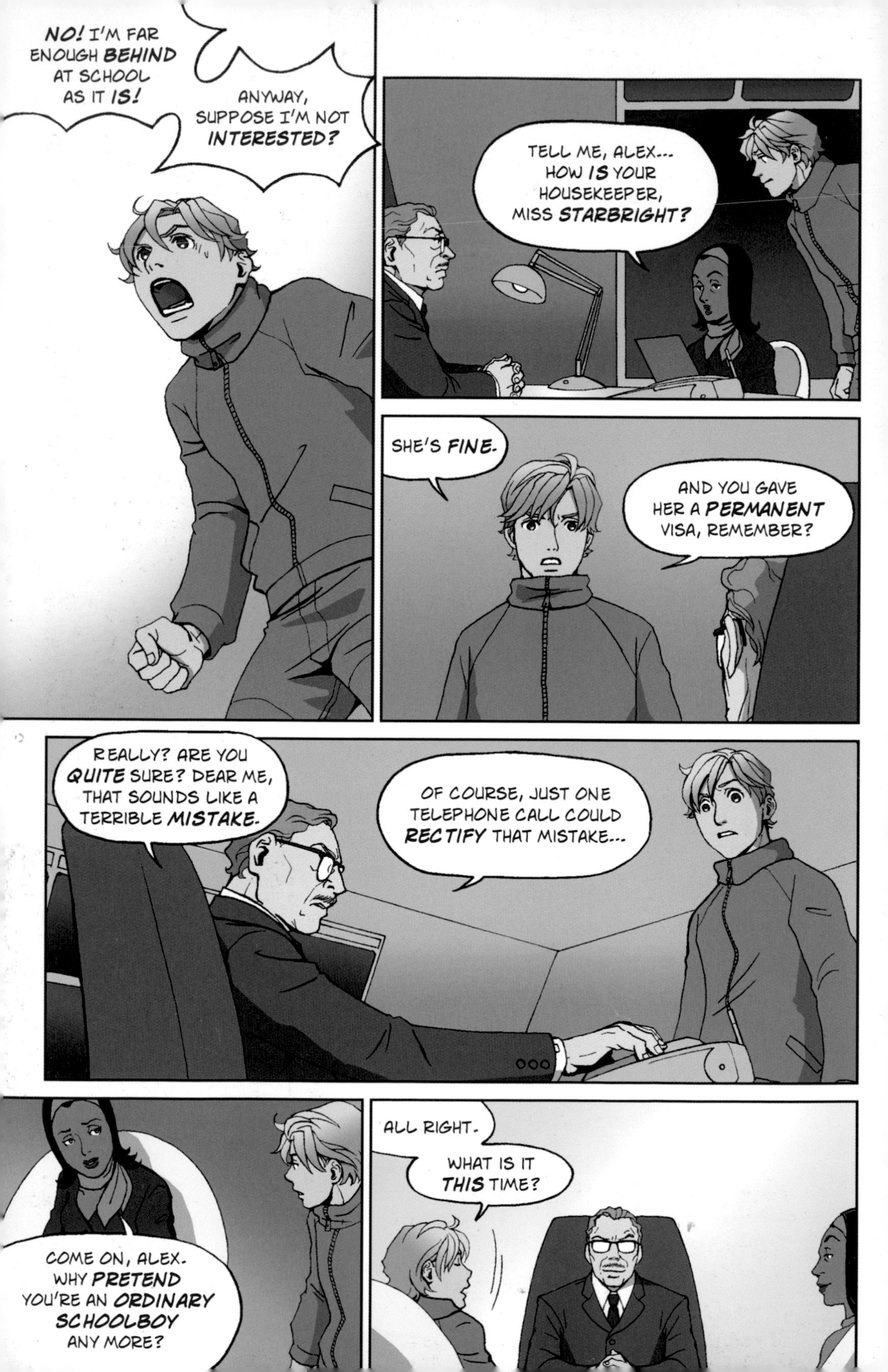
NO! I'M FAR ENOUGH BEHIND AT SCHOOL AS IT IS!
ANYWAY, SUPPOSE I'M NOT INTERESTED?
TELL ME, ALEX... HOW IS YOUR HOUSEKEEPER, MISS STARBRIGHT?
SHE'S FINE.
AND YOU GAVE HER A PERMANENT VISA, REMEMBER?
REALLY? ARE YOU QUITE SURE? DEAR ME, THAT SOUNDS LIKE A TERRIBLE MISTAKE.
OF COURSE, JUST ONE TELEPHONE CALL COULD RECTIFY THAT MISTAKE...
COME ON, ALEX. WHY PRETEND YOU'RE AN ORDINARY SCHOOLBOY ANY MORE?
ALL RIGHT.
WHAT IS IT THIS TIME?

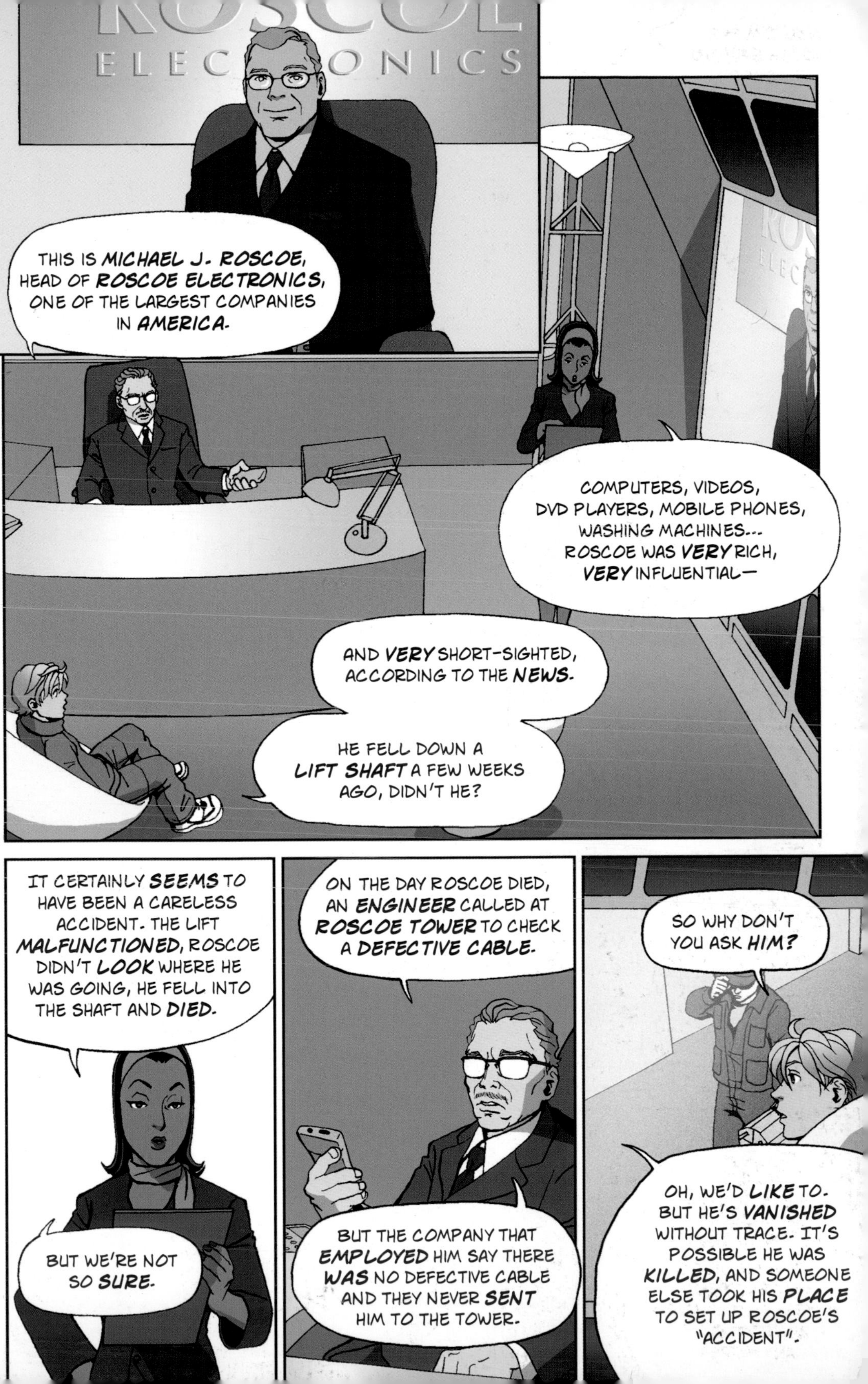
ROSCOE ELECTRONICS
THIS IS MICHAEL J. ROSCOE, HEAD OF ROSCOE ELECTRONICS, ONE OF THE LARGEST COMPANIES IN AMERICA.
COMPUTERS, VIDEOS, DVD PLAYERS, MOBILE PHONES, WASHING MACHINES... ROSCOE WAS VERY RICH, VERY INFLUENTIAL—
AND VERY SHORT-SIGHTED, ACCORDING TO THE NEWS.
HE FELL DOWN A LIFT SHAFT A FEW WEEKS AGO, DIDN'T HE?
IT CERTAINLY SEEMS TO HAVE BEEN A CARELESS ACCIDENT. THE LIFT MALFUNCTIONED, ROSCOE DIDN'T LOOK WHERE HE WAS GOING, HE FELL INTO THE SHAFT AND DIED.
BUT WE'RE NOT SO SURE.
ON THE DAY ROSCOE DIED, AN ENGINEER CALLED AT ROSCOE TOWER TO CHECK A DEFECTIVE CABLE.
BUT THE COMPANY THAT EMPLOYED HIM SAY THERE WAS NO DEFECTIVE CABLE AND THEY NEVER SENT HIM TO THE TOWER.
SO WHY DON'T YOU ASK HIM?
OH, WE'D LIKE TO. BUT HE'S VANISHED WITHOUT TRACE. IT'S POSSIBLE HE WAS KILLED, AND SOMEONE ELSE TOOK HIS PLACE TO SET UP ROSCOE'S "ACCIDENT".

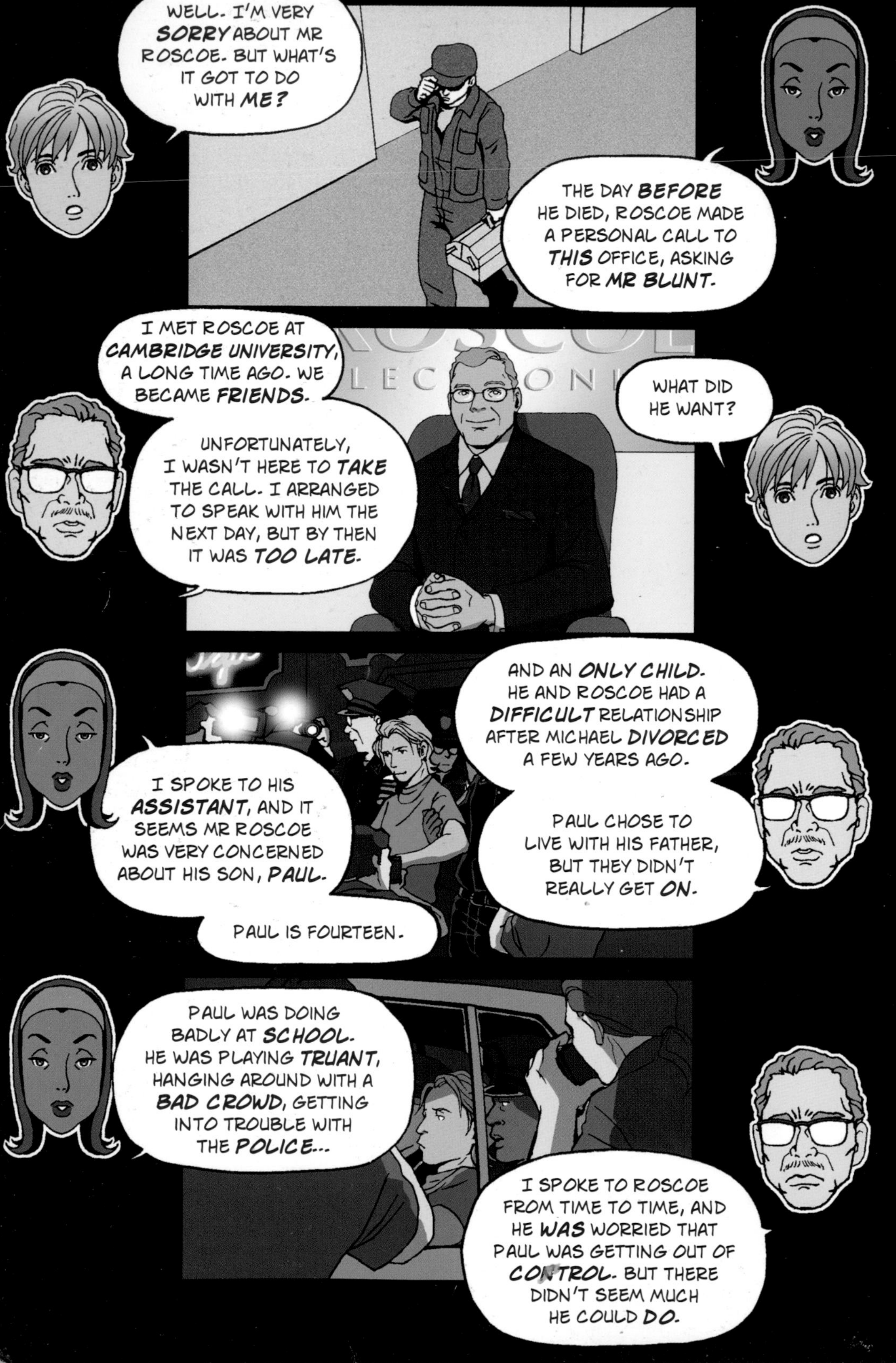
WELL. I'M VERY SORRY ABOUT MR ROSCOE. BUT WHAT'S IT GOT TO DO WITH ME?
THE DAY BEFORE HE DIED, ROSCOE MADE A PERSONAL CALL TO THIS OFFICE, ASKING FOR MR BLUNT.
I MET ROSCOE AT CAMBRIDGE UNIVERSITY, A LONG TIME AGO. WE BECAME FRIENDS.
UNFORTUNATELY, I WASN'T HERE TO TAKE THE CALL. I ARRANGED TO SPEAK WITH HIM THE NEXT DAY, BUT BY THEN IT WAS TOO LATE.
WHAT DID HE WANT?
I SPOKE TO HIS ASSISTANT, AND IT SEEMS MR ROSCOE WAS VERY CONCERNED ABOUT HIS SON, PAUL.
PAUL IS FOURTEEN.
AND AN ONLY CHILD. HE AND ROSCOE HAD A DIFFICULT RELATIONSHIP AFTER MICHAEL DIVORCED A FEW YEARS AGO.
PAUL CHOSE TO LIVE WITH HIS FATHER, BUT THEY DIDN'T REALLY GET ON.
PAUL WAS DOING BADLY AT SCHOOL. HE WAS PLAYING TRUANT, HANGING AROUND WITH A BAD CROWD, GETTING INTO TROUBLE WITH THE POLICE...
I SPOKE TO ROSCOE FROM TIME TO TIME, AND HE WAS WORRIED THAT PAUL WAS GETTING OUT OF CONTROL. BUT THERE DIDN'T SEEM MUCH HE COULD DO.

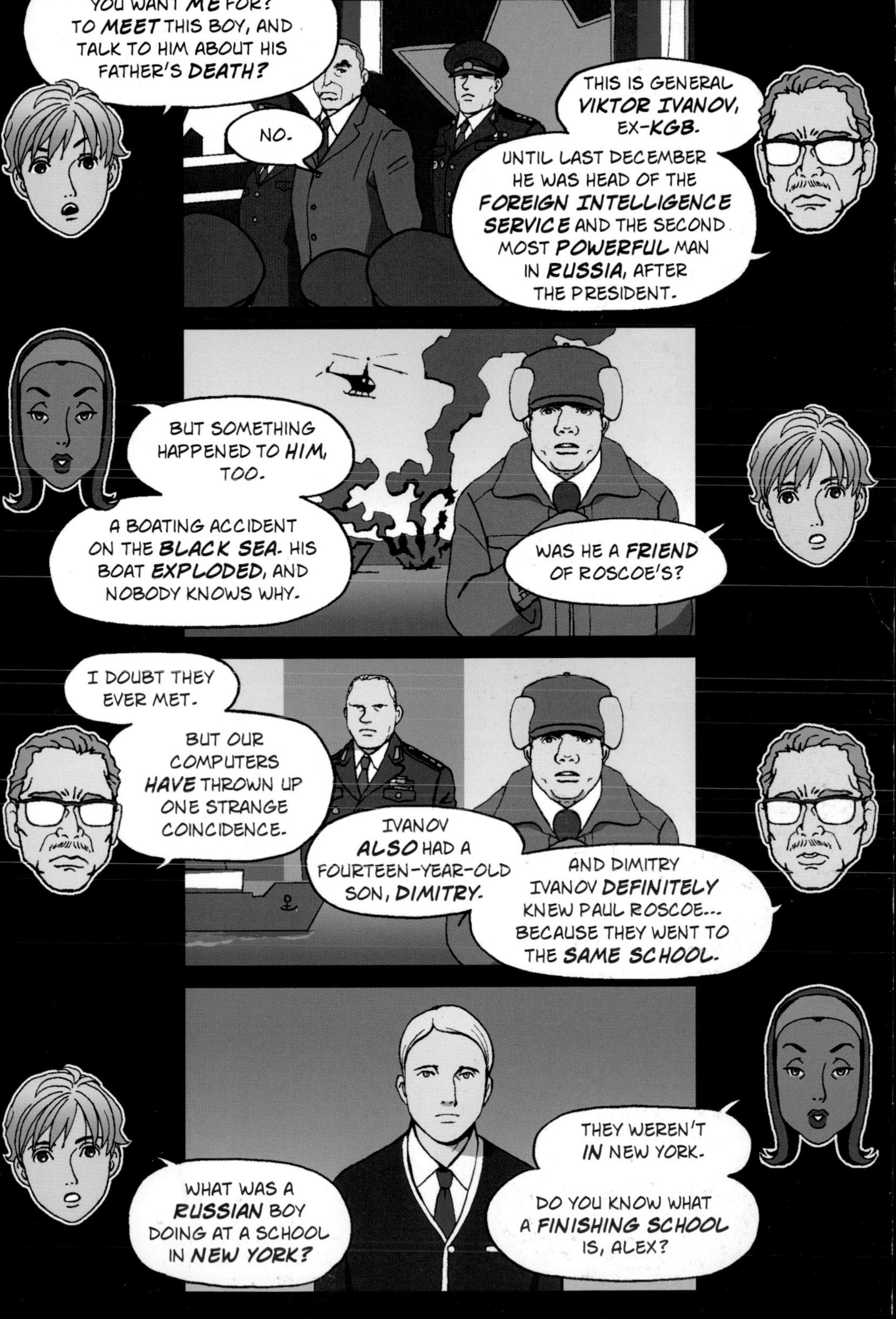
YOU WANT ME FOR? TO MEET THIS BOY, AND TALK TO HIM ABOUT HIS FATHER'S DEATH?
NO.
THIS IS GENERAL VIKTOR IVANOV, EX-KGB.
UNTIL LAST DECEMBER HE WAS HEAD OF THE FOREIGN INTELLIGENCE SERVICE AND THE SECOND MOST POWERFUL MAN IN RUSSIA, AFTER THE PRESIDENT.
BUT SOMETHING HAPPENED TO HIM, TOO.
A BOATING ACCIDENT ON THE BLACK SEA. HIS BOAT EXPLODED, AND NOBODY KNOWS WHY.
WAS HE A FRIEND OF ROSCOE'S?
I DOUBT THEY EVER MET.
BUT OUR COMPUTERS HAVE THROWN UP ONE STRANGE COINCIDENCE.
IVANOV ALSO HAD A FOURTEEN-YEAR-OLD SON, DIMITRY.
AND DIMITRY IVANOV DEFINITELY KNEW PAUL ROSCOE... BECAUSE THEY WENT TO THE SAME SCHOOL.
WHAT WAS A RUSSIAN BOY DOING AT A SCHOOL IN NEW YORK?
THEY WEREN'T IN NEW YORK.
DO YOU KNOW WHAT A FINISHING SCHOOL IS, ALEX?

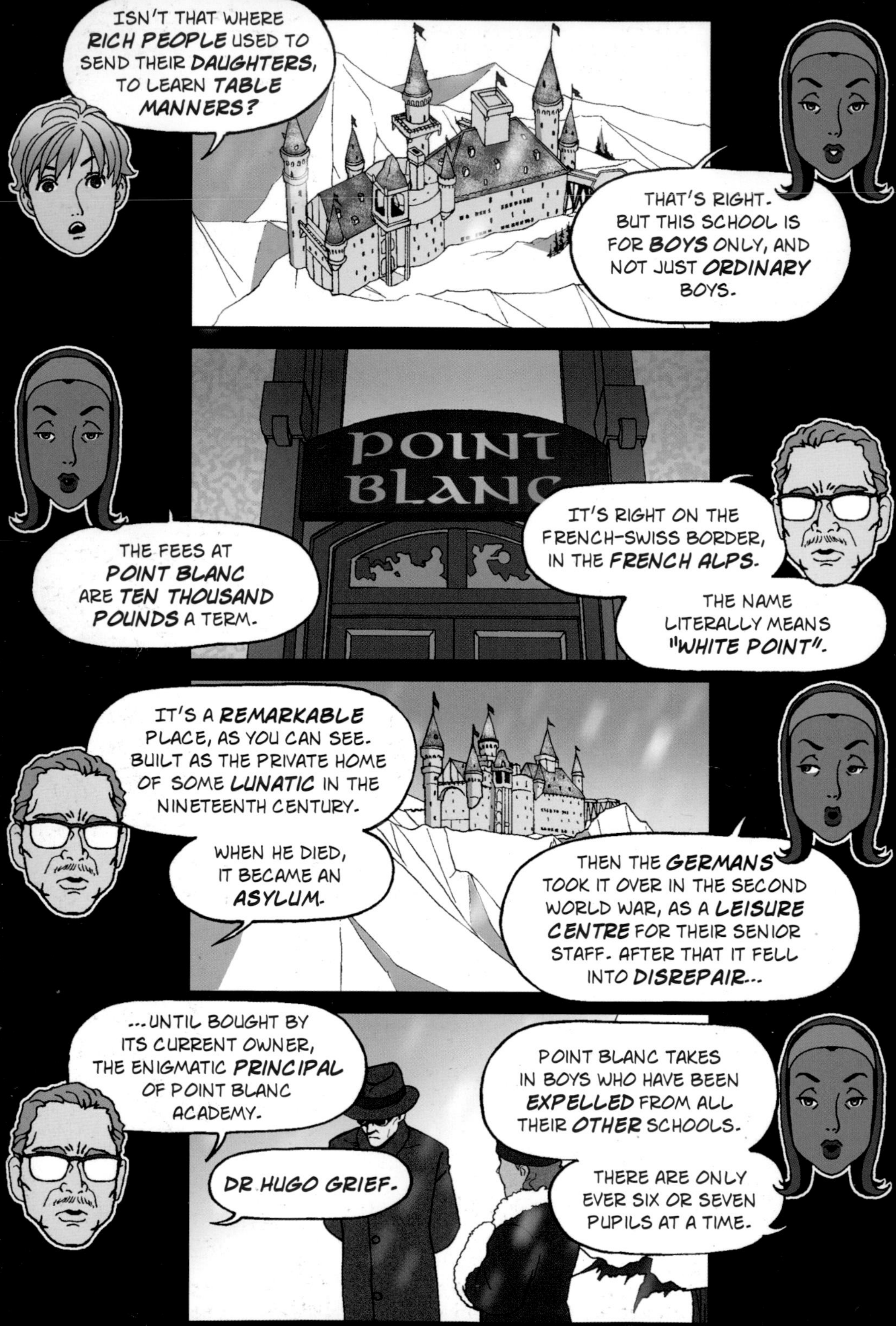
ISN'T THAT WHERE RICH PEOPLE USED TO SEND THEIR DAUGHTERS, TO LEARN TABLE MANNERS?
THAT'S RIGHT. BUT THIS SCHOOL IS FOR BOYS ONLY, AND NOT JUST ORDINARY BOYS.
POINT BLANC
THE FEES AT POINT BLANC ARE TEN THOUSAND POUNDS A TERM.
IT'S RIGHT ON THE FRENCH-SWISS BORDER, IN THE FRENCH ALPS.
THE NAME LITERALLY MEANS "WHITE POINT".
IT'S A REMARKABLE PLACE, AS YOU CAN SEE. BUILT AS THE PRIVATE HOME OF SOME LUNATIC IN THE NINETEENTH CENTURY.
WHEN HE DIED, IT BECAME AN ASYLUM.
THEN THE GERMANS TOOK IT OVER IN THE SECOND WORLD WAR, AS A LEISURE CENTRE FOR THEIR SENIOR STAFF. AFTER THAT IT FELL INTO DISREPAIR...
...UNTIL BOUGHT BY ITS CURRENT OWNER, THE ENIGMATIC PRINCIPAL OF POINT BLANC ACADEMY.
DR HUGO GRIEF.
POINT BLANC TAKES IN BOYS WHO HAVE BEEN EXPELLED FROM ALL THEIR OTHER SCHOOLS.
THERE ARE ONLY EVER SIX OR SEVEN PUPILS AT A TIME.

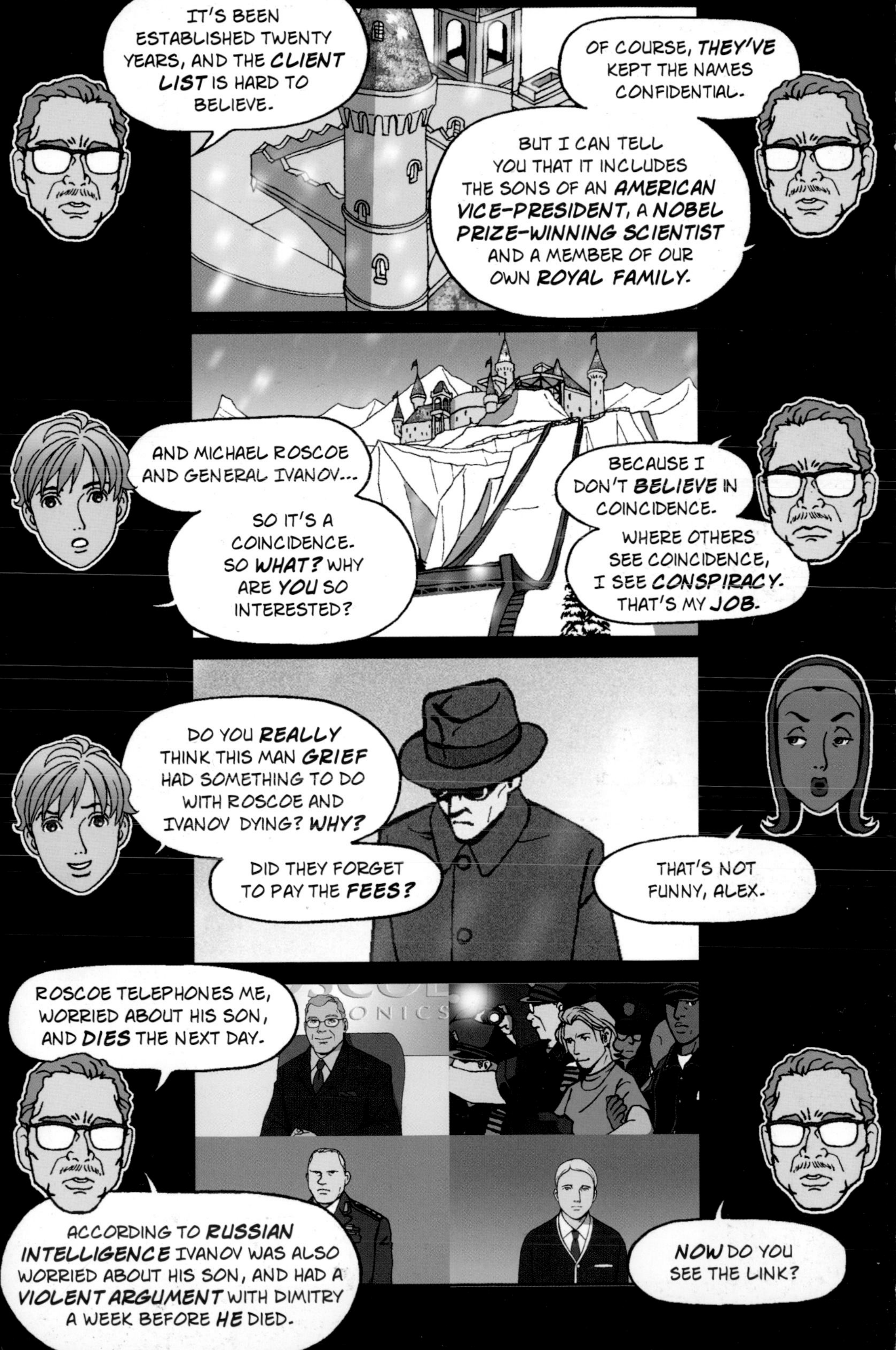
IT'S BEEN ESTABLISHED TWENTY YEARS, AND THE CLIENT LIST IS HARD TO BELIEVE.
OF COURSE, THEY'VE KEPT THE NAMES CONFIDENTIAL.
BUT I CAN TELL YOU THAT IT INCLUDES THE SONS OF AN AMERICAN VICE-PRESIDENT, A NOBEL PRIZE-WINNING SCIENTIST AND A MEMBER OF OUR OWN ROYAL FAMILY.
AND MICHAEL ROSCOE AND GENERAL IVANOV...
SO IT'S A COINCIDENCE. SO WHAT? WHY ARE YOU SO INTERESTED?
BECAUSE I DON'T BELIEVE IN COINCIDENCE.
WHERE OTHERS SEE COINCIDENCE, I SEE CONSPIRACY. THAT'S MY JOB.
DO YOU REALLY THINK THIS MAN GRIEF HAD SOMETHING TO DO WITH ROSCOE AND IVANOV DYING? WHY?
DID THEY FORGET TO PAY THE FEES?
THAT'S NOT FUNNY, ALEX.
ROSCOE TELEPHONES ME, WORRIED ABOUT HIS SON, AND DIES THE NEXT DAY.
ACCORDING TO RUSSIAN INTELLIGENCE IVANOV WAS ALSO WORRIED ABOUT HIS SON, AND HAD A VIOLENT ARGUMENT WITH DIMITRY A WEEK BEFORE HE DIED.
NOW DO YOU SEE THE LINK?

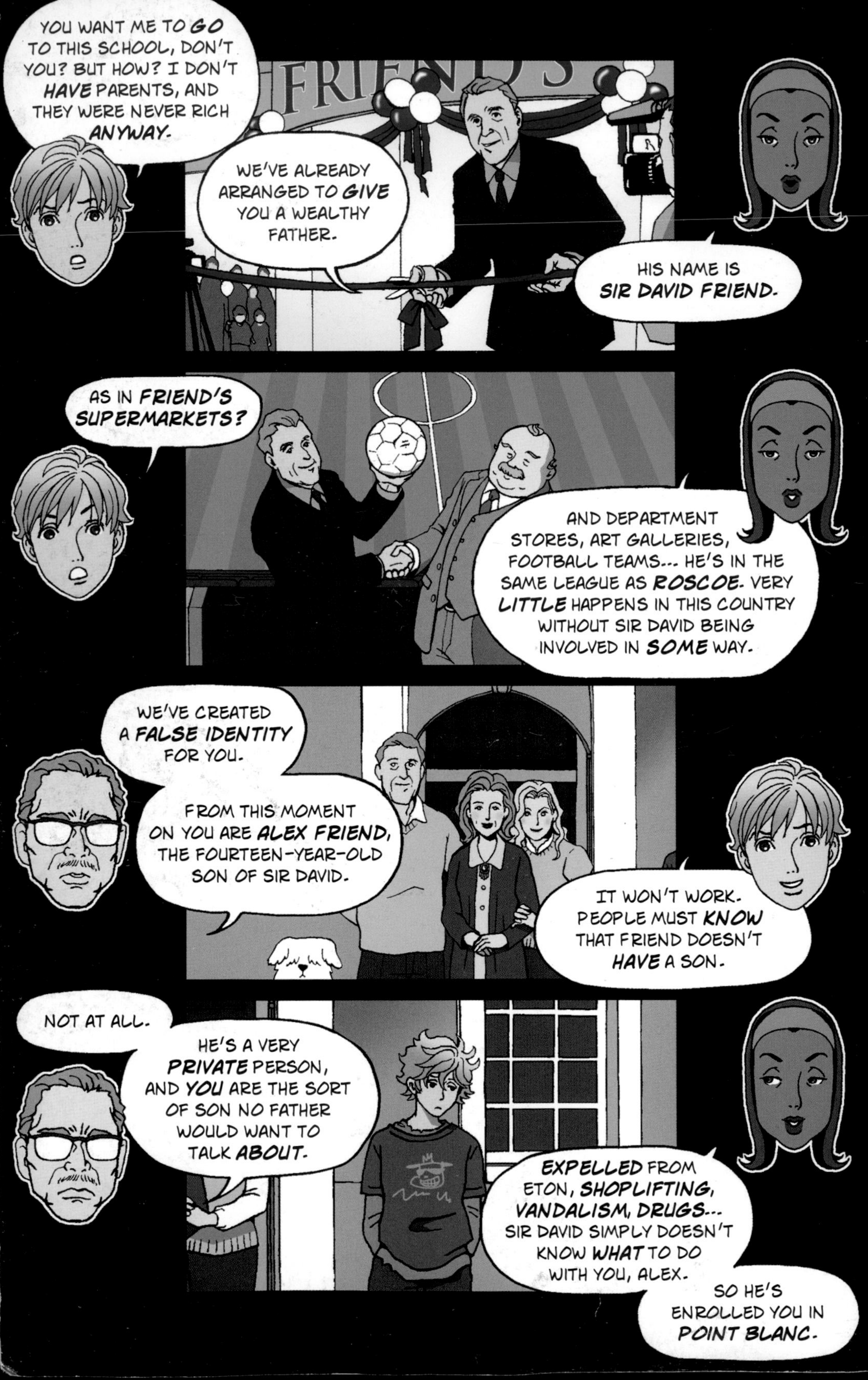
YOU WANT ME TO GO TO THIS SCHOOL, DON'T YOU? BUT HOW? I DON'T HAVE PARENTS, AND THEY WERE NEVER RICH ANYWAY.
WE'VE ALREADY ARRANGED TO GIVE YOU A WEALTHY FATHER.
HIS NAME IS SIR DAVID FRIEND.
AS IN FRIEND'S SUPERMARKETS?
AND DEPARTMENT STORES, ART GALLERIES, FOOTBALL TEAMS... HE'S IN THE SAME LEAGUE AS ROSCOE. VERY LITTLE HAPPENS IN THIS COUNTRY WITHOUT SIR DAVID BEING INVOLVED IN SOME WAY.
WE'VE CREATED A FALSE IDENTITY FOR YOU.
FROM THIS MOMENT ON YOU ARE ALEX FRIEND, THE FOURTEEN-YEAR-OLD SON OF SIR DAVID.
IT WON'T WORK. PEOPLE MUST KNOW THAT FRIEND DOESN'T HAVE A SON.
NOT AT ALL.
HE'S A VERY PRIVATE PERSON, AND YOU ARE THE SORT OF SON NO FATHER WOULD WANT TO TALK ABOUT.
EXPELLED FROM ETON, SHOPLIFTING, VANDALISM, DRUGS... SIR DAVID SIMPLY DOESN'T KNOW WHAT TO DO WITH YOU, ALEX.
SO HE'S ENROLLED YOU IN POINT BLANC.

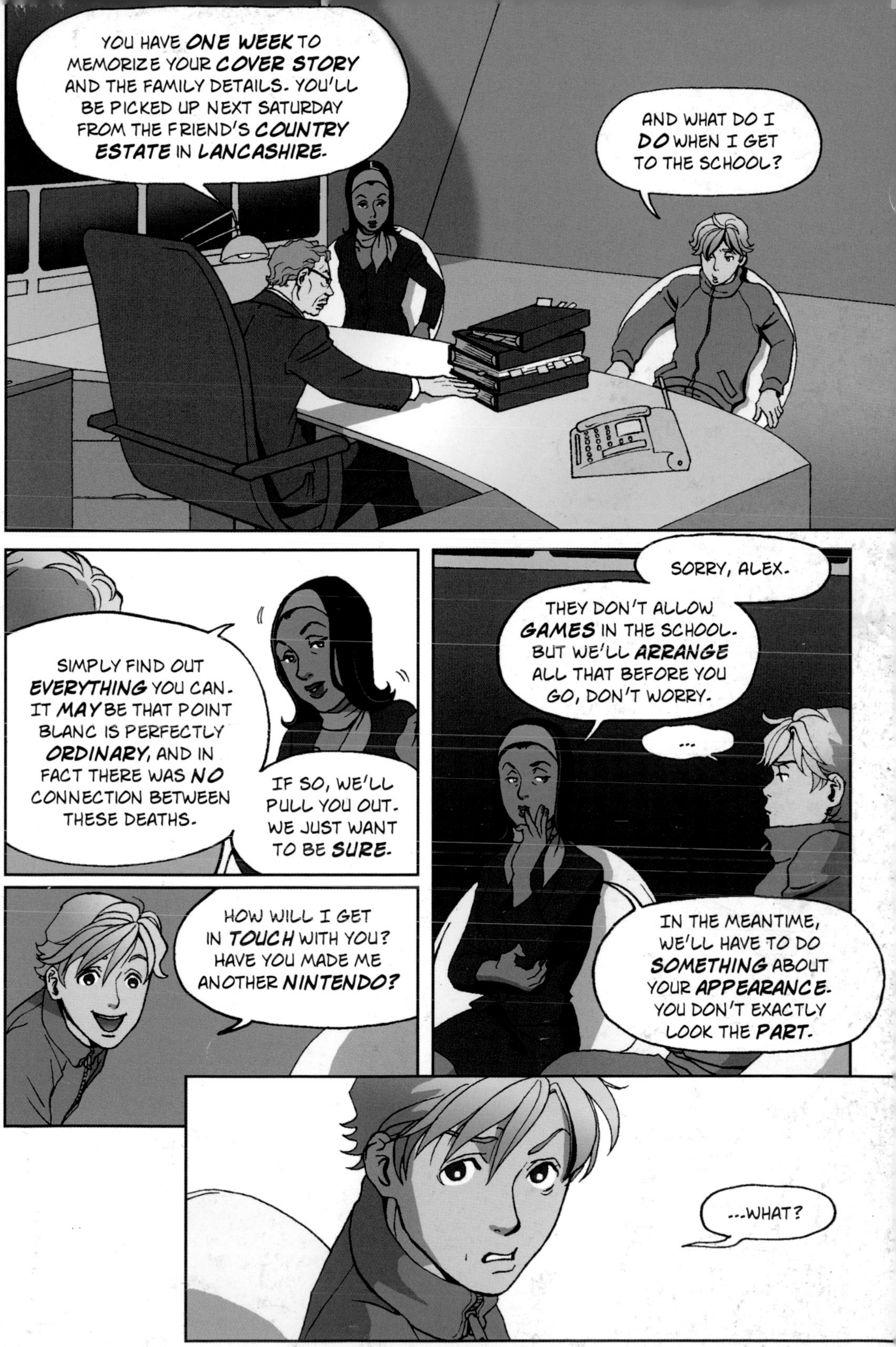
YOU HAVE ONE WEEK TO MEMORIZE YOUR COVER STORY AND THE FAMILY DETAILS. YOU'LL BE PICKED UP NEXT SATURDAY FROM THE FRIEND'S COUNTRY ESTATE IN LANCASHIRE.
AND WHAT DO I DO WHEN I GET TO THE SCHOOL?
SIMPLY FIND OUT EVERYTHING YOU CAN. IT MAY BE THAT POINT BLANC IS PERFECTLY ORDINARY, AND IN FACT THERE WAS NO CONNECTION BETWEEN THESE DEATHS.
IF SO, WE'LL PULL YOU OUT. WE JUST WANT TO BE SURE.
HOW WILL I GET IN TOUCH WITH YOU? HAVE YOU MADE ME ANOTHER NINTENDO?
SORRY, ALEX.
THEY DON'T ALLOW GAMES IN THE SCHOOL. BUT WE'LL ARRANGE ALL THAT BEFORE YOU GO, DON'T WORRY.
...
IN THE MEANTIME, WE'LL HAVE TO DO SOMETHING ABOUT YOUR APPEARANCE. YOU DON'T EXACTLY LOOK THE PART.
...WHAT?

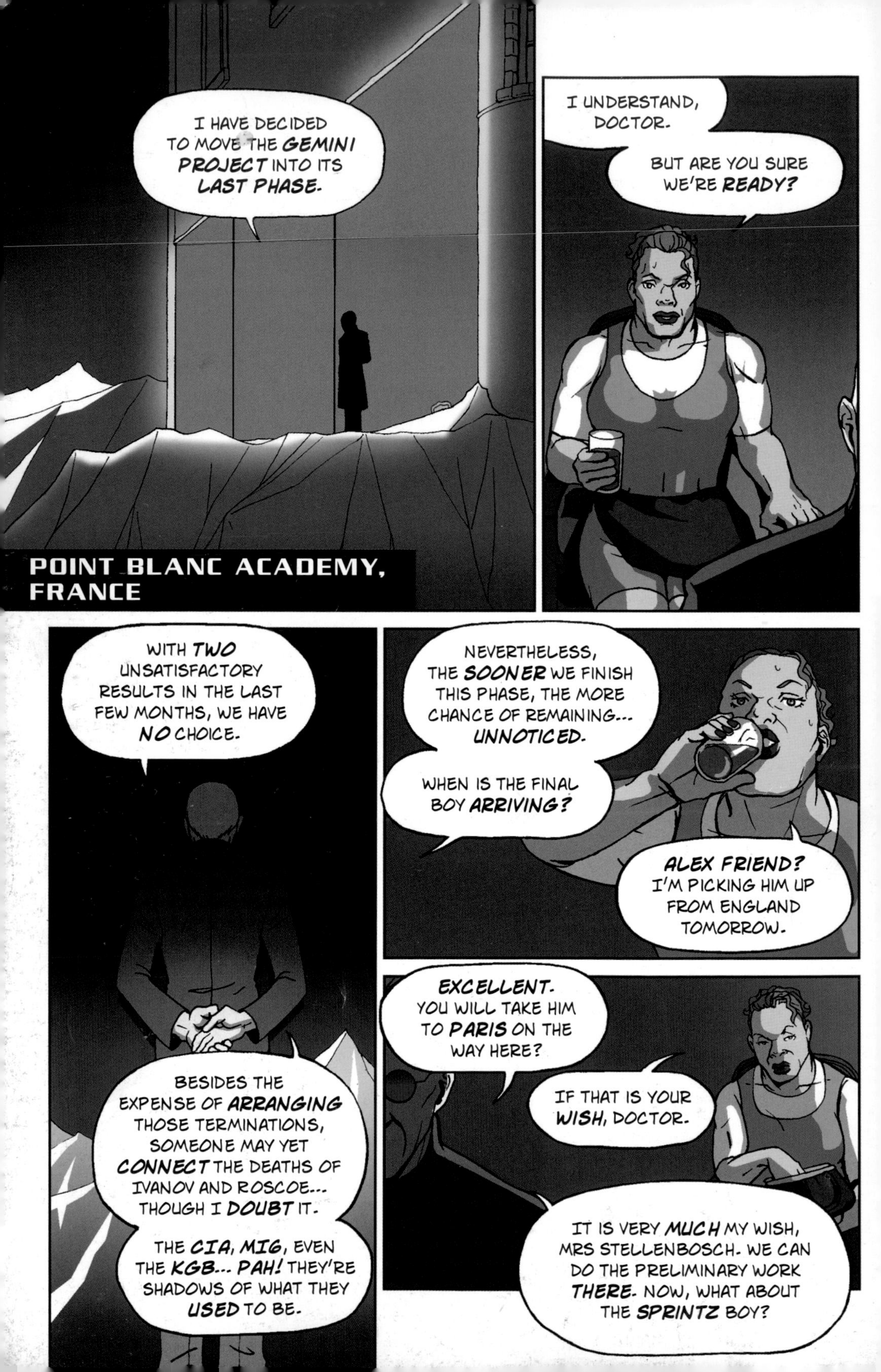
I HAVE DECIDED TO MOVE THE GEMINI PROJECT INTO ITS LAST PHASE.
POINT BLANC ACADEMY, FRANCE
I UNDERSTAND, DOCTOR.
BUT ARE YOU SURE WE'RE READY?
WITH TWO UNSATISFACTORY RESULTS IN THE LAST FEW MONTHS, WE HAVE NO CHOICE.
BESIDES THE EXPENSE OF ARRANGING THOSE TERMINATIONS, SOMEONE MAY YET CONNECT THE DEATHS OF IVANOV AND ROSCOE... THOUGH I DOUBT IT.
THE CIA, MI6, EVEN THE KGB... PAH! THEY'RE SHADOWS OF WHAT THEY USED TO BE.
NEVERTHELESS, THE SOONER WE FINISH THIS PHASE, THE MORE CHANCE OF REMAINING... UNNOTICED.
WHEN IS THE FINAL BOY ARRIVING?
ALEX FRIEND? I'M PICKING HIM UP FROM ENGLAND TOMORROW.
EXCELLENT. YOU WILL TAKE HIM TO PARIS ON THE WAY HERE?
IF THAT IS YOUR WISH, DOCTOR.
IT IS VERY MUCH MY WISH, MRS STELLENBOSCH. WE CAN DO THE PRELIMINARY WORK THERE. NOW, WHAT ABOUT THE SPRINTZ BOY?

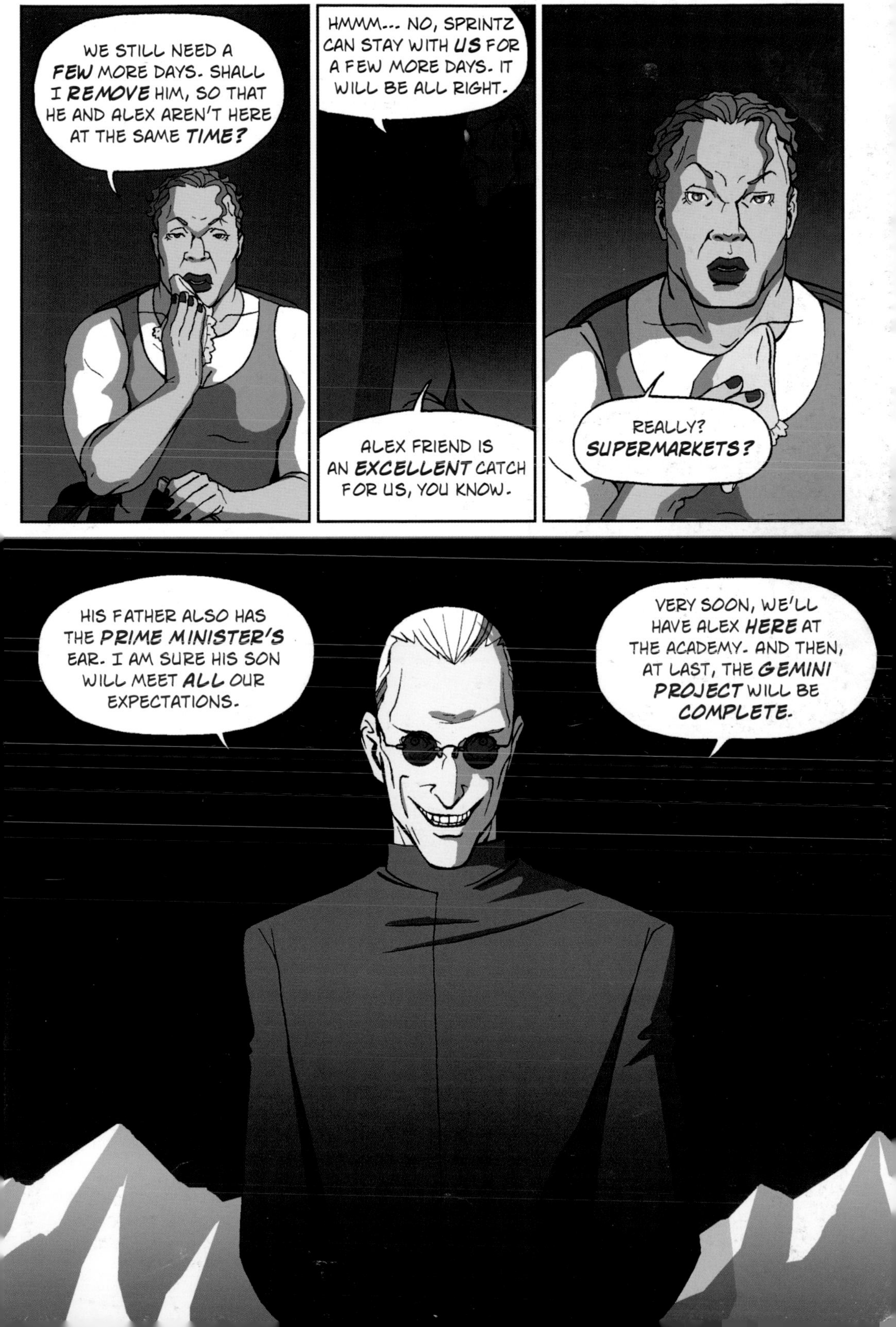
WE STILL NEED A FEW MORE DAYS. SHALL I REMOVE HIM, SO THAT HE AND ALEX AREN'T HERE AT THE SAME TIME?
HMMM... NO, SPRINTZ CAN STAY WITH US FOR A FEW MORE DAYS. IT WILL BE ALL RIGHT.
ALEX FRIEND IS AN EXCELLENT CATCH FOR US, YOU KNOW.
REALLY? SUPERMARKETS?
HIS FATHER ALSO HAS THE PRIME MINISTER'S EAR. I AM SURE HIS SON WILL MEET ALL OUR EXPECTATIONS.
VERY SOON, WE'LL HAVE ALEX HERE AT THE ACADEMY. AND THEN, AT LAST, THE GEMINI PROJECT WILL BE COMPLETE.

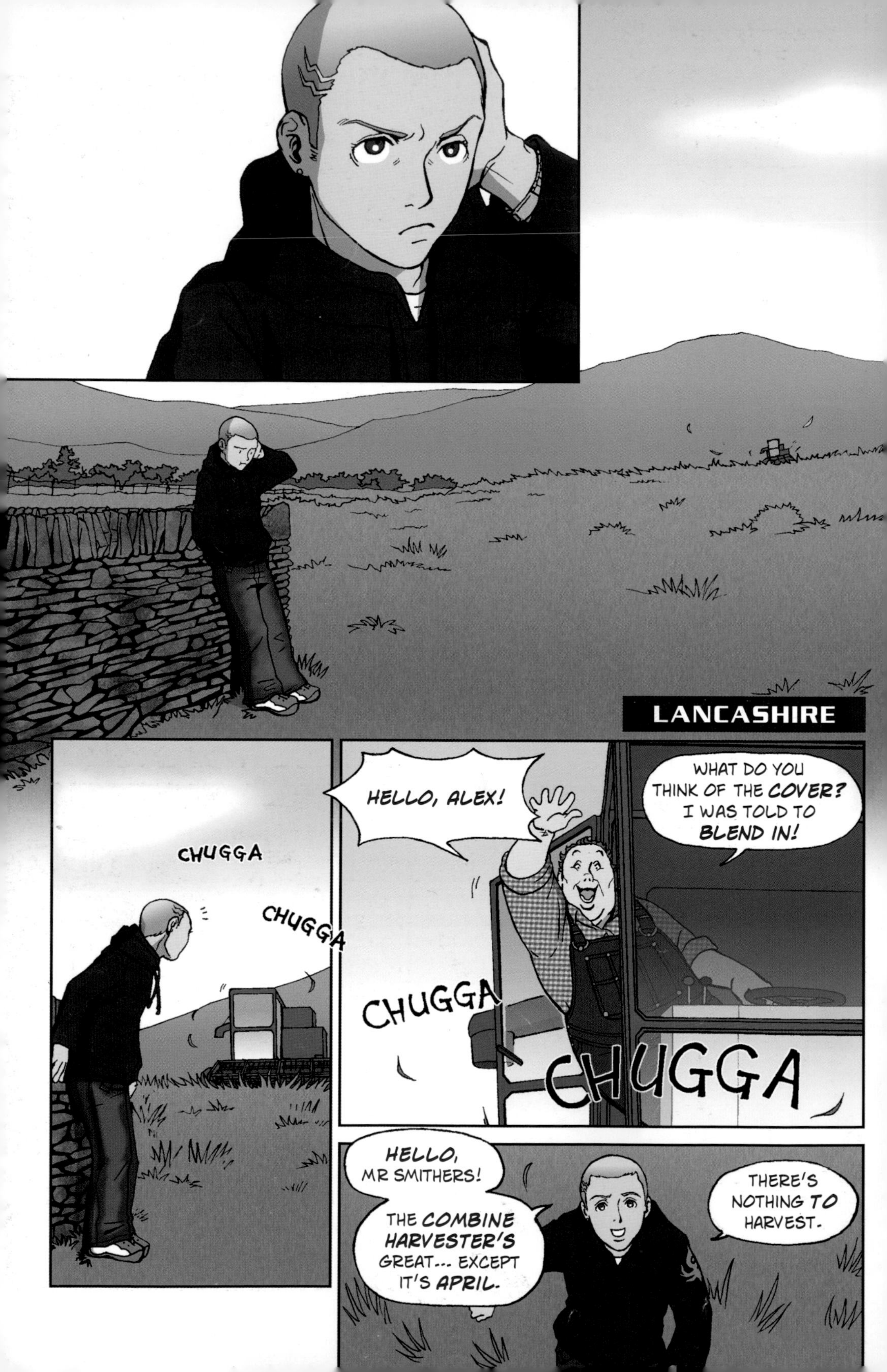
LANCASHIRE
CHUGGA
CHUGGA
HELLO, ALEX!
WHAT DO YOU THINK OF THE COVER? I WAS TOLD TO BLEND IN!
CHUGGA
CHUGGA
HELLO, MR SMITHERS!
THE COMBINE HARVESTER'S GREAT... EXCEPT IT'S APRIL.
THERE'S NOTHING TO HARVEST.

I HADN'T **THOUGHT** OF THAT!

THE TROUBLE IS, I'M NOT REALLY A **FIELD AGENT!**

GET IT?

HAVE YOU GOT ME ANOTHER **NINTENDO?**

NO, THAT'S THE **PROBLEM.** THE ACADEMY DOESN'T **ALLOW** GAMES OF ANY SORT, OR EVEN **COMPUTERS.** THEY SUPPLY ALL THEIR **OWN.**

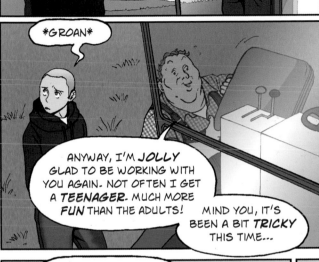

GROAN

ANYWAY, I'M **JOLLY** GLAD TO BE WORKING WITH YOU AGAIN. NOT OFTEN I GET A **TEENAGER.** MUCH MORE **FUN** THAN THE ADULTS!

MIND YOU, IT'S BEEN A BIT **TRICKY** THIS TIME...

NOW, I'M TOLD THERE'S A LOT OF **SNOW** UP ON POINT BLANC, SO YOU'LL NEED **THIS.** KNOW WHAT IT IS?

I'VE BEEN **SKIING** BEFORE, MR SMITHERS.

BUT NOT IN A SUIT LIKE **THIS.** IT'S HIGHLY **INSULATED,** AND ALSO **BULLET-PROOF.**

WOW.

AND THESE ARE **SKI GOGGLES**.

BUT IN CASE YOU HAVE TO BE ANYWHERE AT **NIGHT**, THEY ALSO HAVE AN **INFRARED** MODE.

JUST PRESS THE **SWITCH** AND YOU'LL BE ABLE TO SEE FOR **TWENTY METRES**, EVEN IF THERE'S NO **MOON**.

NOW, YOU'RE NOT ALLOWED **COMPUTERS**...

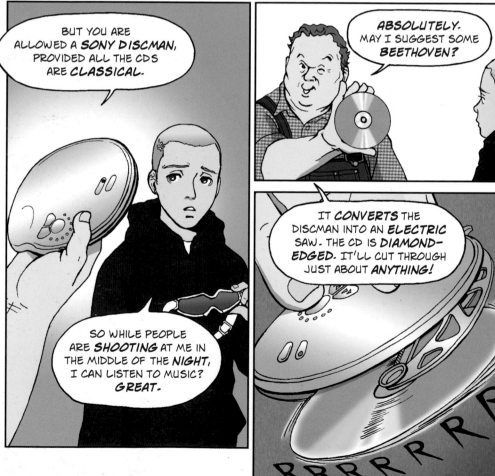

BUT YOU ARE ALLOWED A **SONY DISCMAN**, PROVIDED ALL THE CDS ARE **CLASSICAL**.

ABSOLUTELY. MAY I SUGGEST SOME **BEETHOVEN?**

SO WHILE PEOPLE ARE **SHOOTING** AT ME IN THE MIDDLE OF THE **NIGHT**, I CAN LISTEN TO MUSIC? **GREAT.**

IT **CONVERTS** THE DISCMAN INTO AN **ELECTRIC** SAW. THE CD IS **DIAMOND-EDGED**. IT'LL CUT THROUGH JUST ABOUT **ANYTHING!**

RRRRRRR

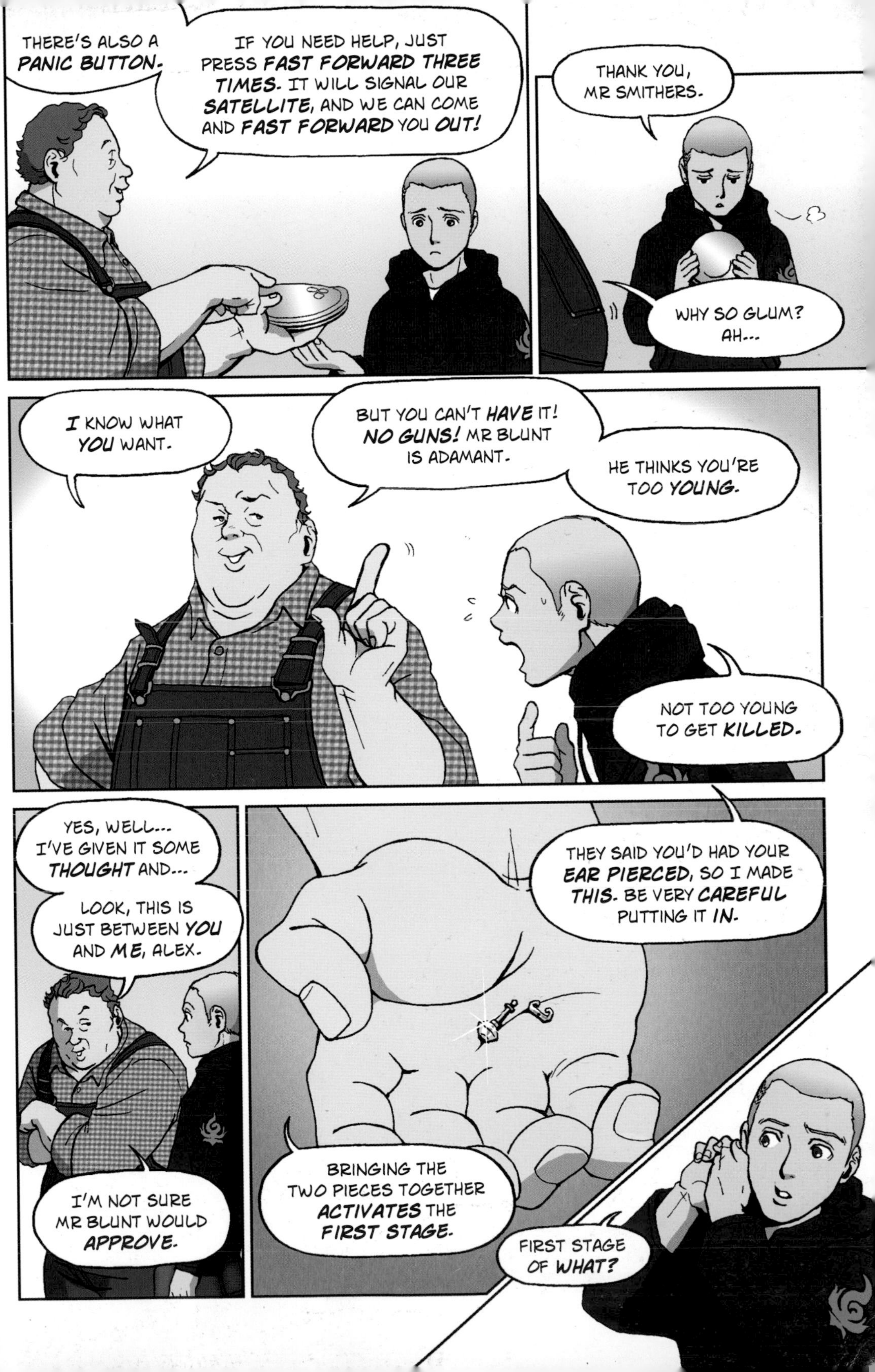
THERE'S ALSO A PANIC BUTTON.
IF YOU NEED HELP, JUST PRESS FAST FORWARD THREE TIMES. IT WILL SIGNAL OUR SATELLITE, AND WE CAN COME AND FAST FORWARD YOU OUT!
THANK YOU, MR SMITHERS.
WHY SO GLUM? AH...
I KNOW WHAT YOU WANT.
BUT YOU CAN'T HAVE IT! NO GUNS! MR BLUNT IS ADAMANT.
HE THINKS YOU'RE TOO YOUNG.
NOT TOO YOUNG TO GET KILLED.
YES, WELL... I'VE GIVEN IT SOME THOUGHT AND...
LOOK, THIS IS JUST BETWEEN YOU AND ME, ALEX.
I'M NOT SURE MR BLUNT WOULD APPROVE.
THEY SAID YOU'D HAD YOUR EAR PIERCED, SO I MADE THIS. BE VERY CAREFUL PUTTING IT IN.
BRINGING THE TWO PIECES TOGETHER ACTIVATES THE FIRST STAGE.
FIRST STAGE OF WHAT?

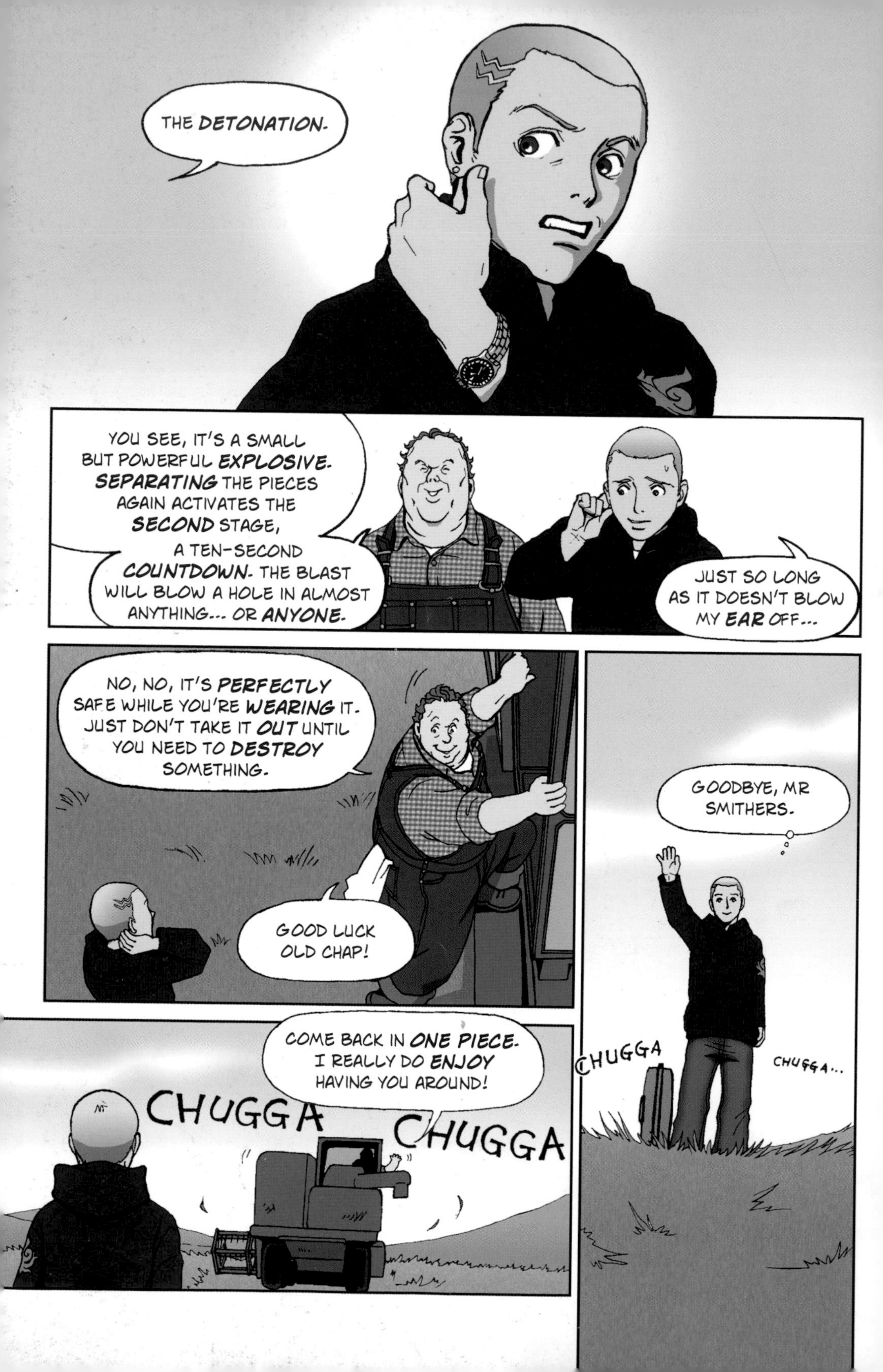
THE DETONATION.
YOU SEE, IT'S A SMALL BUT POWERFUL EXPLOSIVE. SEPARATING THE PIECES AGAIN ACTIVATES THE SECOND STAGE, A TEN-SECOND COUNTDOWN. THE BLAST WILL BLOW A HOLE IN ALMOST ANYTHING... OR ANYONE.
JUST SO LONG AS IT DOESN'T BLOW MY EAR OFF...
NO, NO, IT'S PERFECTLY SAFE WHILE YOU'RE WEARING IT. JUST DON'T TAKE IT OUT UNTIL YOU NEED TO DESTROY SOMETHING.
GOOD LUCK OLD CHAP!
COME BACK IN ONE PIECE. I REALLY DO ENJOY HAVING YOU AROUND!
CHUGGA
CHUGGA
GOODBYE, MR SMITHERS.
CHUGGA
CHUGGA...

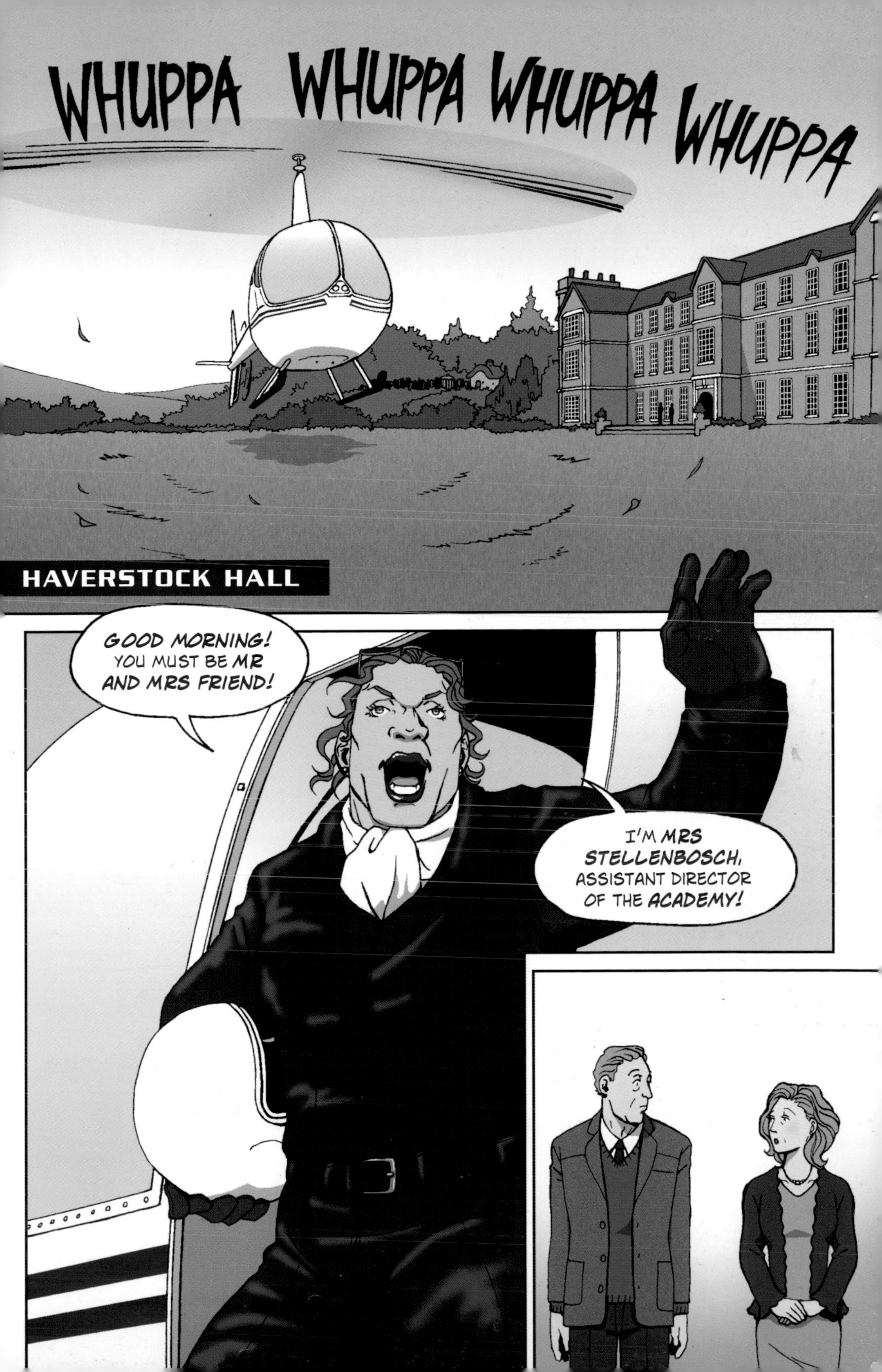
WHUPPA WHUPPA WHUPPA WHUPPA
HAVERSTOCK HALL
GOOD MORNING! YOU MUST BE MR AND MRS FRIEND!
I'M MRS STELLENBOSCH, ASSISTANT DIRECTOR OF THE ACADEMY!

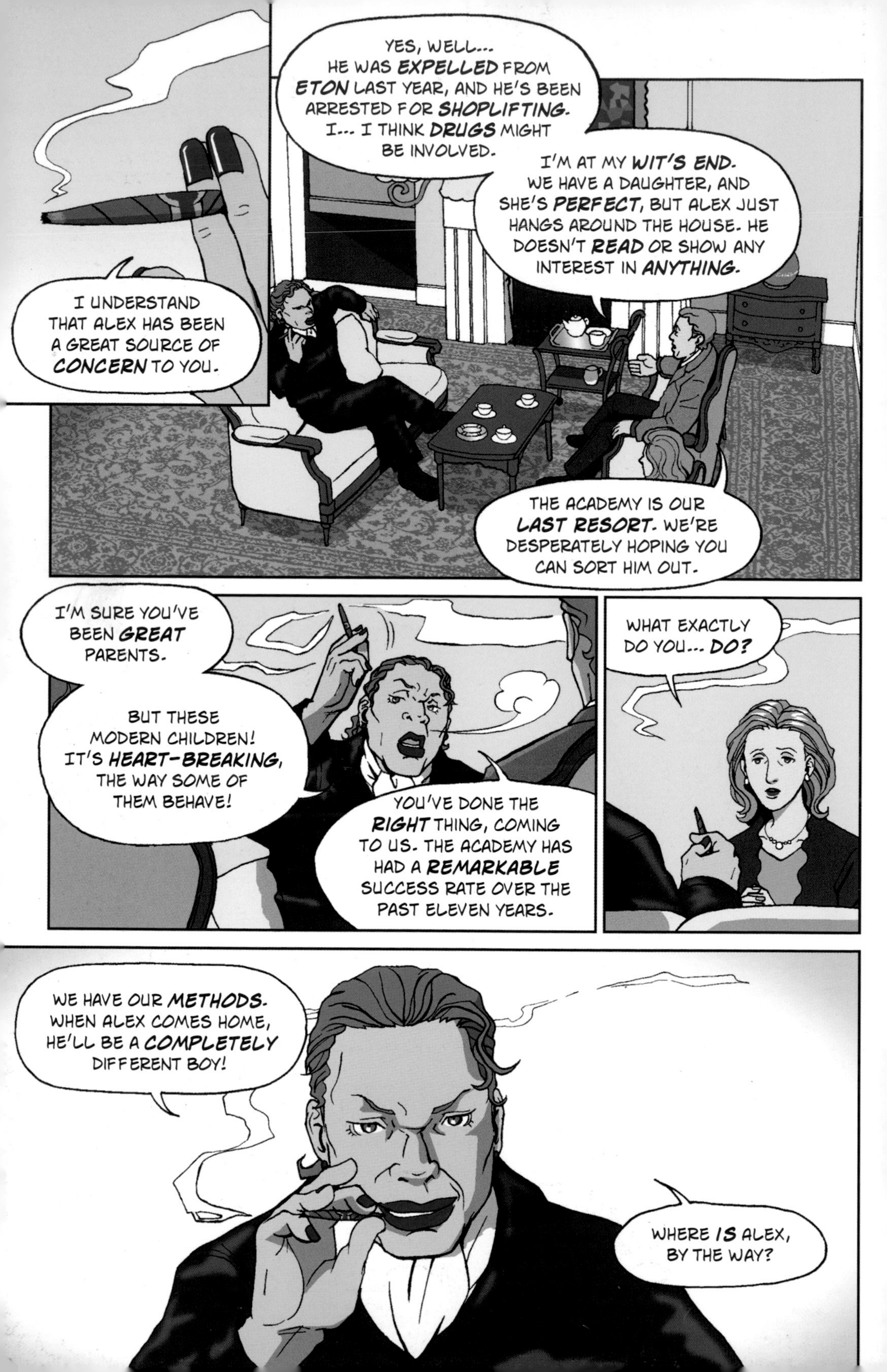

I UNDERSTAND THAT ALEX HAS BEEN A GREAT SOURCE OF CONCERN TO YOU.
YES, WELL... HE WAS EXPELLED FROM ETON LAST YEAR, AND HE'S BEEN ARRESTED FOR SHOPLIFTING. I... I THINK DRUGS MIGHT BE INVOLVED.
I'M AT MY WIT'S END. WE HAVE A DAUGHTER, AND SHE'S PERFECT, BUT ALEX JUST HANGS AROUND THE HOUSE. HE DOESN'T READ OR SHOW ANY INTEREST IN ANYTHING.
THE ACADEMY IS OUR LAST RESORT. WE'RE DESPERATELY HOPING YOU CAN SORT HIM OUT.
I'M SURE YOU'VE BEEN GREAT PARENTS.
BUT THESE MODERN CHILDREN! IT'S HEART-BREAKING, THE WAY SOME OF THEM BEHAVE!
YOU'VE DONE THE RIGHT THING, COMING TO US. THE ACADEMY HAS HAD A REMARKABLE SUCCESS RATE OVER THE PAST ELEVEN YEARS.
WHAT EXACTLY DO YOU... DO?
WE HAVE OUR METHODS. WHEN ALEX COMES HOME, HE'LL BE A COMPLETELY DIFFERENT BOY!
WHERE IS ALEX, BY THE WAY?

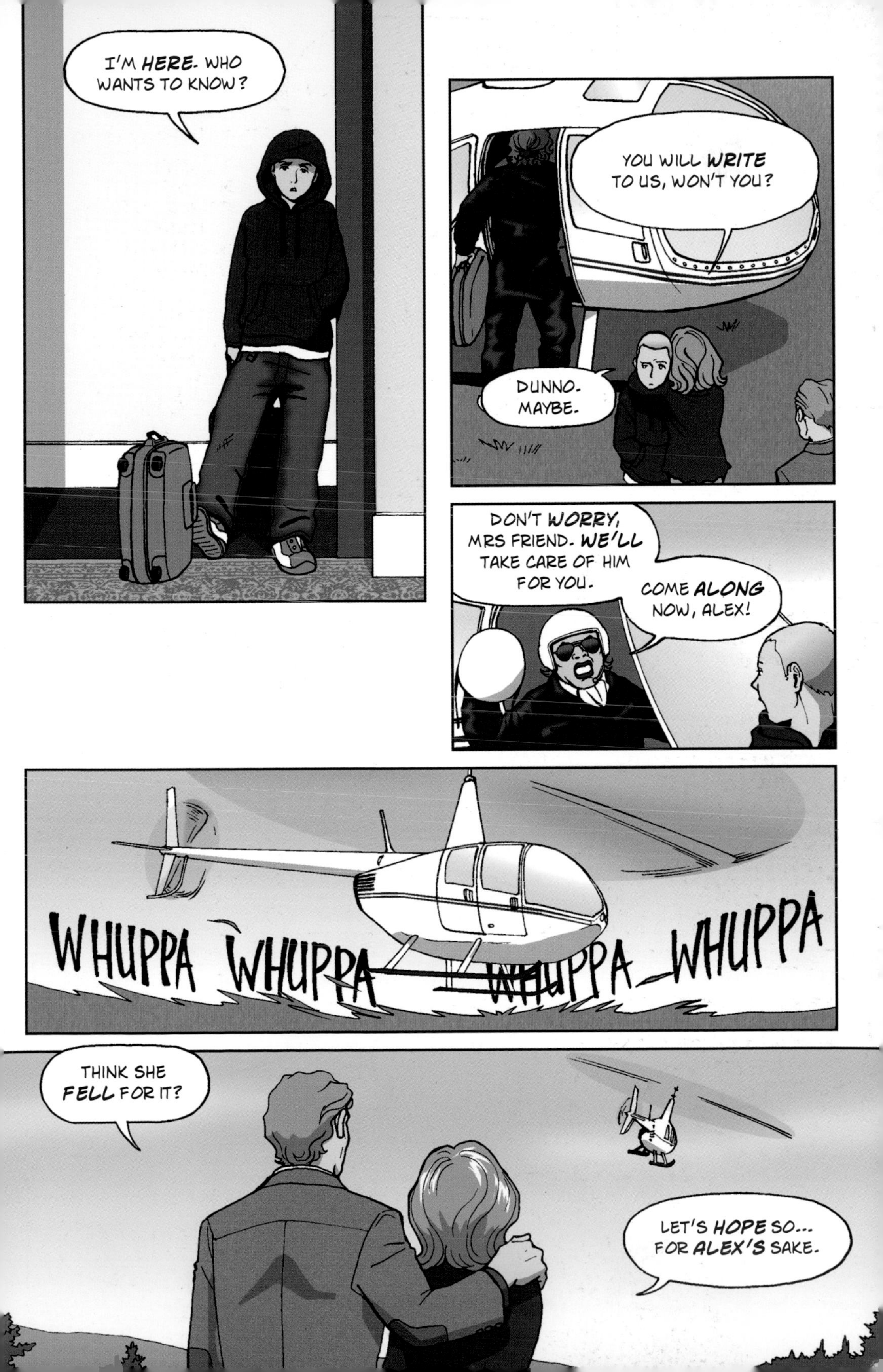
I'M HERE. WHO WANTS TO KNOW?
YOU WILL WRITE TO US, WON'T YOU?
DUNNO. MAYBE.
DON'T WORRY, MRS FRIEND. WE'LL TAKE CARE OF HIM FOR YOU.
COME ALONG NOW, ALEX!
WHUPPA WHUPPA WHUPPA WHUPPA
THINK SHE FELL FOR IT?
LET'S HOPE SO... FOR ALEX'S SAKE.

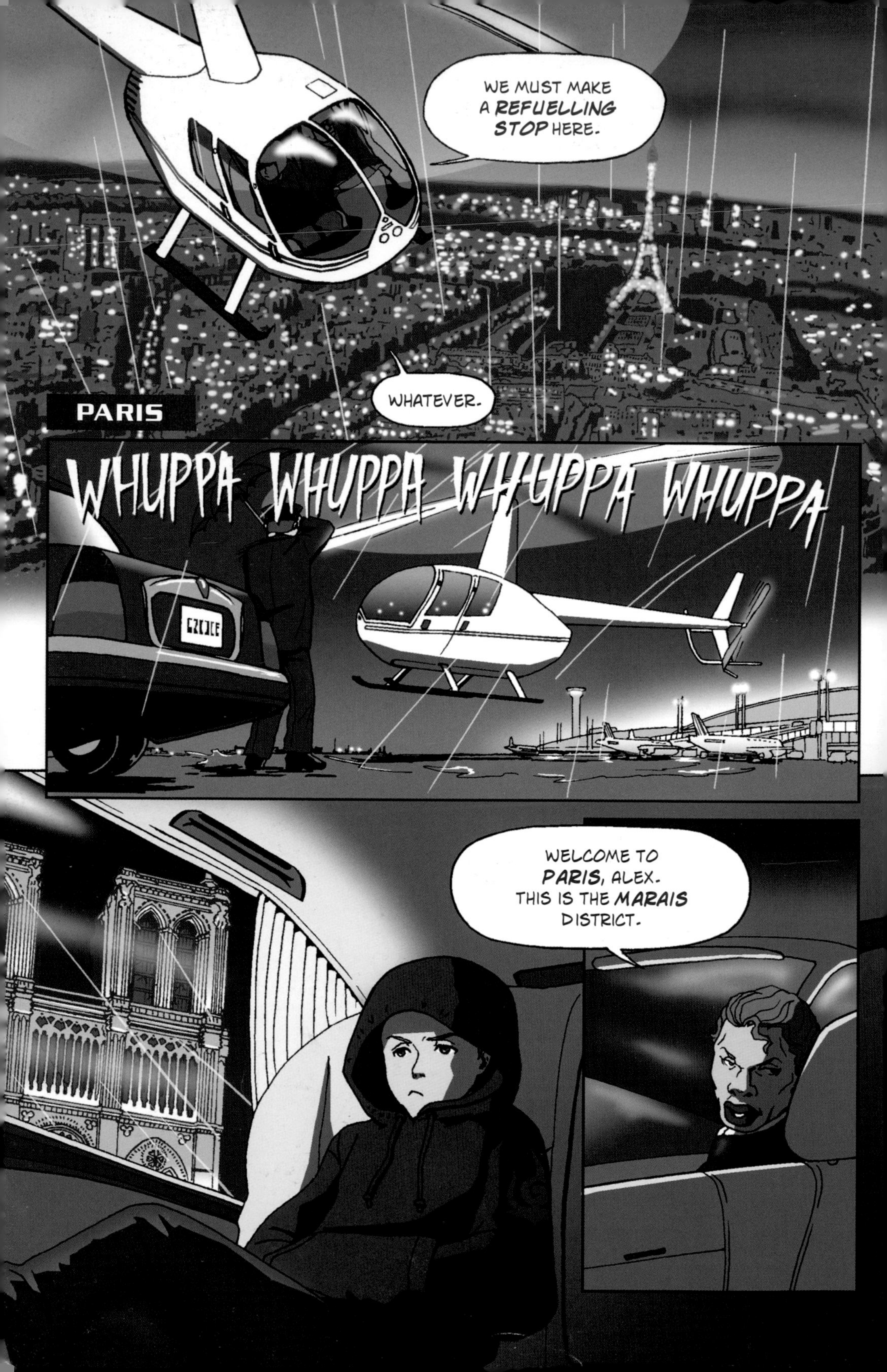
WE MUST MAKE A REFUELLING STOP HERE.
WHATEVER.
PARIS
WHUPPA WHUPPA WHUPPA WHUPPA
WELCOME TO PARIS, ALEX. THIS IS THE MARAIS DISTRICT.

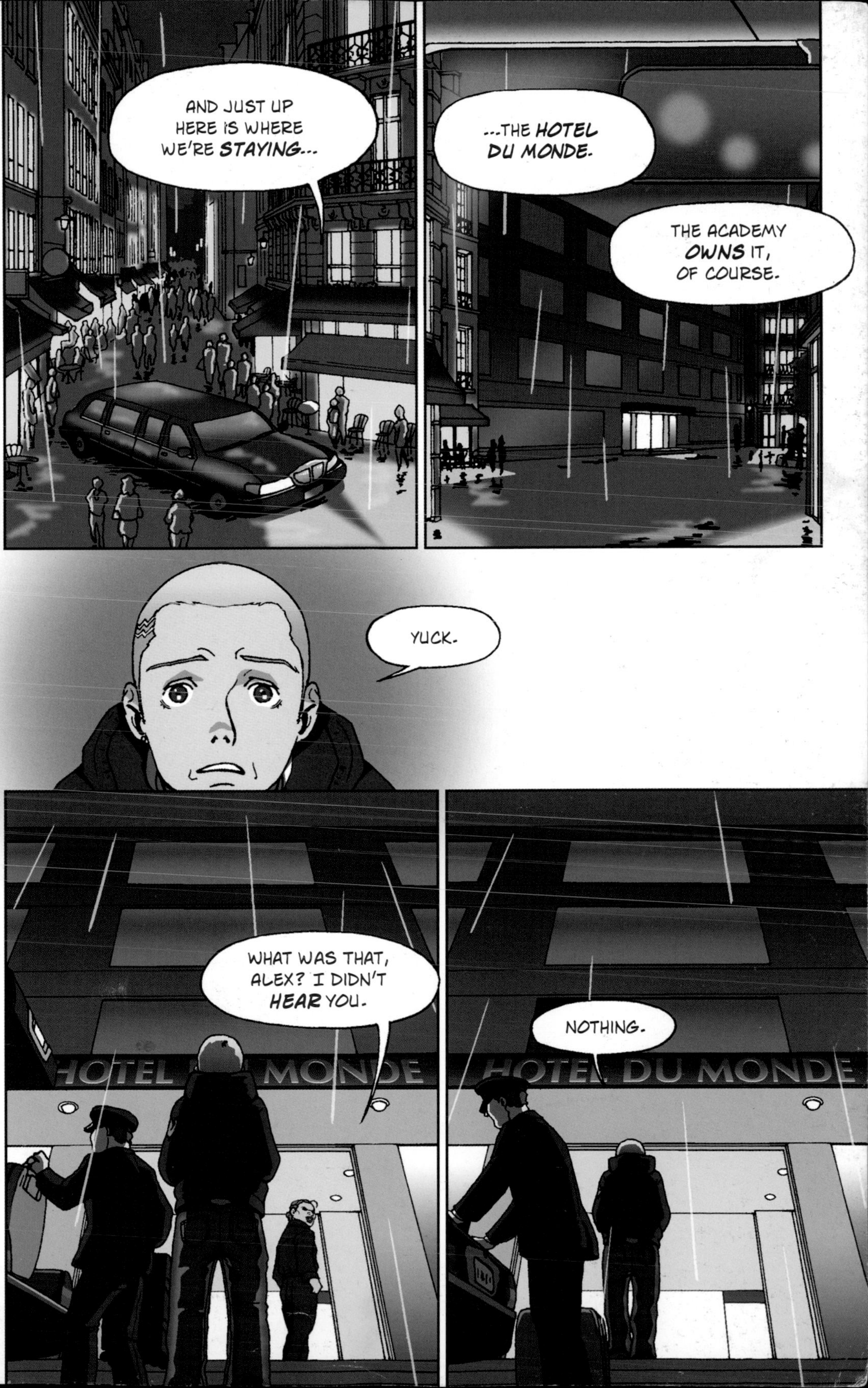
AND JUST UP HERE IS WHERE WE'RE STAYING...
...THE HOTEL DU MONDE.
THE ACADEMY OWNS IT, OF COURSE.
YUCK.
WHAT WAS THAT, ALEX? I DIDN'T HEAR YOU.
HOTEL DU MONDE
NOTHING.
HOTEL DU MONDE

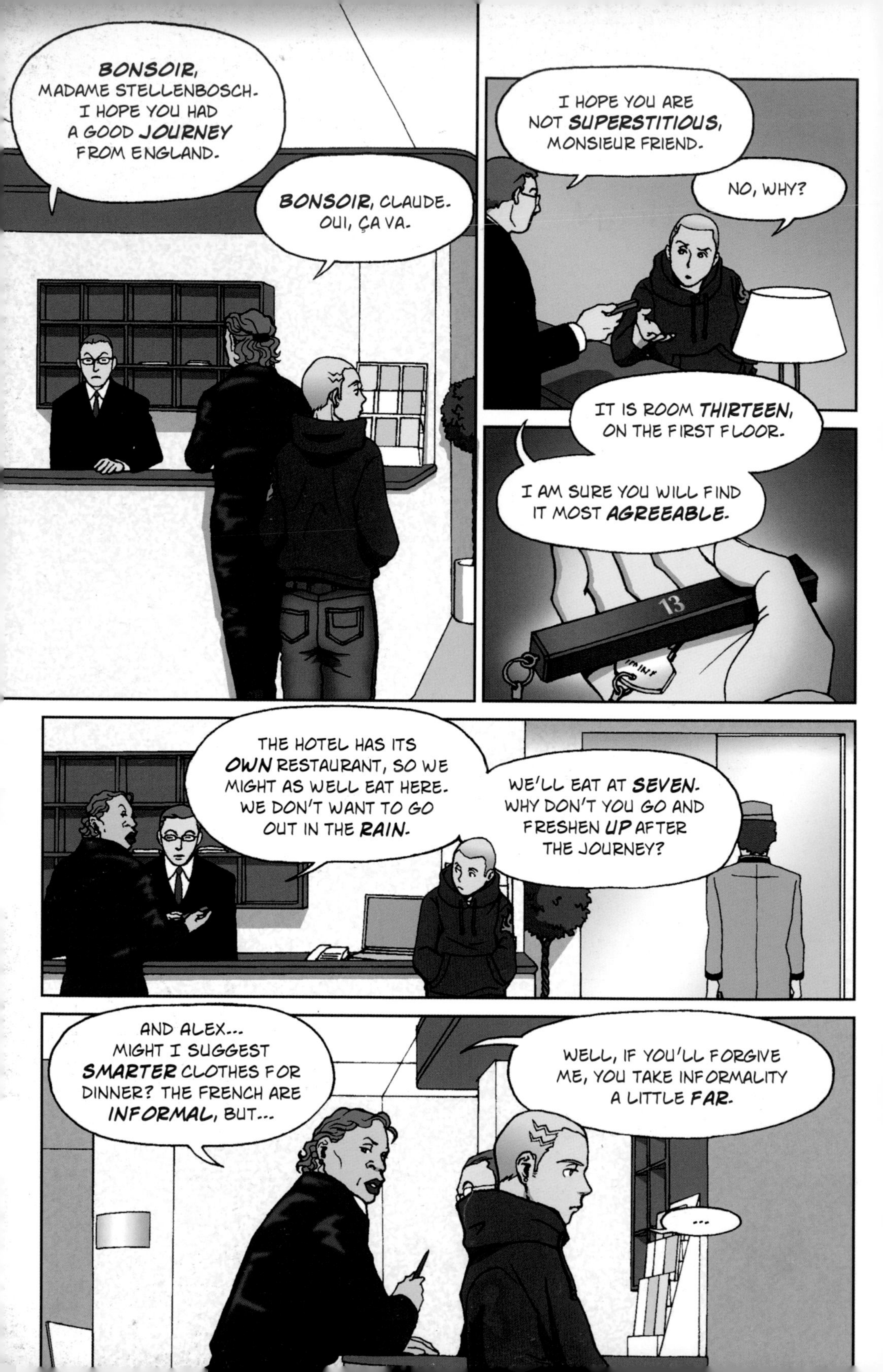
BONSOIR, MADAME STELLENBOSCH. I HOPE YOU HAD A GOOD JOURNEY FROM ENGLAND.
BONSOIR, CLAUDE. OUI, ÇA VA.
I HOPE YOU ARE NOT SUPERSTITIOUS, MONSIEUR FRIEND.
NO, WHY?
IT IS ROOM THIRTEEN, ON THE FIRST FLOOR.
I AM SURE YOU WILL FIND IT MOST AGREEABLE.
13
THE HOTEL HAS ITS OWN RESTAURANT, SO WE MIGHT AS WELL EAT HERE. WE DON'T WANT TO GO OUT IN THE RAIN.
WE'LL EAT AT SEVEN. WHY DON'T YOU GO AND FRESHEN UP AFTER THE JOURNEY?
AND ALEX... MIGHT I SUGGEST SMARTER CLOTHES FOR DINNER? THE FRENCH ARE INFORMAL, BUT...
WELL, IF YOU'LL FORGIVE ME, YOU TAKE INFORMALITY A LITTLE FAR.
...

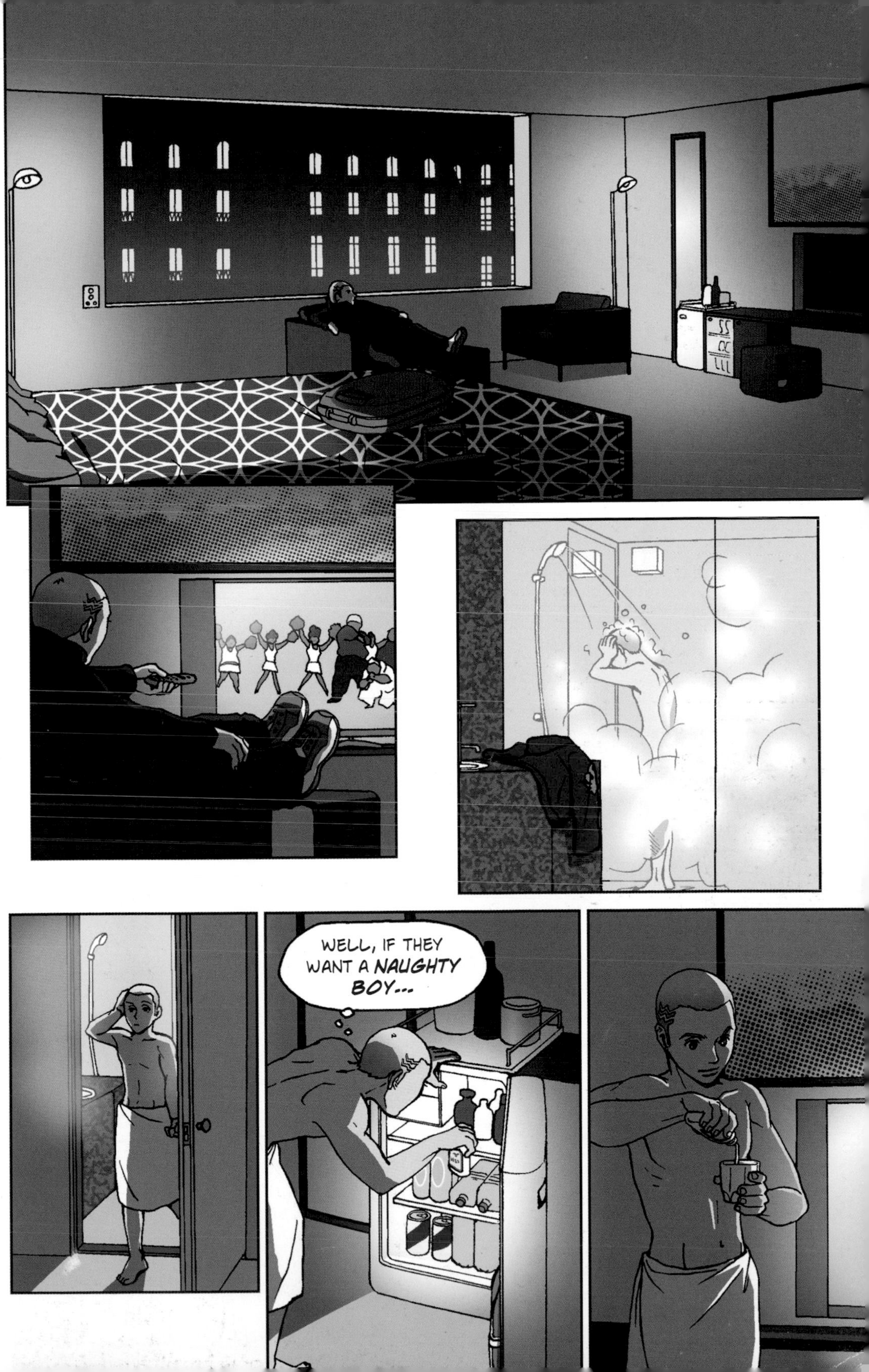
WELL, IF THEY WANT A *NAUGHTY* BOY...

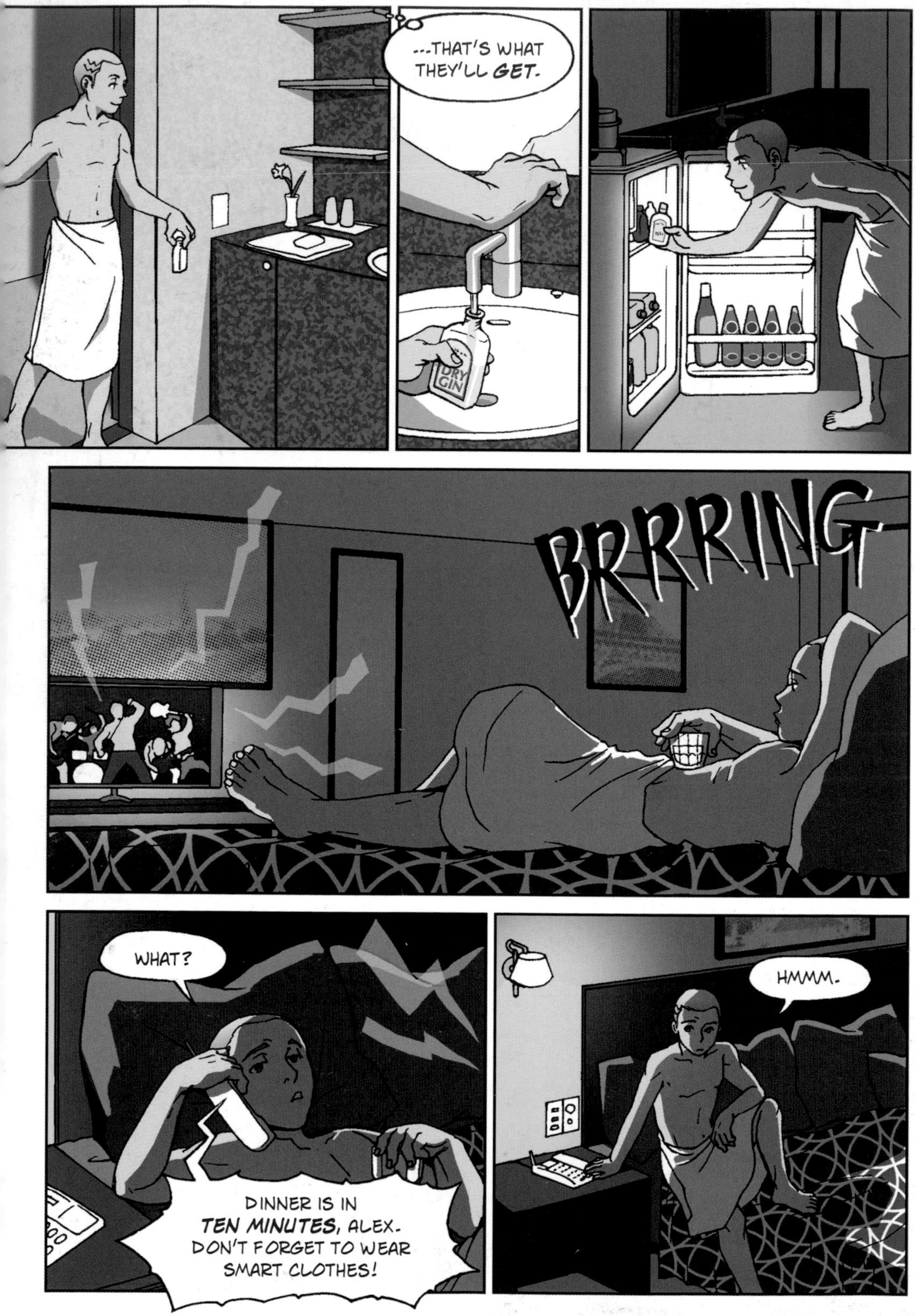
...THAT'S WHAT THEY'LL GET.
DRY GIN
BRRRING
WHAT?
DINNER IS IN TEN MINUTES, ALEX. DON'T FORGET TO WEAR SMART CLOTHES!
HMMM.

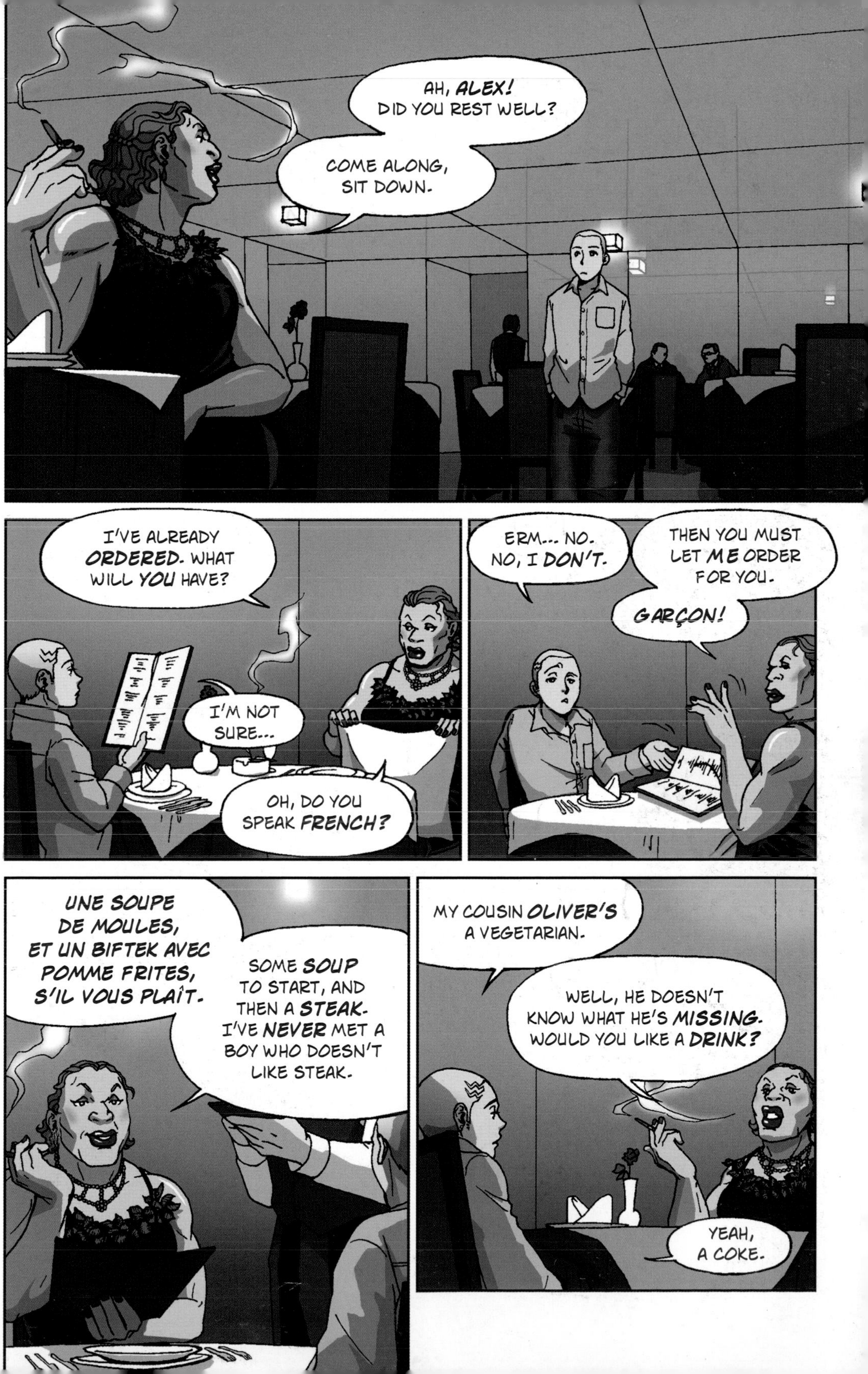
AH, ALEX! DID YOU REST WELL?
COME ALONG, SIT DOWN.
I'VE ALREADY ORDERED. WHAT WILL YOU HAVE?
I'M NOT SURE...
OH, DO YOU SPEAK FRENCH?
ERM... NO. NO, I DON'T.
THEN YOU MUST LET ME ORDER FOR YOU.
GARÇON!
UNE SOUPE DE MOULES, ET UN BIFTEK AVEC POMME FRITES, S'IL VOUS PLAÎT.
SOME SOUP TO START, AND THEN A STEAK. I'VE NEVER MET A BOY WHO DOESN'T LIKE STEAK.
MY COUSIN OLIVER'S A VEGETARIAN.
WELL, HE DOESN'T KNOW WHAT HE'S MISSING. WOULD YOU LIKE A DRINK?
YEAH, A COKE.

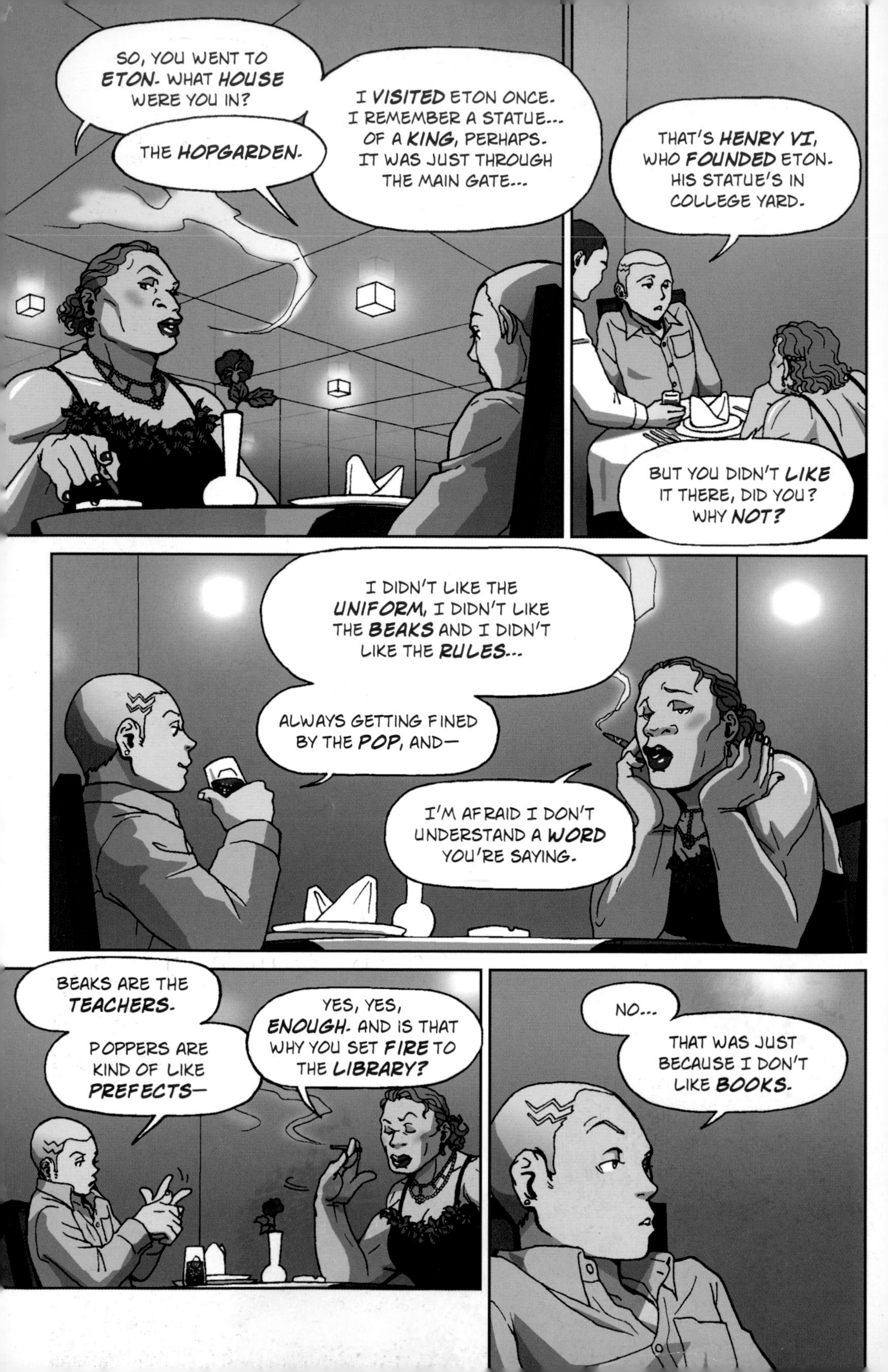
SO, YOU WENT TO ETON. WHAT HOUSE WERE YOU IN?
THE HOPGARDEN.
I VISITED ETON ONCE. I REMEMBER A STATUE... OF A KING, PERHAPS. IT WAS JUST THROUGH THE MAIN GATE...
THAT'S HENRY VI, WHO FOUNDED ETON. HIS STATUE'S IN COLLEGE YARD.
BUT YOU DIDN'T LIKE IT THERE, DID YOU? WHY NOT?
I DIDN'T LIKE THE UNIFORM, I DIDN'T LIKE THE BEAKS AND I DIDN'T LIKE THE RULES...
ALWAYS GETTING FINED BY THE POP, AND—
I'M AFRAID I DON'T UNDERSTAND A WORD YOU'RE SAYING.
BEAKS ARE THE TEACHERS.
POPPERS ARE KIND OF LIKE PREFECTS—
YES, YES, ENOUGH. AND IS THAT WHY YOU SET FIRE TO THE LIBRARY?
NO...
THAT WAS JUST BECAUSE I DON'T LIKE BOOKS.

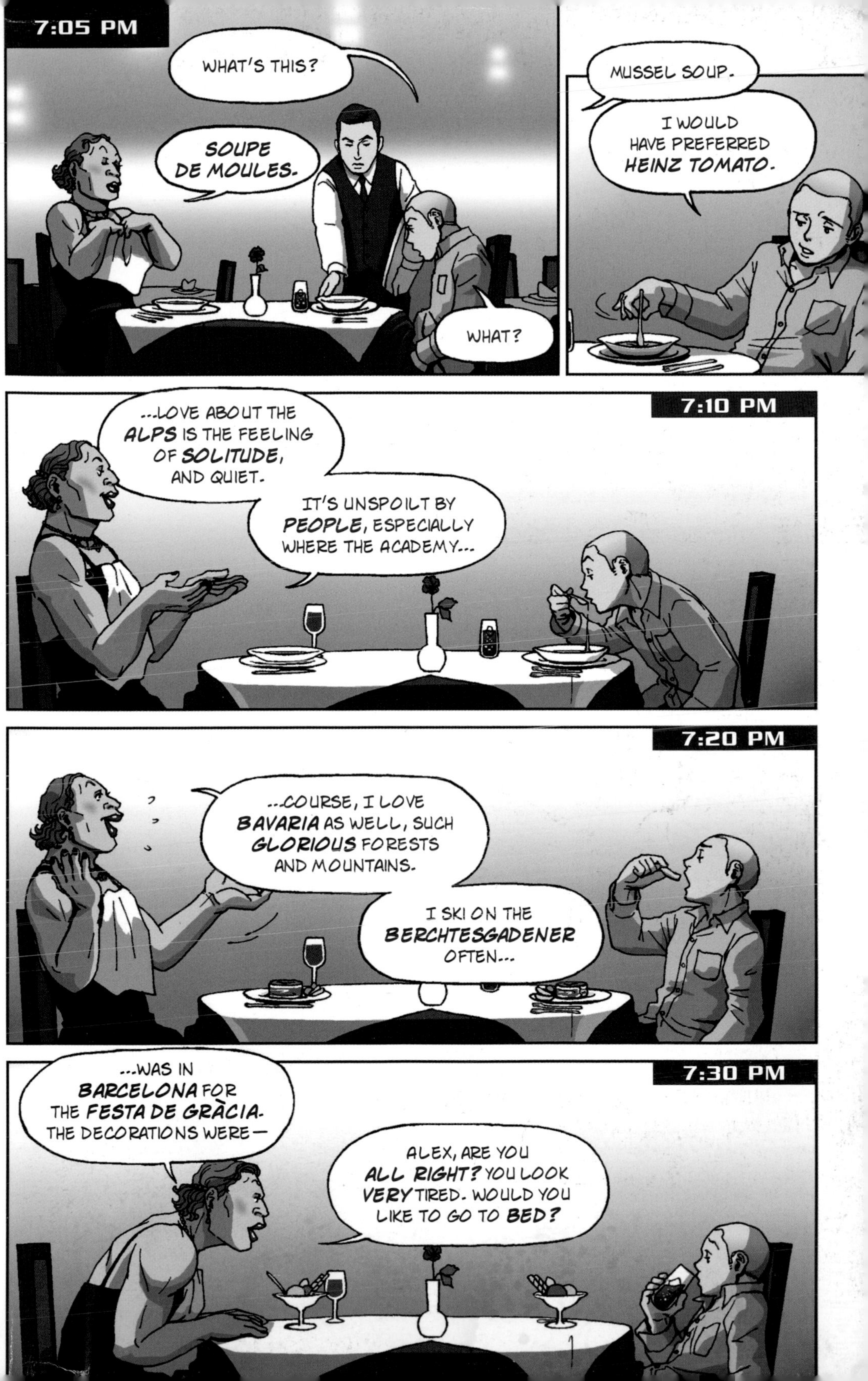
7:05 PM
WHAT'S THIS?
SOUPE DE MOULES.
WHAT?
MUSSEL SOUP.
I WOULD HAVE PREFERRED HEINZ TOMATO.
7:10 PM
...LOVE ABOUT THE ALPS IS THE FEELING OF SOLITUDE, AND QUIET.
IT'S UNSPOILT BY PEOPLE, ESPECIALLY WHERE THE ACADEMY...
7:20 PM
...COURSE, I LOVE BAVARIA AS WELL, SUCH GLORIOUS FORESTS AND MOUNTAINS.
I SKI ON THE BERCHTESGADENER OFTEN...
7:30 PM
...WAS IN BARCELONA FOR THE FESTA DE GRÀCIA. THE DECORATIONS WERE—
ALEX, ARE YOU ALL RIGHT? YOU LOOK VERY TIRED. WOULD YOU LIKE TO GO TO BED?

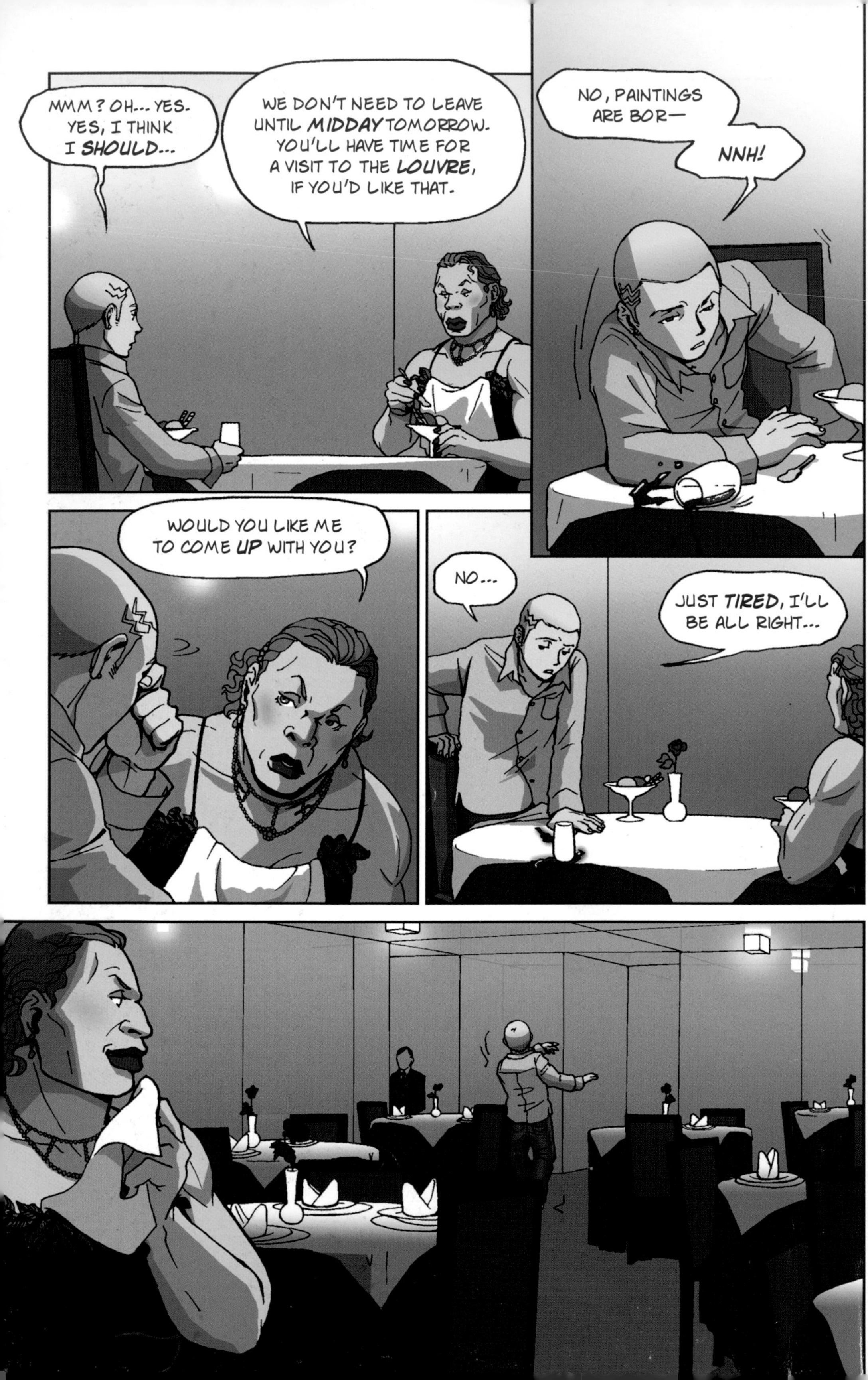
MMM? OH... YES. YES, I THINK I SHOULD...
WE DON'T NEED TO LEAVE UNTIL MIDDAY TOMORROW. YOU'LL HAVE TIME FOR A VISIT TO THE LOUVRE, IF YOU'D LIKE THAT.
NO, PAINTINGS ARE BOR—
NNH!
WOULD YOU LIKE ME TO COME UP WITH YOU?
NO...
JUST TIRED, I'LL BE ALL RIGHT...

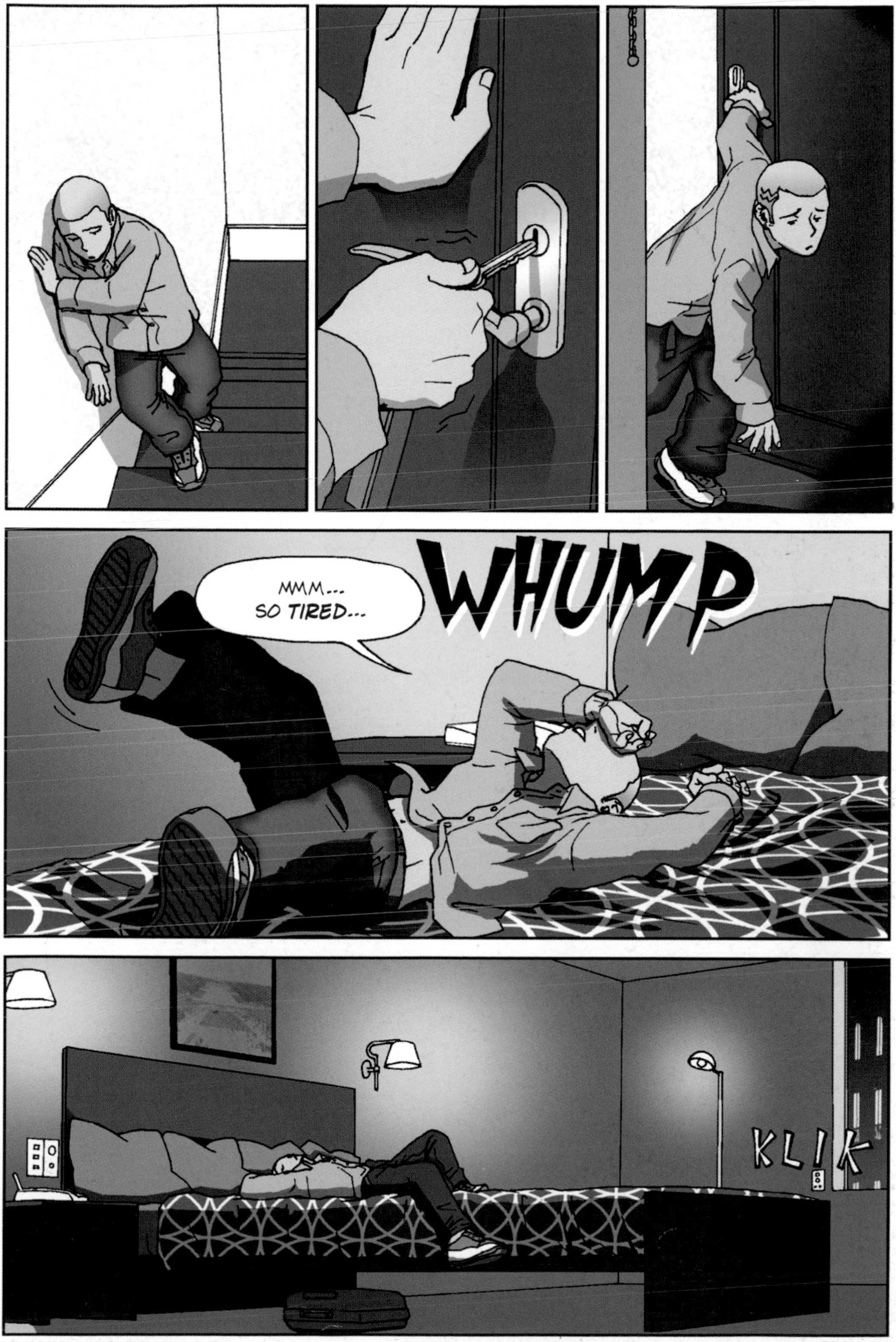
MMM...
SO TIRED...
WHUMP
KLIK

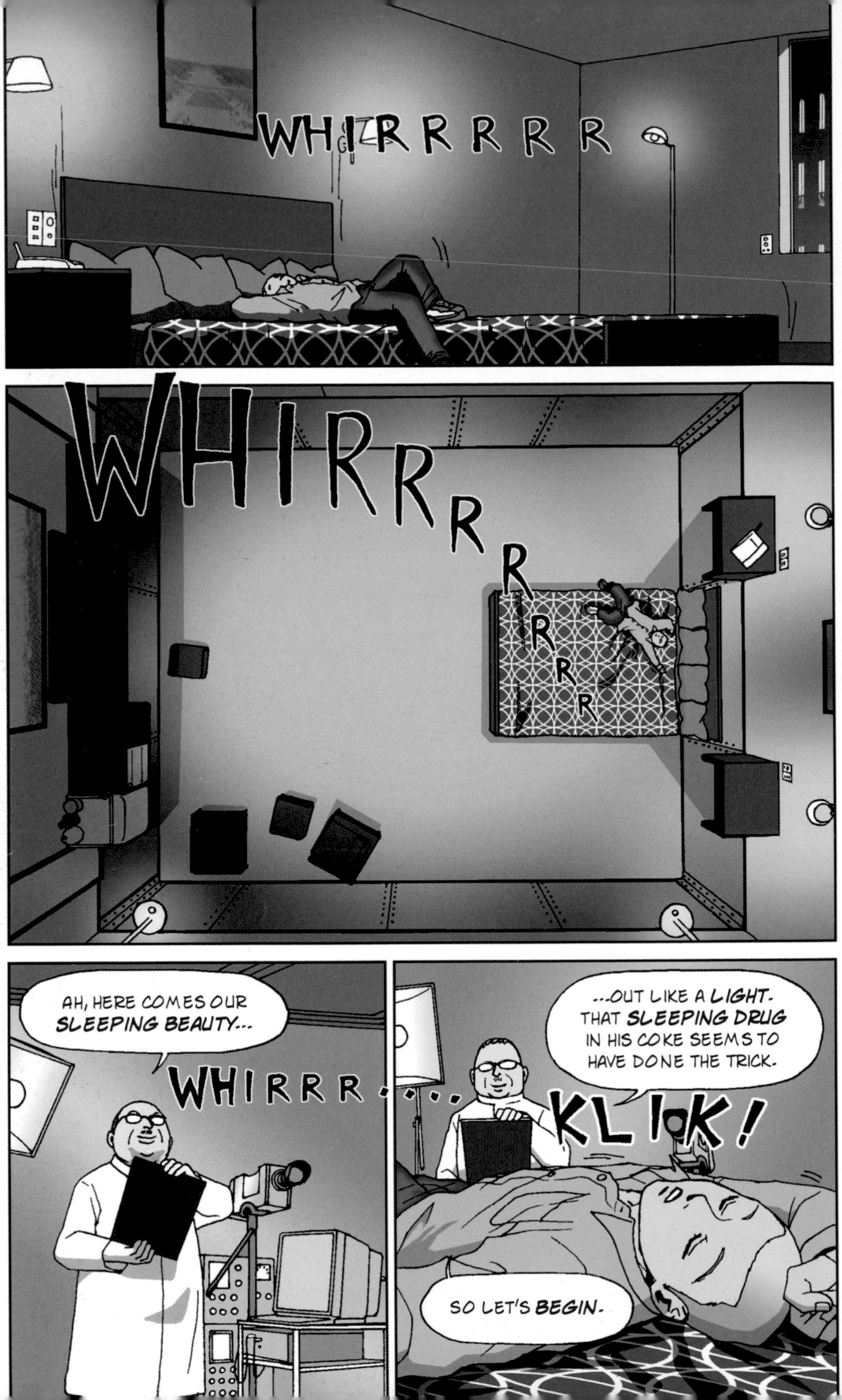
WHIRRRRR
WHIRRRRRRR
AH, HERE COMES OUR SLEEPING BEAUTY...
WHIRRR...
...OUT LIKE A LIGHT. THAT SLEEPING DRUG IN HIS COKE SEEMS TO HAVE DONE THE TRICK.
KLICK!
SO LET'S BEGIN.

KLIK!
KLIK!
WHIRRRRRRR
FRIEND, ALEX
FULL BODY SCAN
BEEP
BEEP
BEEP
ZMMMMMMM

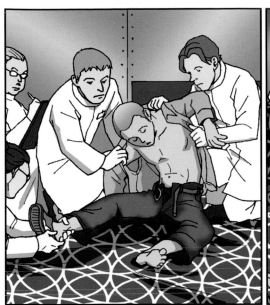

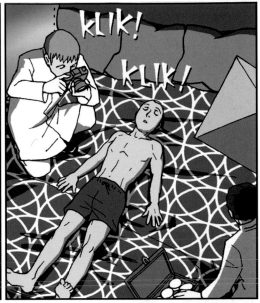

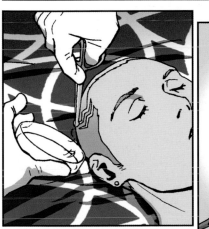

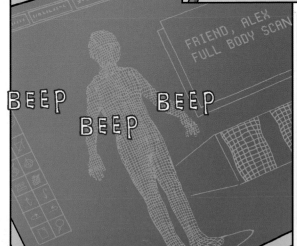

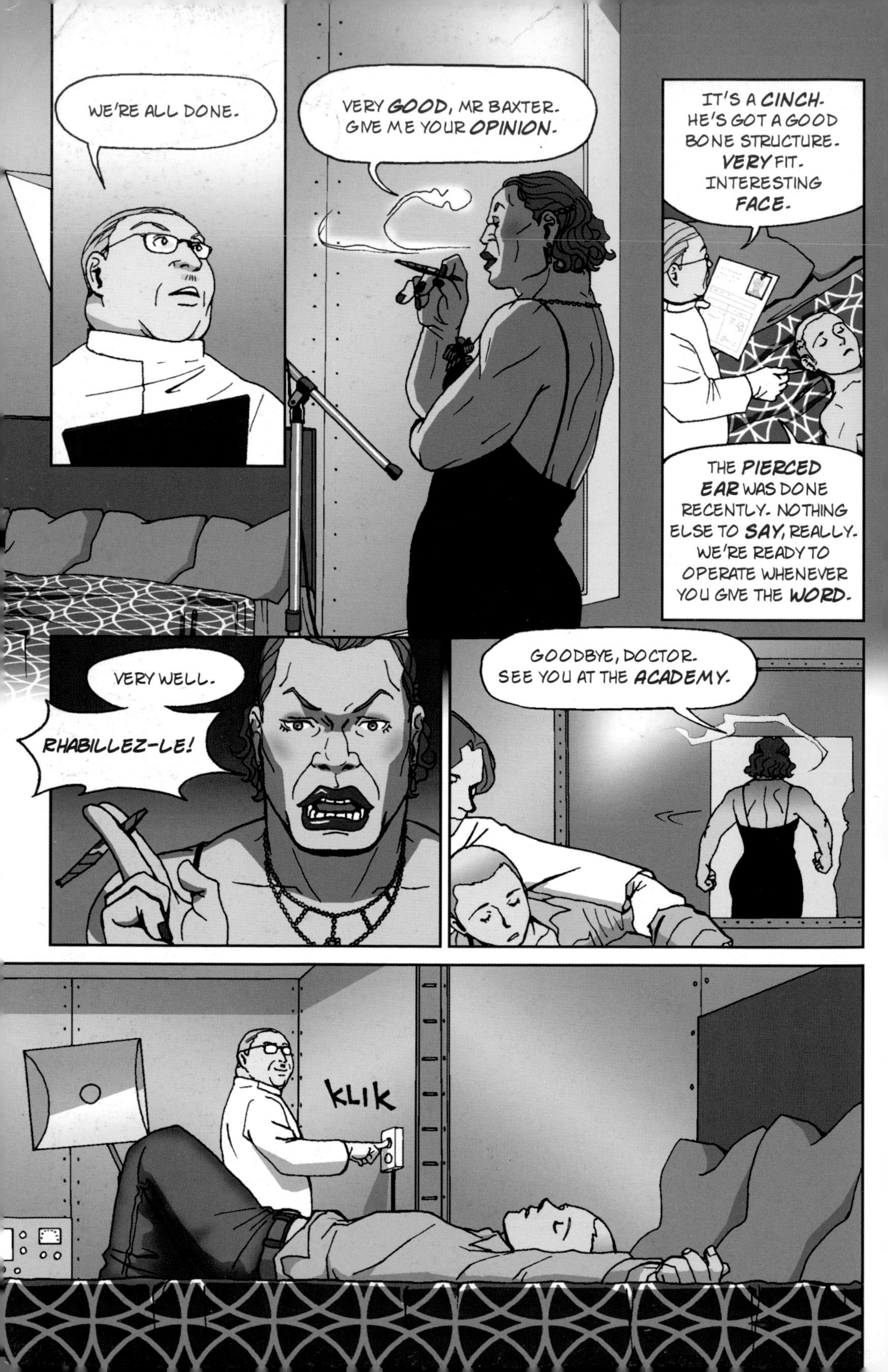
WE'RE ALL DONE.
VERY GOOD, MR BAXTER. GIVE ME YOUR OPINION.
IT'S A CINCH. HE'S GOT A GOOD BONE STRUCTURE. VERY FIT. INTERESTING FACE.
THE PIERCED EAR WAS DONE RECENTLY. NOTHING ELSE TO SAY, REALLY. WE'RE READY TO OPERATE WHENEVER YOU GIVE THE WORD.
VERY WELL.
RHABILLEZ-LE!
GOODBYE, DOCTOR. SEE YOU AT THE ACADEMY.
KLIK

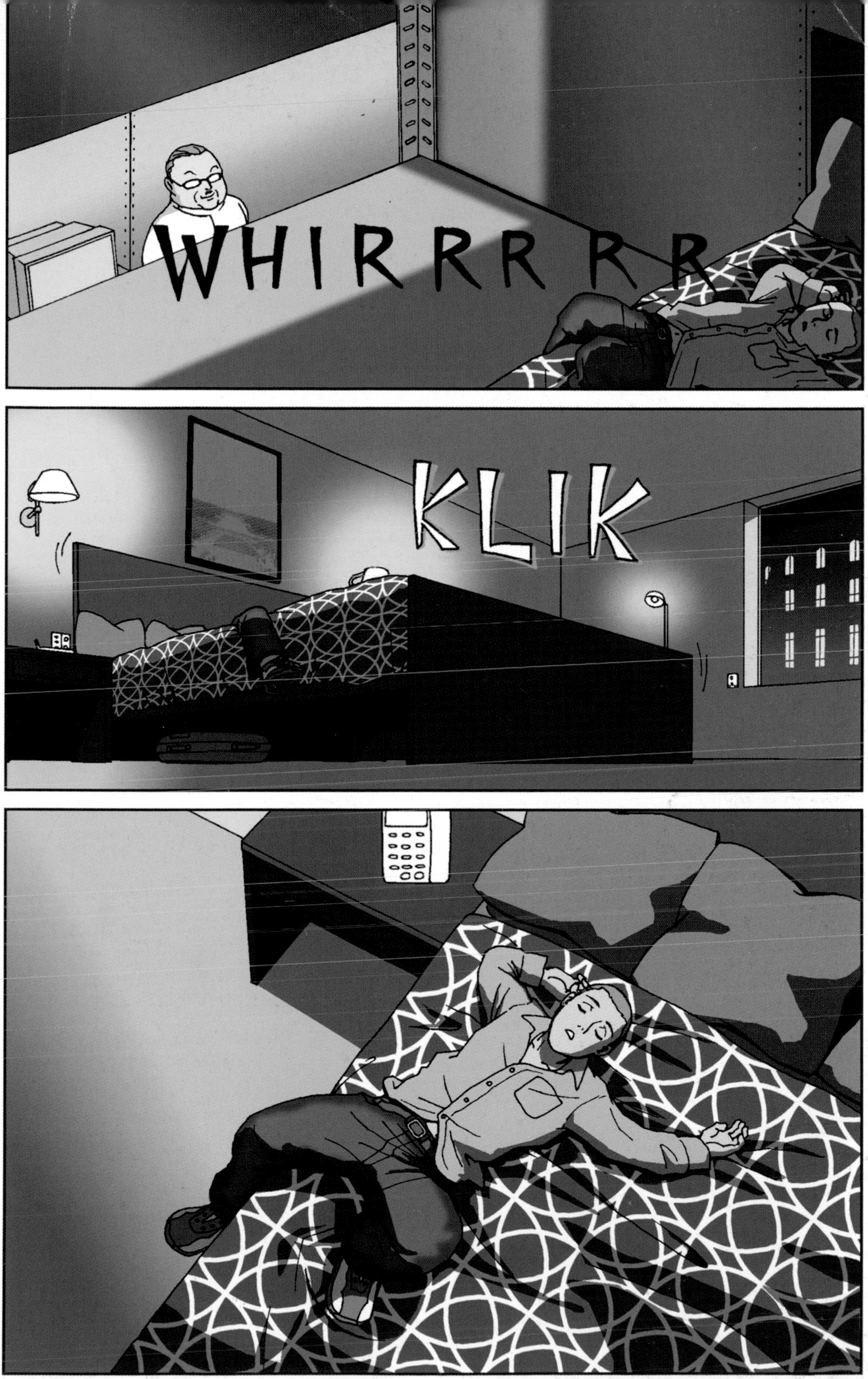
WHIRRRRR
KLIK

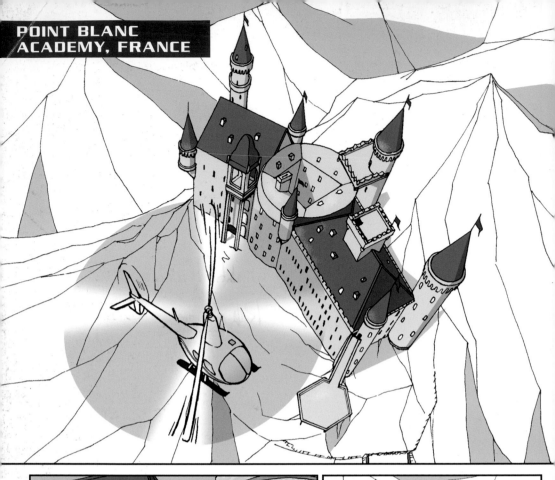

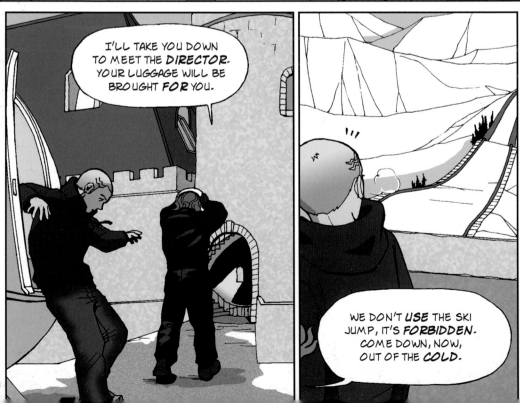

POINT BLANC ACADEMY, FRANCE
I'LL TAKE YOU DOWN TO MEET THE DIRECTOR. YOUR LUGGAGE WILL BE BROUGHT FOR YOU.
WE DON'T USE THE SKI JUMP, IT'S FORBIDDEN. COME DOWN, NOW, OUT OF THE COLD.

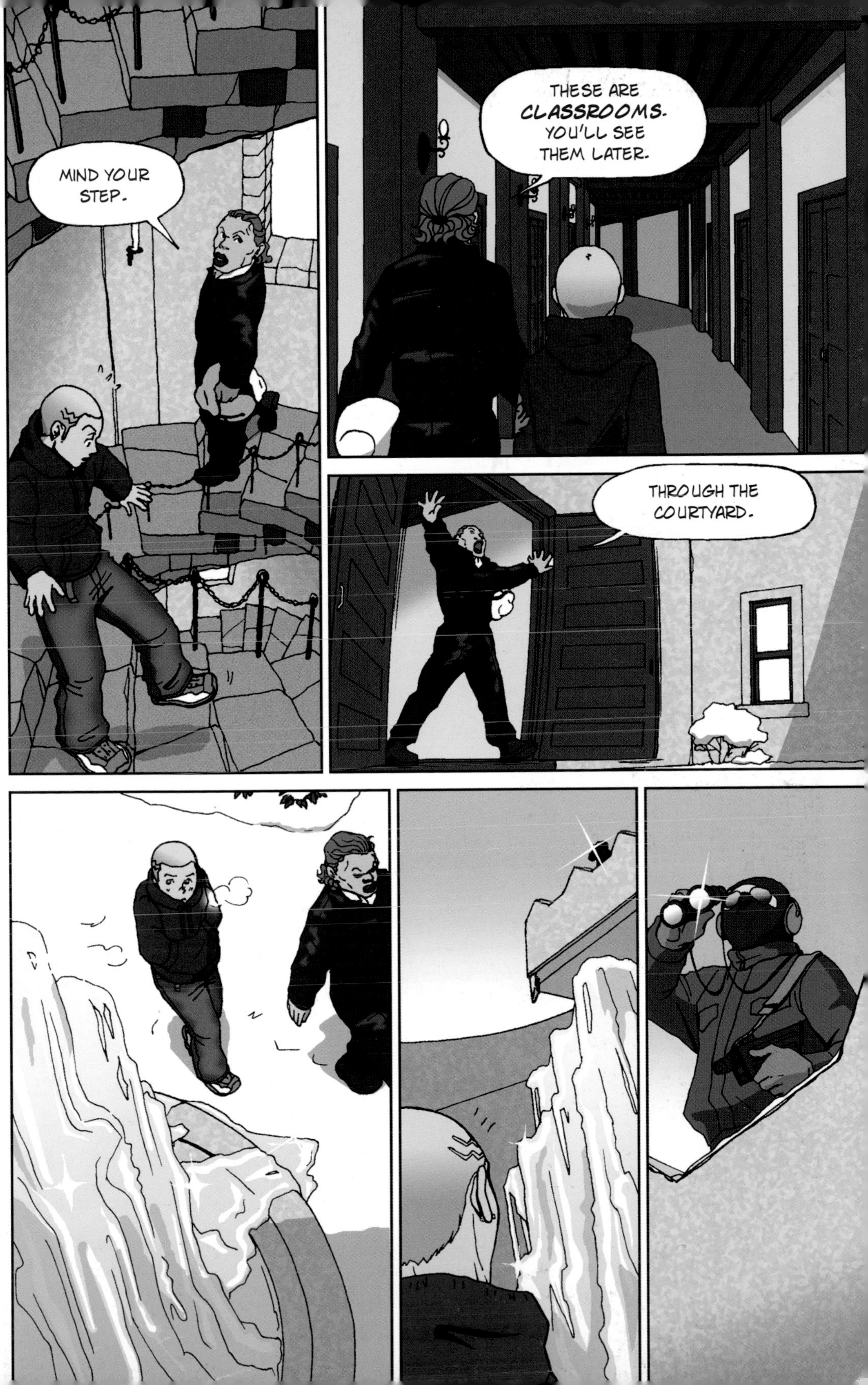
MIND YOUR STEP.
THESE ARE CLASSROOMS. YOU'LL SEE THEM LATER.
THROUGH THE COURTYARD.

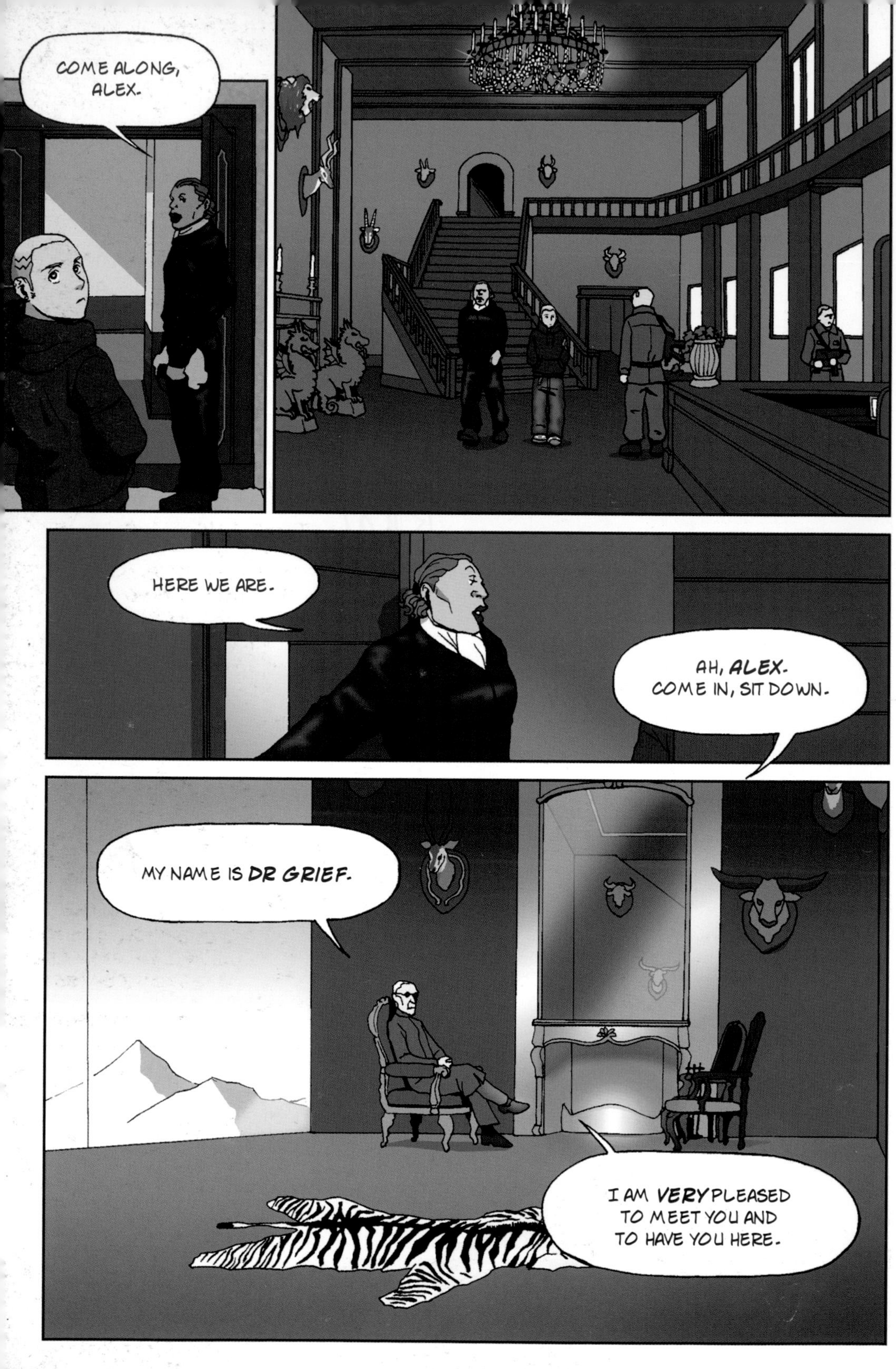
COME ALONG, ALEX.
HERE WE ARE.
AH, ALEX. COME IN, SIT DOWN.
MY NAME IS DR GRIEF.
I AM VERY PLEASED TO MEET YOU AND TO HAVE YOU HERE.

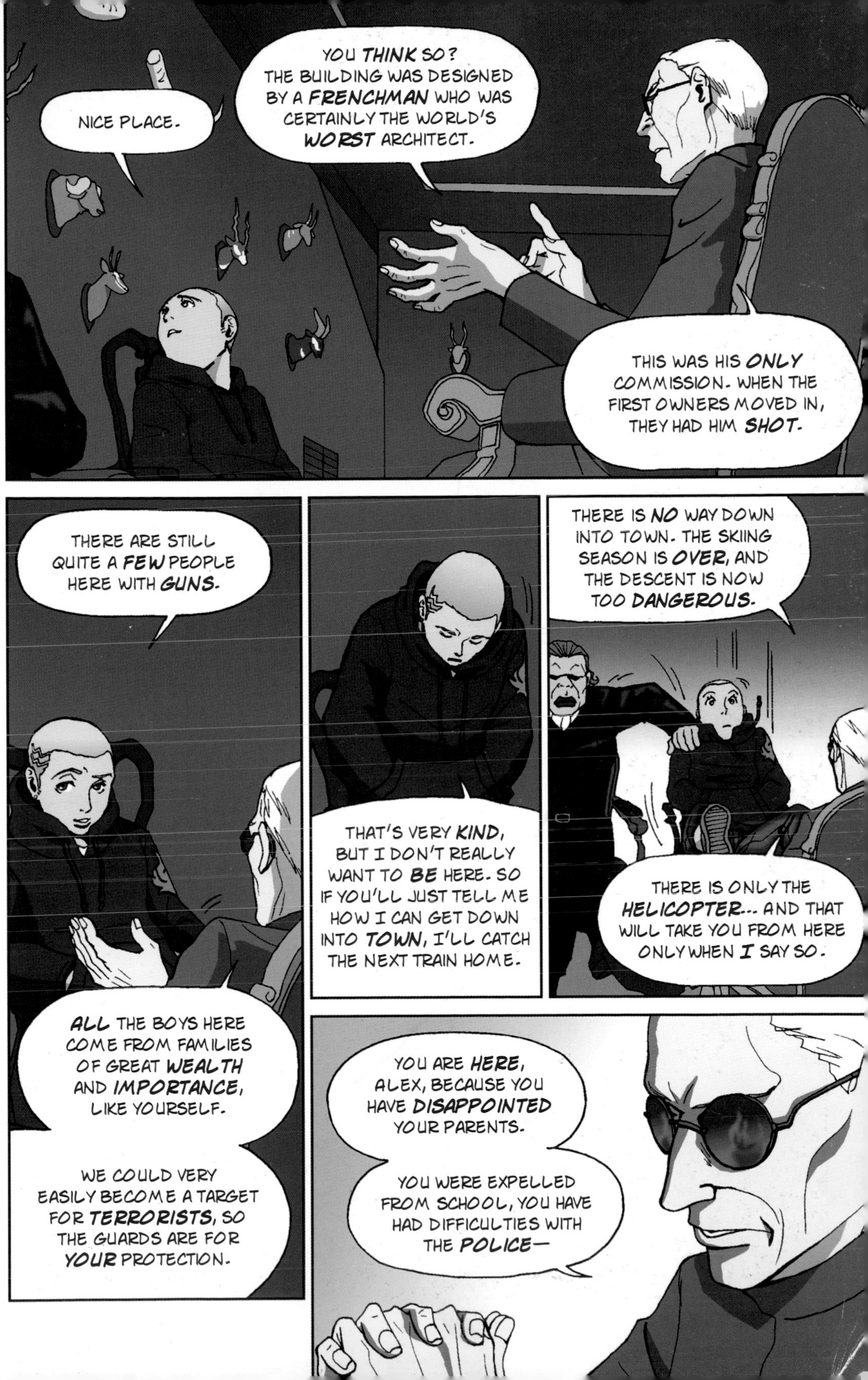
NICE PLACE.
YOU THINK SO? THE BUILDING WAS DESIGNED BY A FRENCHMAN WHO WAS CERTAINLY THE WORLD'S WORST ARCHITECT.
THIS WAS HIS ONLY COMMISSION. WHEN THE FIRST OWNERS MOVED IN, THEY HAD HIM SHOT.
THERE ARE STILL QUITE A FEW PEOPLE HERE WITH GUNS.
ALL THE BOYS HERE COME FROM FAMILIES OF GREAT WEALTH AND IMPORTANCE, LIKE YOURSELF.
WE COULD VERY EASILY BECOME A TARGET FOR TERRORISTS, SO THE GUARDS ARE FOR YOUR PROTECTION.
THAT'S VERY KIND, BUT I DON'T REALLY WANT TO BE HERE. SO IF YOU'LL JUST TELL ME HOW I CAN GET DOWN INTO TOWN, I'LL CATCH THE NEXT TRAIN HOME.
THERE IS NO WAY DOWN INTO TOWN. THE SKIING SEASON IS OVER, AND THE DESCENT IS NOW TOO DANGEROUS.
THERE IS ONLY THE HELICOPTER... AND THAT WILL TAKE YOU FROM HERE ONLY WHEN I SAY SO.
YOU ARE HERE, ALEX, BECAUSE YOU HAVE DISAPPOINTED YOUR PARENTS.
YOU WERE EXPELLED FROM SCHOOL, YOU HAVE HAD DIFFICULTIES WITH THE POLICE—

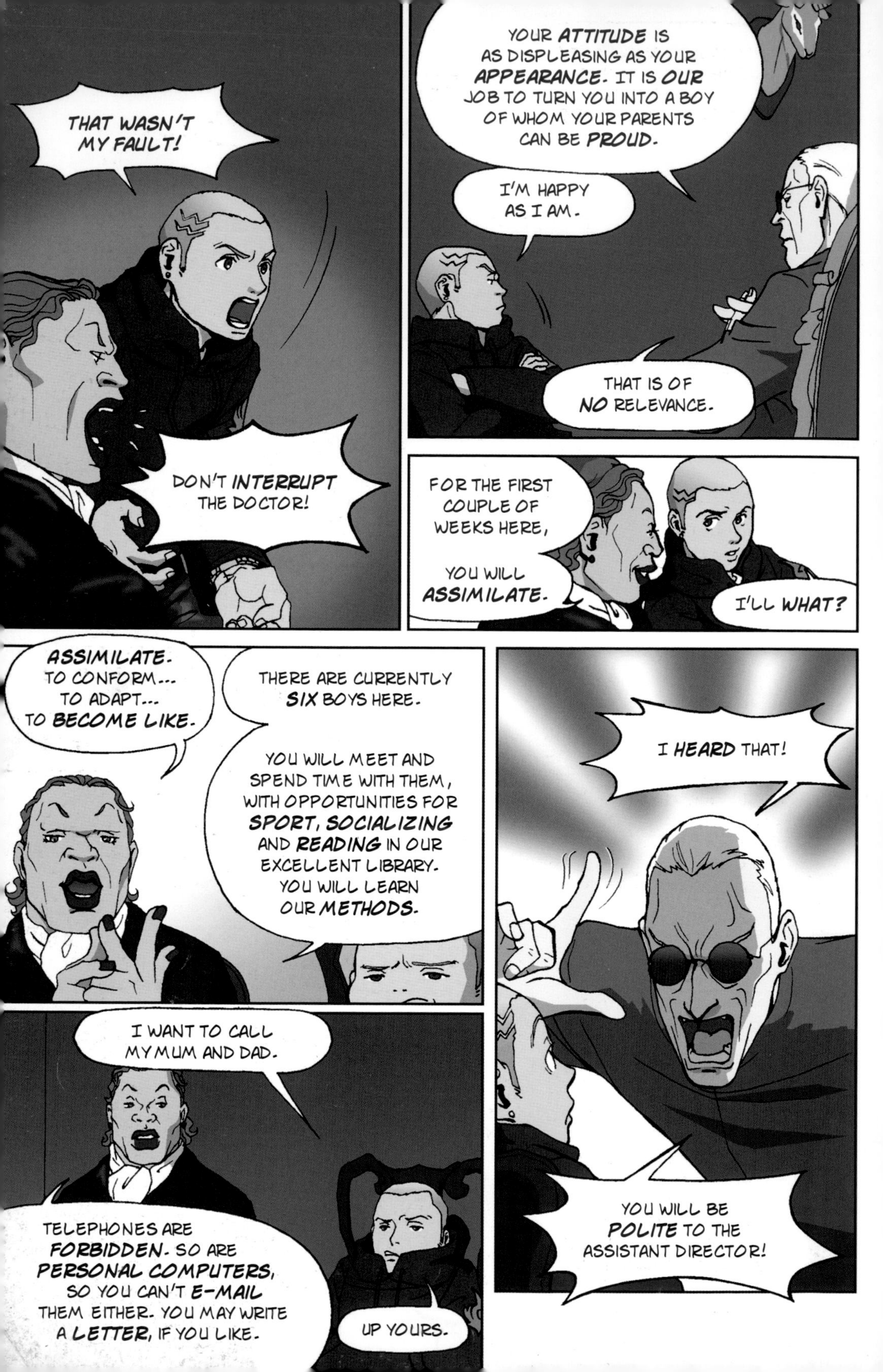
THAT WASN'T MY FAULT!
DON'T INTERRUPT THE DOCTOR!
YOUR ATTITUDE IS AS DISPLEASING AS YOUR APPEARANCE. IT IS OUR JOB TO TURN YOU INTO A BOY OF WHOM YOUR PARENTS CAN BE PROUD.
I'M HAPPY AS I AM.
THAT IS OF NO RELEVANCE.
FOR THE FIRST COUPLE OF WEEKS HERE,
YOU WILL ASSIMILATE.
I'LL WHAT?
ASSIMILATE. TO CONFORM... TO ADAPT... TO BECOME LIKE.
THERE ARE CURRENTLY SIX BOYS HERE.
YOU WILL MEET AND SPEND TIME WITH THEM, WITH OPPORTUNITIES FOR SPORT, SOCIALIZING AND READING IN OUR EXCELLENT LIBRARY. YOU WILL LEARN OUR METHODS.
I WANT TO CALL MY MUM AND DAD.
TELEPHONES ARE FORBIDDEN. SO ARE PERSONAL COMPUTERS, SO YOU CAN'T E-MAIL THEM EITHER. YOU MAY WRITE A LETTER, IF YOU LIKE.
UP YOURS.
I HEARD THAT!
YOU WILL BE POLITE TO THE ASSISTANT DIRECTOR!

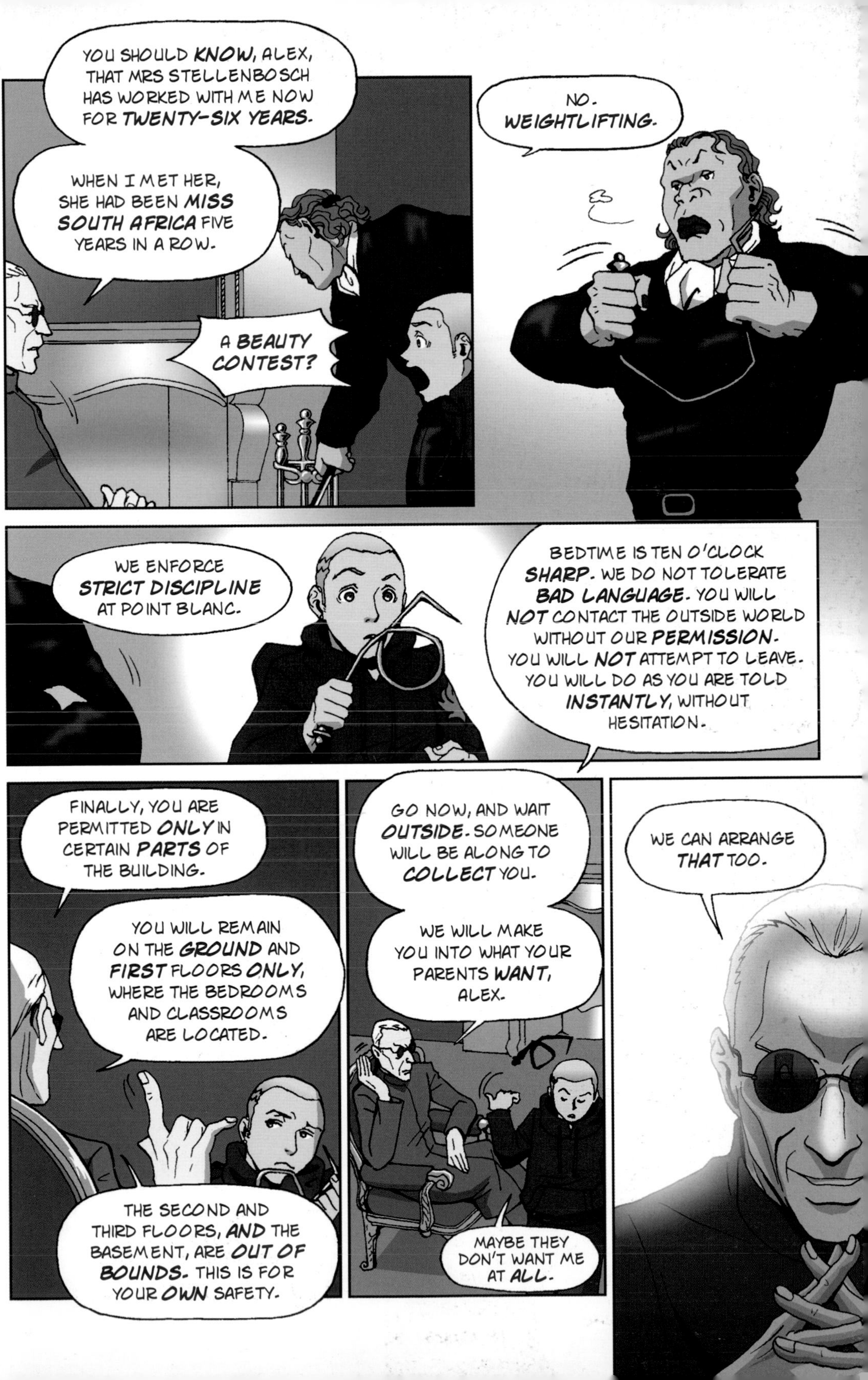
YOU SHOULD KNOW, ALEX, THAT MRS STELLENBOSCH HAS WORKED WITH ME NOW FOR TWENTY-SIX YEARS.
WHEN I MET HER, SHE HAD BEEN MISS SOUTH AFRICA FIVE YEARS IN A ROW.
A BEAUTY CONTEST?
NO. WEIGHTLIFTING.
WE ENFORCE STRICT DISCIPLINE AT POINT BLANC.
BEDTIME IS TEN O'CLOCK SHARP. WE DO NOT TOLERATE BAD LANGUAGE. YOU WILL NOT CONTACT THE OUTSIDE WORLD WITHOUT OUR PERMISSION. YOU WILL NOT ATTEMPT TO LEAVE. YOU WILL DO AS YOU ARE TOLD INSTANTLY, WITHOUT HESITATION.
FINALLY, YOU ARE PERMITTED ONLY IN CERTAIN PARTS OF THE BUILDING.
YOU WILL REMAIN ON THE GROUND AND FIRST FLOORS ONLY, WHERE THE BEDROOMS AND CLASSROOMS ARE LOCATED.
THE SECOND AND THIRD FLOORS, AND THE BASEMENT, ARE OUT OF BOUNDS. THIS IS FOR YOUR OWN SAFETY.
GO NOW, AND WAIT OUTSIDE. SOMEONE WILL BE ALONG TO COLLECT YOU.
WE WILL MAKE YOU INTO WHAT YOUR PARENTS WANT, ALEX.
MAYBE THEY DON'T WANT ME AT ALL.
WE CAN ARRANGE THAT TOO.

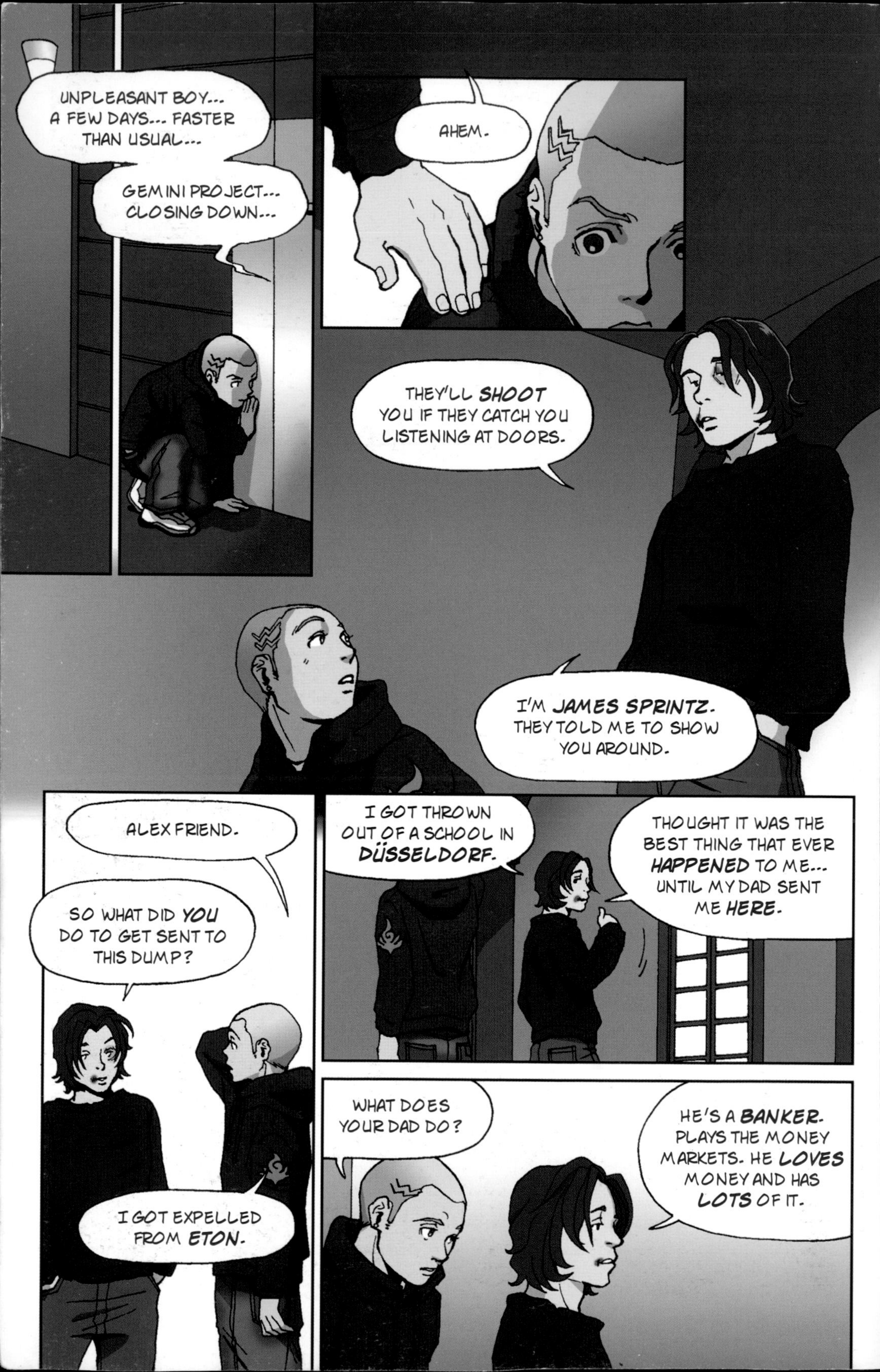
UNPLEASANT BOY... A FEW DAYS... FASTER THAN USUAL...
GEMINI PROJECT... CLOSING DOWN...
AHEM.
THEY'LL SHOOT YOU IF THEY CATCH YOU LISTENING AT DOORS.
I'M JAMES SPRINTZ. THEY TOLD ME TO SHOW YOU AROUND.
ALEX FRIEND.
SO WHAT DID YOU DO TO GET SENT TO THIS DUMP?
I GOT EXPELLED FROM ETON.
I GOT THROWN OUT OF A SCHOOL IN DÜSSELDORF.
THOUGHT IT WAS THE BEST THING THAT EVER HAPPENED TO ME... UNTIL MY DAD SENT ME HERE.
WHAT DOES YOUR DAD DO?
HE'S A BANKER. PLAYS THE MONEY MARKETS. HE LOVES MONEY AND HAS LOTS OF IT.

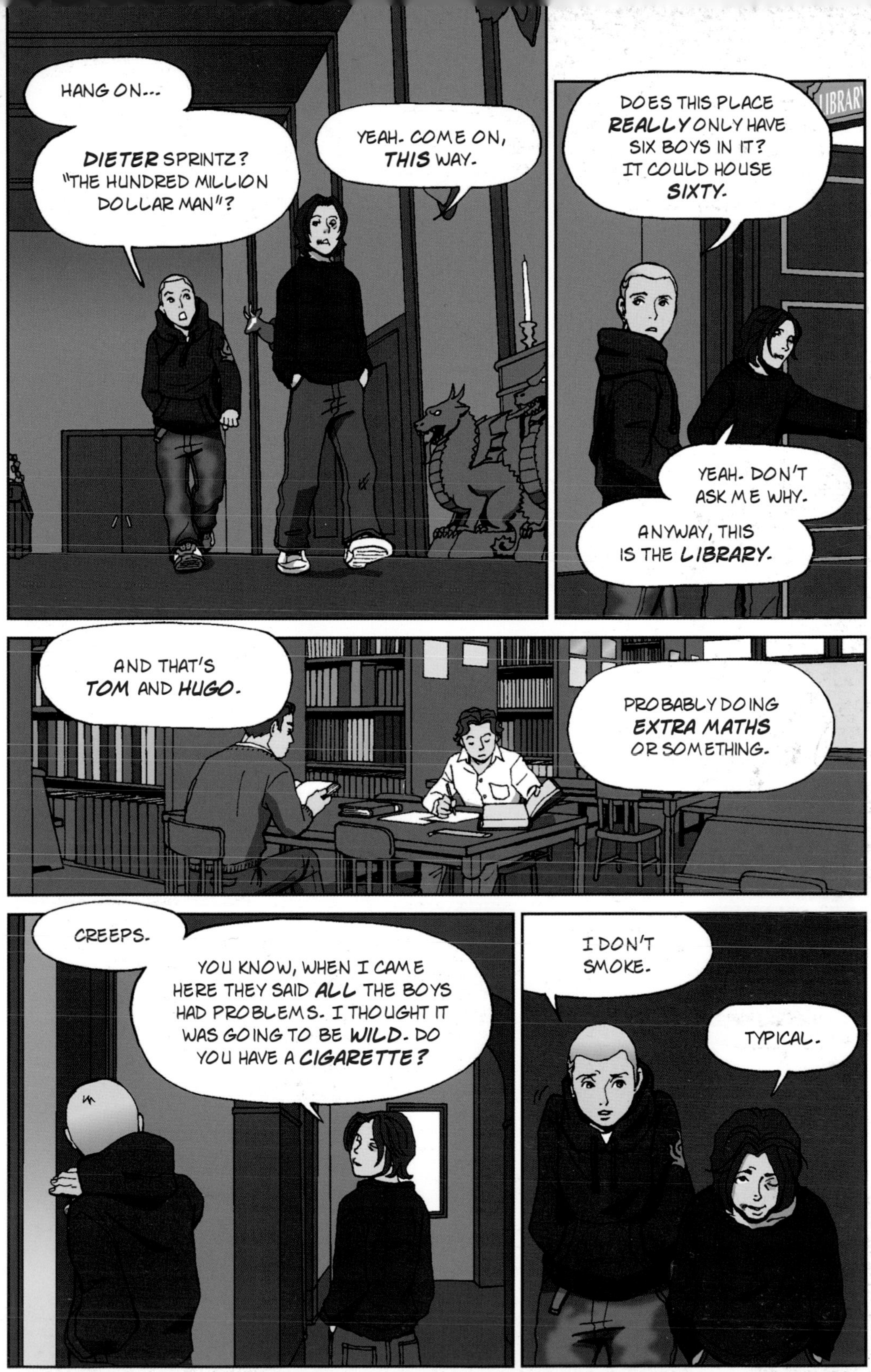

HANG ON...
DIETER SPRINTZ? "THE HUNDRED MILLION DOLLAR MAN"?
YEAH. COME ON, THIS WAY.
LIBRARY
DOES THIS PLACE REALLY ONLY HAVE SIX BOYS IN IT? IT COULD HOUSE SIXTY.
YEAH. DON'T ASK ME WHY.
ANYWAY, THIS IS THE LIBRARY.
AND THAT'S TOM AND HUGO.
PROBABLY DOING EXTRA MATHS OR SOMETHING.
CREEPS.
YOU KNOW, WHEN I CAME HERE THEY SAID ALL THE BOYS HAD PROBLEMS. I THOUGHT IT WAS GOING TO BE WILD. DO YOU HAVE A CIGARETTE?
I DON'T SMOKE.
TYPICAL.

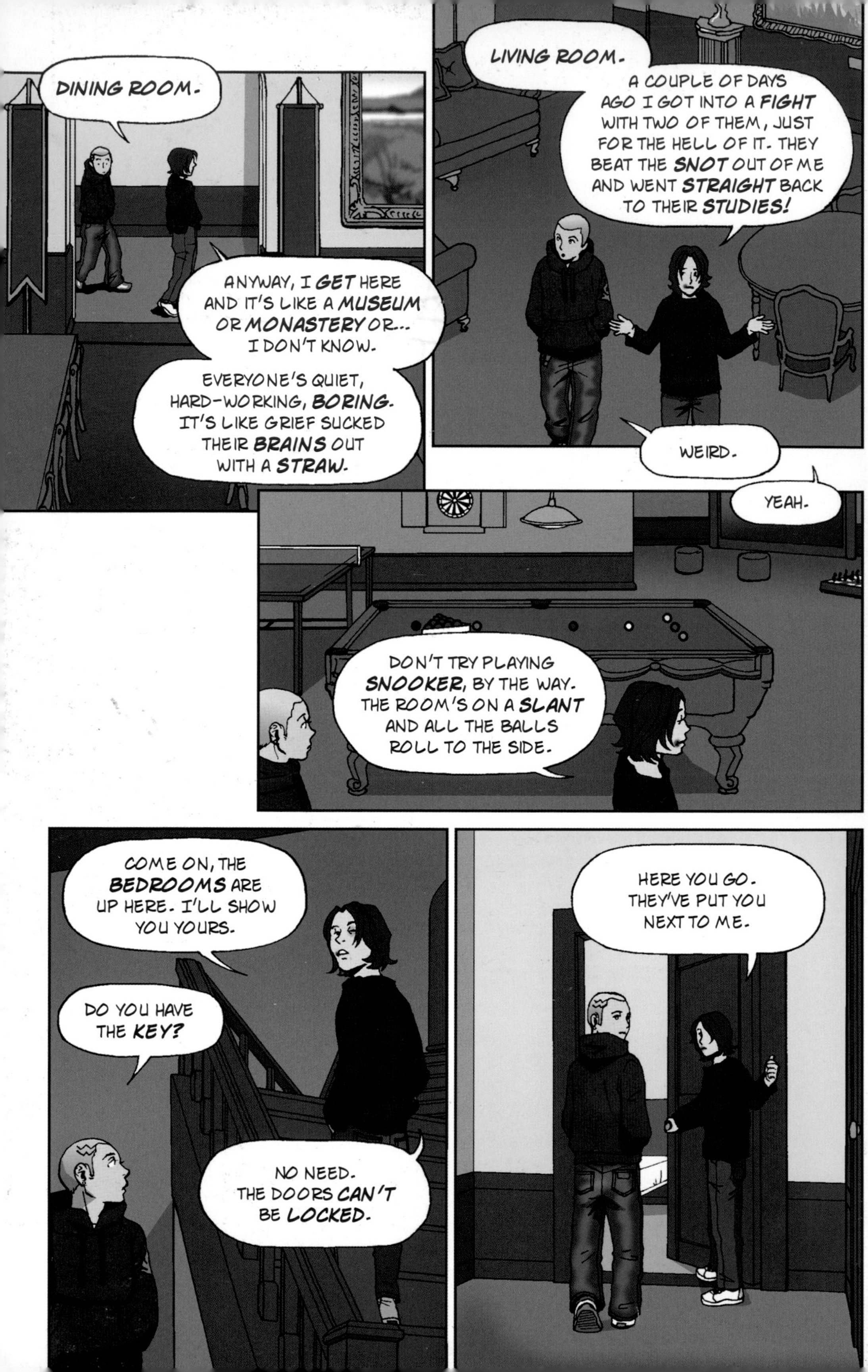
DINING ROOM.
ANYWAY, I GET HERE AND IT'S LIKE A MUSEUM OR MONASTERY OR... I DON'T KNOW.
EVERYONE'S QUIET, HARD-WORKING, BORING. IT'S LIKE GRIEF SUCKED THEIR BRAINS OUT WITH A STRAW.
LIVING ROOM.
A COUPLE OF DAYS AGO I GOT INTO A FIGHT WITH TWO OF THEM, JUST FOR THE HELL OF IT. THEY BEAT THE SNOT OUT OF ME AND WENT STRAIGHT BACK TO THEIR STUDIES!
WEIRD.
YEAH.
DON'T TRY PLAYING SNOOKER, BY THE WAY. THE ROOM'S ON A SLANT AND ALL THE BALLS ROLL TO THE SIDE.
COME ON, THE BEDROOMS ARE UP HERE. I'LL SHOW YOU YOURS.
DO YOU HAVE THE KEY?
NO NEED. THE DOORS CAN'T BE LOCKED.
HERE YOU GO. THEY'VE PUT YOU NEXT TO ME.

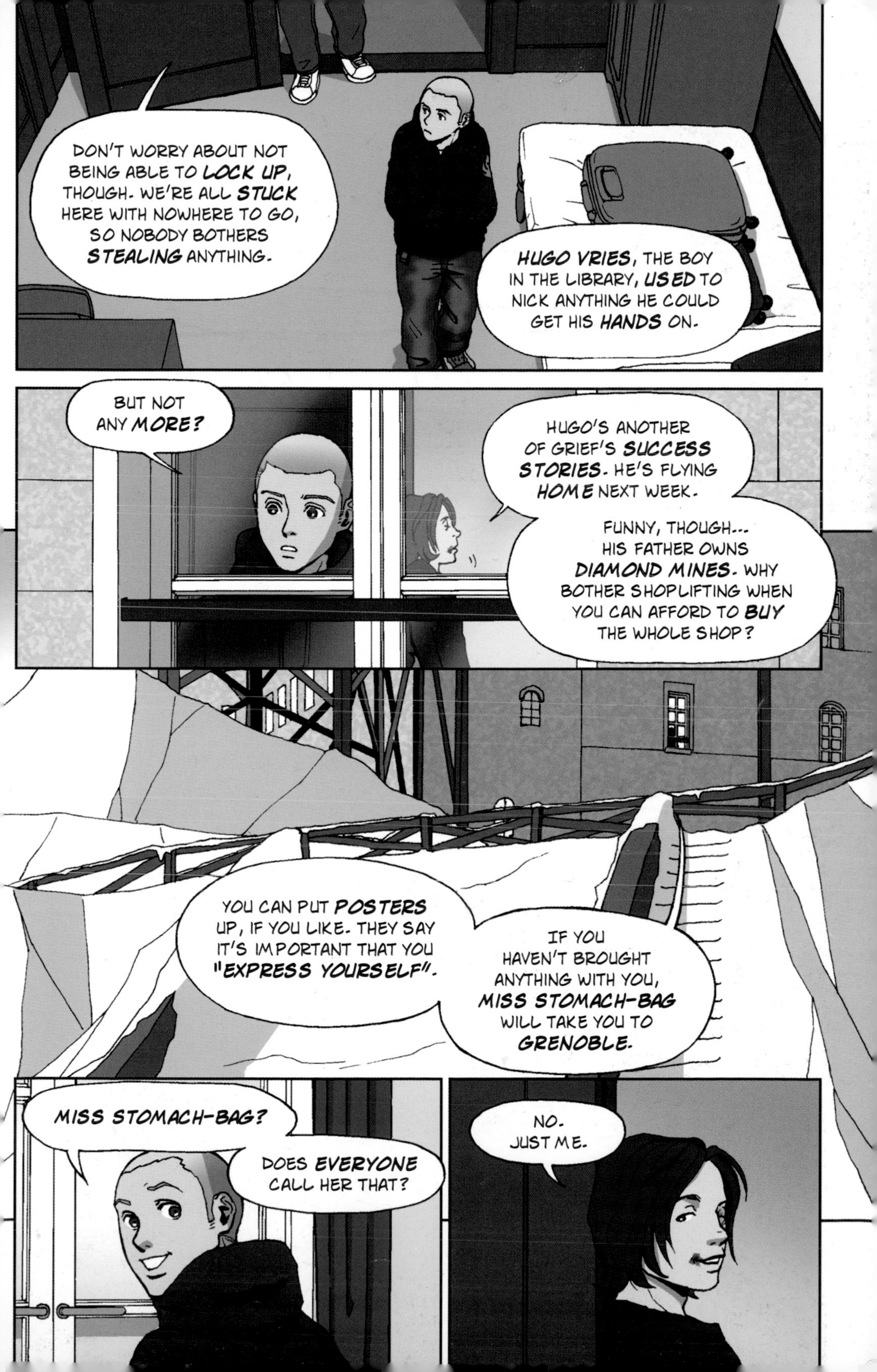
DON'T WORRY ABOUT NOT BEING ABLE TO LOCK UP, THOUGH. WE'RE ALL STUCK HERE WITH NOWHERE TO GO, SO NOBODY BOTHERS STEALING ANYTHING.
HUGO VRIES, THE BOY IN THE LIBRARY, USED TO NICK ANYTHING HE COULD GET HIS HANDS ON.
BUT NOT ANY MORE?
HUGO'S ANOTHER OF GRIEF'S SUCCESS STORIES. HE'S FLYING HOME NEXT WEEK.
FUNNY, THOUGH... HIS FATHER OWNS DIAMOND MINES. WHY BOTHER SHOPLIFTING WHEN YOU CAN AFFORD TO BUY THE WHOLE SHOP?
YOU CAN PUT POSTERS UP, IF YOU LIKE. THEY SAY IT'S IMPORTANT THAT YOU "EXPRESS YOURSELF".
IF YOU HAVEN'T BROUGHT ANYTHING WITH YOU, MISS STOMACH-BAG WILL TAKE YOU TO GRENOBLE.
MISS STOMACH-BAG?
DOES EVERYONE CALL HER THAT?
NO. JUST ME.

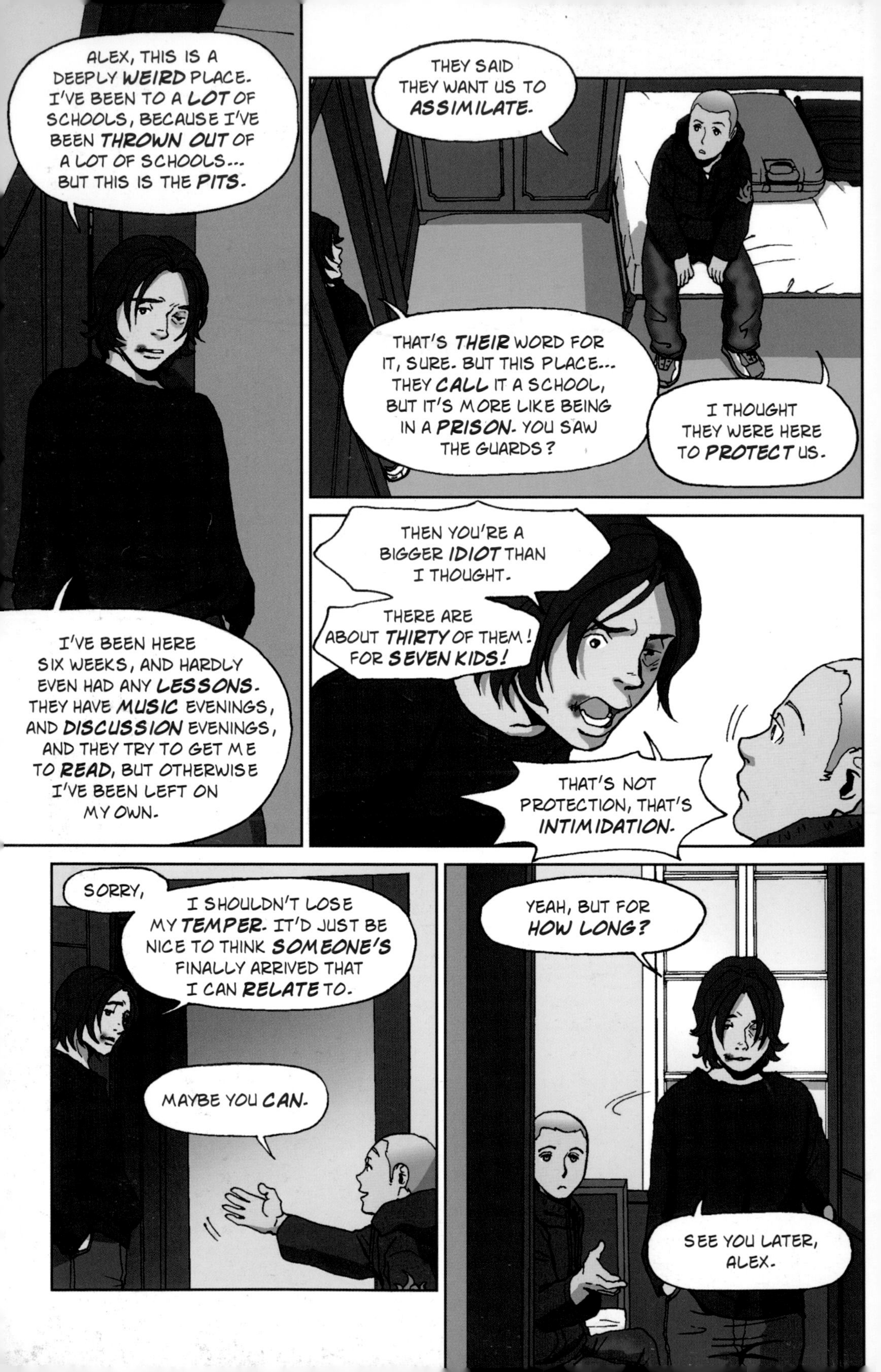

ALEX, THIS IS A DEEPLY WEIRD PLACE. I'VE BEEN TO A LOT OF SCHOOLS, BECAUSE I'VE BEEN THROWN OUT OF A LOT OF SCHOOLS... BUT THIS IS THE PITS.
THEY SAID THEY WANT US TO ASSIMILATE.
THAT'S THEIR WORD FOR IT, SURE. BUT THIS PLACE... THEY CALL IT A SCHOOL, BUT IT'S MORE LIKE BEING IN A PRISON. YOU SAW THE GUARDS?
I THOUGHT THEY WERE HERE TO PROTECT US.
I'VE BEEN HERE SIX WEEKS, AND HARDLY EVEN HAD ANY LESSONS. THEY HAVE MUSIC EVENINGS, AND DISCUSSION EVENINGS, AND THEY TRY TO GET ME TO READ, BUT OTHERWISE I'VE BEEN LEFT ON MY OWN.
THEN YOU'RE A BIGGER IDIOT THAN I THOUGHT.
THERE ARE ABOUT THIRTY OF THEM! FOR SEVEN KIDS!
THAT'S NOT PROTECTION, THAT'S INTIMIDATION.
SORRY,
I SHOULDN'T LOSE MY TEMPER. IT'D JUST BE NICE TO THINK SOMEONE'S FINALLY ARRIVED THAT I CAN RELATE TO.
MAYBE YOU CAN.
YEAH, BUT FOR HOW LONG?
SEE YOU LATER, ALEX.

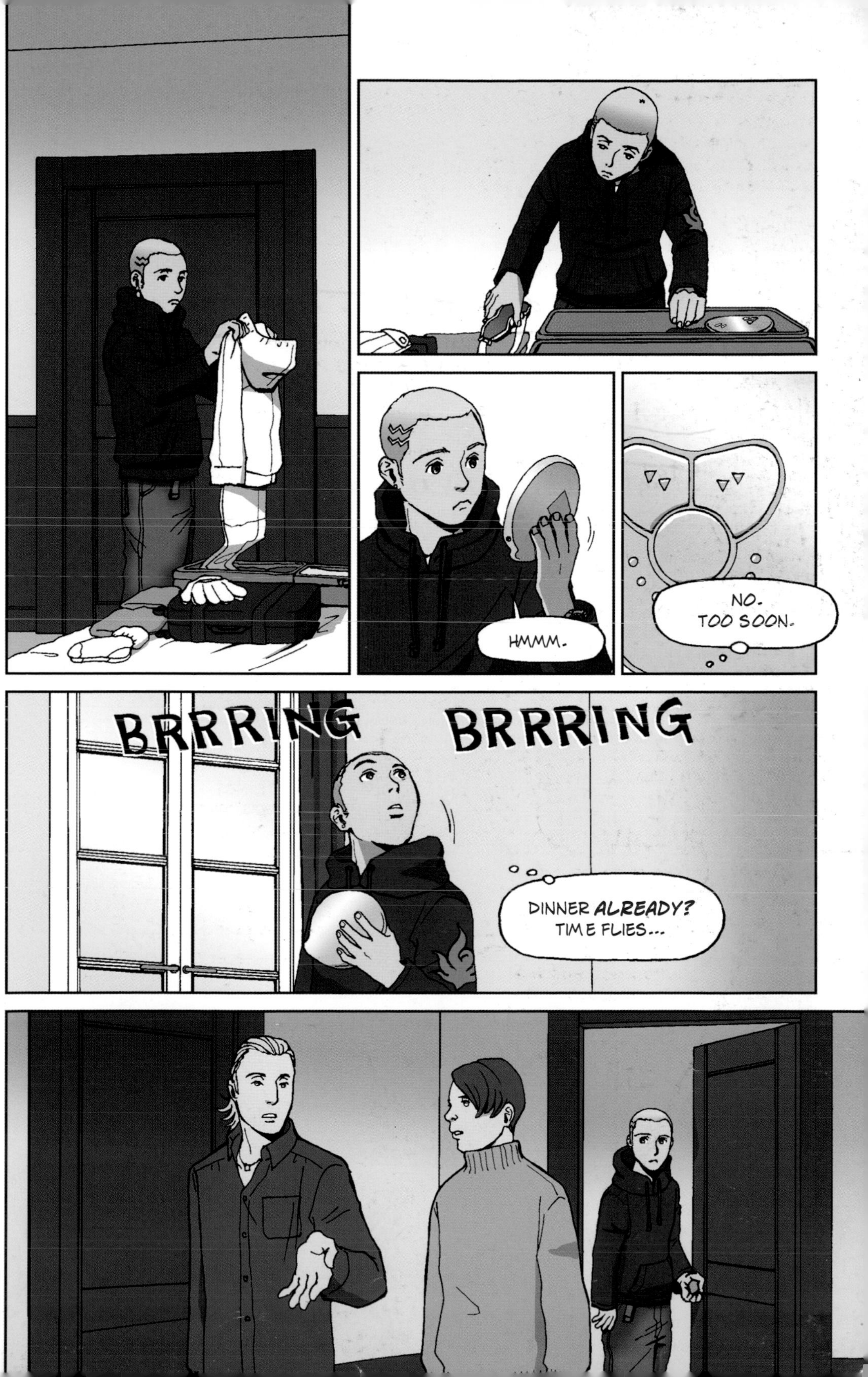
HMMM.
NO. TOO SOON.
BRRRING BRRRING
DINNER ALREADY? TIME FLIES...

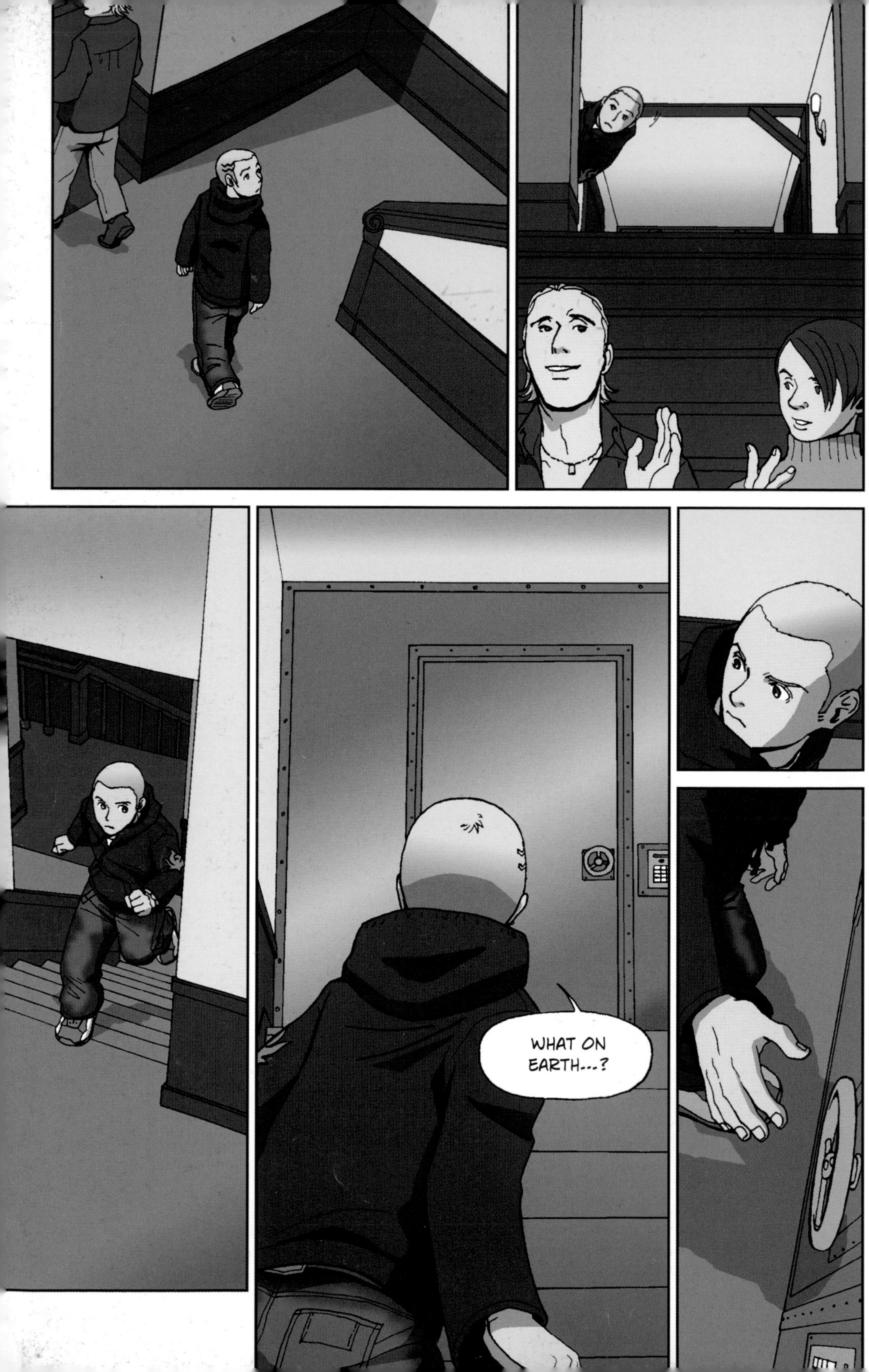
WHAT ON EARTH...?

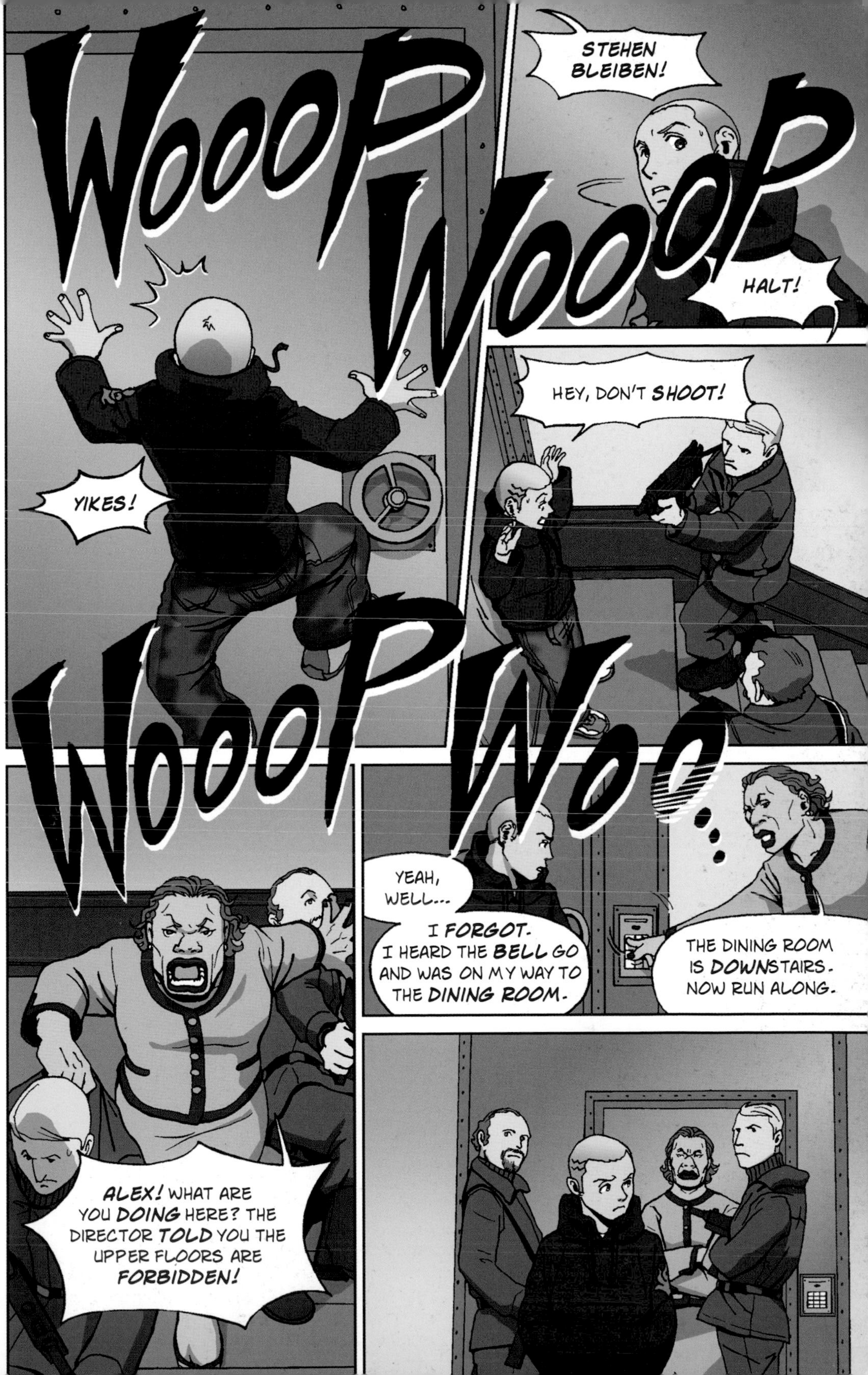
WOOOP
STEHEN BLEIBEN!
WOOOP
HALT!
YIKES!
HEY, DON'T SHOOT!
WOOOP
WOO...
ALEX! WHAT ARE YOU DOING HERE? THE DIRECTOR TOLD YOU THE UPPER FLOORS ARE FORBIDDEN!
YEAH, WELL...
I FORGOT. I HEARD THE BELL GO AND WAS ON MY WAY TO THE DINING ROOM.
THE DINING ROOM IS DOWNSTAIRS. NOW RUN ALONG.

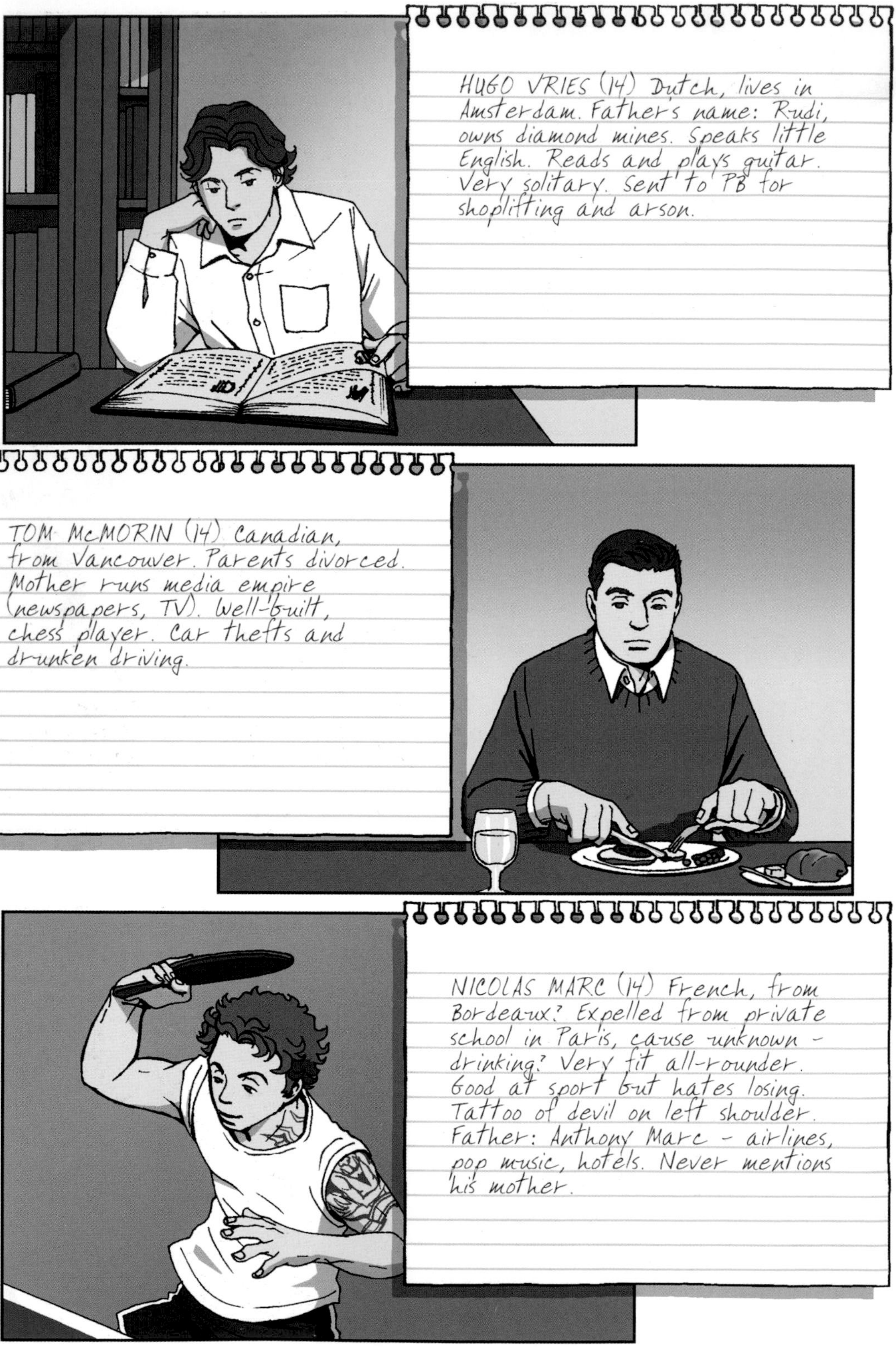
HUGO VRIES (14) Dutch, lives in Amsterdam. Father's name: Rudi, owns diamond mines. Speaks little English. Reads and plays guitar. Very solitary. Sent to PB for shoplifting and arson.
TOM McMORIN (14) Canadian, from Vancouver. Parents divorced. Mother runs media empire (newspapers, TV). Well-built, chess player. Car thefts and drunken driving.
NICOLAS MARC (14) French, from Bordeaux? Expelled from private school in Paris, cause unknown - drinking? Very fit all-rounder. Good at sport but hates losing. Tattoo of devil on left shoulder. Father: Anthony Marc - airlines, pop music, hotels. Never mentions his mother.

CASSIAN JAMES (14) American. Mother: Jill, studio chief in Hollywood. Parents divorced. Loud voice. Swears a lot. Plays jazz piano. Expelled from three schools. Various drug offences - sent to PB after smuggling arrest but won't talk about it now. One of the kids who beat up James. Stronger than he looks.

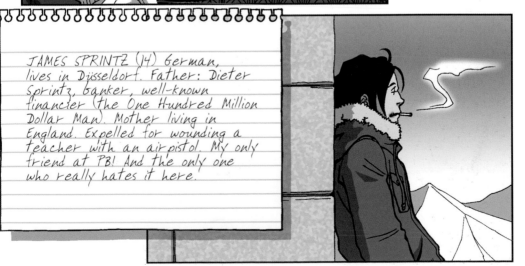

JOE CANTERBURY (14) American. Spends a lot of time with Cassian (helped him with James). Mother (name unknown) New York Senator. Father something big at the Pentagon. Vandalism, truancy, shoplifting. Sent to PB after stealing and smashing up car. Vegetarian. Permanently chewing gum. Has he given up smoking?

JAMES SPRINTZ (14) German, lives in Düsseldorf. Father: Dieter Sprintz, banker, well-known financier (the One Hundred Million Dollar Man). Mother living in England. Expelled for wounding a teacher with an air pistol. My only friend at PB! And the only one who really hates it here.

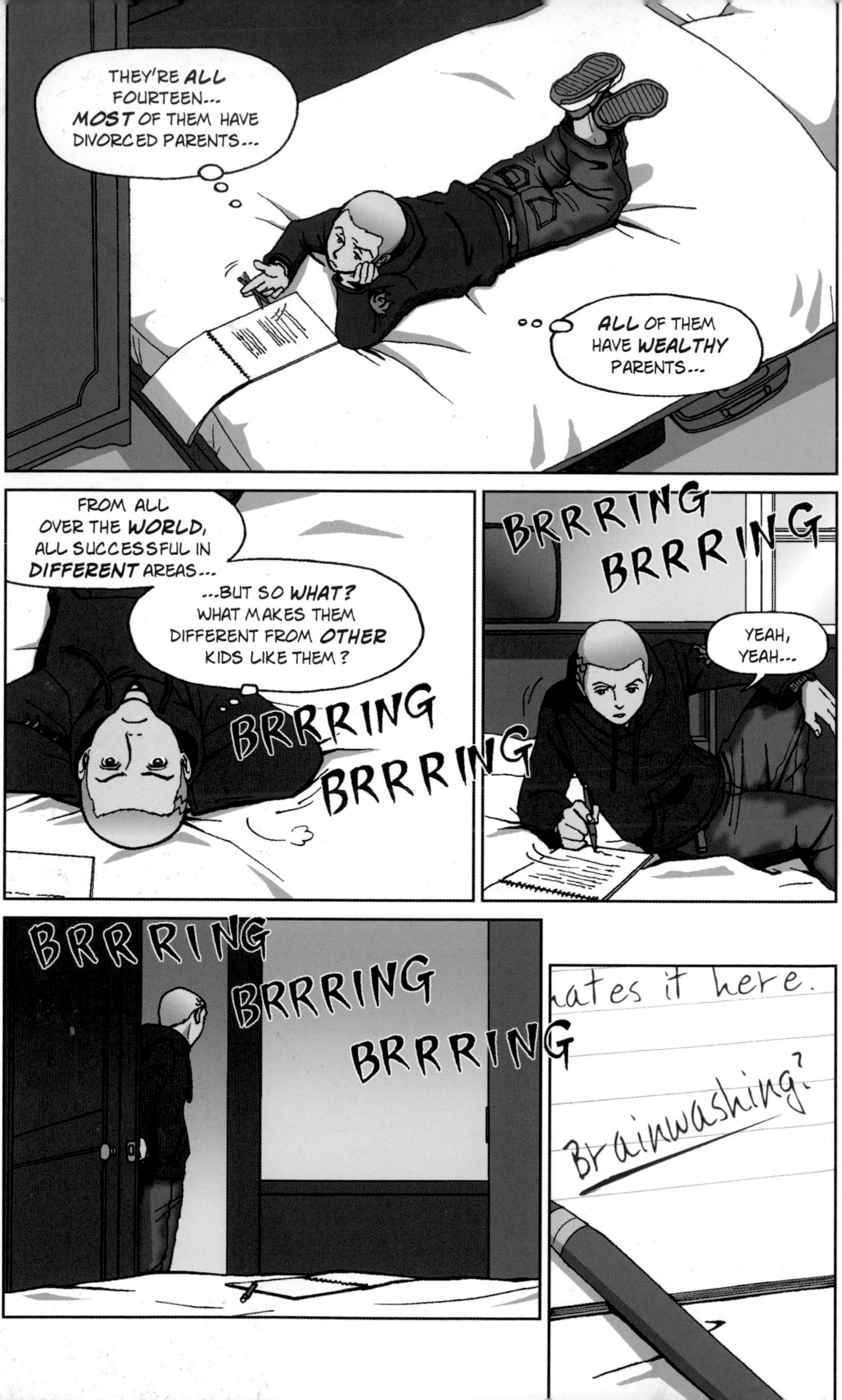
THEY'RE ALL FOURTEEN... MOST OF THEM HAVE DIVORCED PARENTS...
ALL OF THEM HAVE WEALTHY PARENTS...
FROM ALL OVER THE WORLD, ALL SUCCESSFUL IN DIFFERENT AREAS...
...BUT SO WHAT? WHAT MAKES THEM DIFFERENT FROM OTHER KIDS LIKE THEM?
BRRRING
BRRRING
BRRRING
BRRRING
YEAH, YEAH...
BRRRING
BRRRING
BRRRING
ates it here.
Brainwashing?

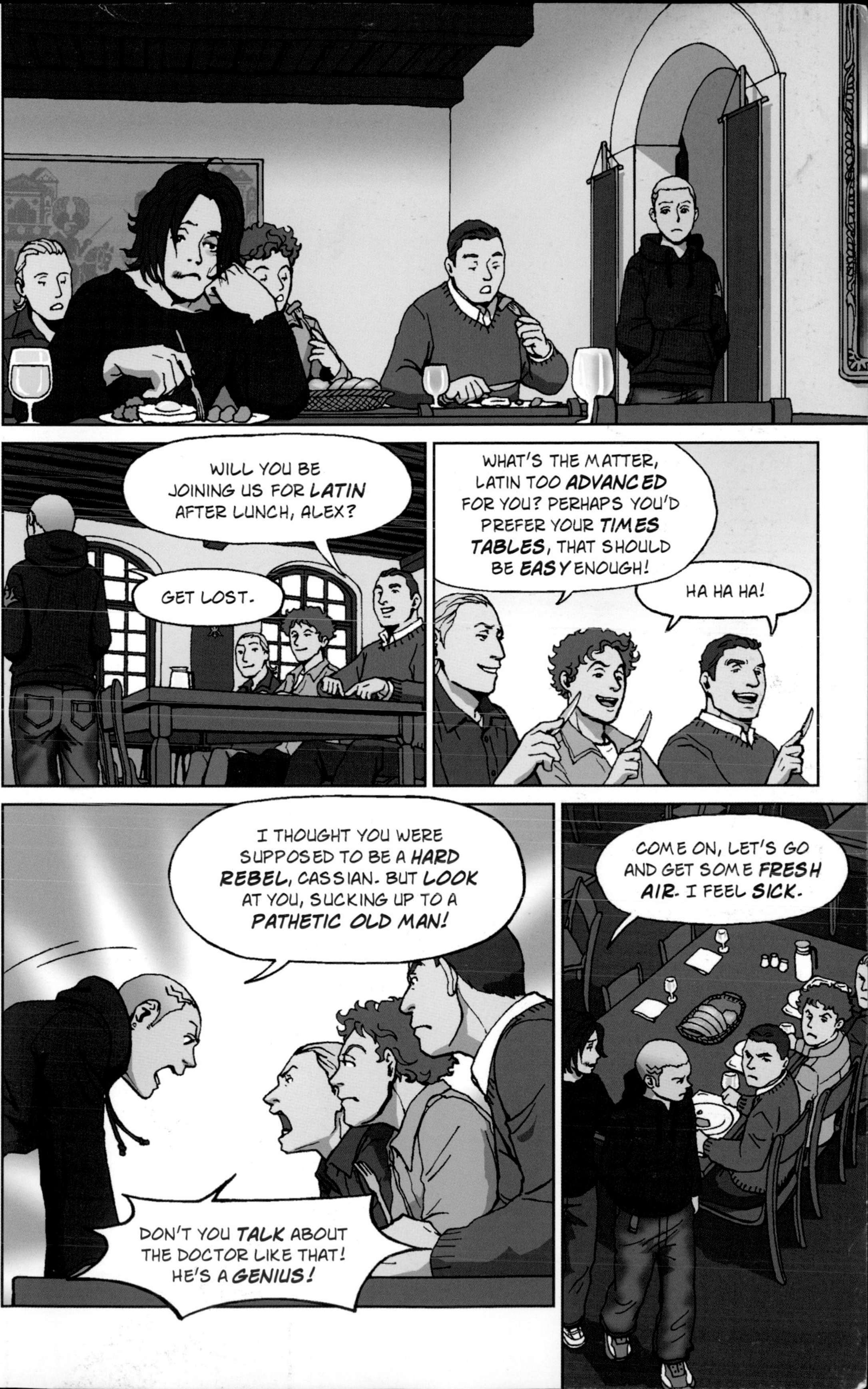
WILL YOU BE JOINING US FOR LATIN AFTER LUNCH, ALEX?
GET LOST.
WHAT'S THE MATTER, LATIN TOO ADVANCED FOR YOU? PERHAPS YOU'D PREFER YOUR TIMES TABLES, THAT SHOULD BE EASY ENOUGH!
HA HA HA!
I THOUGHT YOU WERE SUPPOSED TO BE A HARD REBEL, CASSIAN. BUT LOOK AT YOU, SUCKING UP TO A PATHETIC OLD MAN!
DON'T YOU TALK ABOUT THE DOCTOR LIKE THAT! HE'S A GENIUS!
COME ON, LET'S GO AND GET SOME FRESH AIR. I FEEL SICK.

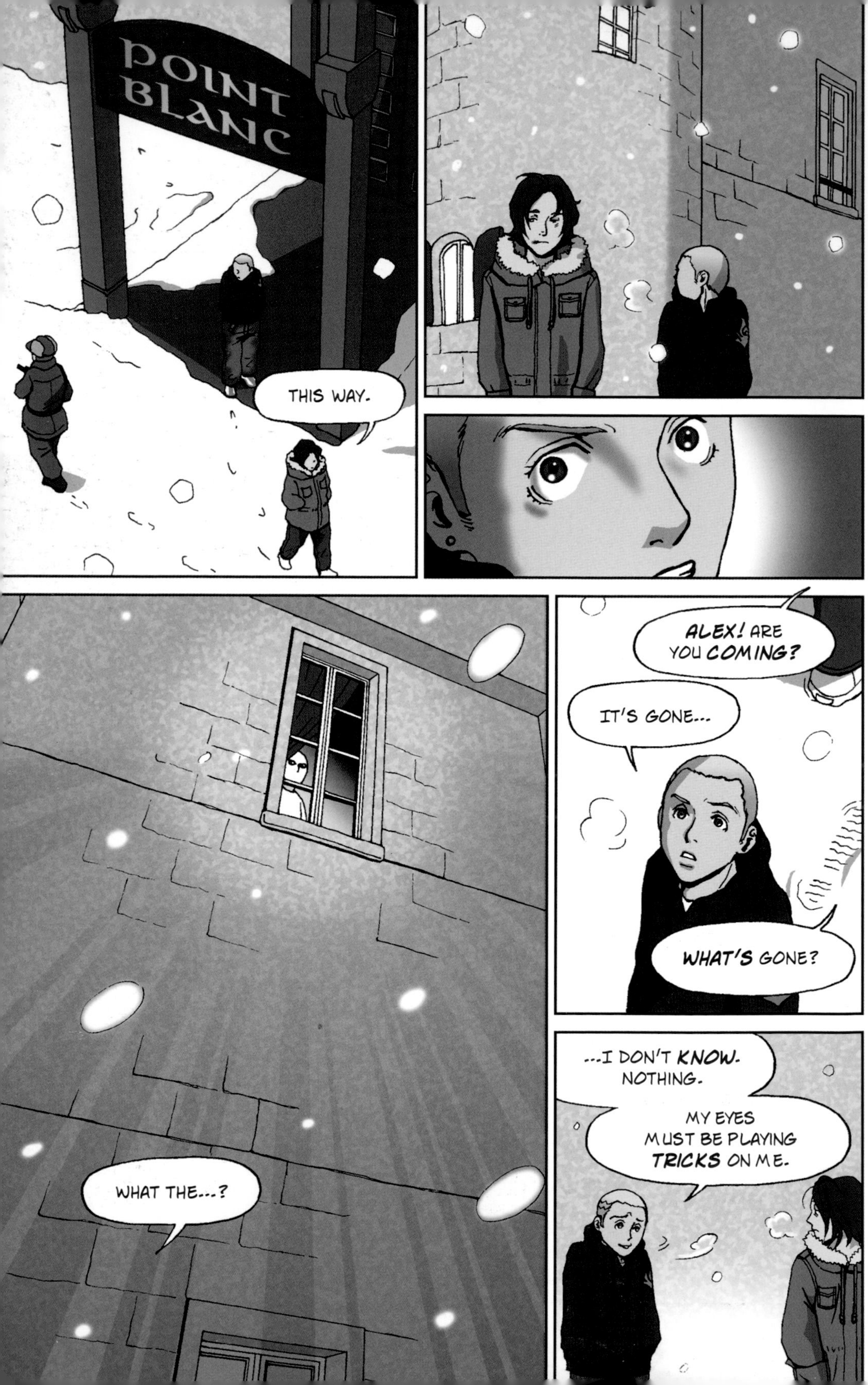
POINT BLANC
THIS WAY.
ALEX! ARE YOU COMING?
IT'S GONE...
WHAT'S GONE?
WHAT THE...?
...I DON'T KNOW. NOTHING.
MY EYES MUST BE PLAYING TRICKS ON ME.

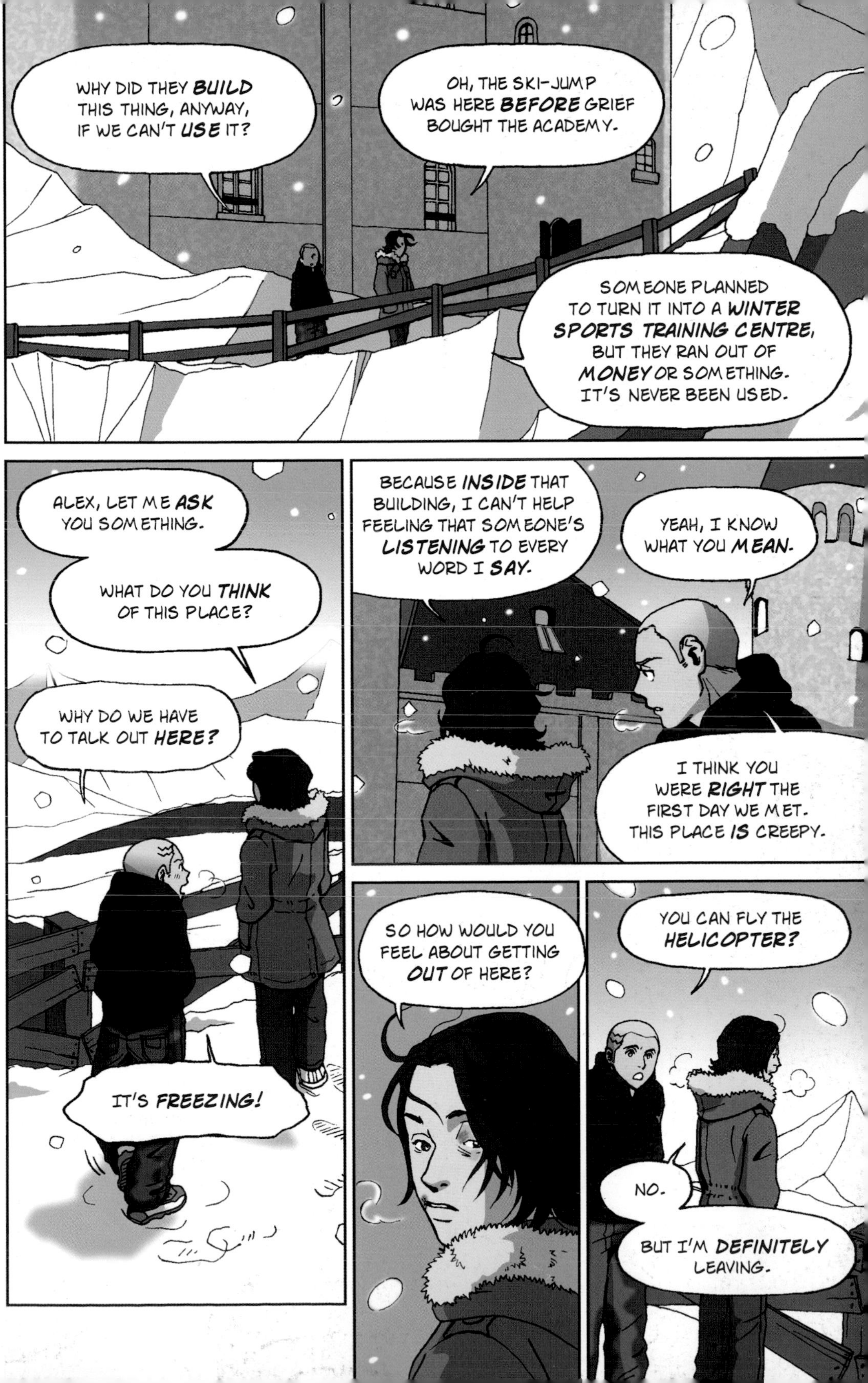
WHY DID THEY BUILD THIS THING, ANYWAY, IF WE CAN'T USE IT?
OH, THE SKI-JUMP WAS HERE BEFORE GRIEF BOUGHT THE ACADEMY.
SOMEONE PLANNED TO TURN IT INTO A WINTER SPORTS TRAINING CENTRE, BUT THEY RAN OUT OF MONEY OR SOMETHING. IT'S NEVER BEEN USED.
ALEX, LET ME ASK YOU SOMETHING.
WHAT DO YOU THINK OF THIS PLACE?
WHY DO WE HAVE TO TALK OUT HERE?
IT'S FREEZING!
BECAUSE INSIDE THAT BUILDING, I CAN'T HELP FEELING THAT SOMEONE'S LISTENING TO EVERY WORD I SAY.
YEAH, I KNOW WHAT YOU MEAN.
I THINK YOU WERE RIGHT THE FIRST DAY WE MET. THIS PLACE IS CREEPY.
SO HOW WOULD YOU FEEL ABOUT GETTING OUT OF HERE?
YOU CAN FLY THE HELICOPTER?
NO.
BUT I'M DEFINITELY LEAVING.

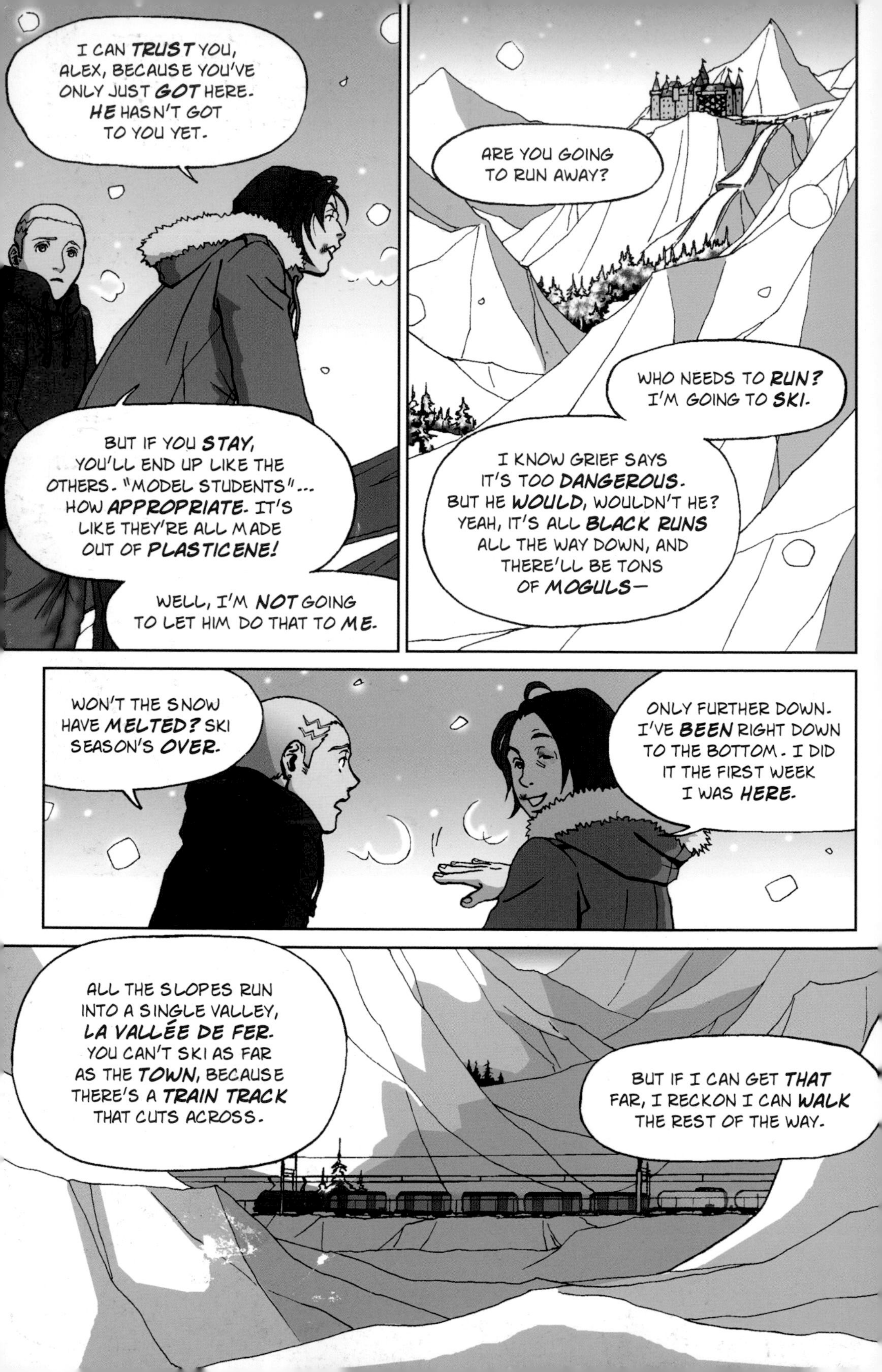
I CAN TRUST YOU, ALEX, BECAUSE YOU'VE ONLY JUST GOT HERE. HE HASN'T GOT TO YOU YET.
BUT IF YOU STAY, YOU'LL END UP LIKE THE OTHERS. "MODEL STUDENTS"... HOW APPROPRIATE. IT'S LIKE THEY'RE ALL MADE OUT OF PLASTICENE!
WELL, I'M NOT GOING TO LET HIM DO THAT TO ME.
ARE YOU GOING TO RUN AWAY?
WHO NEEDS TO RUN? I'M GOING TO SKI.
I KNOW GRIEF SAYS IT'S TOO DANGEROUS. BUT HE WOULD, WOULDN'T HE? YEAH, IT'S ALL BLACK RUNS ALL THE WAY DOWN, AND THERE'LL BE TONS OF MOGULS—
WON'T THE SNOW HAVE MELTED? SKI SEASON'S OVER.
ONLY FURTHER DOWN. I'VE BEEN RIGHT DOWN TO THE BOTTOM. I DID IT THE FIRST WEEK I WAS HERE.
ALL THE SLOPES RUN INTO A SINGLE VALLEY, LA VALLÉE DE FER. YOU CAN'T SKI AS FAR AS THE TOWN, BECAUSE THERE'S A TRAIN TRACK THAT CUTS ACROSS.
BUT IF I CAN GET THAT FAR, I RECKON I CAN WALK THE REST OF THE WAY.

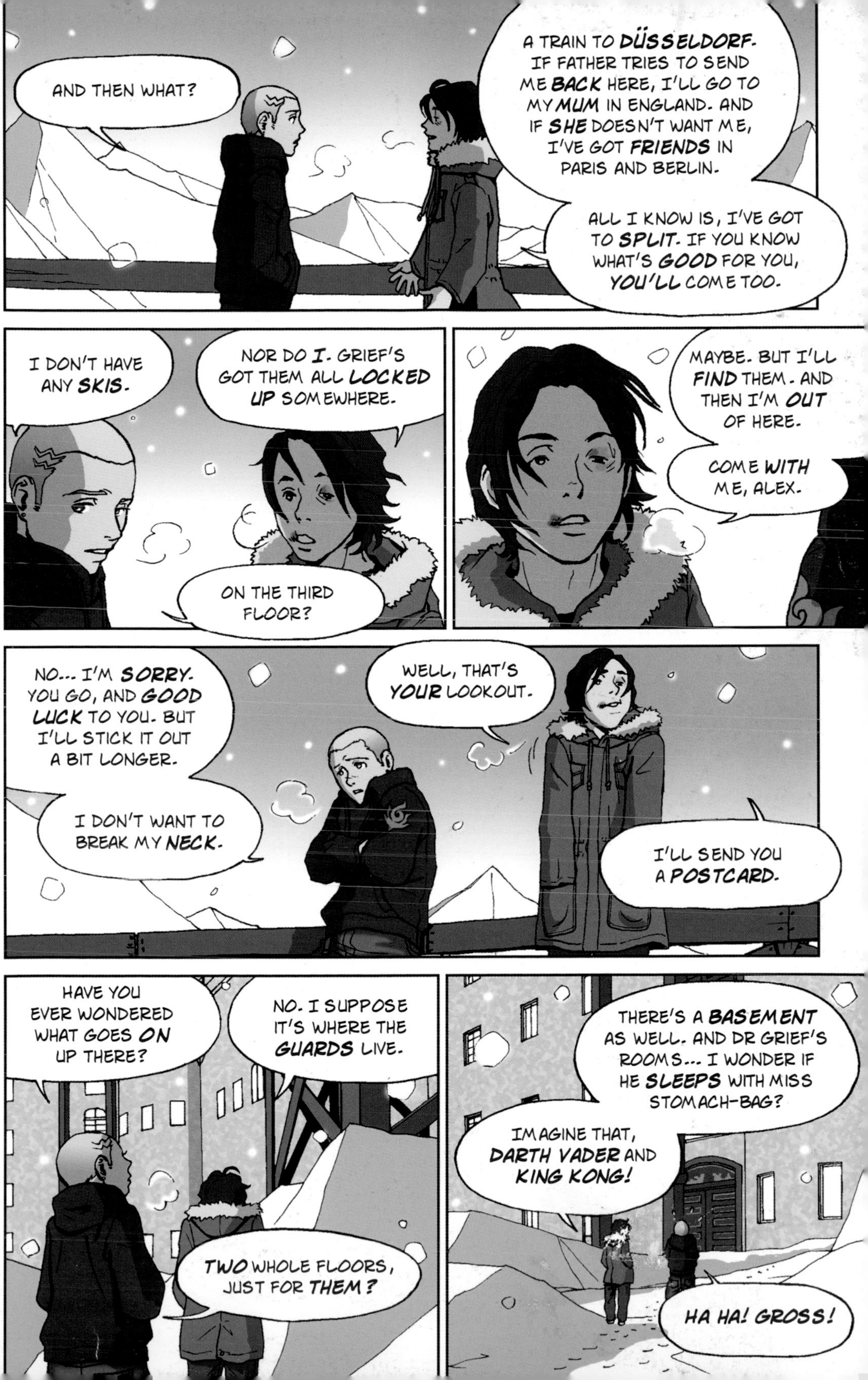
AND THEN WHAT?
A TRAIN TO DÜSSELDORF. IF FATHER TRIES TO SEND ME BACK HERE, I'LL GO TO MY MUM IN ENGLAND. AND IF SHE DOESN'T WANT ME, I'VE GOT FRIENDS IN PARIS AND BERLIN.
ALL I KNOW IS, I'VE GOT TO SPLIT. IF YOU KNOW WHAT'S GOOD FOR YOU, YOU'LL COME TOO.
I DON'T HAVE ANY SKIS.
NOR DO I. GRIEF'S GOT THEM ALL LOCKED UP SOMEWHERE.
ON THE THIRD FLOOR?
MAYBE. BUT I'LL FIND THEM. AND THEN I'M OUT OF HERE.
COME WITH ME, ALEX.
NO... I'M SORRY. YOU GO, AND GOOD LUCK TO YOU. BUT I'LL STICK IT OUT A BIT LONGER.
I DON'T WANT TO BREAK MY NECK.
WELL, THAT'S YOUR LOOKOUT.
I'LL SEND YOU A POSTCARD.
HAVE YOU EVER WONDERED WHAT GOES ON UP THERE?
NO. I SUPPOSE IT'S WHERE THE GUARDS LIVE.
TWO WHOLE FLOORS, JUST FOR THEM?
THERE'S A BASEMENT AS WELL. AND DR GRIEF'S ROOMS... I WONDER IF HE SLEEPS WITH MISS STOMACH-BAG?
IMAGINE THAT, DARTH VADER AND KING KONG!
HA HA! GROSS!

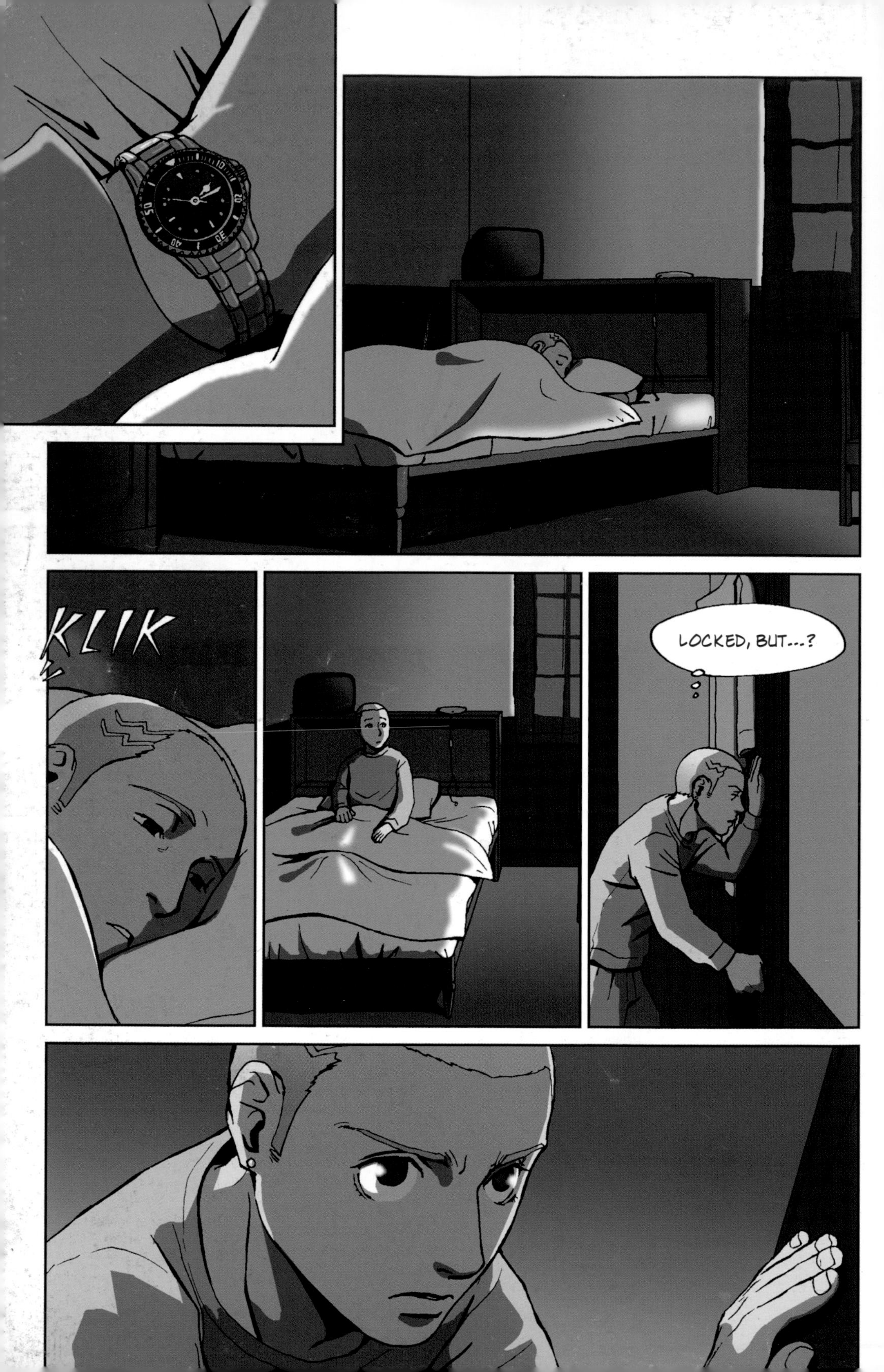
KLIK
LOCKED, BUT...?

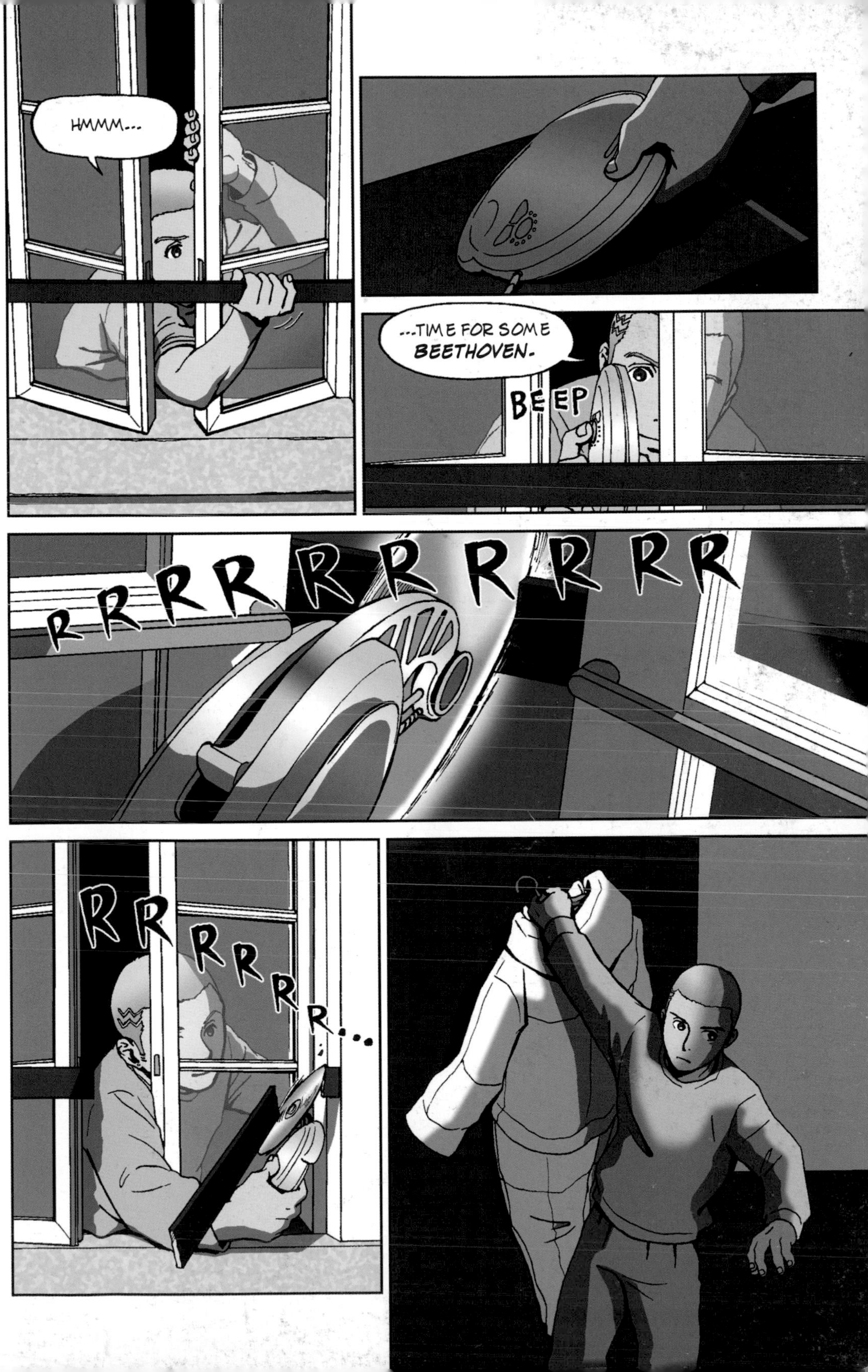

HMMM...
...TIME FOR SOME BEETHOVEN.
BEEP
RRRRRRRRRR
RRRRRRR...

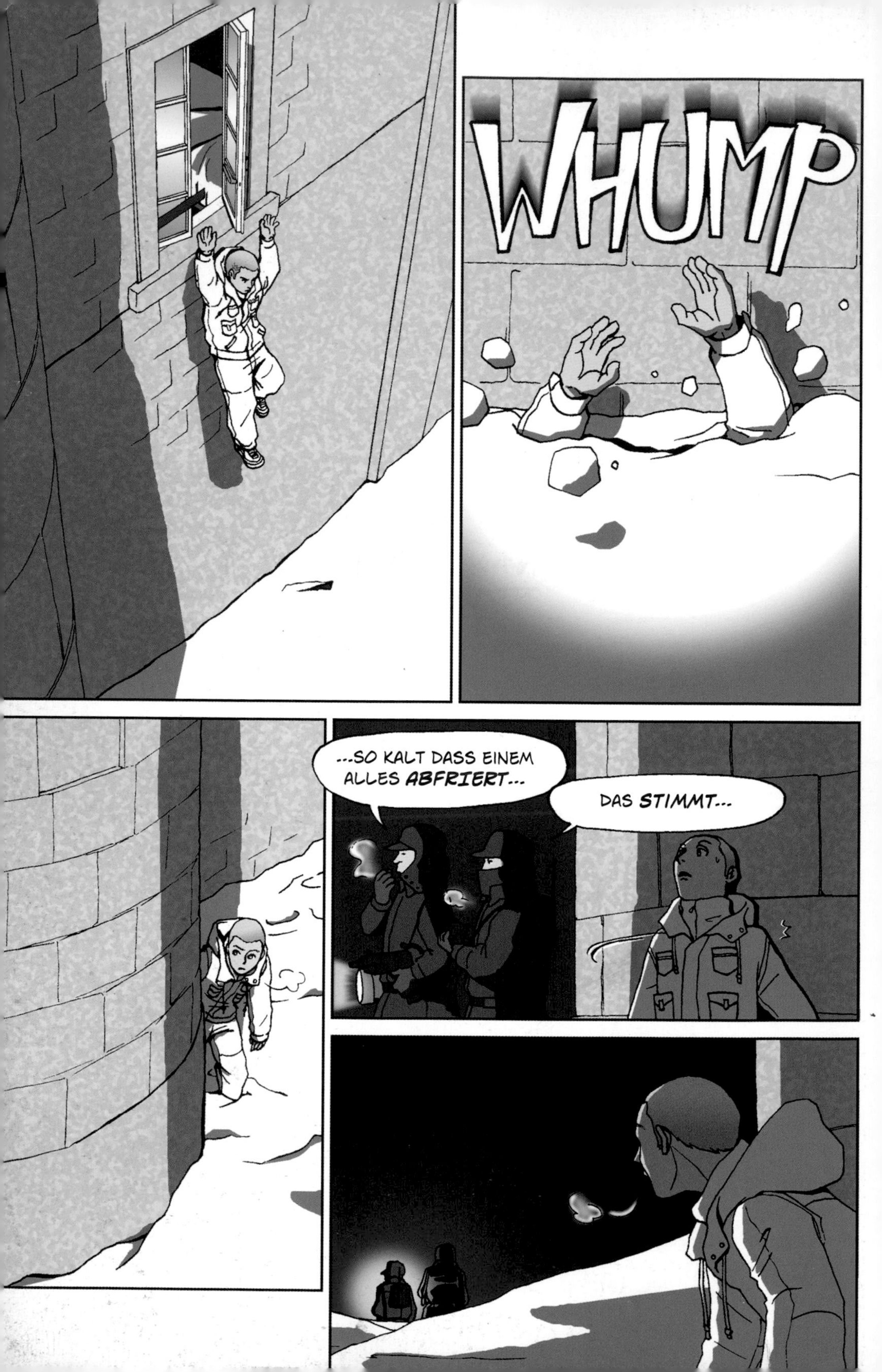
WHUMP
...SO KALT DASS EINEM ALLES ABFRIERT...
DAS STIMMT...

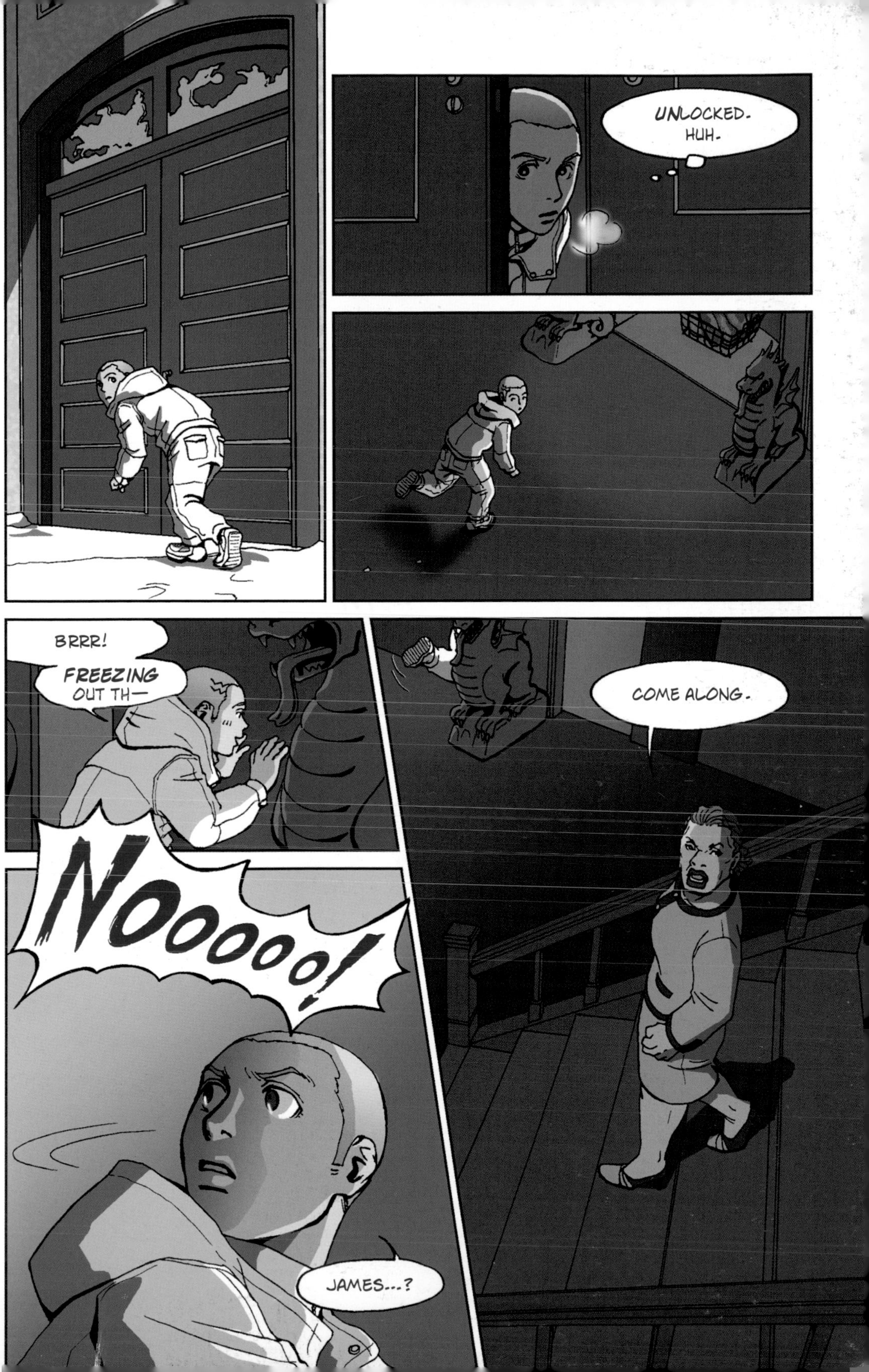
UNLOCKED.
HUH.
BRRR!
FREEZING OUT TH—
COME ALONG.
NOOOOO!
JAMES...?

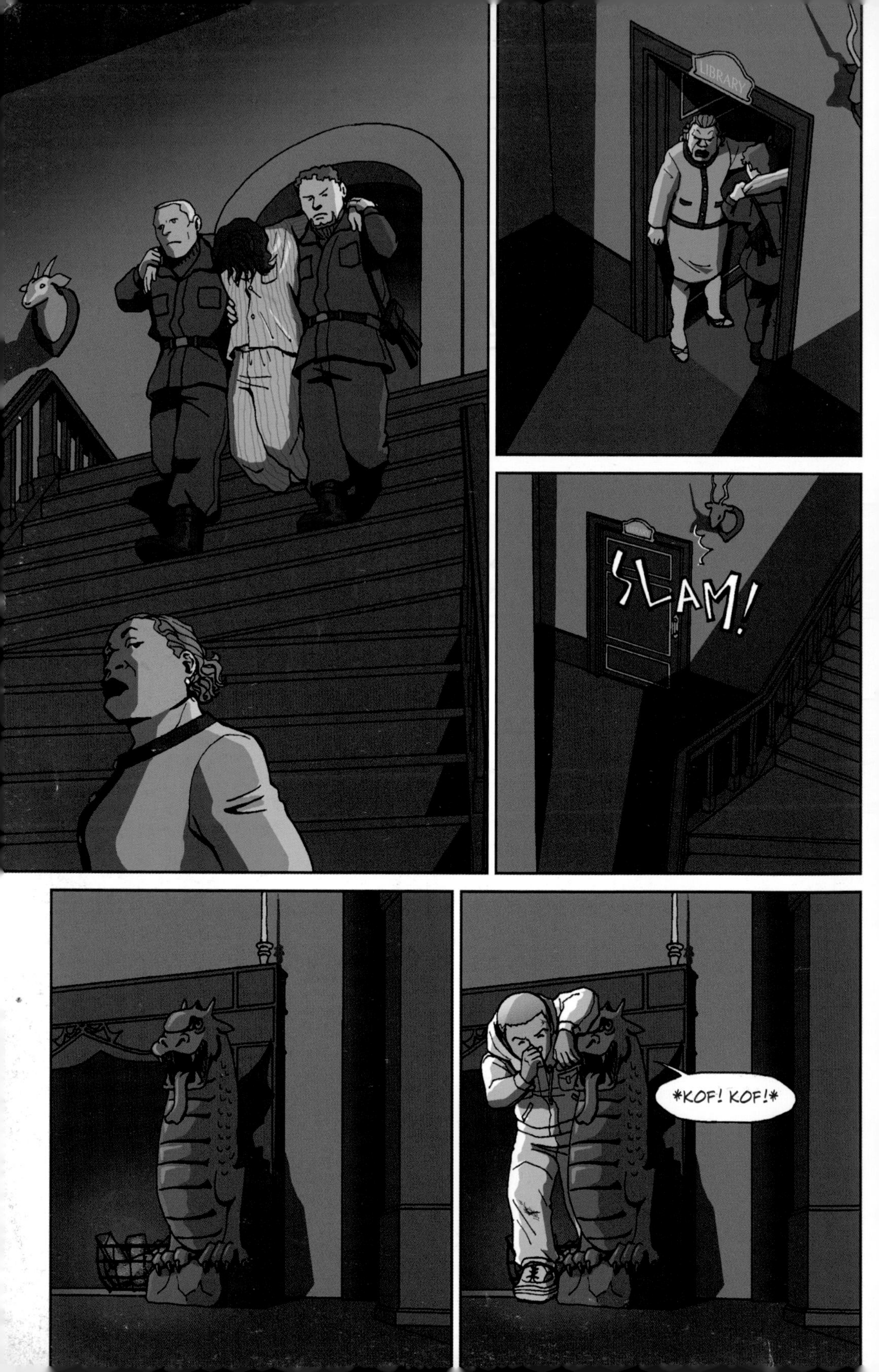
LIBRARY
SLAM!
KOF! KOF!

BUT... WHERE...?

THAT'S THE ONLY DOOR...

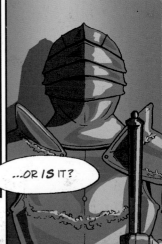

...OR IS IT?

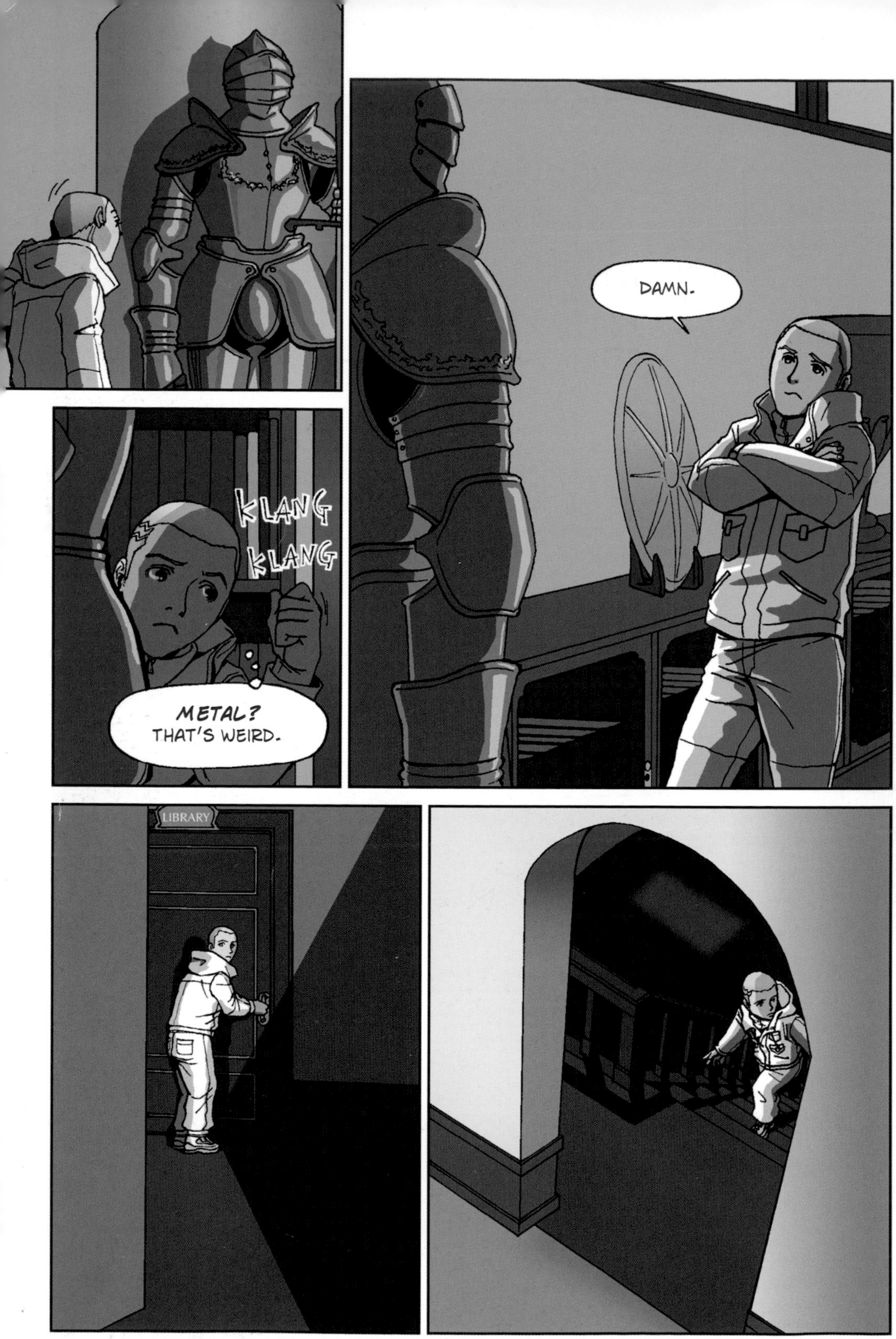

KLANG
KLANG
METAL? THAT'S WEIRD.
DAMN.
LIBRARY

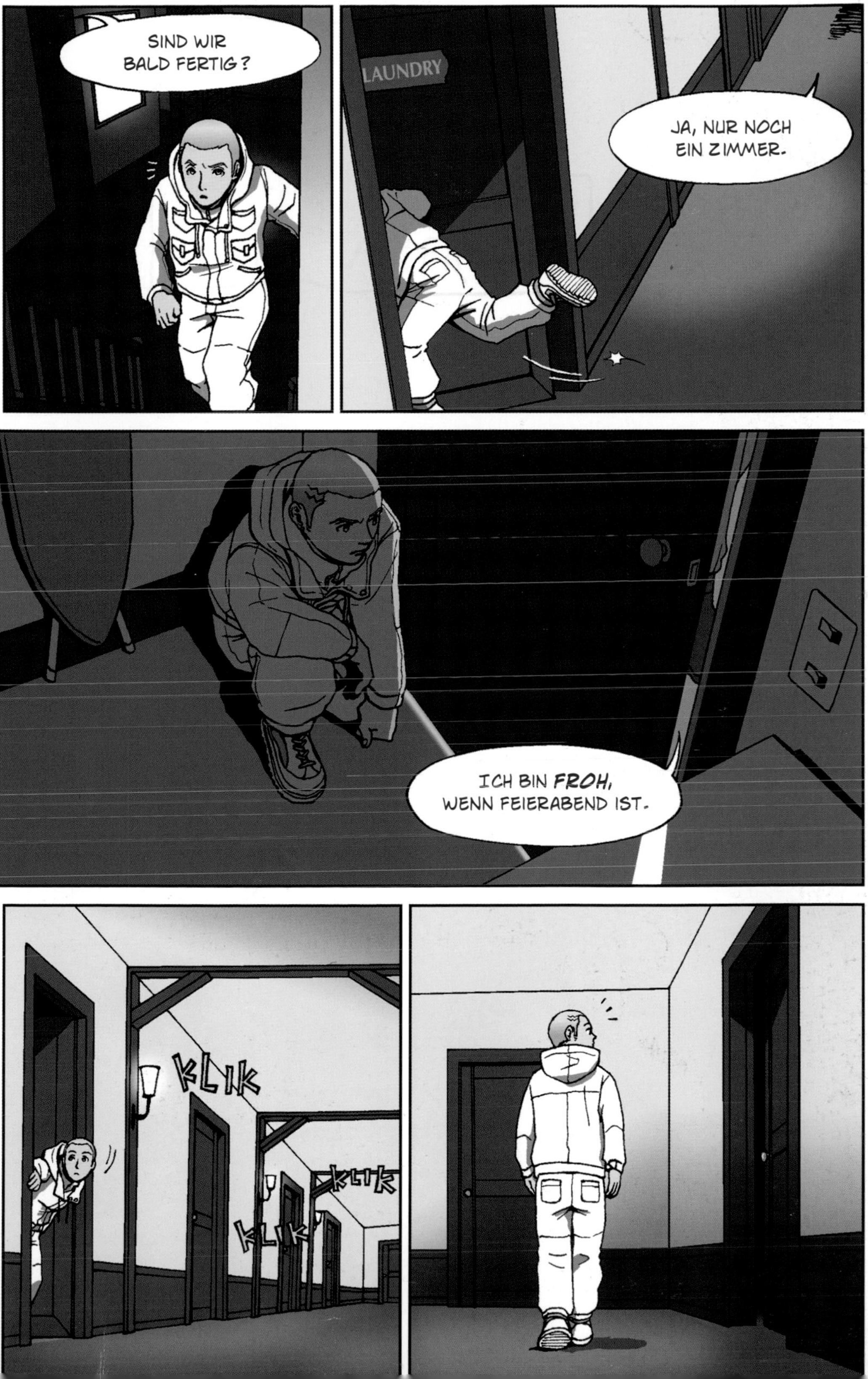
SIND WIR BALD FERTIG?
LAUNDRY
JA, NUR NOCH EIN ZIMMER.
ICH BIN FROH, WENN FEIERABEND IST.
KLIK
KLIK
KLIK

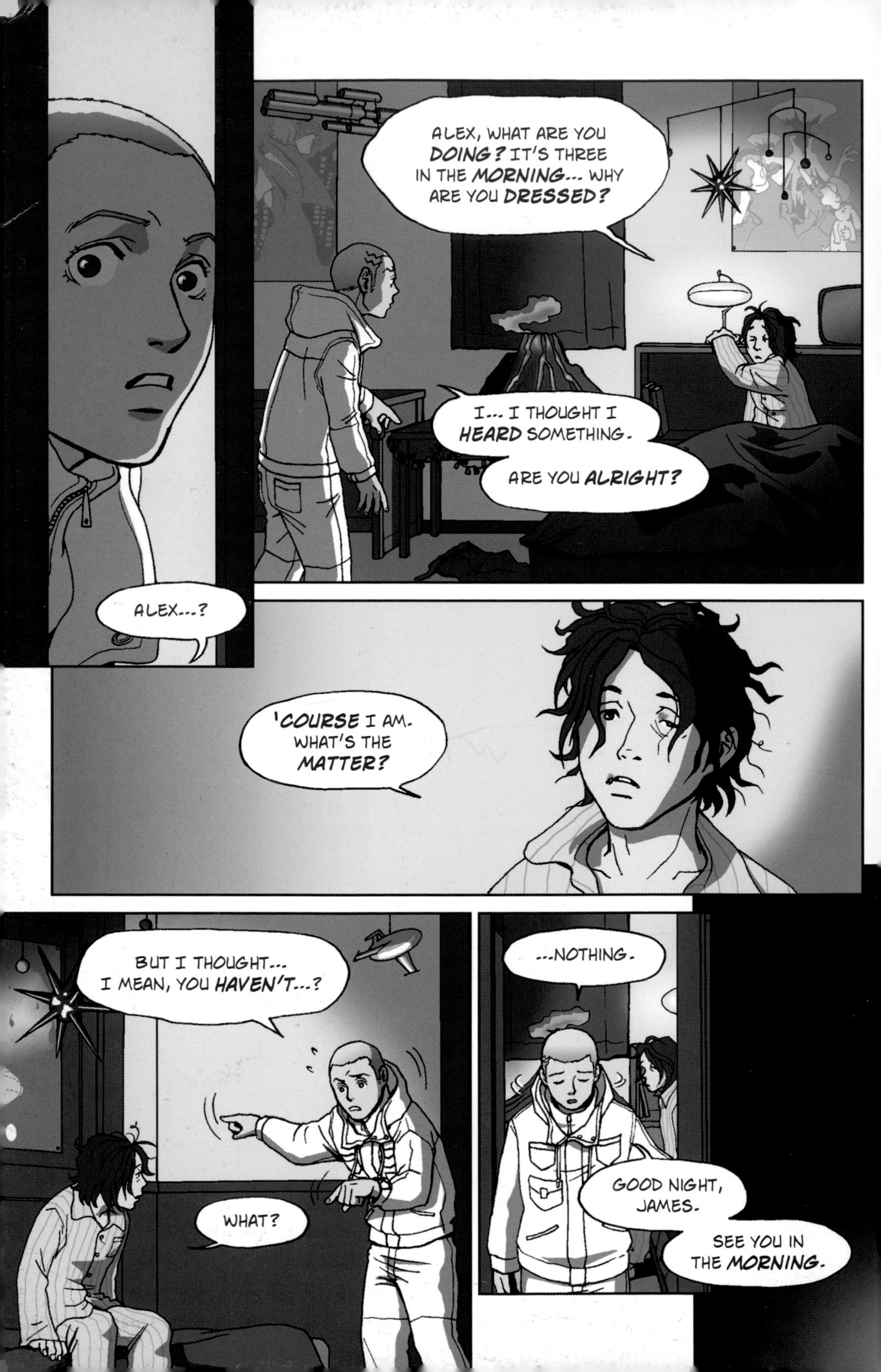
ALEX, WHAT ARE YOU DOING? IT'S THREE IN THE MORNING... WHY ARE YOU DRESSED?
I... I THOUGHT I HEARD SOMETHING.
ARE YOU ALRIGHT?
ALEX...?
'COURSE I AM. WHAT'S THE MATTER?
BUT I THOUGHT... I MEAN, YOU HAVEN'T...?
WHAT?
...NOTHING.
GOOD NIGHT, JAMES.
SEE YOU IN THE MORNING.

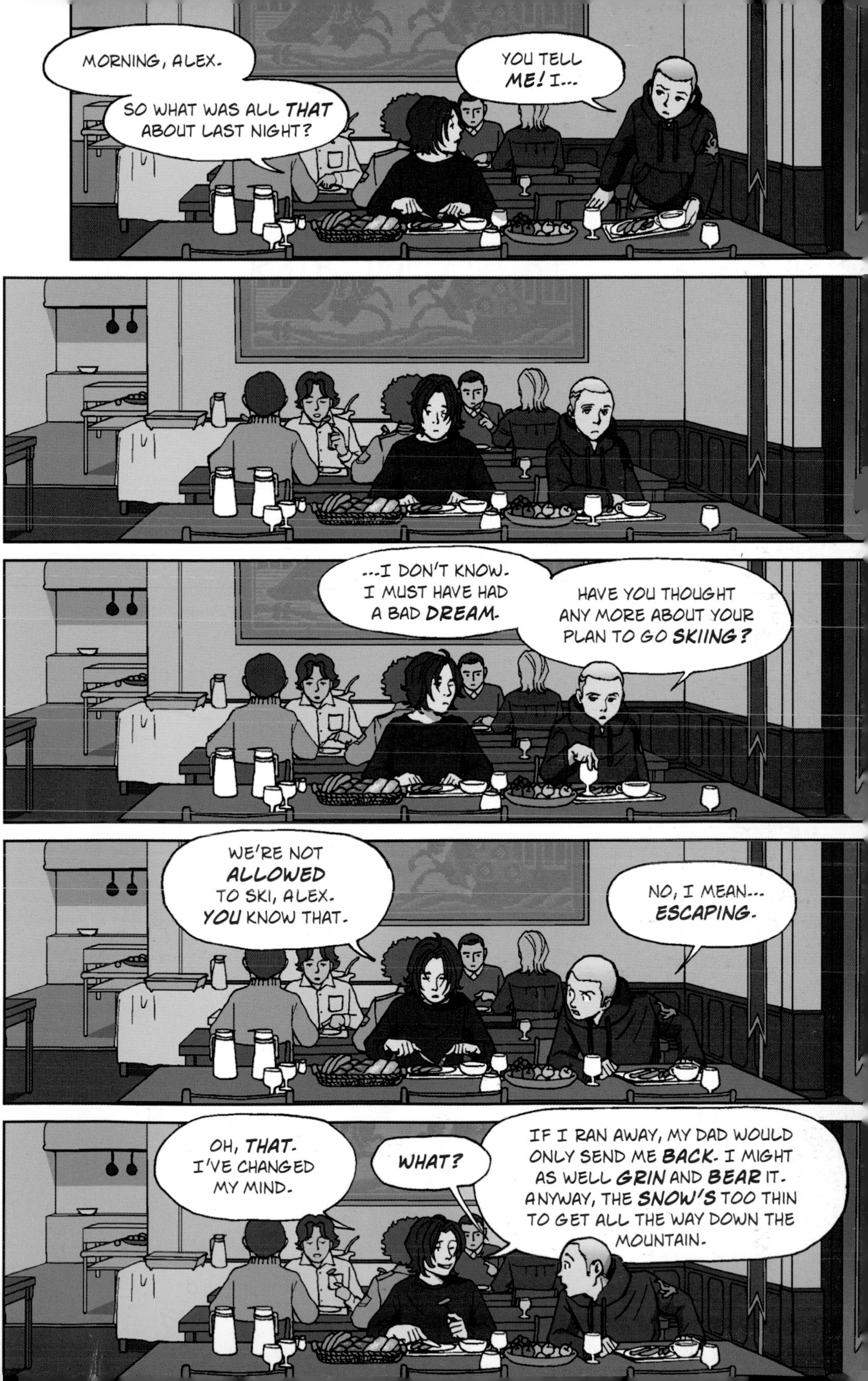
MORNING, ALEX.
SO WHAT WAS ALL THAT ABOUT LAST NIGHT?
YOU TELL ME! I...
...I DON'T KNOW. I MUST HAVE HAD A BAD DREAM.
HAVE YOU THOUGHT ANY MORE ABOUT YOUR PLAN TO GO SKIING?
WE'RE NOT ALLOWED TO SKI, ALEX. YOU KNOW THAT.
NO, I MEAN... ESCAPING.
OH, THAT. I'VE CHANGED MY MIND.
WHAT?
IF I RAN AWAY, MY DAD WOULD ONLY SEND ME BACK. I MIGHT AS WELL GRIN AND BEAR IT. ANYWAY, THE SNOW'S TOO THIN TO GET ALL THE WAY DOWN THE MOUNTAIN.

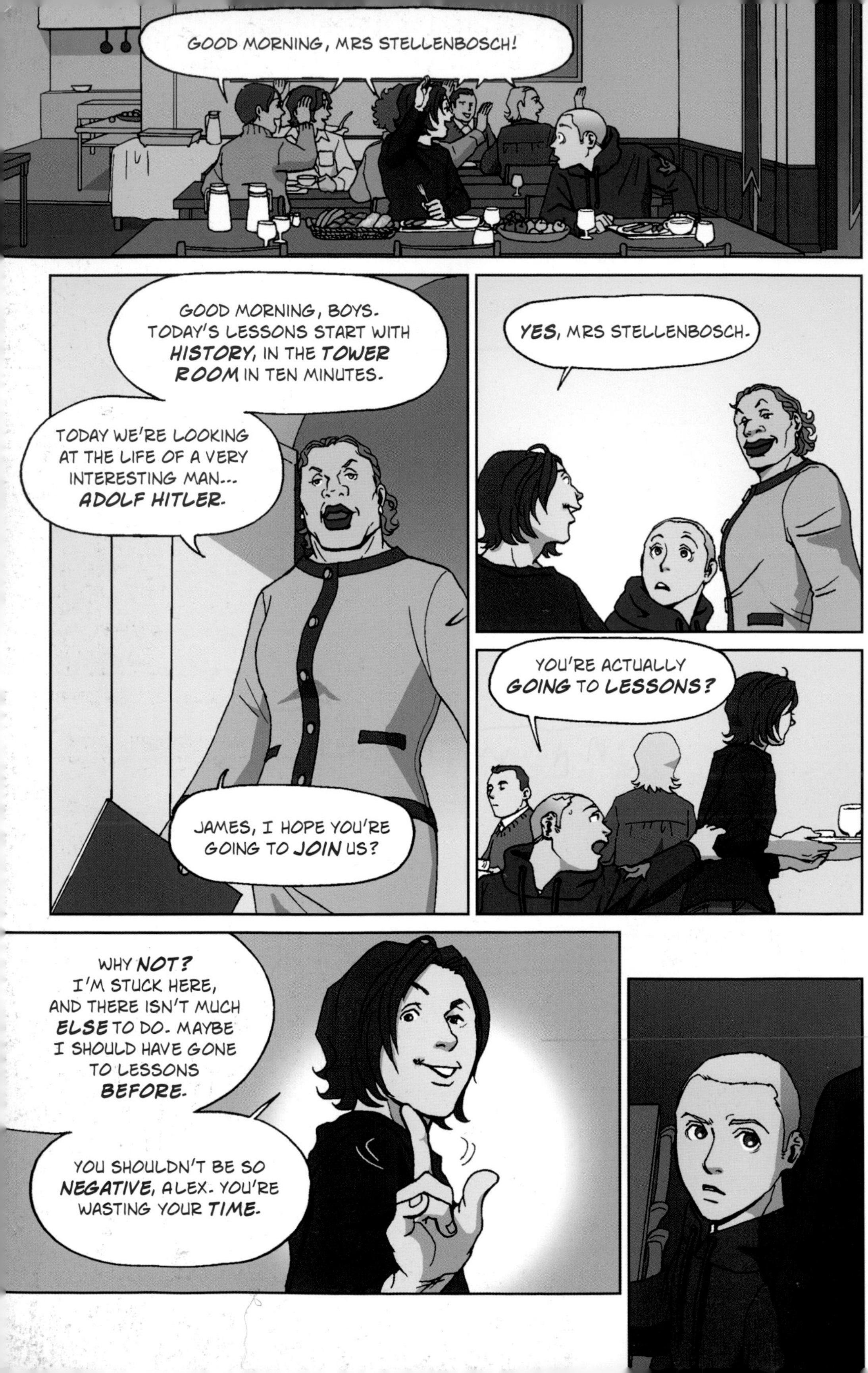
GOOD MORNING, MRS STELLENBOSCH!
GOOD MORNING, BOYS. TODAY'S LESSONS START WITH HISTORY, IN THE TOWER ROOM IN TEN MINUTES.
TODAY WE'RE LOOKING AT THE LIFE OF A VERY INTERESTING MAN... ADOLF HITLER.
JAMES, I HOPE YOU'RE GOING TO JOIN US?
YES, MRS STELLENBOSCH.
YOU'RE ACTUALLY GOING TO LESSONS?
WHY NOT? I'M STUCK HERE, AND THERE ISN'T MUCH ELSE TO DO. MAYBE I SHOULD HAVE GONE TO LESSONS BEFORE.
YOU SHOULDN'T BE SO NEGATIVE, ALEX. YOU'RE WASTING YOUR TIME.

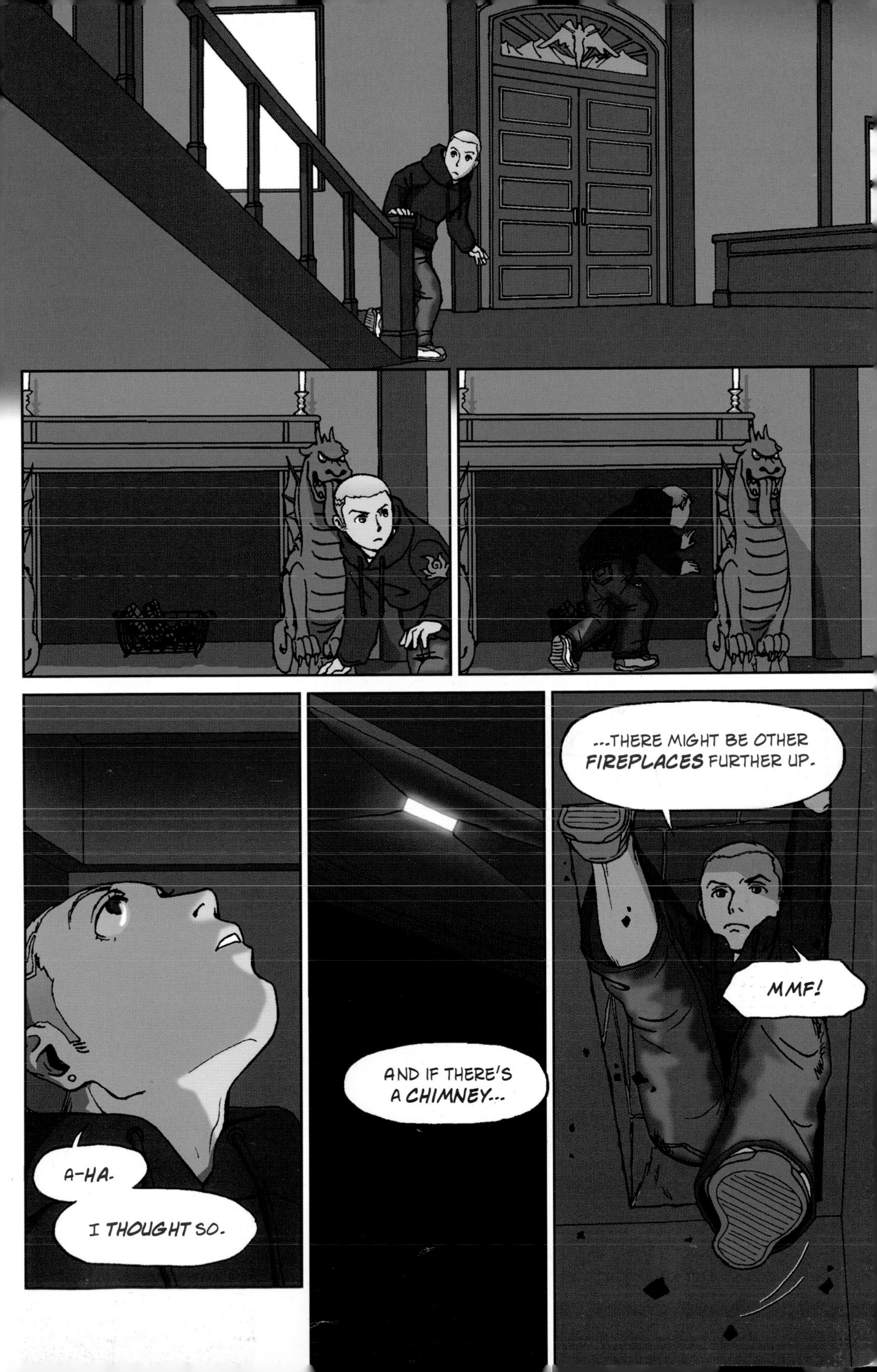
A-HA.
I THOUGHT SO.
AND IF THERE'S A CHIMNEY...
...THERE MIGHT BE OTHER FIREPLACES FURTHER UP.
MMF!

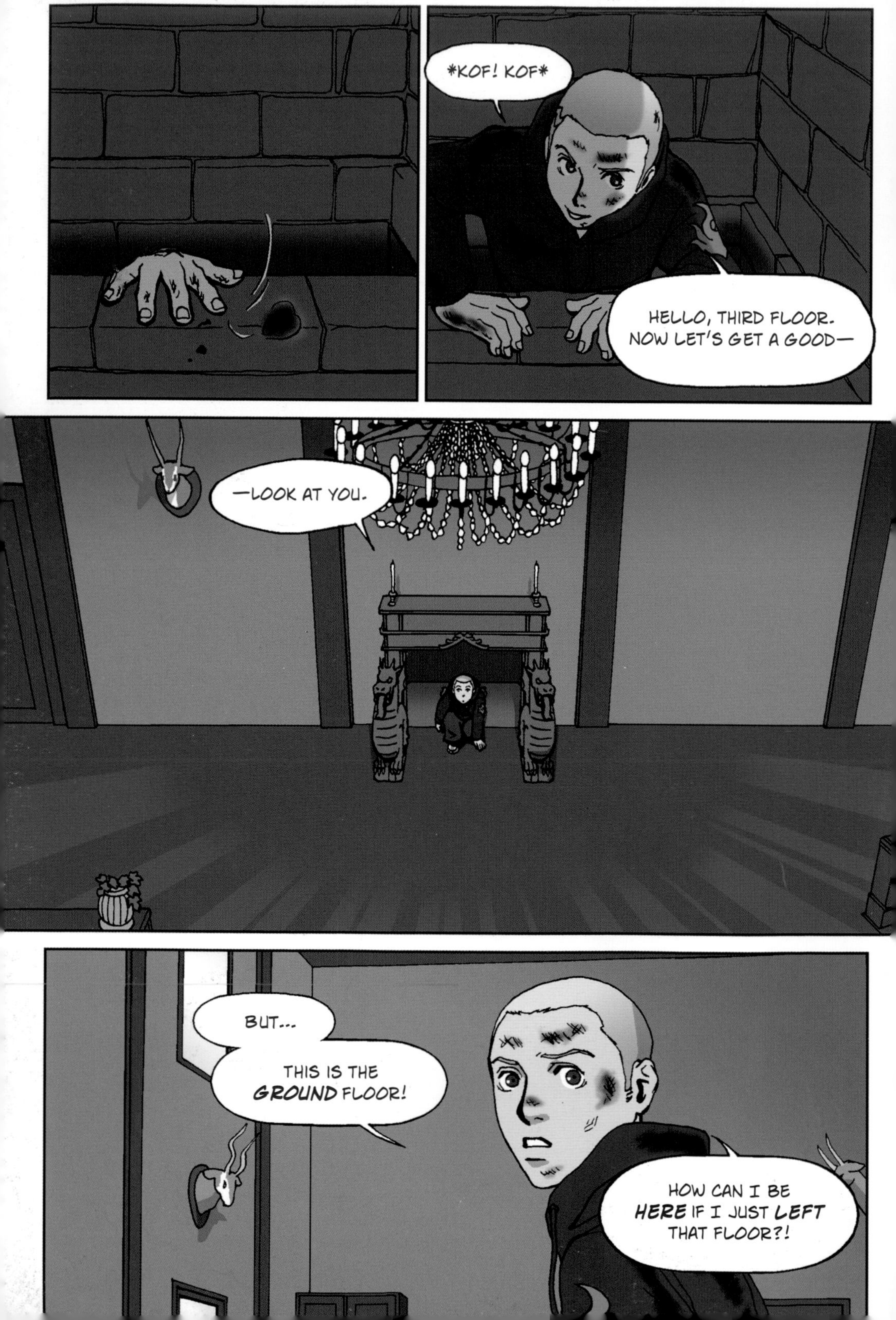
KOF! KOF
HELLO, THIRD FLOOR. NOW LET'S GET A GOOD—
—LOOK AT YOU.
BUT...
THIS IS THE GROUND FLOOR!
HOW CAN I BE HERE IF I JUST LEFT THAT FLOOR?!

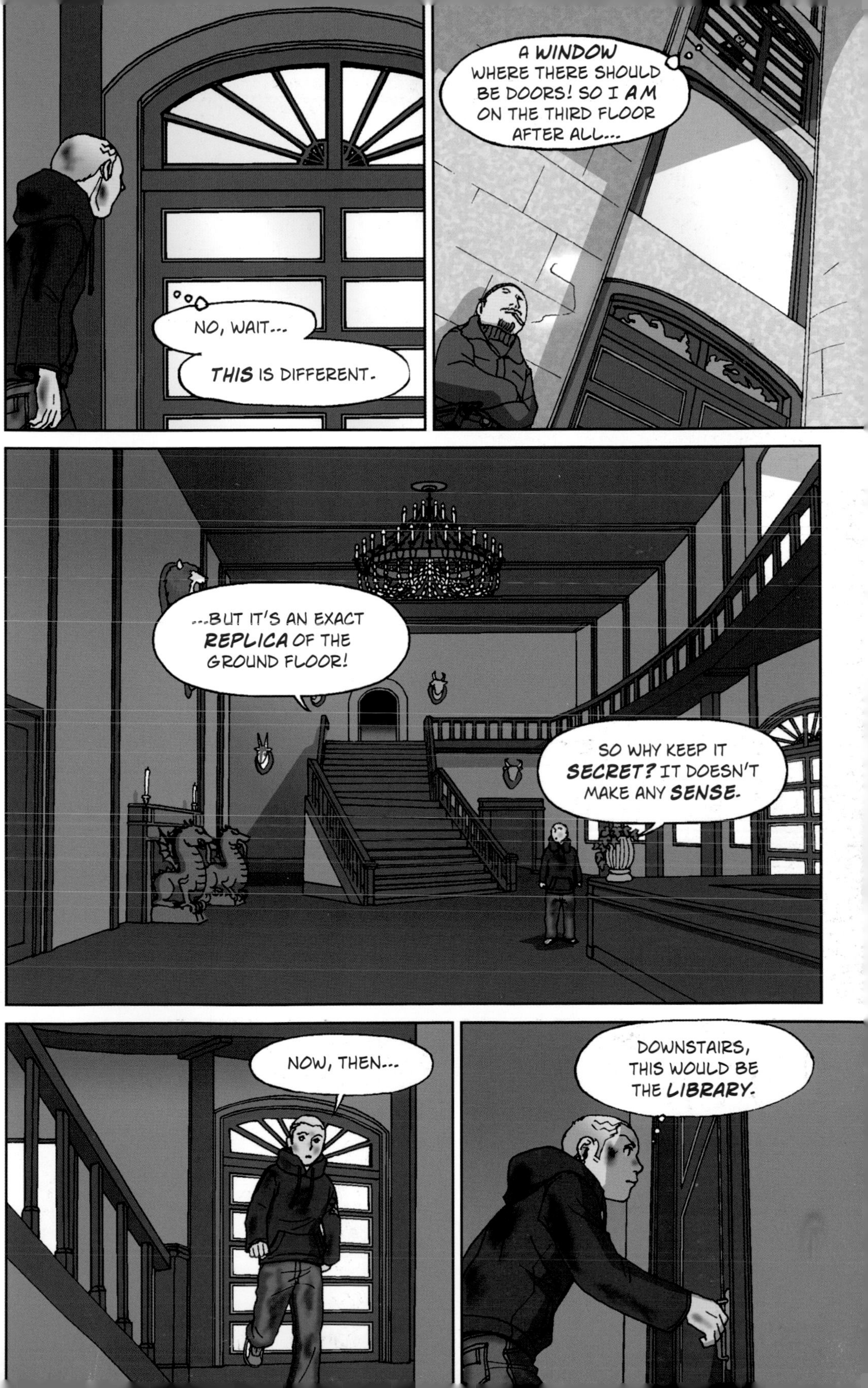
NO, WAIT...
THIS IS DIFFERENT.
A WINDOW WHERE THERE SHOULD BE DOORS! SO I AM ON THE THIRD FLOOR AFTER ALL...
...BUT IT'S AN EXACT REPLICA OF THE GROUND FLOOR!
SO WHY KEEP IT SECRET? IT DOESN'T MAKE ANY SENSE.
NOW, THEN...
DOWNSTAIRS, THIS WOULD BE THE LIBRARY.

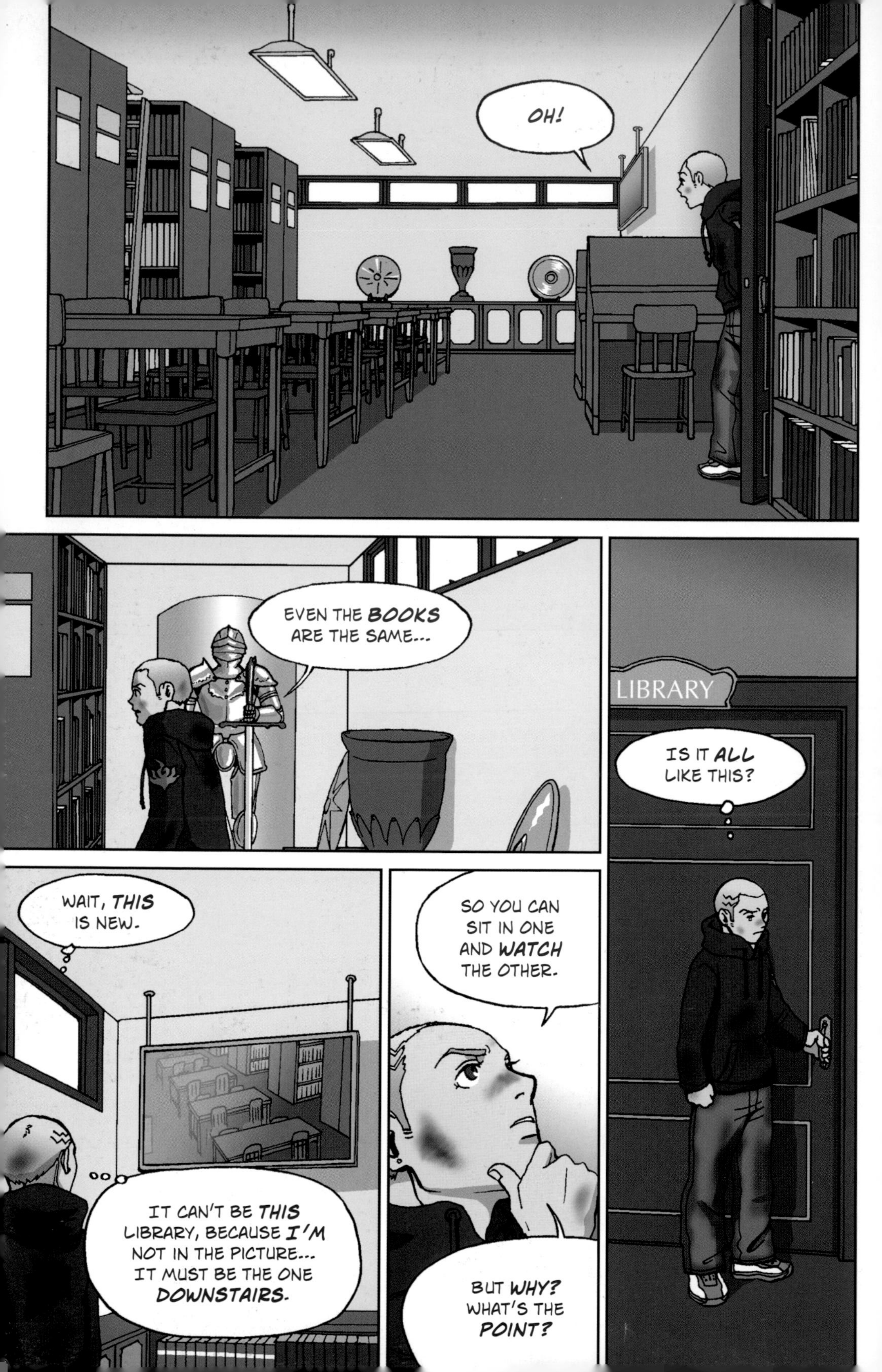

OH!
EVEN THE BOOKS ARE THE SAME...
LIBRARY
IS IT ALL LIKE THIS?
WAIT, THIS IS NEW.
IT CAN'T BE THIS LIBRARY, BECAUSE I'M NOT IN THE PICTURE... IT MUST BE THE ONE DOWNSTAIRS.
SO YOU CAN SIT IN ONE AND WATCH THE OTHER.
BUT WHY? WHAT'S THE POINT?

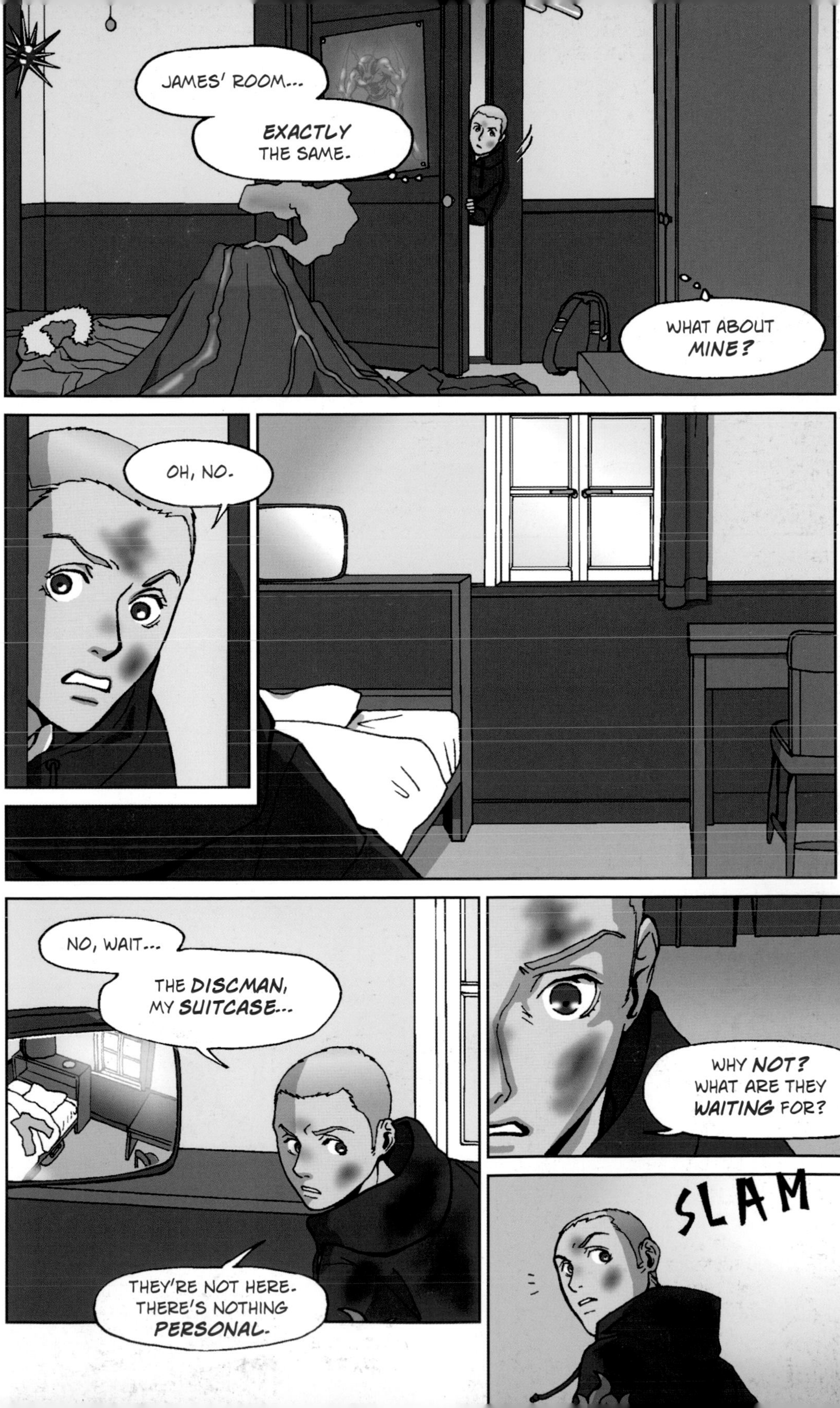

JAMES' ROOM...
EXACTLY THE SAME.
WHAT ABOUT MINE?
OH, NO.
NO, WAIT...
THE DISCMAN, MY SUITCASE...
THEY'RE NOT HERE. THERE'S NOTHING PERSONAL.
WHY NOT? WHAT ARE THEY WAITING FOR?
SLAM

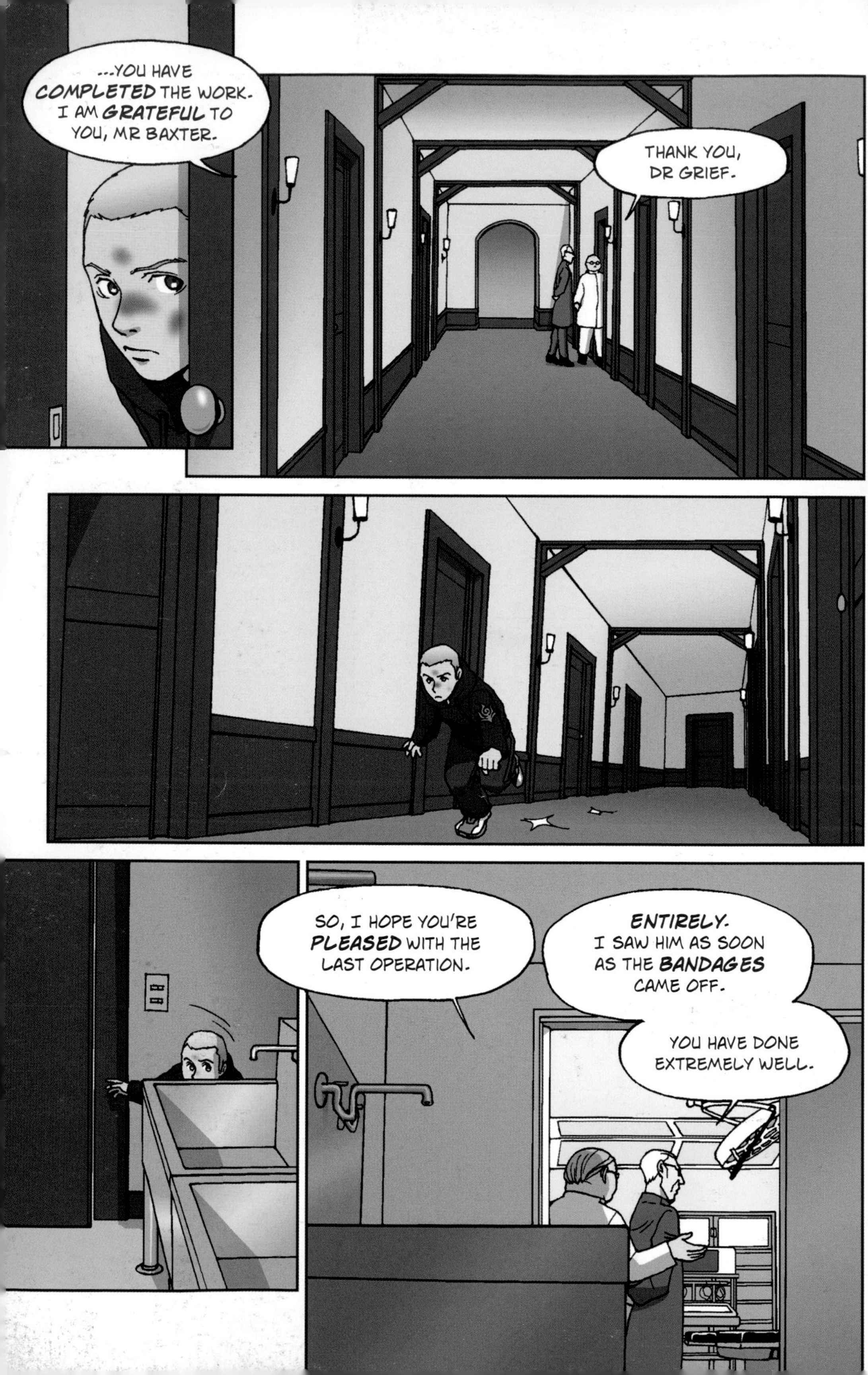
...YOU HAVE COMPLETED THE WORK. I AM GRATEFUL TO YOU, MR BAXTER.
THANK YOU, DR GRIEF.
SO, I HOPE YOU'RE PLEASED WITH THE LAST OPERATION.
ENTIRELY. I SAW HIM AS SOON AS THE BANDAGES CAME OFF.
YOU HAVE DONE EXTREMELY WELL.

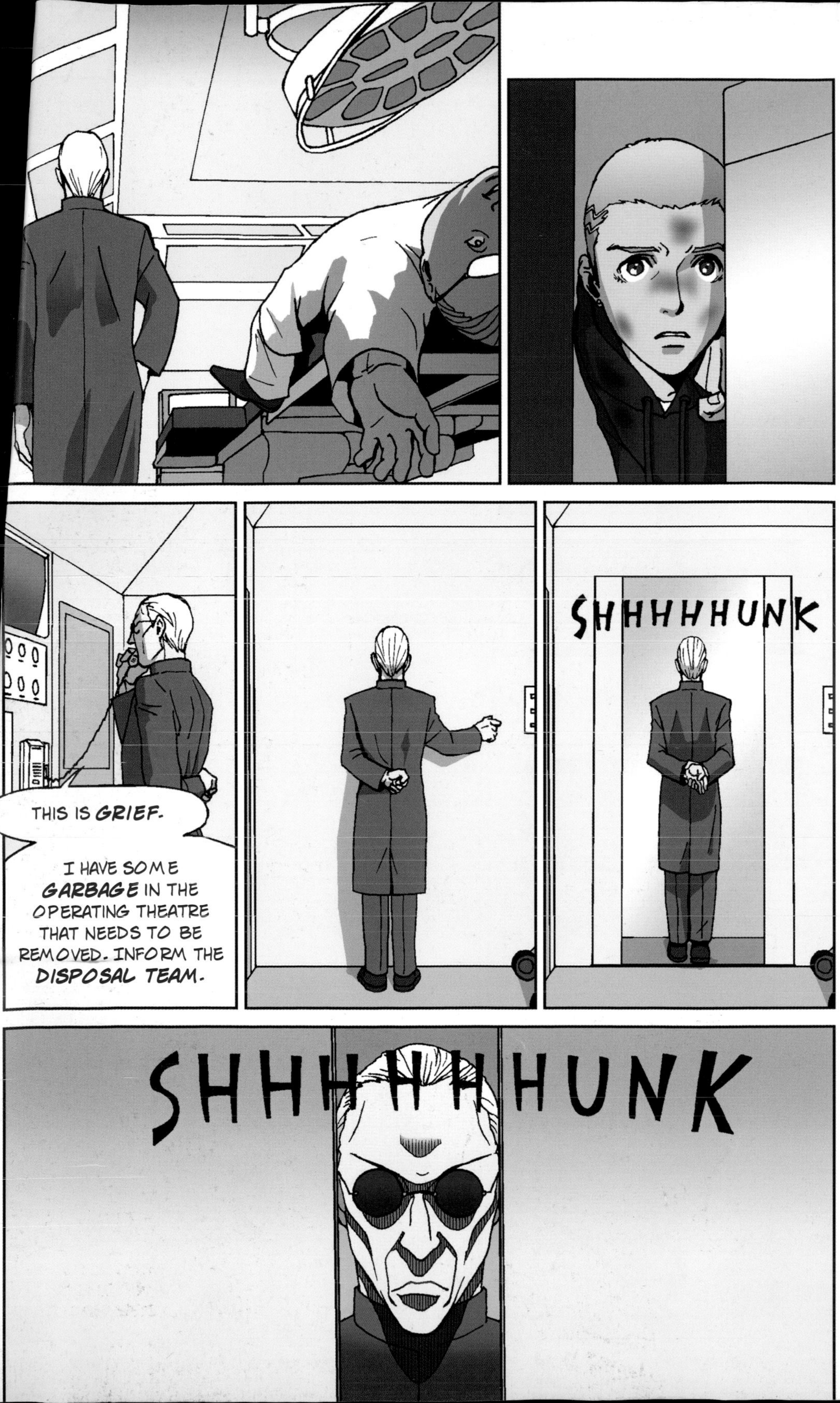
THIS IS GRIEF.
I HAVE SOME GARBAGE IN THE OPERATING THEATRE THAT NEEDS TO BE REMOVED. INFORM THE DISPOSAL TEAM.
SHHHHHUNK
SHHHHHHUNK

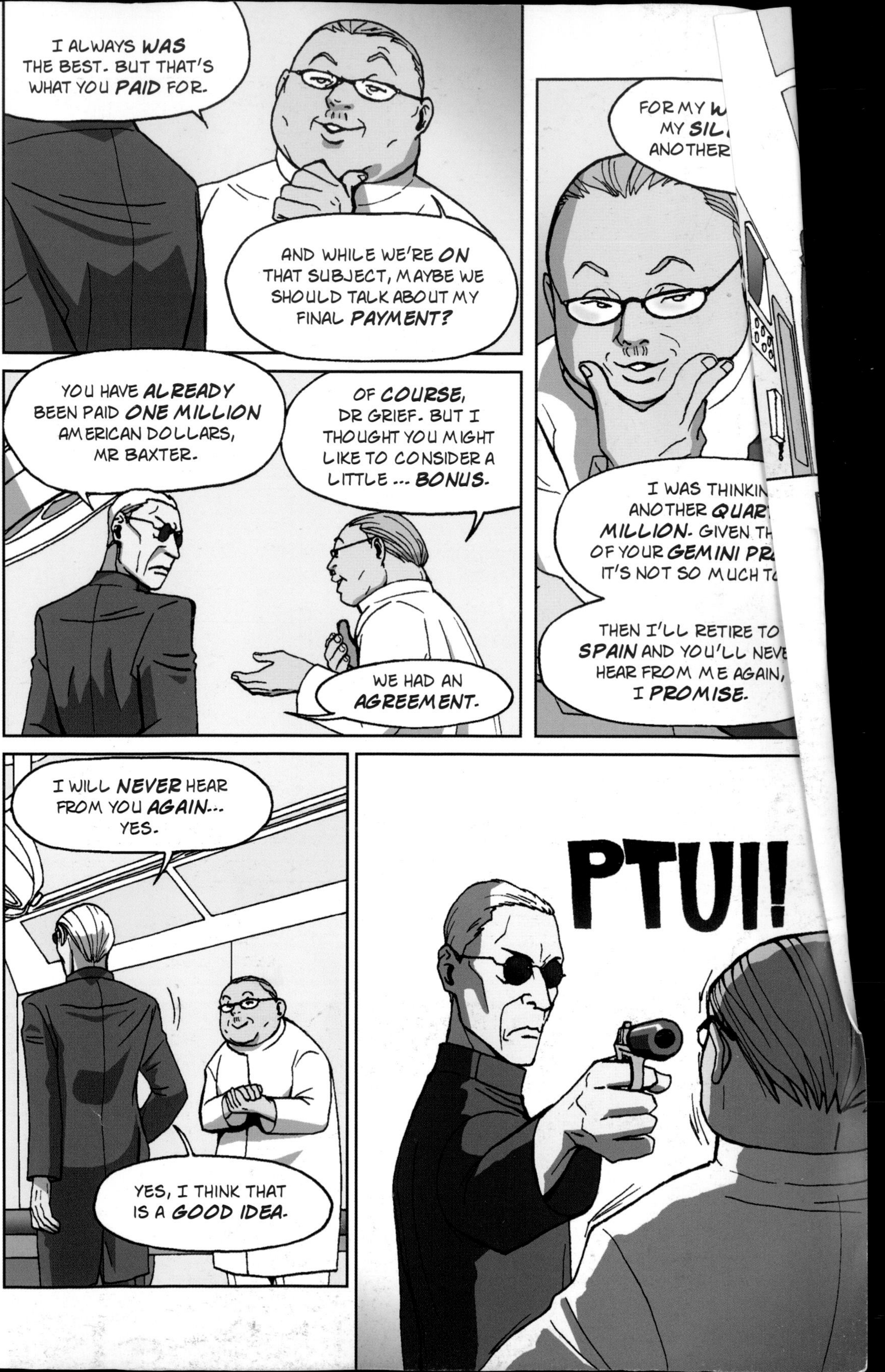
I ALWAYS **WAS** THE BEST. BUT THAT'S WHAT YOU **PAID** FOR.
AND WHILE WE'RE **ON** THAT SUBJECT, MAYBE WE SHOULD TALK ABOUT MY FINAL **PAYMENT?**
YOU HAVE **ALREADY** BEEN PAID **ONE MILLION** AMERICAN DOLLARS, MR BAXTER.
OF **COURSE**, DR GRIEF. BUT I THOUGHT YOU MIGHT LIKE TO CONSIDER A LITTLE ... **BONUS**.
WE HAD AN **AGREEMENT**.
FOR MY
MY
ANOTHER
I WAS THINKIN
ANOTHER
MILLION. GIVEN TH
OF YOUR **GEMINI**
IT'S NOT SO MUCH
THEN I'LL RETIRE TO
SPAIN AND YOU'LL NEVE
HEAR FROM ME AGAIN,
I **PROMISE**.
I WILL **NEVER** HEAR FROM YOU **AGAIN**... YES.
YES, I THINK THAT IS A **GOOD IDEA**.
PTUI!

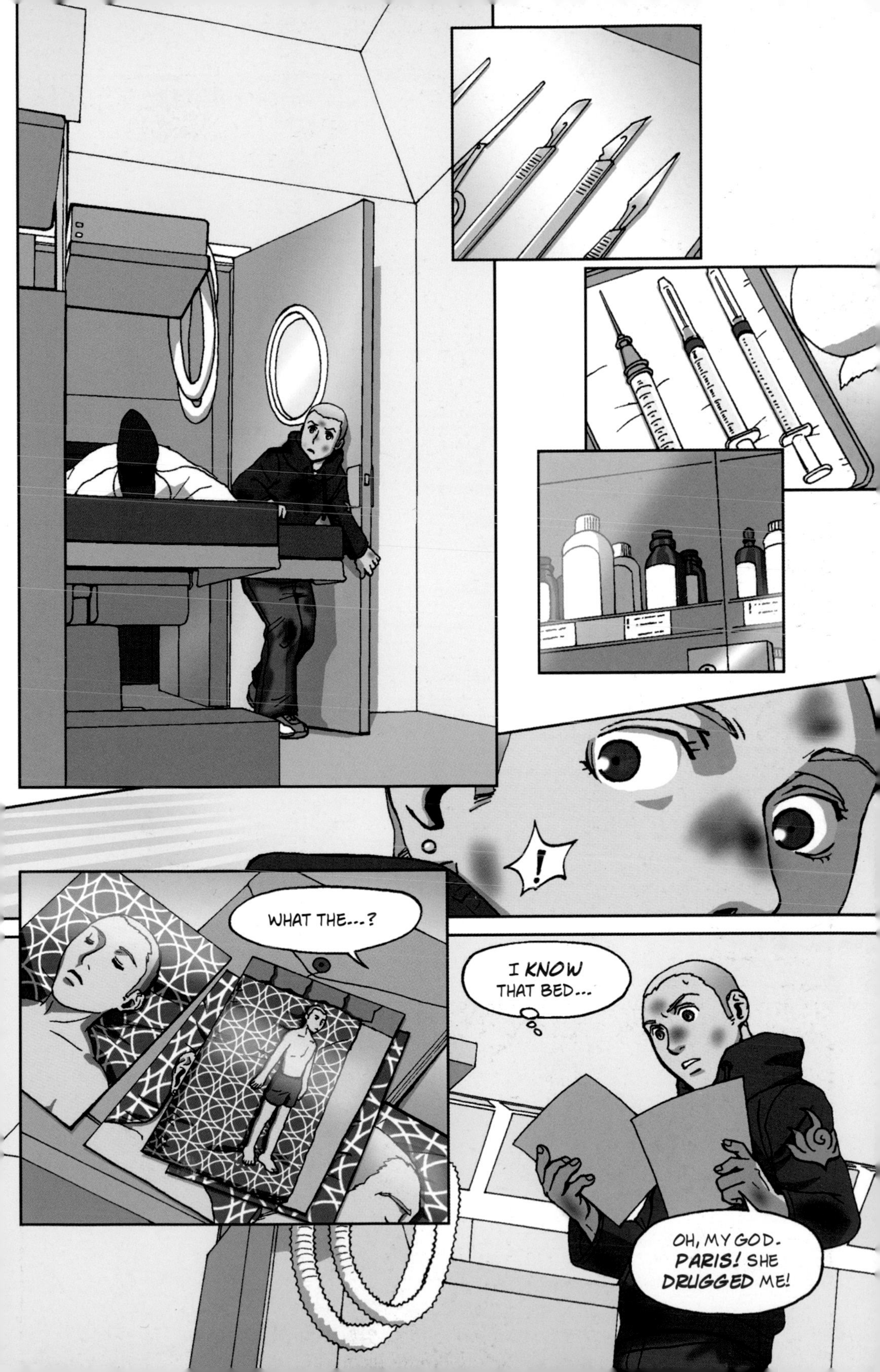
!
WHAT THE...?
I KNOW THAT BED...
OH, MY GOD. PARIS! SHE DRUGGED ME!

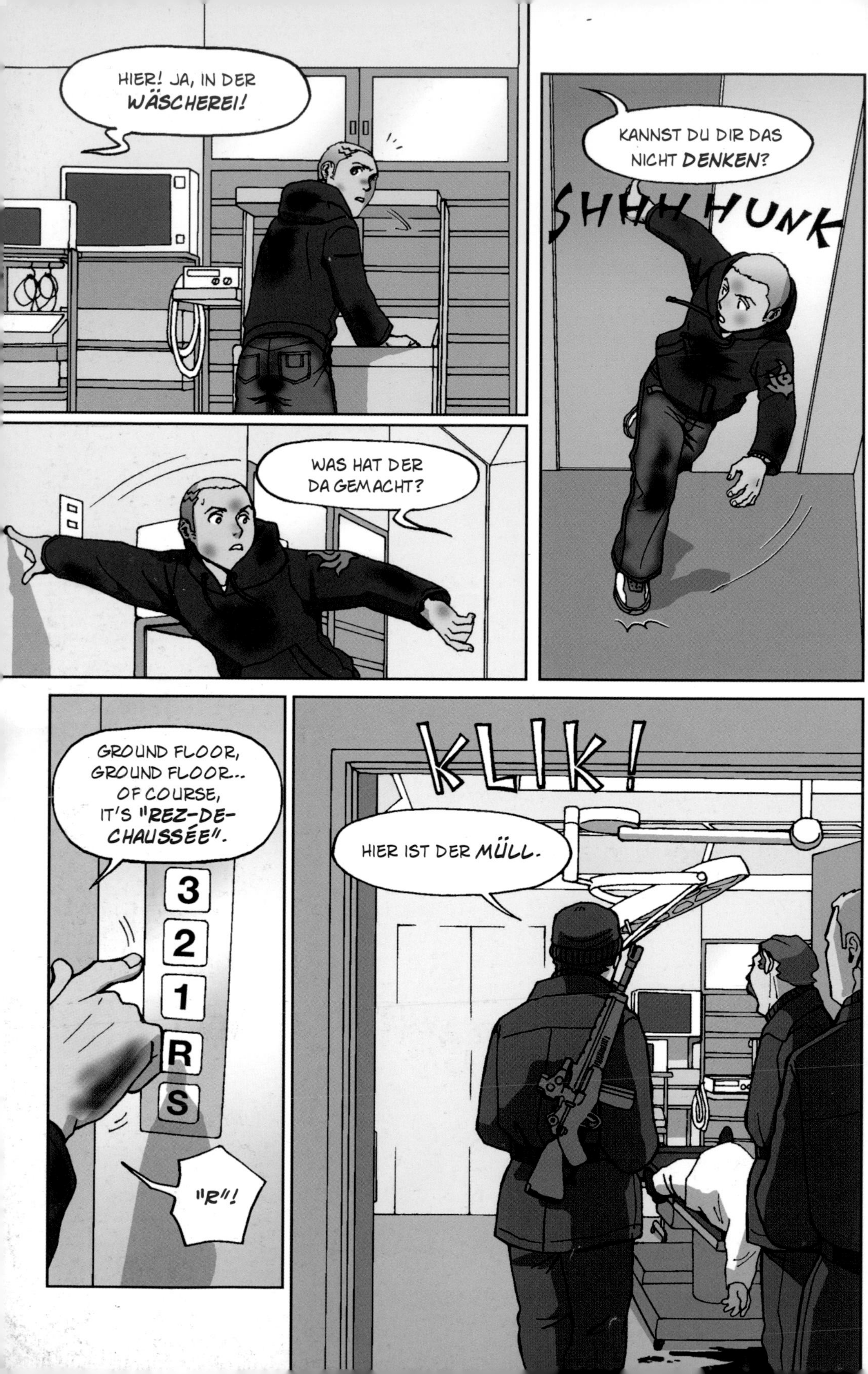
HIER! JA, IN DER WÄSCHEREI!
KANNST DU DIR DAS NICHT DENKEN?
SHHHHUNK
WAS HAT DER DA GEMACHT?
GROUND FLOOR, GROUND FLOOR... OF COURSE, IT'S "REZ-DE-CHAUSSÉE".
3
2
1
R
S
"R"!
KLIK!
HIER IST DER MÜLL.

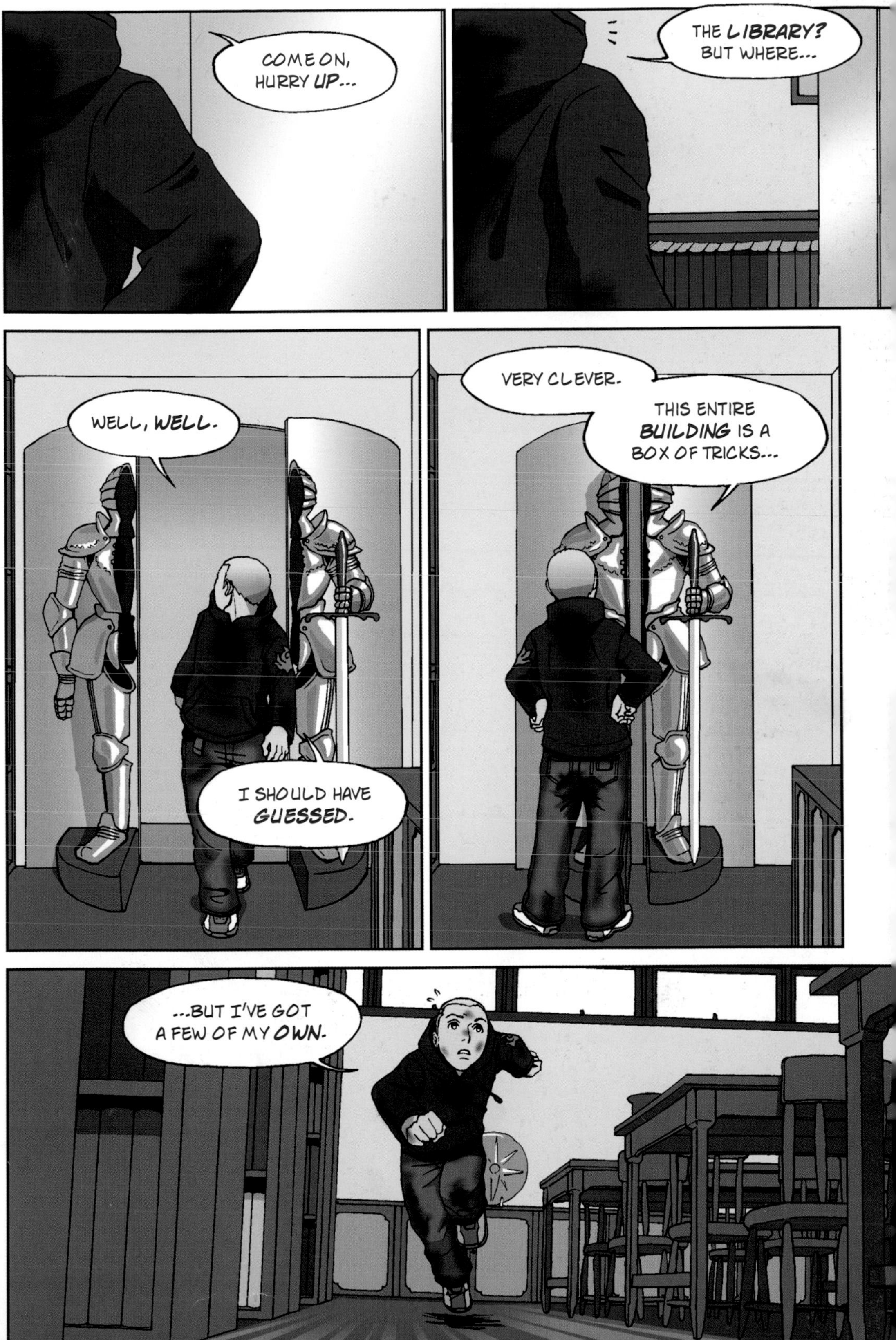

COME ON, HURRY UP...
THE LIBRARY? BUT WHERE...
WELL, WELL.
I SHOULD HAVE GUESSED.
VERY CLEVER.
THIS ENTIRE BUILDING IS A BOX OF TRICKS...
...BUT I'VE GOT A FEW OF MY OWN.

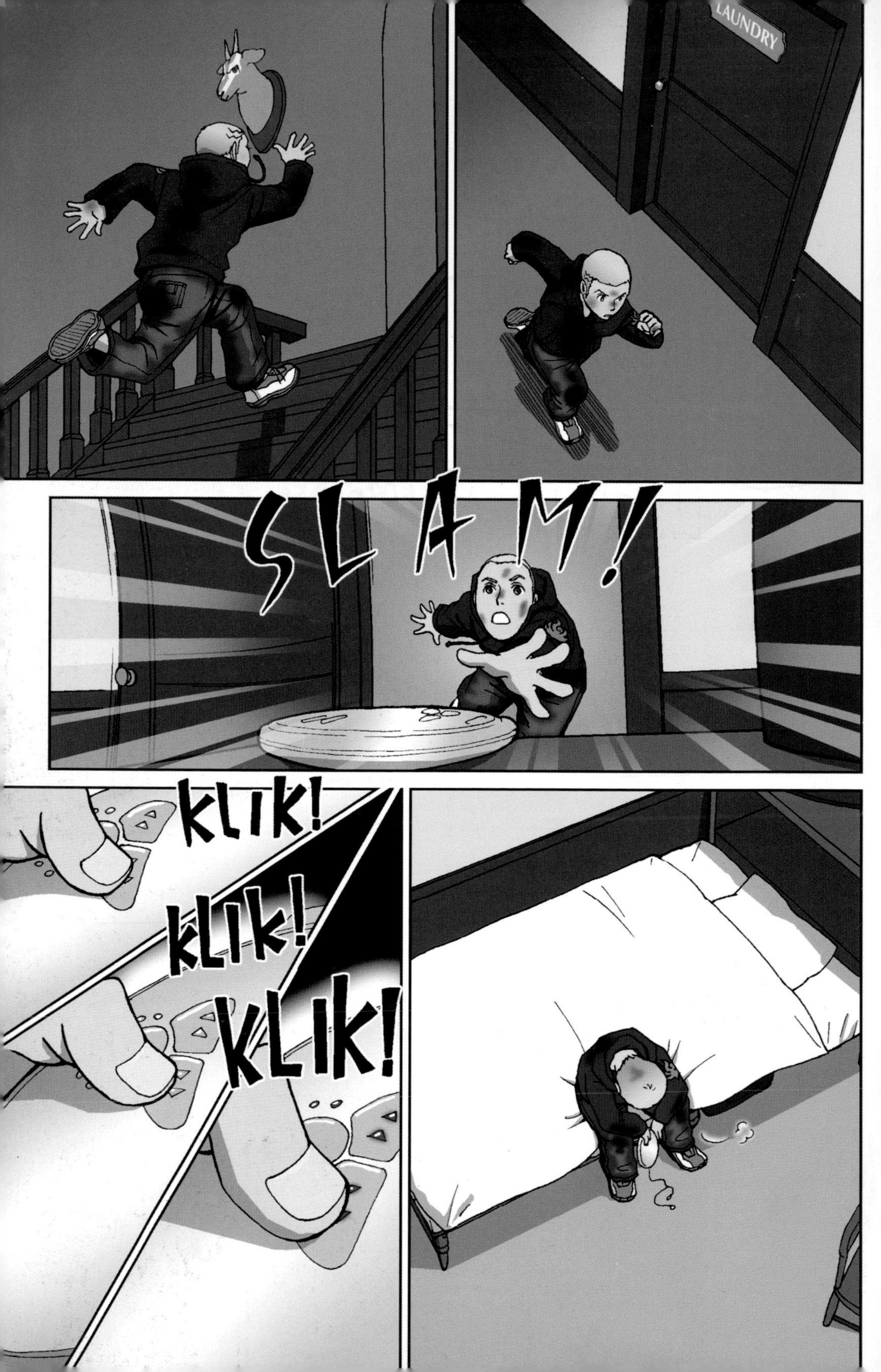
LAUNDRY
SLAM!
KLIK!
KLIK!
KLIK!

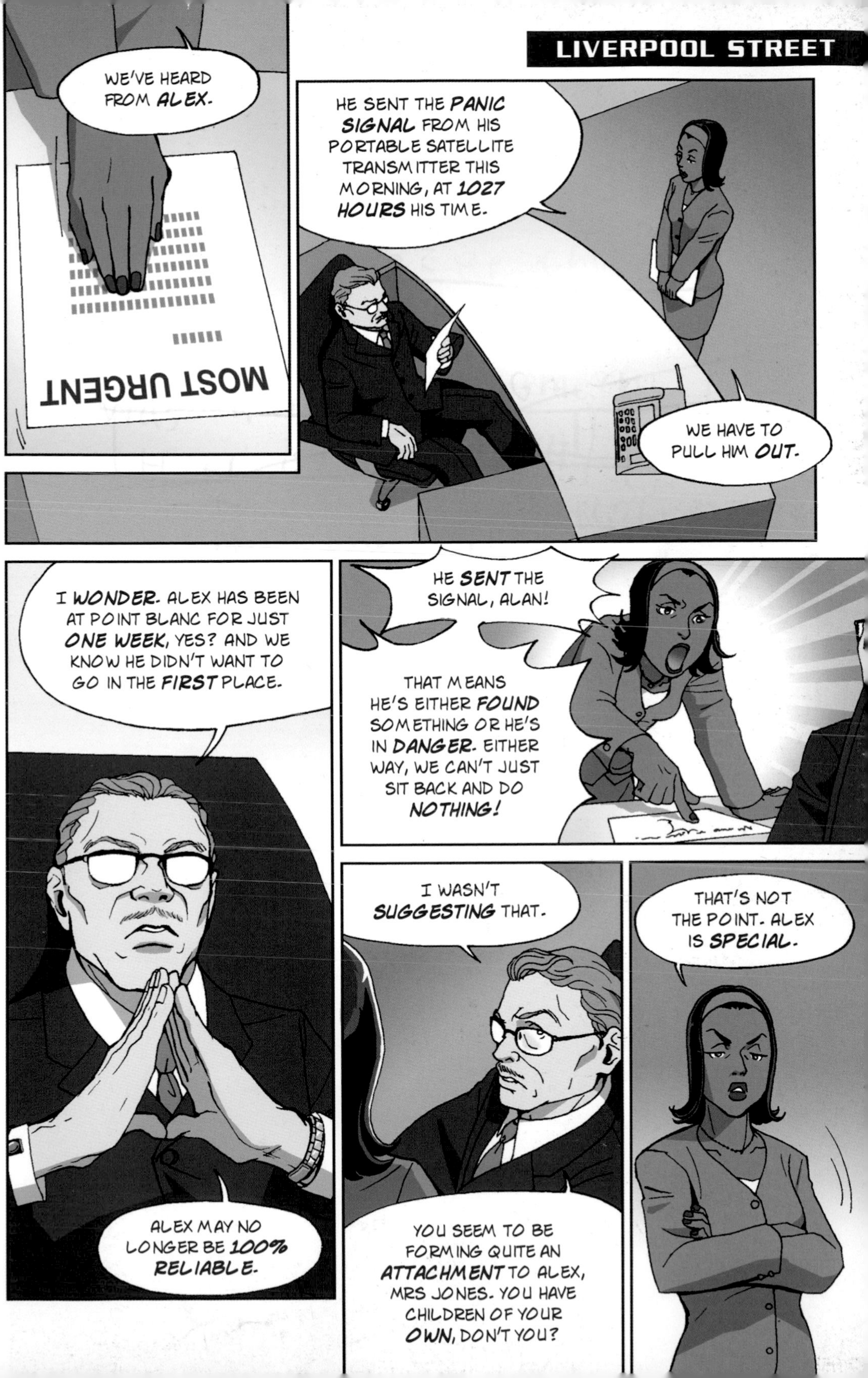
LIVERPOOL STREET
WE'VE HEARD FROM ALEX.
MOST URGENT
HE SENT THE PANIC SIGNAL FROM HIS PORTABLE SATELLITE TRANSMITTER THIS MORNING, AT 1027 HOURS HIS TIME.
WE HAVE TO PULL HIM OUT.
I WONDER. ALEX HAS BEEN AT POINT BLANC FOR JUST ONE WEEK, YES? AND WE KNOW HE DIDN'T WANT TO GO IN THE FIRST PLACE.
ALEX MAY NO LONGER BE 100% RELIABLE.
HE SENT THE SIGNAL, ALAN!
THAT MEANS HE'S EITHER FOUND SOMETHING OR HE'S IN DANGER. EITHER WAY, WE CAN'T JUST SIT BACK AND DO NOTHING!
I WASN'T SUGGESTING THAT.
YOU SEEM TO BE FORMING QUITE AN ATTACHMENT TO ALEX, MRS JONES. YOU HAVE CHILDREN OF YOUR OWN, DON'T YOU?
THAT'S NOT THE POINT. ALEX IS SPECIAL.

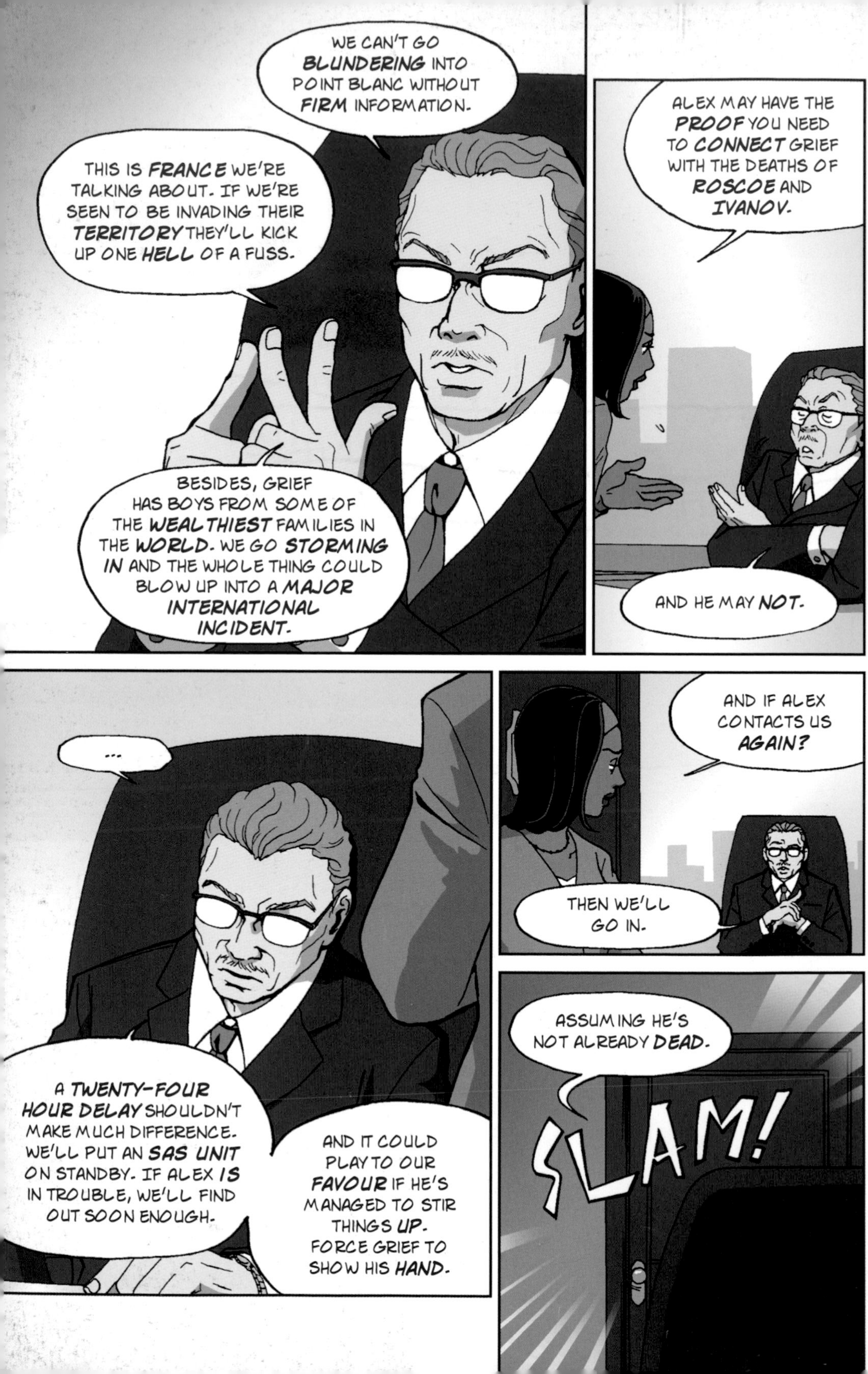
WE CAN'T GO BLUNDERING INTO POINT BLANC WITHOUT FIRM INFORMATION.
THIS IS FRANCE WE'RE TALKING ABOUT. IF WE'RE SEEN TO BE INVADING THEIR TERRITORY THEY'LL KICK UP ONE HELL OF A FUSS.
BESIDES, GRIEF HAS BOYS FROM SOME OF THE WEALTHIEST FAMILIES IN THE WORLD. WE GO STORMING IN AND THE WHOLE THING COULD BLOW UP INTO A MAJOR INTERNATIONAL INCIDENT.
ALEX MAY HAVE THE PROOF YOU NEED TO CONNECT GRIEF WITH THE DEATHS OF ROSCOE AND IVANOV.
AND HE MAY NOT.
...
A TWENTY-FOUR HOUR DELAY SHOULDN'T MAKE MUCH DIFFERENCE. WE'LL PUT AN SAS UNIT ON STANDBY. IF ALEX IS IN TROUBLE, WE'LL FIND OUT SOON ENOUGH.
AND IT COULD PLAY TO OUR FAVOUR IF HE'S MANAGED TO STIR THINGS UP. FORCE GRIEF TO SHOW HIS HAND.
AND IF ALEX CONTACTS US AGAIN?
THEN WE'LL GO IN.
ASSUMING HE'S NOT ALREADY DEAD.
SLAM!

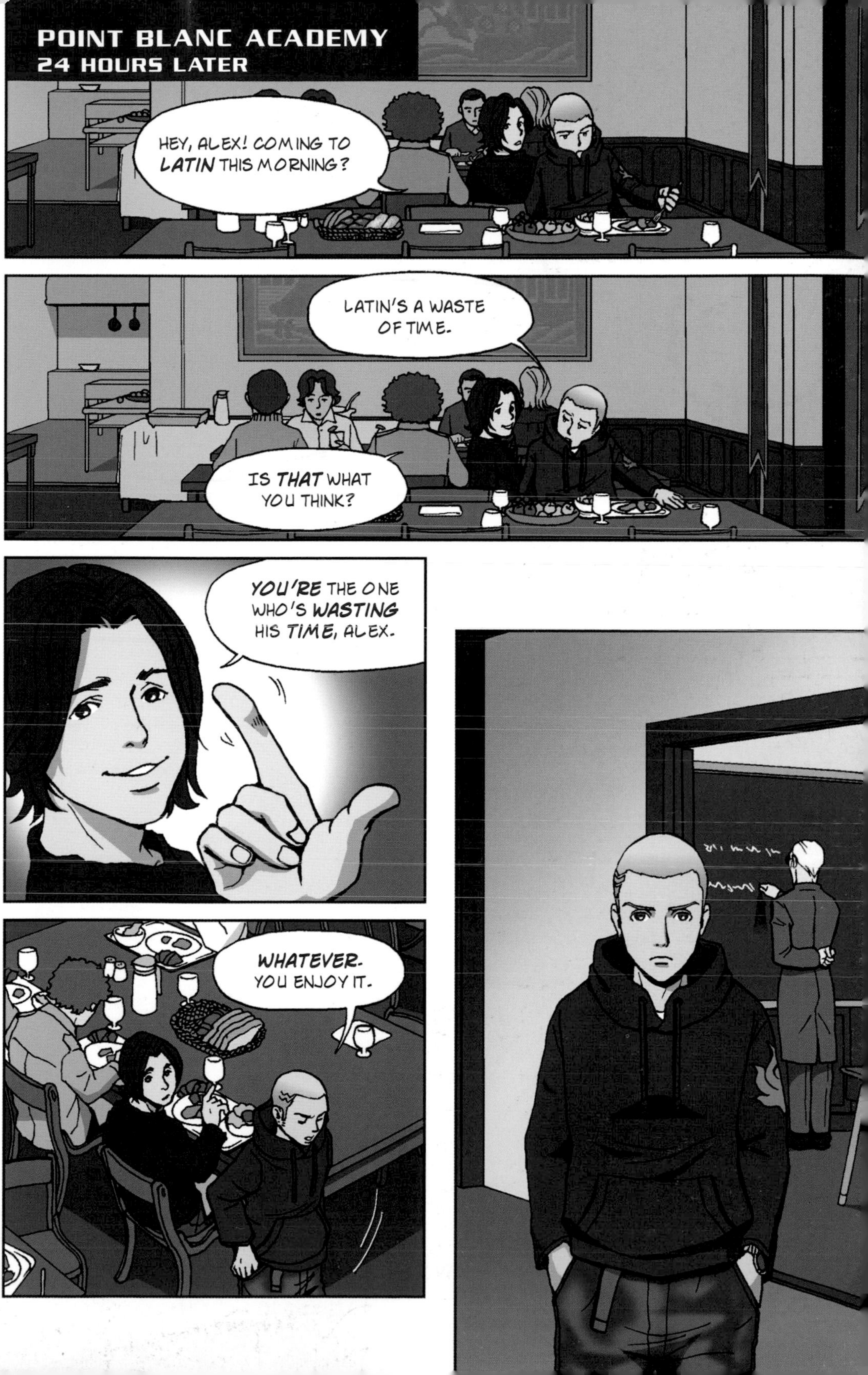
POINT BLANC ACADEMY
24 HOURS LATER
HEY, ALEX! COMING TO LATIN THIS MORNING?
LATIN'S A WASTE OF TIME.
IS THAT WHAT YOU THINK?
YOU'RE THE ONE WHO'S WASTING HIS TIME, ALEX.
WHATEVER. YOU ENJOY IT.

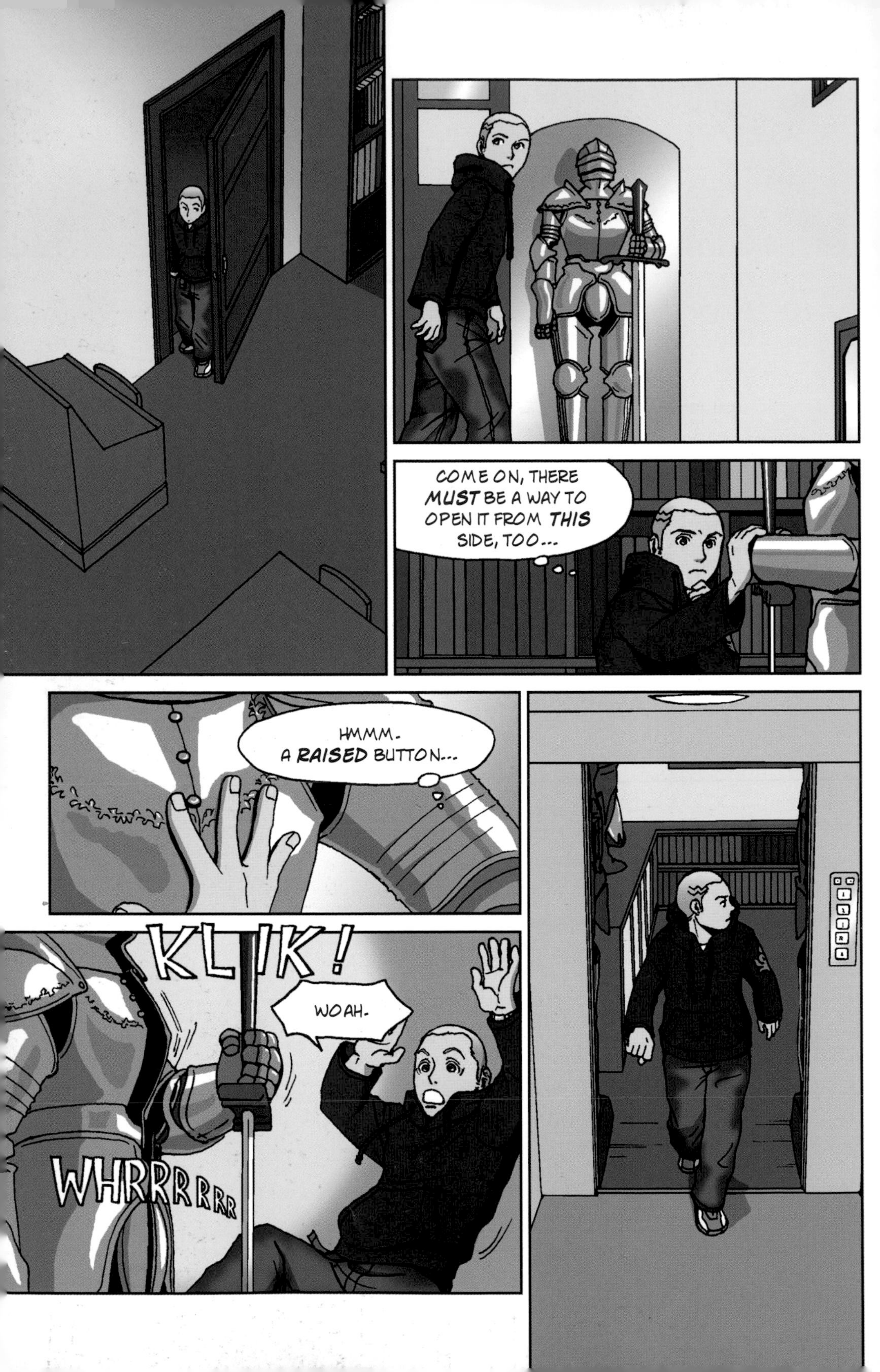
COME ON, THERE MUST BE A WAY TO OPEN IT FROM THIS SIDE, TOO...
HMMM. A RAISED BUTTON...
KLIK!
WOAH.
WHRRRRRRR

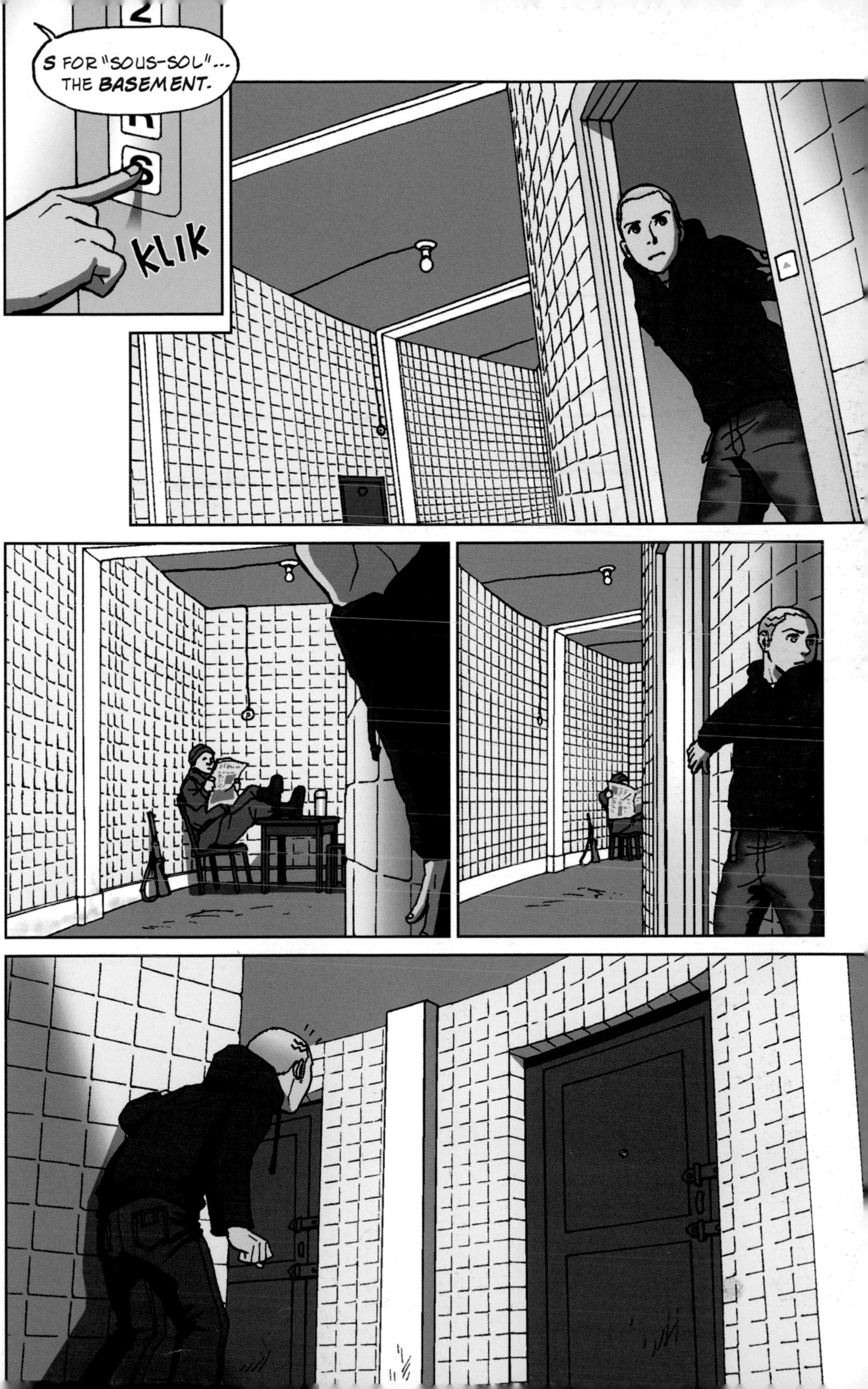
S FOR "SOUS-SOL"... THE BASEMENT.
KLIK

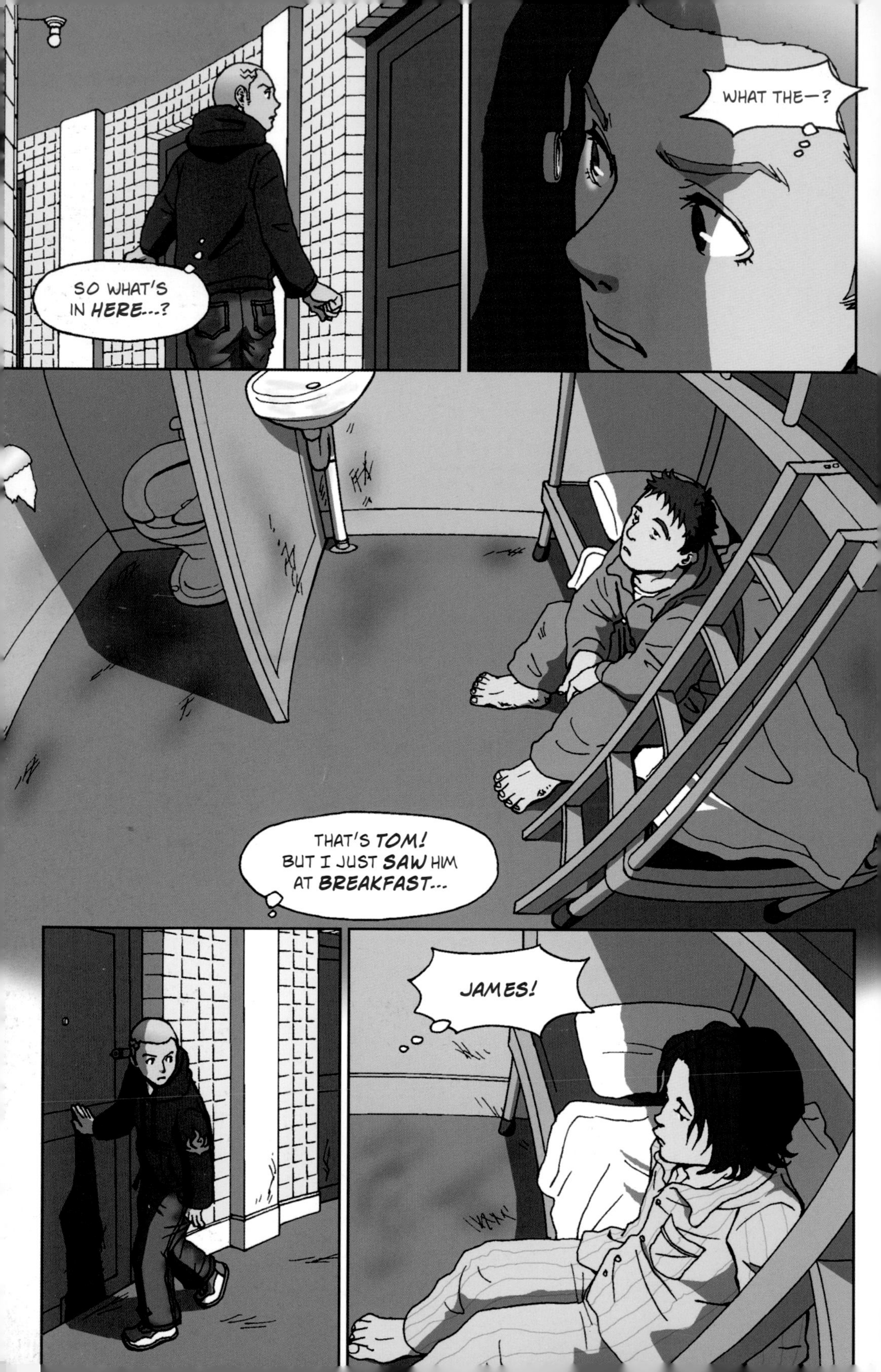
SO WHAT'S IN HERE...?
WHAT THE—?
THAT'S TOM! BUT I JUST SAW HIM AT BREAKFAST...
JAMES!

MMMMMMM

COME ON, COME ON...

ALEX! WHAT ARE YOU *DOING* HERE?

SHHH, KEEP YOUR VOICE *DOWN!* WE HAVEN'T GOT MUCH TIME... WHAT *HAPPENED* TO YOU?

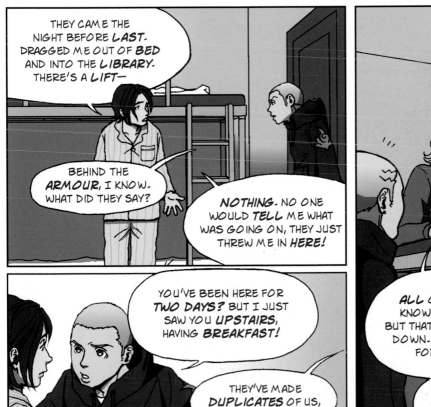

THEY CAME THE NIGHT BEFORE *LAST.* DRAGGED ME OUT OF *BED* AND INTO THE *LIBRARY.* THERE'S A *LIFT*—

BEHIND THE *ARMOUR,* I KNOW. WHAT DID THEY SAY?

NOTHING. NO ONE WOULD *TELL* ME WHAT WAS GOING ON, THEY JUST THREW ME IN *HERE!*

YOU'VE BEEN HERE FOR *TWO DAYS?* BUT I JUST SAW YOU *UPSTAIRS,* HAVING *BREAKFAST!*

THEY'VE MADE *DUPLICATES* OF US, DUDE.

ALL OF US. I DON'T KNOW *HOW OR WHY,* BUT THAT'S WHAT'S GOING DOWN. I'VE BEEN HERE FOR *MONTHS.*

I'M PAUL, BY THE WAY. *PAUL ROSCOE.*

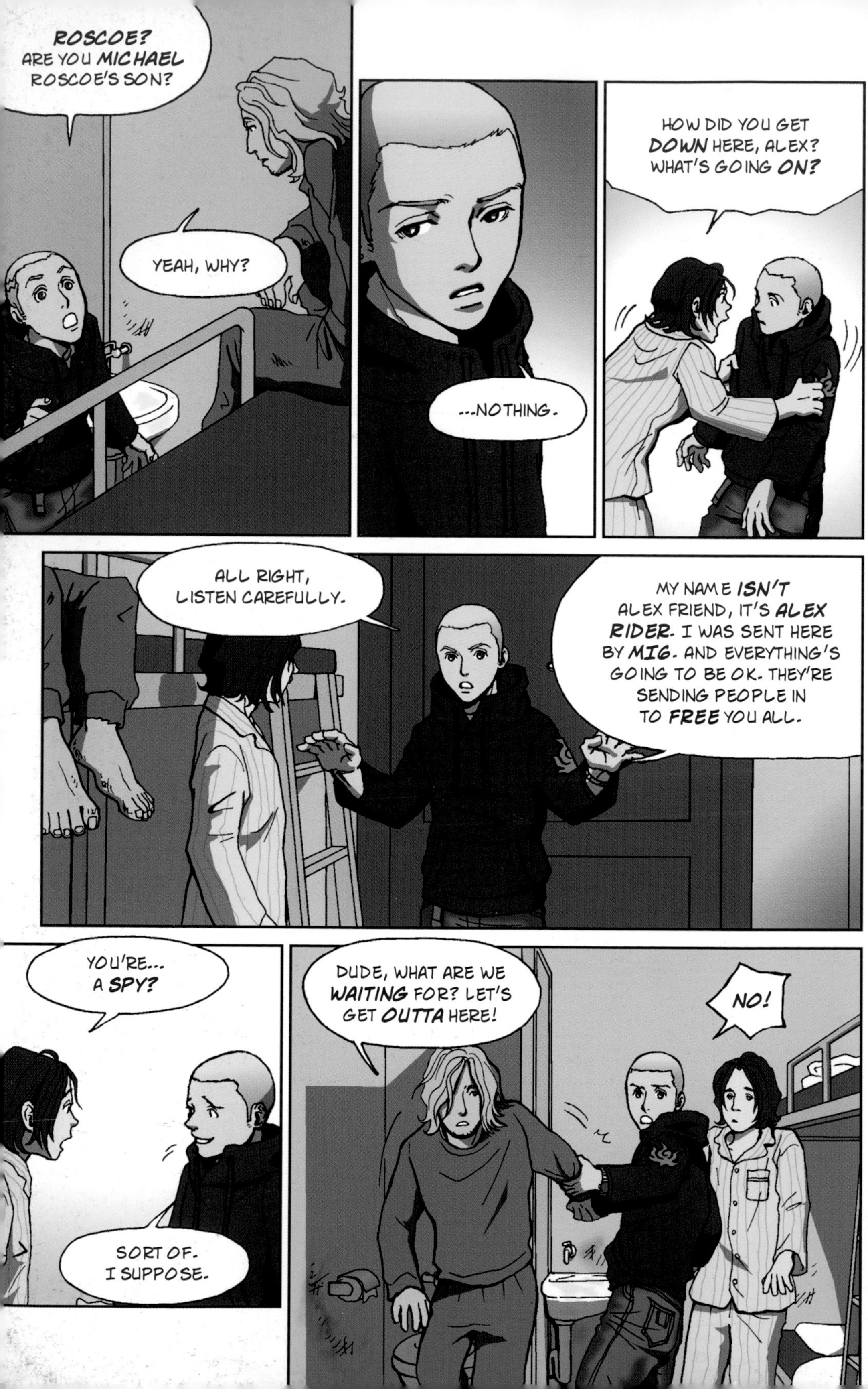
ROSCOE? ARE YOU MICHAEL ROSCOE'S SON?
YEAH, WHY?
...NOTHING.
HOW DID YOU GET DOWN HERE, ALEX? WHAT'S GOING ON?
ALL RIGHT, LISTEN CAREFULLY.
MY NAME ISN'T ALEX FRIEND, IT'S ALEX RIDER. I WAS SENT HERE BY MI6. AND EVERYTHING'S GOING TO BE OK. THEY'RE SENDING PEOPLE IN TO FREE YOU ALL.
YOU'RE... A SPY?
SORT OF. I SUPPOSE.
DUDE, WHAT ARE WE WAITING FOR? LET'S GET OUTTA HERE!
NO!

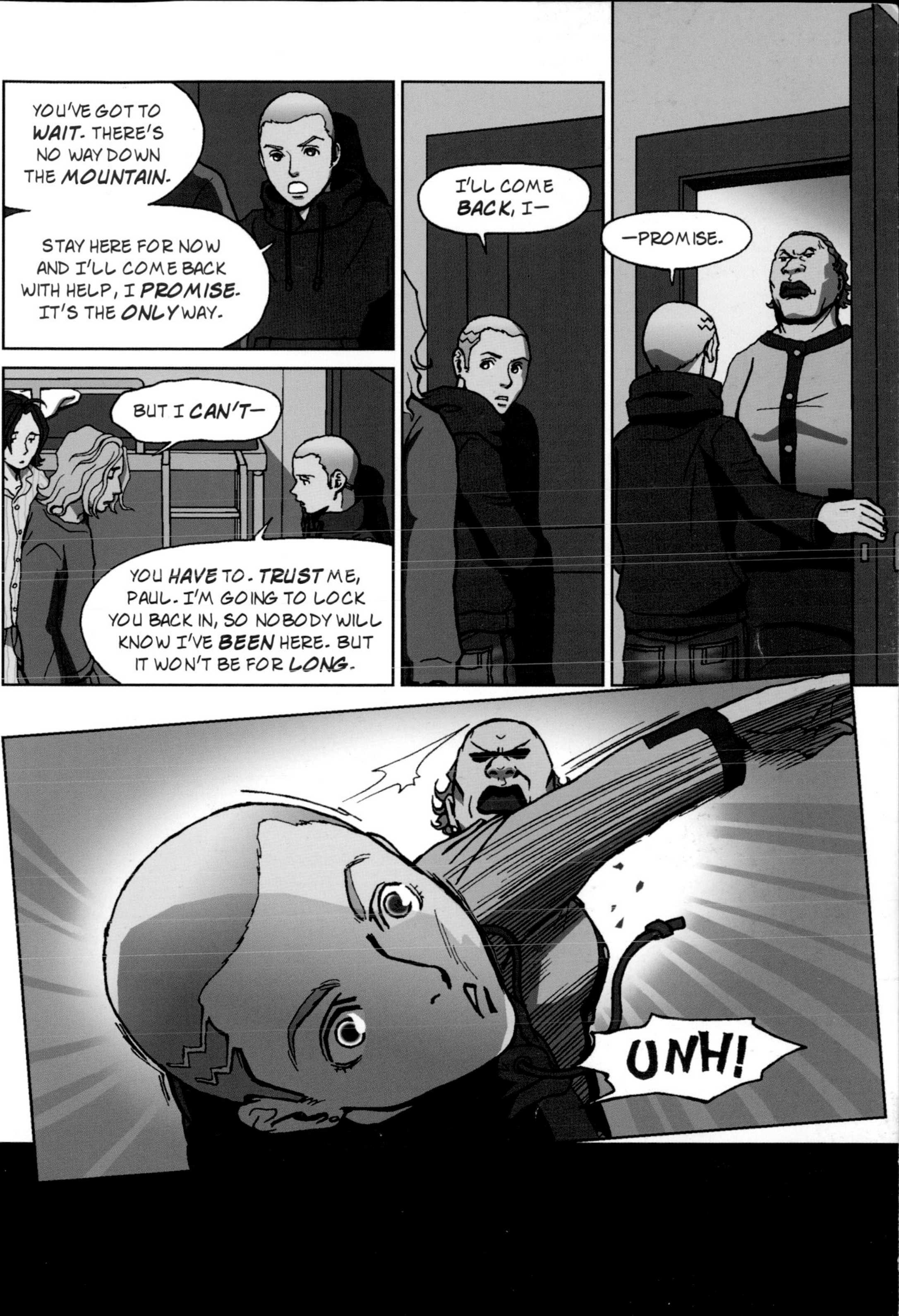
YOU'VE GOT TO WAIT. THERE'S NO WAY DOWN THE MOUNTAIN.
STAY HERE FOR NOW AND I'LL COME BACK WITH HELP, I PROMISE. IT'S THE ONLY WAY.
BUT I CAN'T—
YOU HAVE TO. TRUST ME, PAUL. I'M GOING TO LOCK YOU BACK IN, SO NOBODY WILL KNOW I'VE BEEN HERE. BUT IT WON'T BE FOR LONG.
I'LL COME BACK, I—
—PROMISE.
UNH!

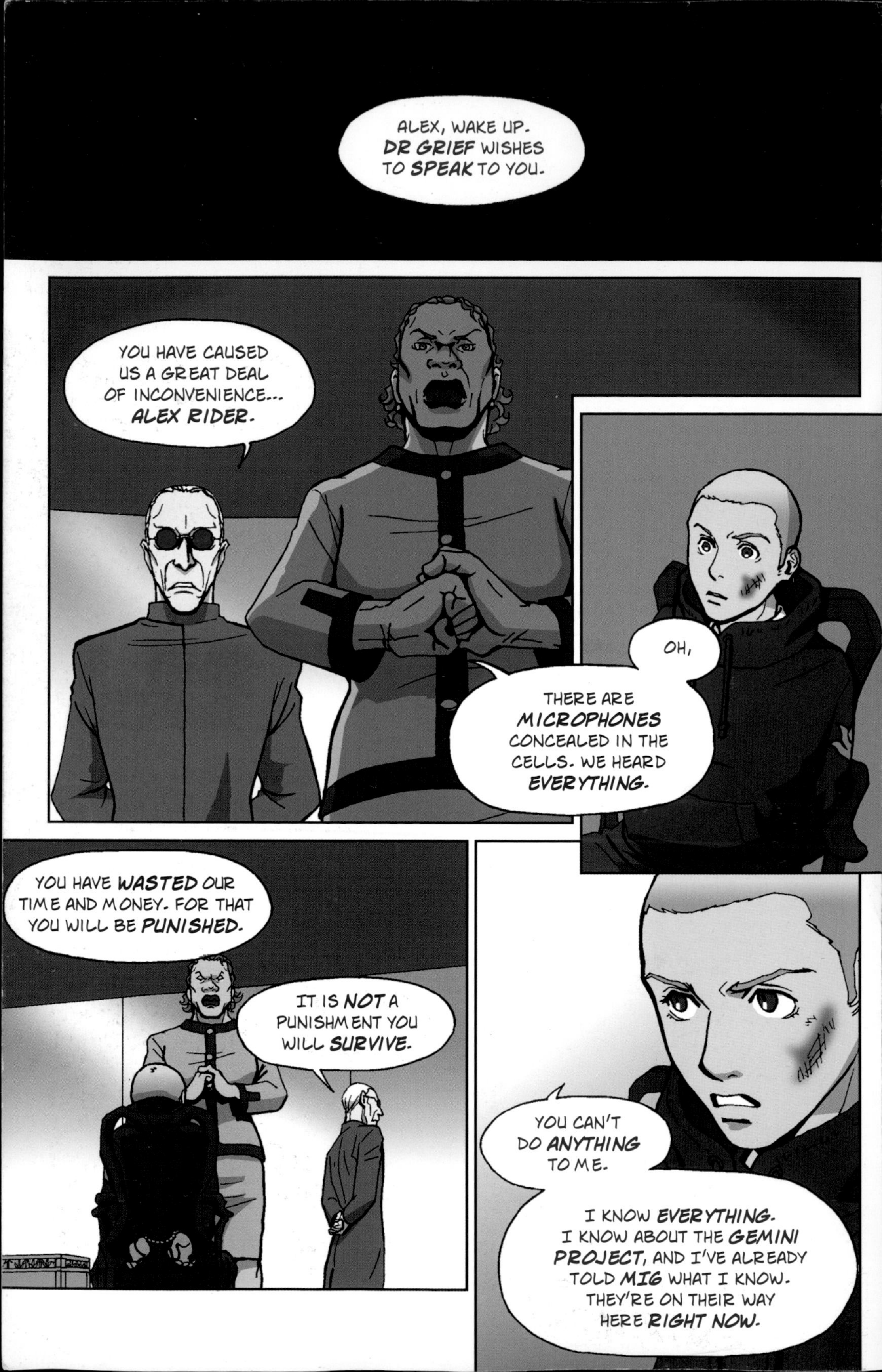
ALEX, WAKE UP. DR GRIEF WISHES TO SPEAK TO YOU.
YOU HAVE CAUSED US A GREAT DEAL OF INCONVENIENCE... ALEX RIDER.
OH,
THERE ARE MICROPHONES CONCEALED IN THE CELLS. WE HEARD EVERYTHING.
YOU HAVE WASTED OUR TIME AND MONEY. FOR THAT YOU WILL BE PUNISHED.
IT IS NOT A PUNISHMENT YOU WILL SURVIVE.
YOU CAN'T DO ANYTHING TO ME.
I KNOW EVERYTHING. I KNOW ABOUT THE GEMINI PROJECT, AND I'VE ALREADY TOLD MI6 WHAT I KNOW. THEY'RE ON THEIR WAY HERE RIGHT NOW.

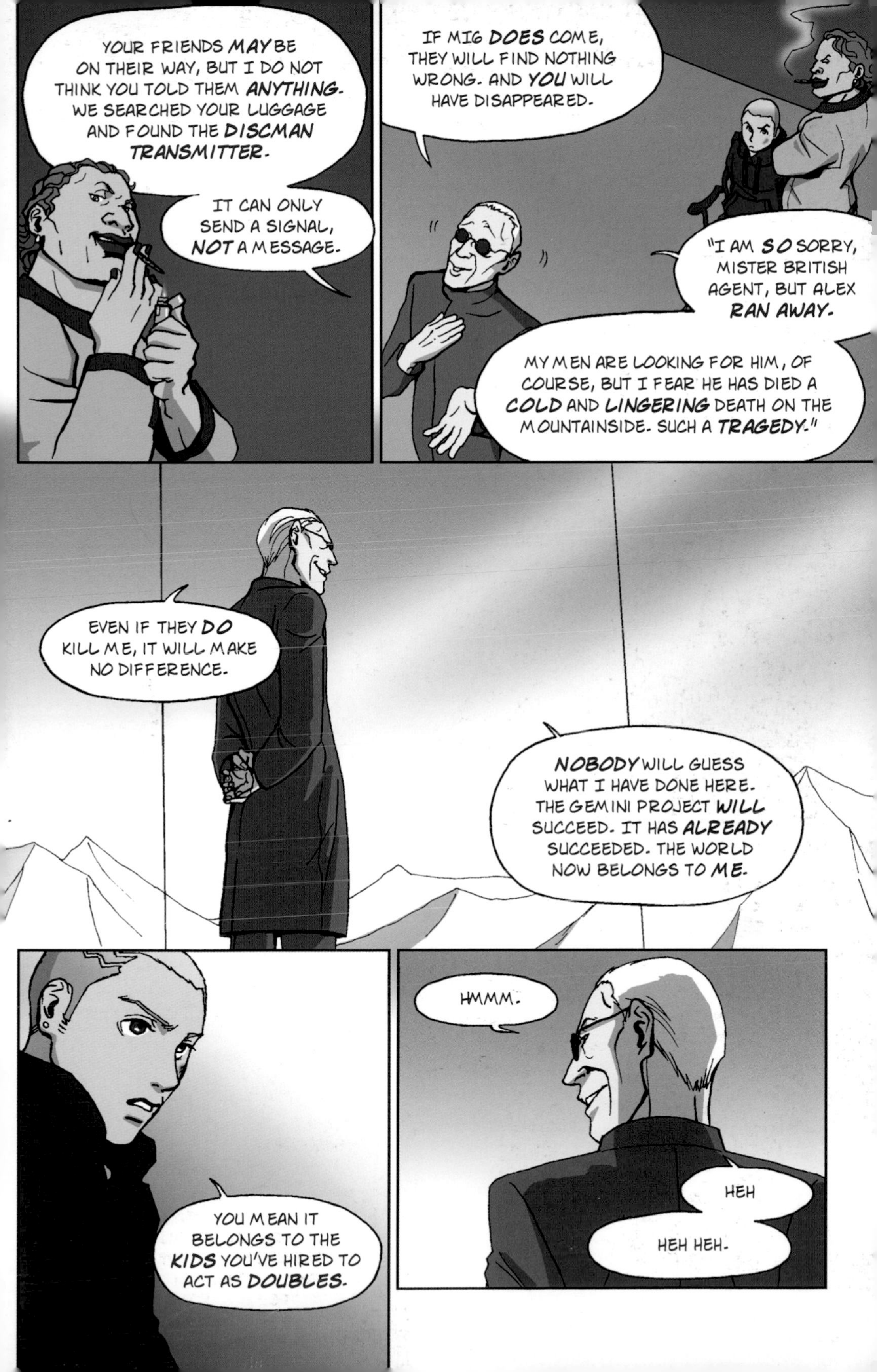
YOUR FRIENDS MAY BE ON THEIR WAY, BUT I DO NOT THINK YOU TOLD THEM ANYTHING. WE SEARCHED YOUR LUGGAGE AND FOUND THE DISCMAN TRANSMITTER.
IT CAN ONLY SEND A SIGNAL, NOT A MESSAGE.
IF MIG DOES COME, THEY WILL FIND NOTHING WRONG. AND YOU WILL HAVE DISAPPEARED.
"I AM SO SORRY, MISTER BRITISH AGENT, BUT ALEX RAN AWAY.
MY MEN ARE LOOKING FOR HIM, OF COURSE, BUT I FEAR HE HAS DIED A COLD AND LINGERING DEATH ON THE MOUNTAINSIDE. SUCH A TRAGEDY."
EVEN IF THEY DO KILL ME, IT WILL MAKE NO DIFFERENCE.
NOBODY WILL GUESS WHAT I HAVE DONE HERE. THE GEMINI PROJECT WILL SUCCEED. IT HAS ALREADY SUCCEEDED. THE WORLD NOW BELONGS TO ME.
YOU MEAN IT BELONGS TO THE KIDS YOU'VE HIRED TO ACT AS DOUBLES.
HMMM.
HEH
HEH HEH.

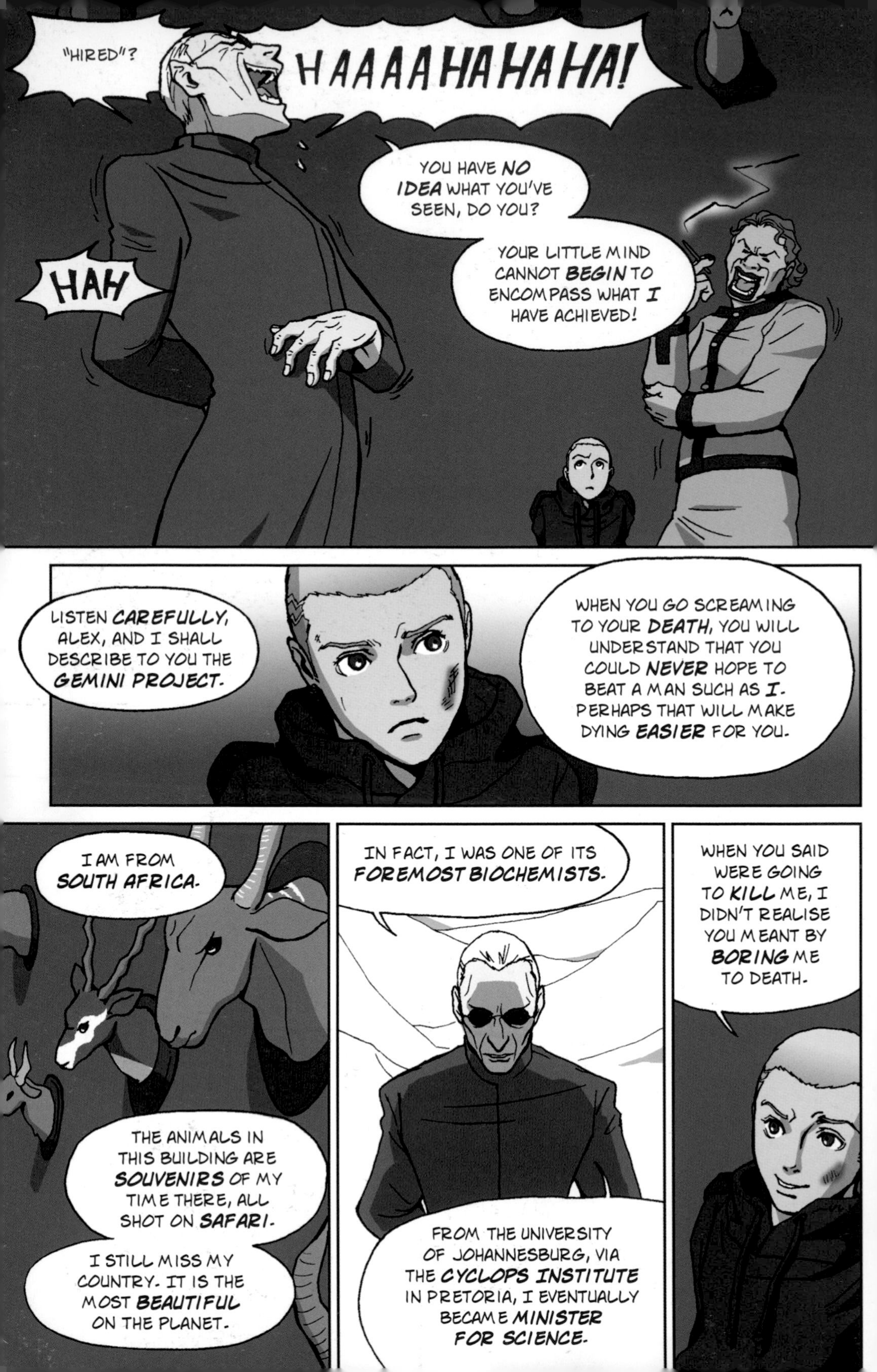
"HIRED"? HAAAAHAHAHAHA!
HAH
YOU HAVE NO IDEA WHAT YOU'VE SEEN, DO YOU?
YOUR LITTLE MIND CANNOT BEGIN TO ENCOMPASS WHAT I HAVE ACHIEVED!
LISTEN CAREFULLY, ALEX, AND I SHALL DESCRIBE TO YOU THE GEMINI PROJECT.
WHEN YOU GO SCREAMING TO YOUR DEATH, YOU WILL UNDERSTAND THAT YOU COULD NEVER HOPE TO BEAT A MAN SUCH AS I. PERHAPS THAT WILL MAKE DYING EASIER FOR YOU.
I AM FROM SOUTH AFRICA.
THE ANIMALS IN THIS BUILDING ARE SOUVENIRS OF MY TIME THERE, ALL SHOT ON SAFARI.
I STILL MISS MY COUNTRY. IT IS THE MOST BEAUTIFUL ON THE PLANET.
IN FACT, I WAS ONE OF ITS FOREMOST BIOCHEMISTS.
FROM THE UNIVERSITY OF JOHANNESBURG, VIA THE CYCLOPS INSTITUTE IN PRETORIA, I EVENTUALLY BECAME MINISTER FOR SCIENCE.
WHEN YOU SAID WERE GOING TO KILL ME, I DIDN'T REALISE YOU MEANT BY BORING ME TO DEATH.

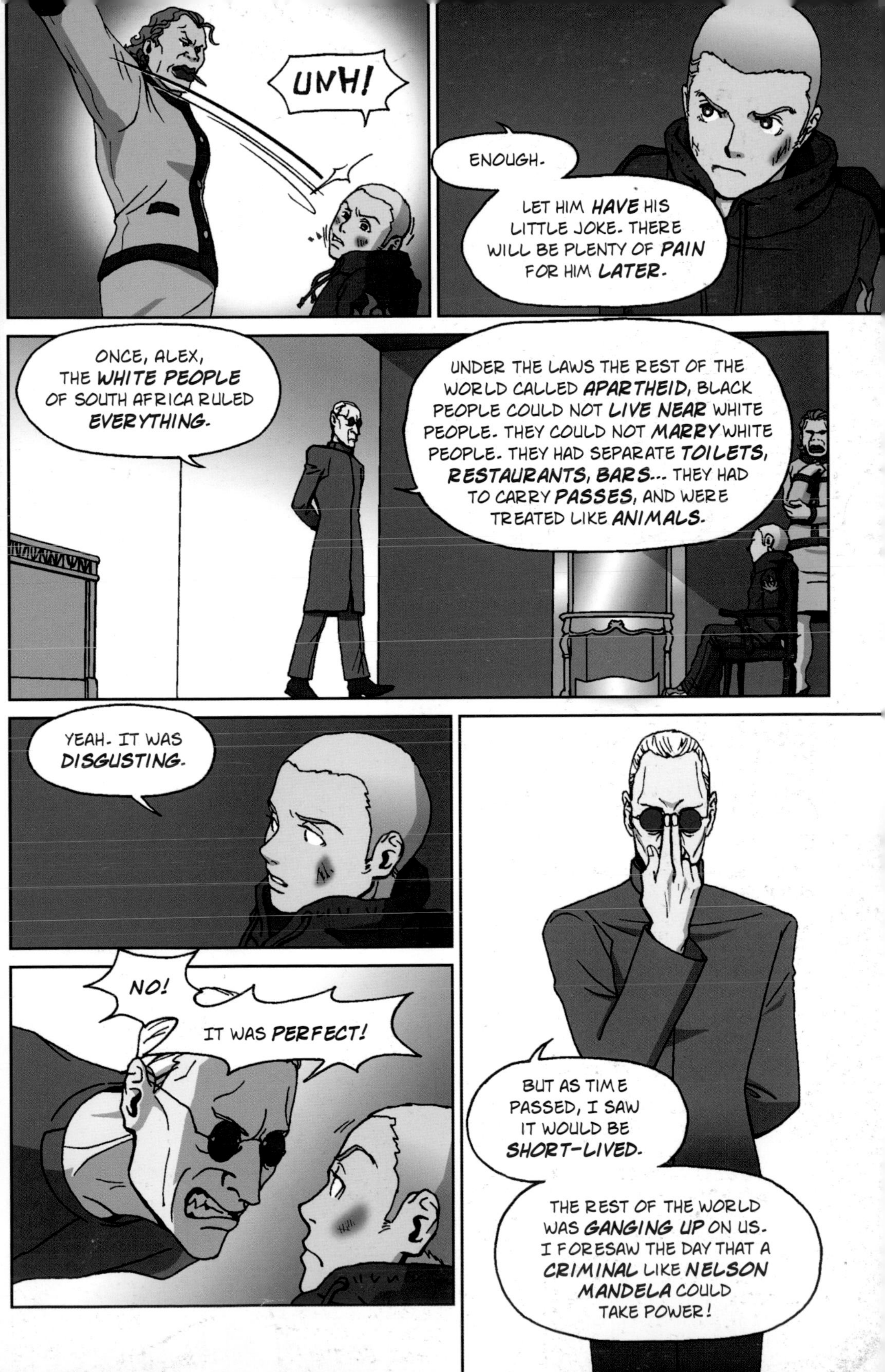
UNH!
ENOUGH.
LET HIM HAVE HIS LITTLE JOKE. THERE WILL BE PLENTY OF PAIN FOR HIM LATER.
ONCE, ALEX, THE WHITE PEOPLE OF SOUTH AFRICA RULED EVERYTHING.
UNDER THE LAWS THE REST OF THE WORLD CALLED APARTHEID, BLACK PEOPLE COULD NOT LIVE NEAR WHITE PEOPLE. THEY COULD NOT MARRY WHITE PEOPLE. THEY HAD SEPARATE TOILETS, RESTAURANTS, BARS... THEY HAD TO CARRY PASSES, AND WERE TREATED LIKE ANIMALS.
YEAH. IT WAS DISGUSTING.
NO!
IT WAS PERFECT!
BUT AS TIME PASSED, I SAW IT WOULD BE SHORT-LIVED.
THE REST OF THE WORLD WAS GANGING UP ON US. I FORESAW THE DAY THAT A CRIMINAL LIKE NELSON MANDELA COULD TAKE POWER!

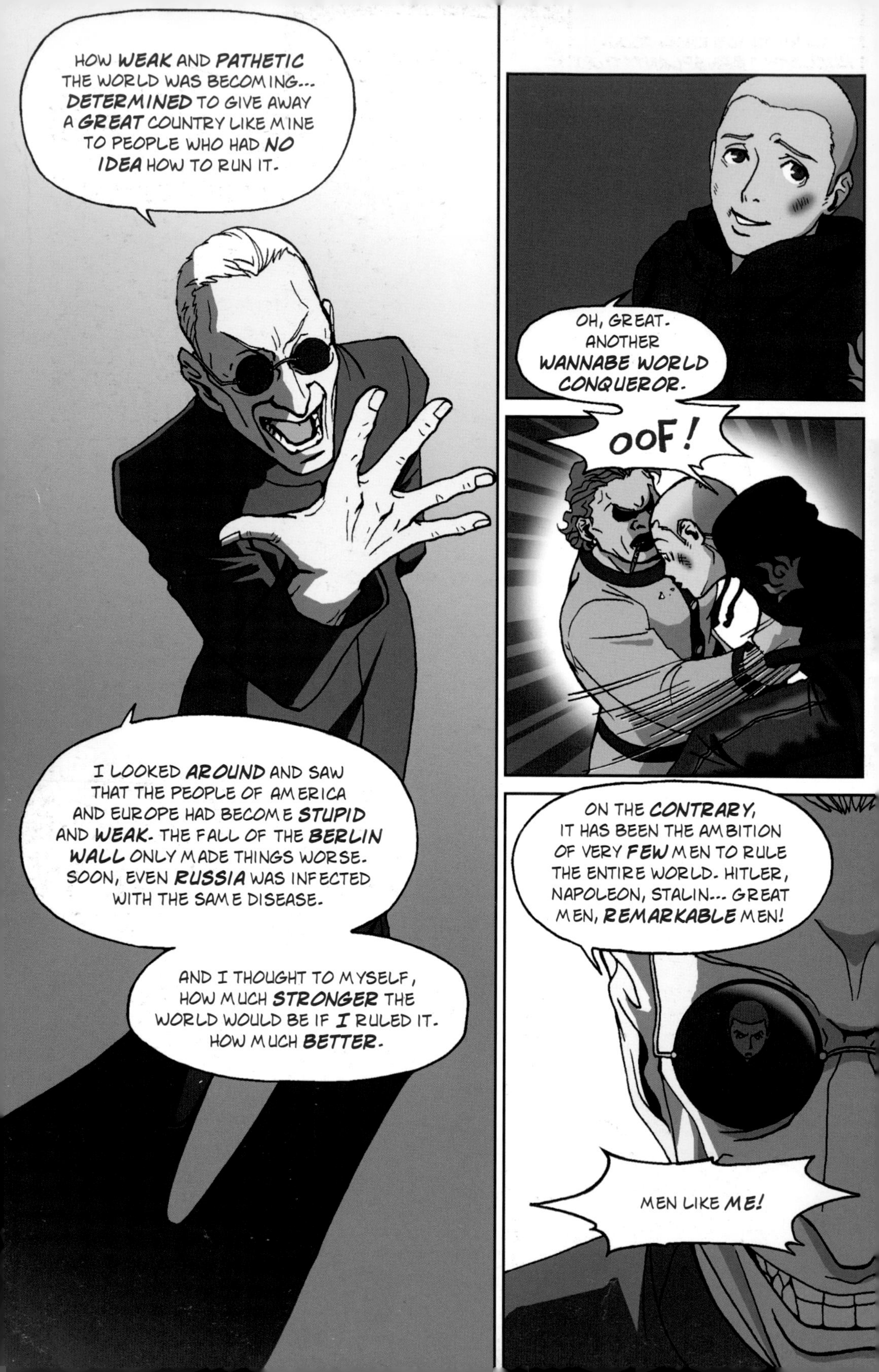
HOW WEAK AND PATHETIC THE WORLD WAS BECOMING... DETERMINED TO GIVE AWAY A GREAT COUNTRY LIKE MINE TO PEOPLE WHO HAD NO IDEA HOW TO RUN IT.
I LOOKED AROUND AND SAW THAT THE PEOPLE OF AMERICA AND EUROPE HAD BECOME STUPID AND WEAK. THE FALL OF THE BERLIN WALL ONLY MADE THINGS WORSE. SOON, EVEN RUSSIA WAS INFECTED WITH THE SAME DISEASE.
AND I THOUGHT TO MYSELF, HOW MUCH STRONGER THE WORLD WOULD BE IF I RULED IT. HOW MUCH BETTER.
OH, GREAT. ANOTHER WANNABE WORLD CONQUEROR.
OOF!
ON THE CONTRARY, IT HAS BEEN THE AMBITION OF VERY FEW MEN TO RULE THE ENTIRE WORLD. HITLER, NAPOLEON, STALIN... GREAT MEN, REMARKABLE MEN!
MEN LIKE ME!

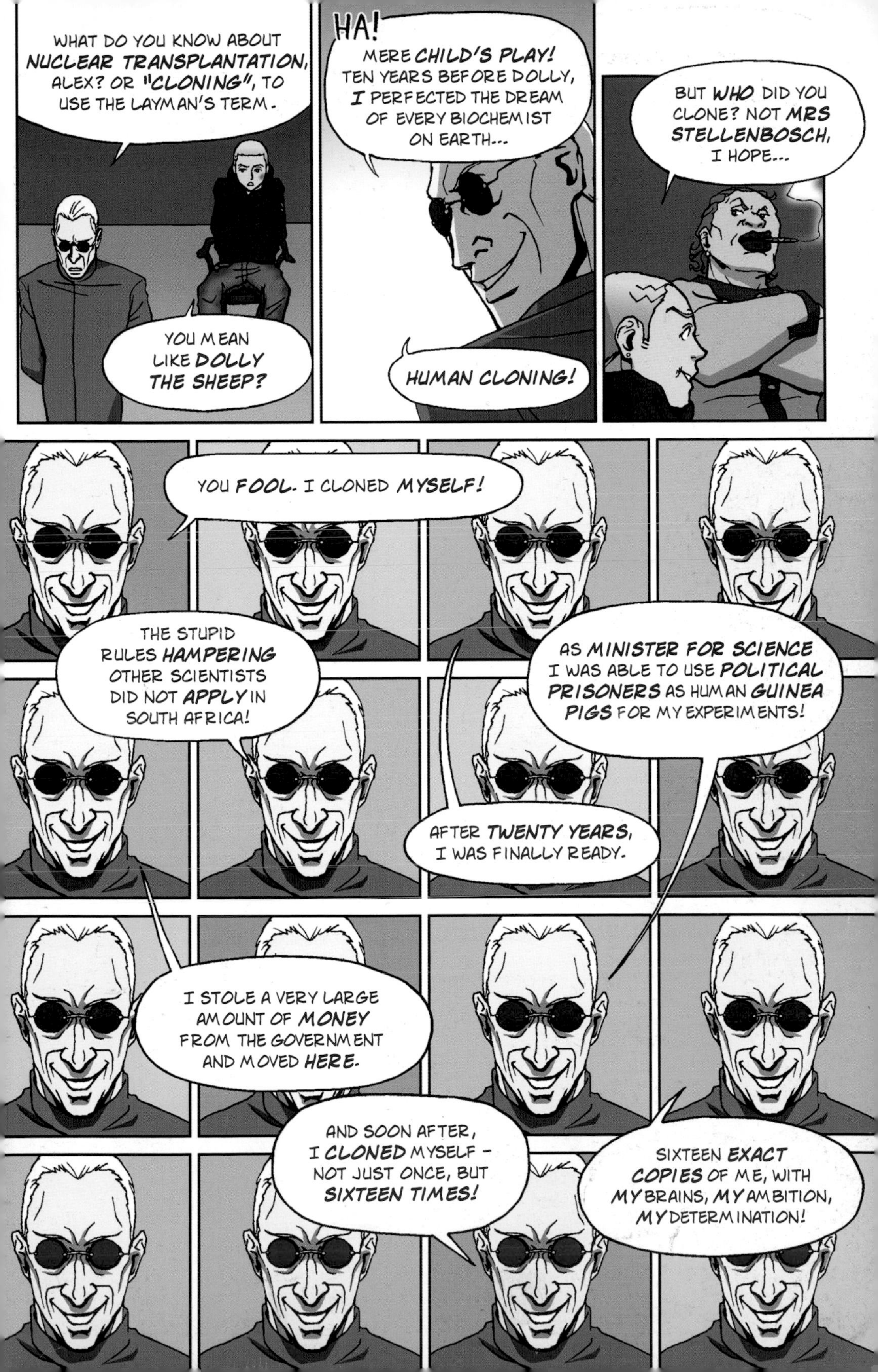
WHAT DO YOU KNOW ABOUT NUCLEAR TRANSPLANTATION, ALEX? OR "CLONING", TO USE THE LAYMAN'S TERM.
YOU MEAN LIKE DOLLY THE SHEEP?
HA!
MERE CHILD'S PLAY! TEN YEARS BEFORE DOLLY, I PERFECTED THE DREAM OF EVERY BIOCHEMIST ON EARTH...
HUMAN CLONING!
BUT WHO DID YOU CLONE? NOT MRS STELLENBOSCH, I HOPE...
YOU FOOL. I CLONED MYSELF!
THE STUPID RULES HAMPERING OTHER SCIENTISTS DID NOT APPLY IN SOUTH AFRICA!
AS MINISTER FOR SCIENCE I WAS ABLE TO USE POLITICAL PRISONERS AS HUMAN GUINEA PIGS FOR MY EXPERIMENTS!
AFTER TWENTY YEARS, I WAS FINALLY READY.
I STOLE A VERY LARGE AMOUNT OF MONEY FROM THE GOVERNMENT AND MOVED HERE.
AND SOON AFTER, I CLONED MYSELF - NOT JUST ONCE, BUT SIXTEEN TIMES!
SIXTEEN EXACT COPIES OF ME, WITH MY BRAINS, MY AMBITION, MY DETERMINATION!

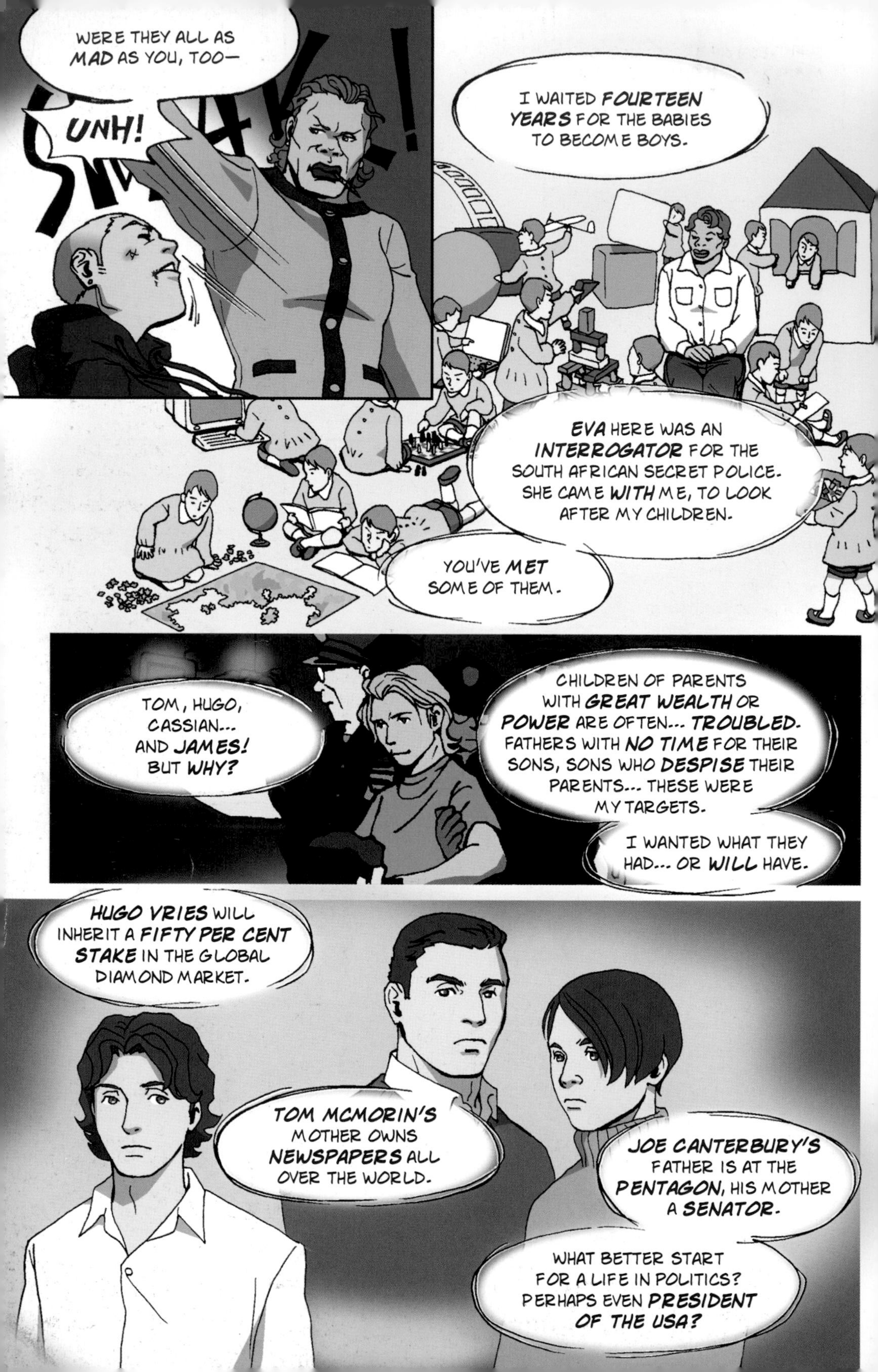
WERE THEY ALL AS MAD AS YOU, TOO—
UNH!
I WAITED FOURTEEN YEARS FOR THE BABIES TO BECOME BOYS.
EVA HERE WAS AN INTERROGATOR FOR THE SOUTH AFRICAN SECRET POLICE. SHE CAME WITH ME, TO LOOK AFTER MY CHILDREN.
YOU'VE MET SOME OF THEM.
TOM, HUGO, CASSIAN... AND JAMES! BUT WHY?
CHILDREN OF PARENTS WITH GREAT WEALTH OR POWER ARE OFTEN... TROUBLED. FATHERS WITH NO TIME FOR THEIR SONS, SONS WHO DESPISE THEIR PARENTS... THESE WERE MY TARGETS.
I WANTED WHAT THEY HAD... OR WILL HAVE.
HUGO VRIES WILL INHERIT A FIFTY PER CENT STAKE IN THE GLOBAL DIAMOND MARKET.
TOM MCMORIN'S MOTHER OWNS NEWSPAPERS ALL OVER THE WORLD.
JOE CANTERBURY'S FATHER IS AT THE PENTAGON, HIS MOTHER A SENATOR.
WHAT BETTER START FOR A LIFE IN POLITICS? PERHAPS EVEN PRESIDENT OF THE USA?

FIFTEEN OF THE WORLD'S MOST **PROMISING** CHILDREN CAME HERE TO POINT BLANC, AND WERE **REPLACED** WITH SURGICALLY ALTERED **CLONES** OF MYSELF.

SURGICALLY ALTERED? THAT MAN, **BAXTER**...

YOU REALLY **HAVE** BEEN BUSY, ALEX.

BAXTER WAS A HARLEY STREET **PLASTIC SURGEON** WITH GAMBLING DEBTS. IT WAS HIS JOB TO **OPERATE** ON MY FAMILY. TO ALTER THEIR **SKIN COLOUR, FACES,** EVEN THEIR **BODIES.**

FROM THEIR **ARRIVAL,** THE BOYS WERE KEPT UNDER **OBSERVATION.**

MY DOUBLES **WATCHED** THEIR TARGETS TO LEARN THEIR MANNERISMS AND HABITS, EVEN THEIR **VOICES.**

BUT ANY PARENT WOULD KNOW IT **WASN'T** THEIR SON, EVEN IF HE **LOOKED** THE SAME!

WRONG!

THESE ARE BUSY PEOPLE, WITH **NO TIME** FOR THEIR CHILDREN. THEY SENT THEIR BOYS HERE BECAUSE THEY **WANTED** THEM TO CHANGE!

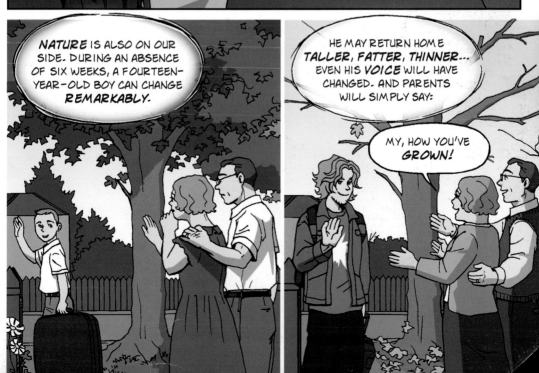

NATURE IS ALSO ON OUR SIDE. DURING AN ABSENCE OF SIX WEEKS, A FOURTEEN-YEAR-OLD BOY CAN CHANGE **REMARKABLY.**

HE MAY RETURN HOME **TALLER, FATTER, THINNER**... EVEN HIS **VOICE** WILL HAVE CHANGED. AND PARENTS WILL SIMPLY SAY:

MY, HOW YOU'VE **GROWN!**

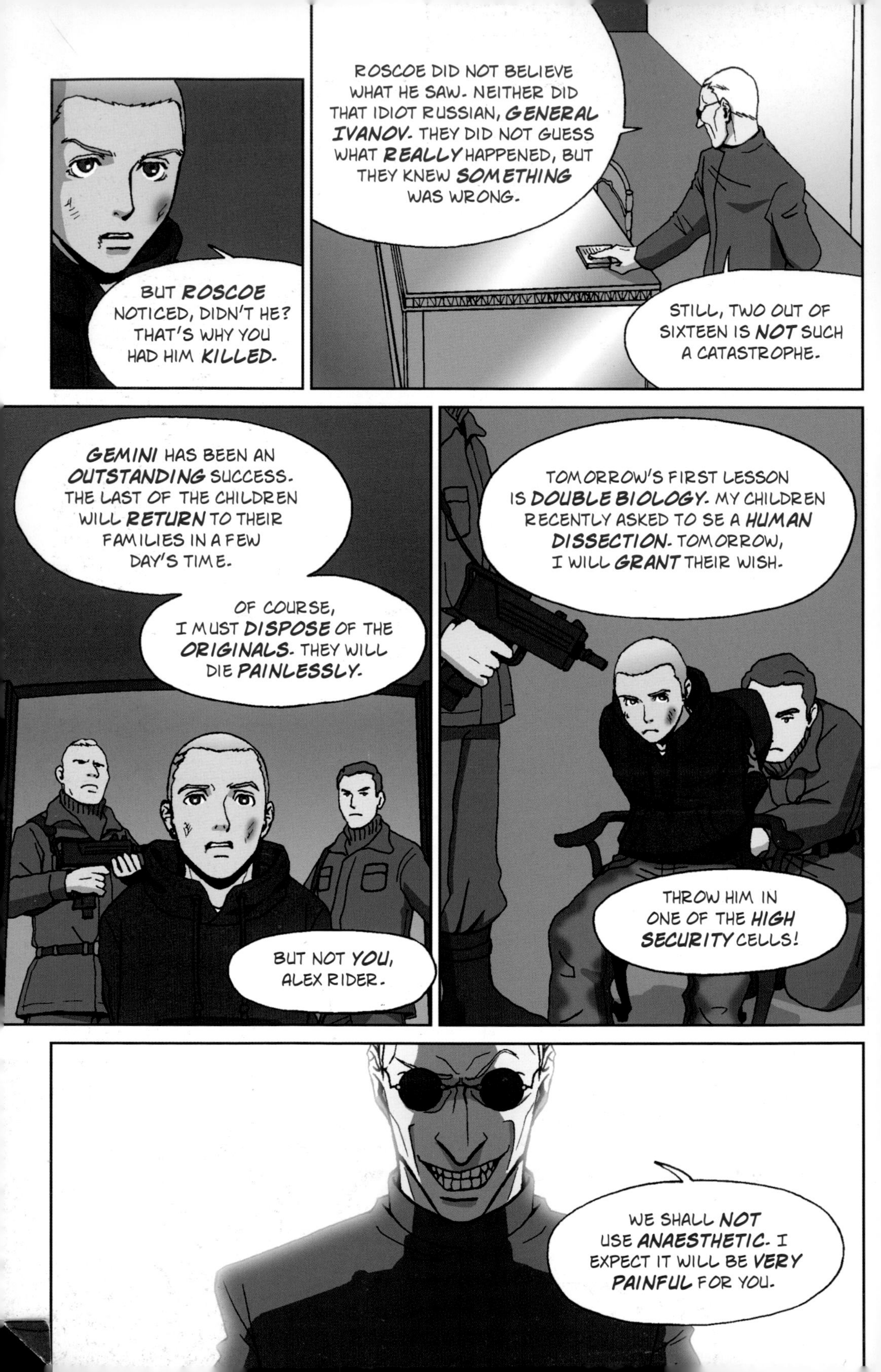
ROSCOE DID NOT BELIEVE WHAT HE SAW. NEITHER DID THAT IDIOT RUSSIAN, GENERAL IVANOV. THEY DID NOT GUESS WHAT REALLY HAPPENED, BUT THEY KNEW SOMETHING WAS WRONG.
BUT ROSCOE NOTICED, DIDN'T HE? THAT'S WHY YOU HAD HIM KILLED.
STILL, TWO OUT OF SIXTEEN IS NOT SUCH A CATASTROPHE.
GEMINI HAS BEEN AN OUTSTANDING SUCCESS. THE LAST OF THE CHILDREN WILL RETURN TO THEIR FAMILIES IN A FEW DAY'S TIME.
OF COURSE, I MUST DISPOSE OF THE ORIGINALS. THEY WILL DIE PAINLESSLY.
BUT NOT YOU, ALEX RIDER.
TOMORROW'S FIRST LESSON IS DOUBLE BIOLOGY. MY CHILDREN RECENTLY ASKED TO SE A HUMAN DISSECTION. TOMORROW, I WILL GRANT THEIR WISH.
THROW HIM IN ONE OF THE HIGH SECURITY CELLS!
WE SHALL NOT USE ANAESTHETIC. I EXPECT IT WILL BE VERY PAINFUL FOR YOU.

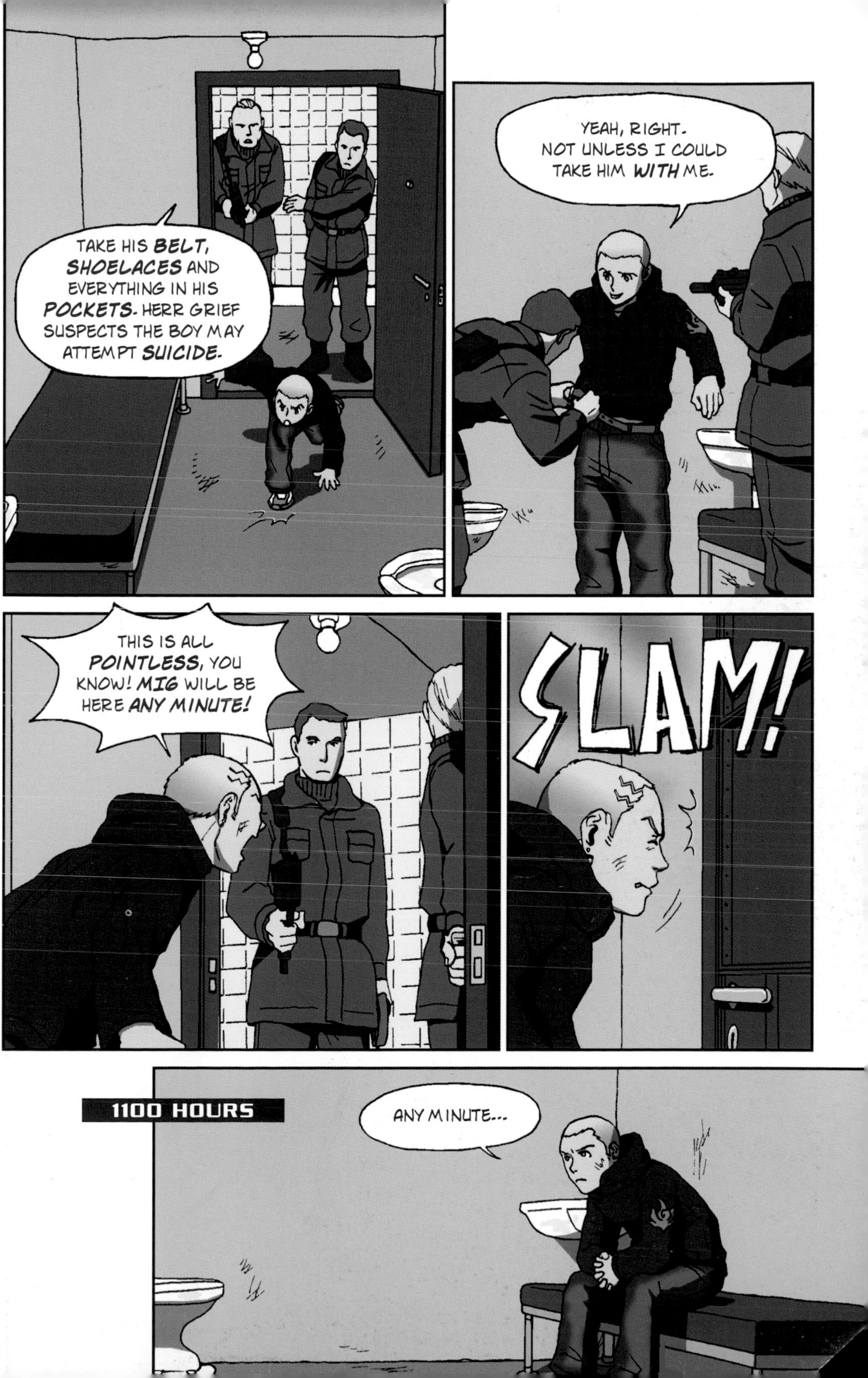
TAKE HIS BELT, SHOELACES AND EVERYTHING IN HIS POCKETS. HERR GRIEF SUSPECTS THE BOY MAY ATTEMPT SUICIDE.
YEAH, RIGHT. NOT UNLESS I COULD TAKE HIM WITH ME.
THIS IS ALL POINTLESS, YOU KNOW! MIG WILL BE HERE ANY MINUTE!
SLAM!
1100 HOURS
ANY MINUTE...

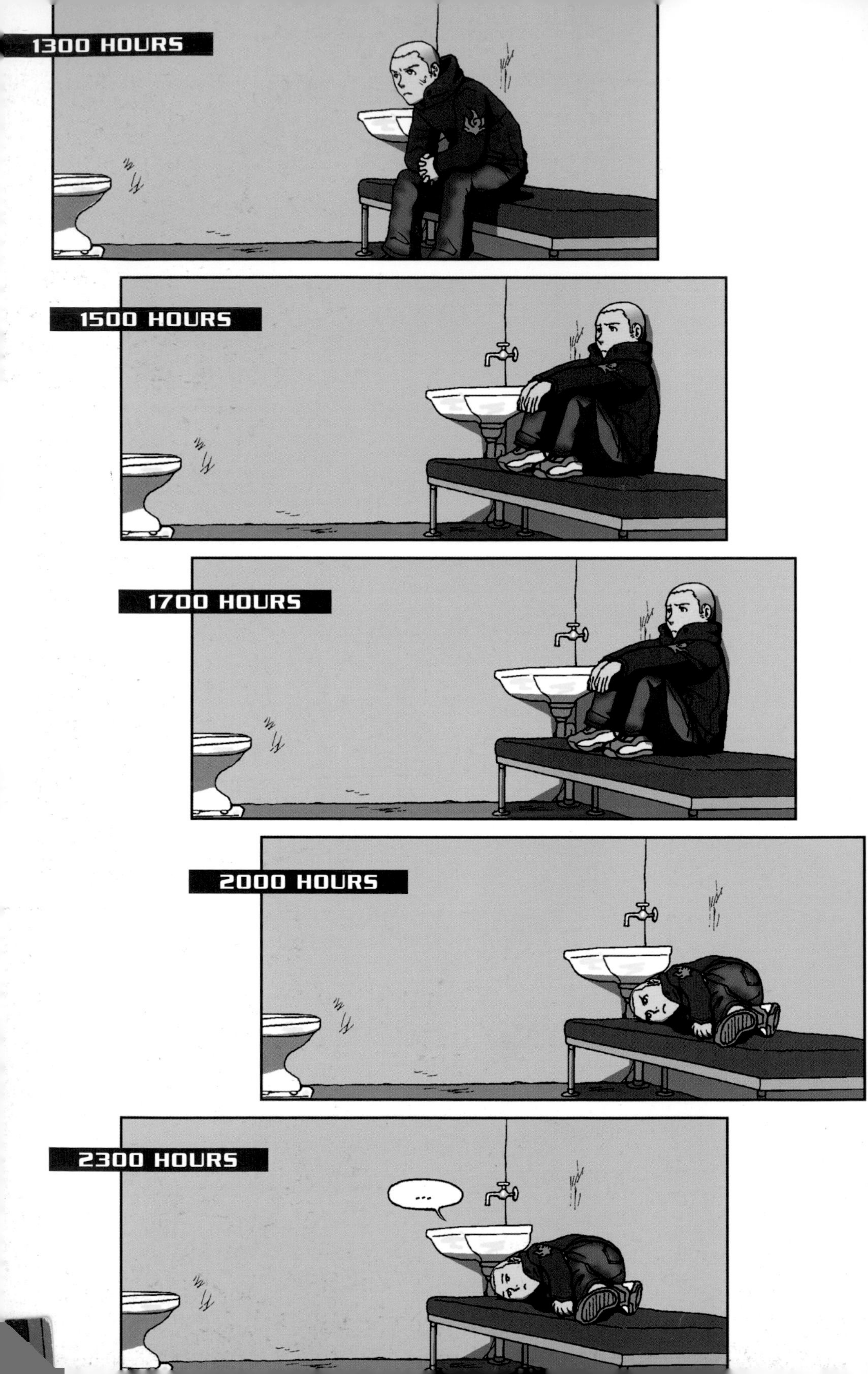
1300 HOURS
1500 HOURS
1700 HOURS
2000 HOURS
2300 HOURS
...

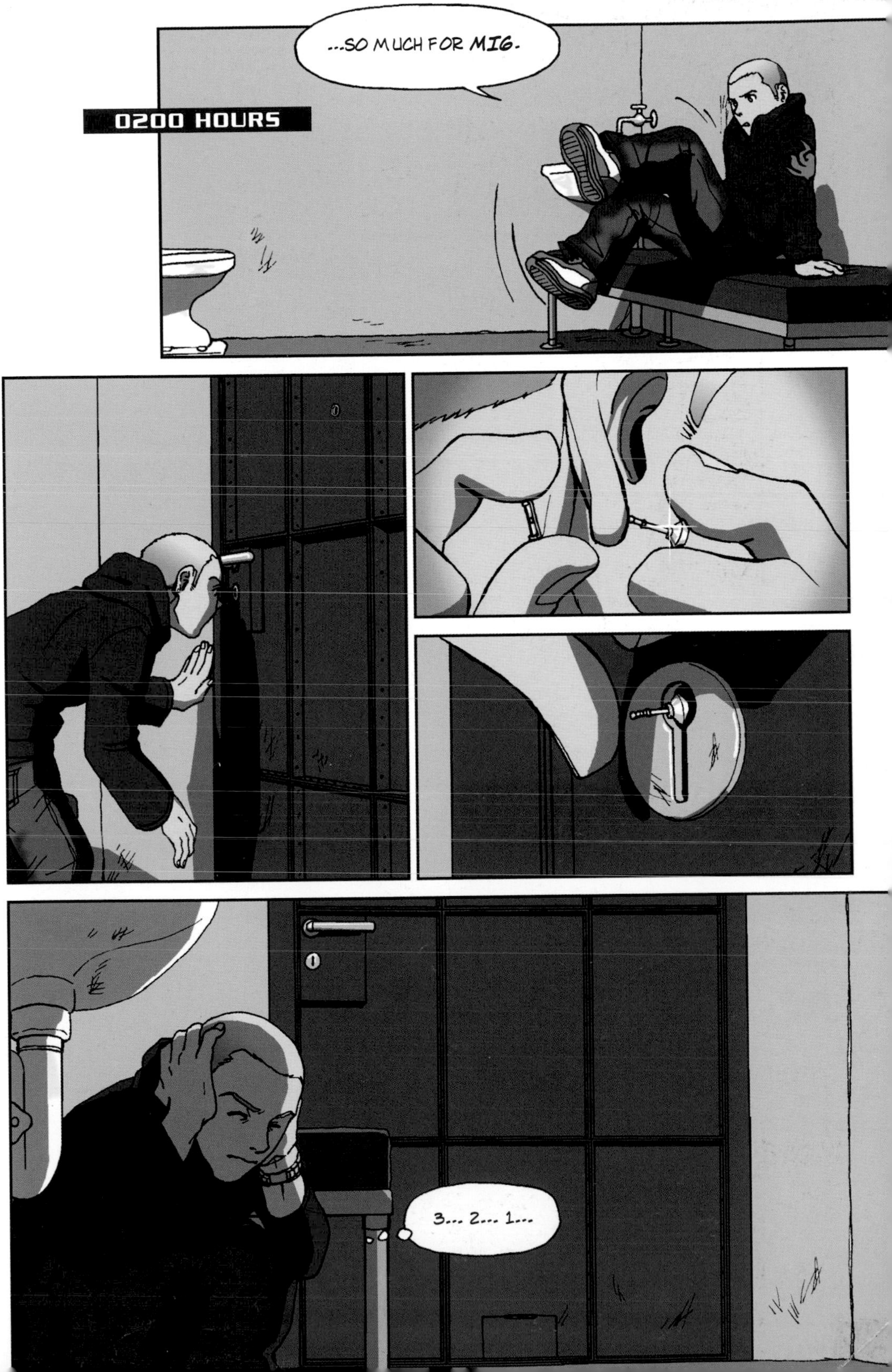
0200 HOURS
...SO MUCH FOR MI6.
3... 2... 1...

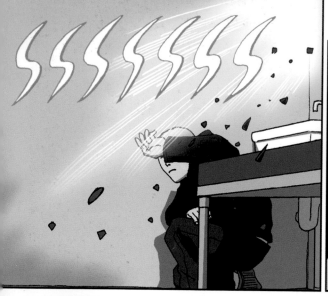

COOL.

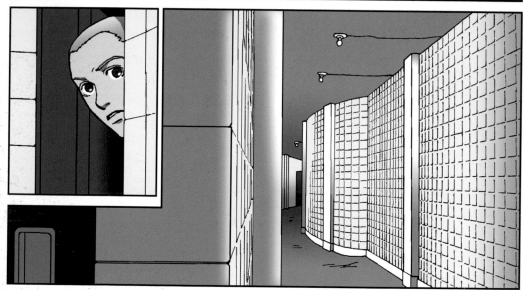

DON'T WORRY, BOYS, I'LL BE **BACK** FOR YOU...

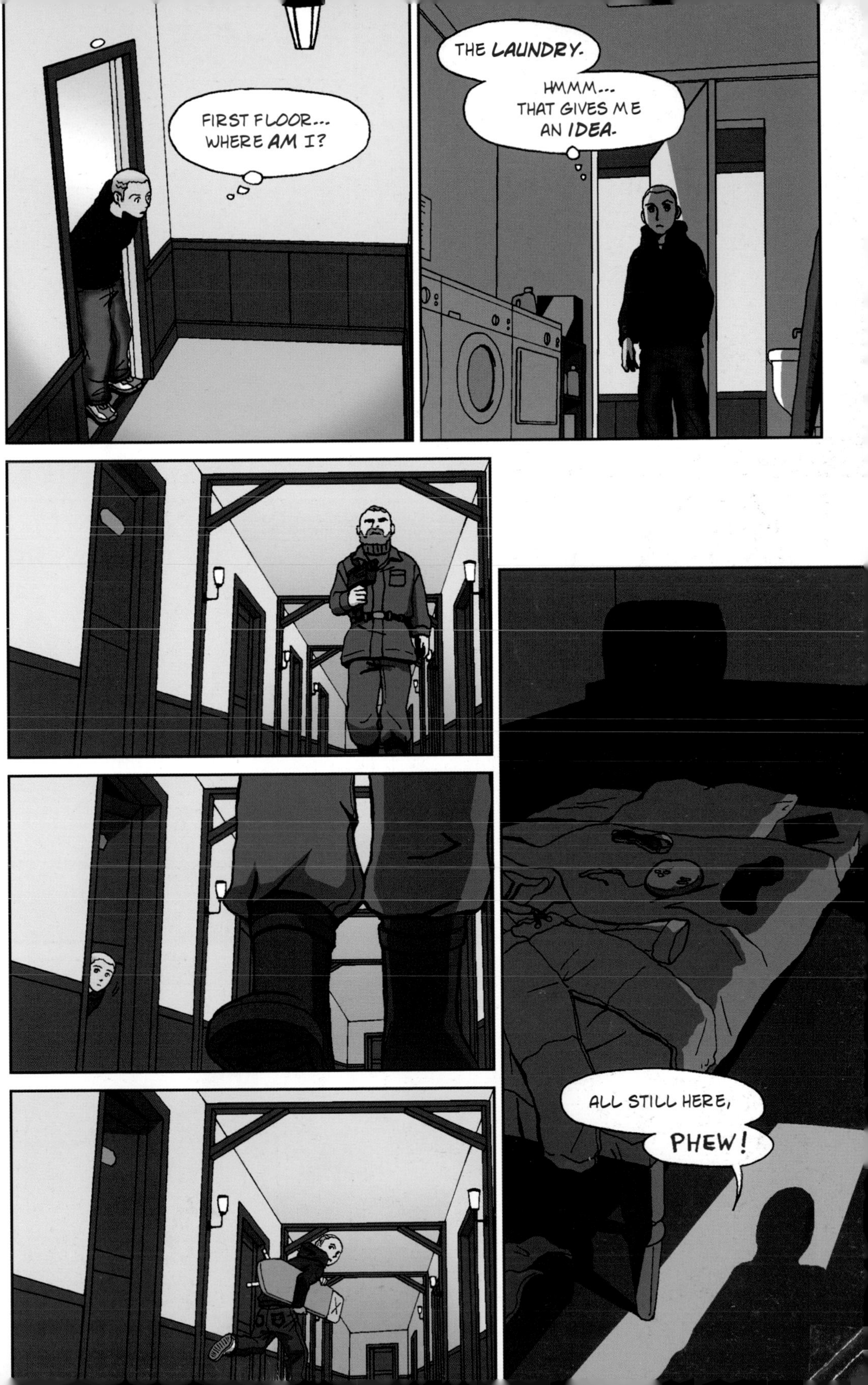
FIRST FLOOR... WHERE AM I?
THE LAUNDRY.
HMMM... THAT GIVES ME AN IDEA.
ALL STILL HERE,
PHEW!

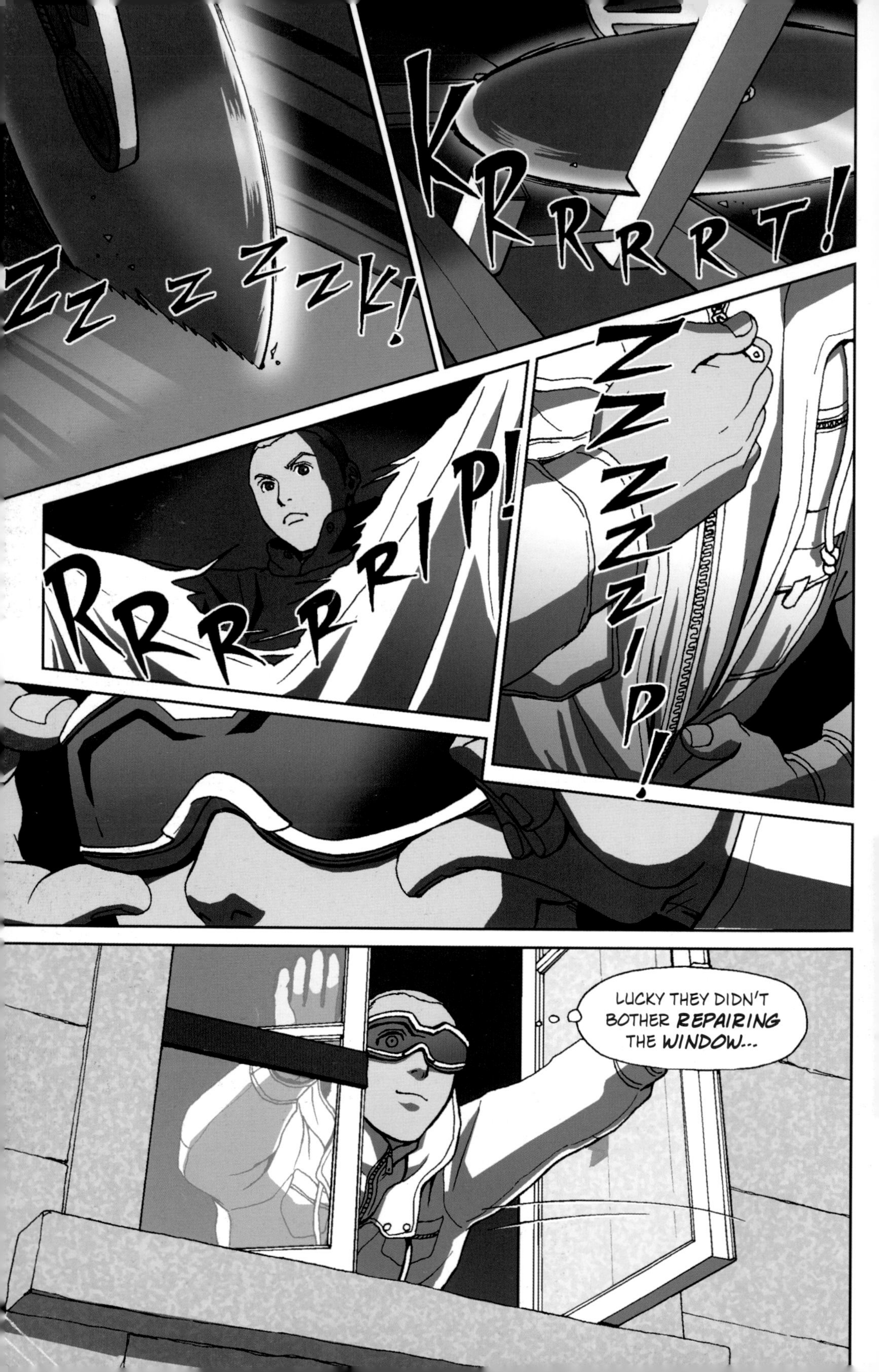
ZZZZZK!
KRRRRRT!
RRRRRIP!
ZZZZZIP!
LUCKY THEY DIDN'T BOTHER REPAIRING THE WINDOW...

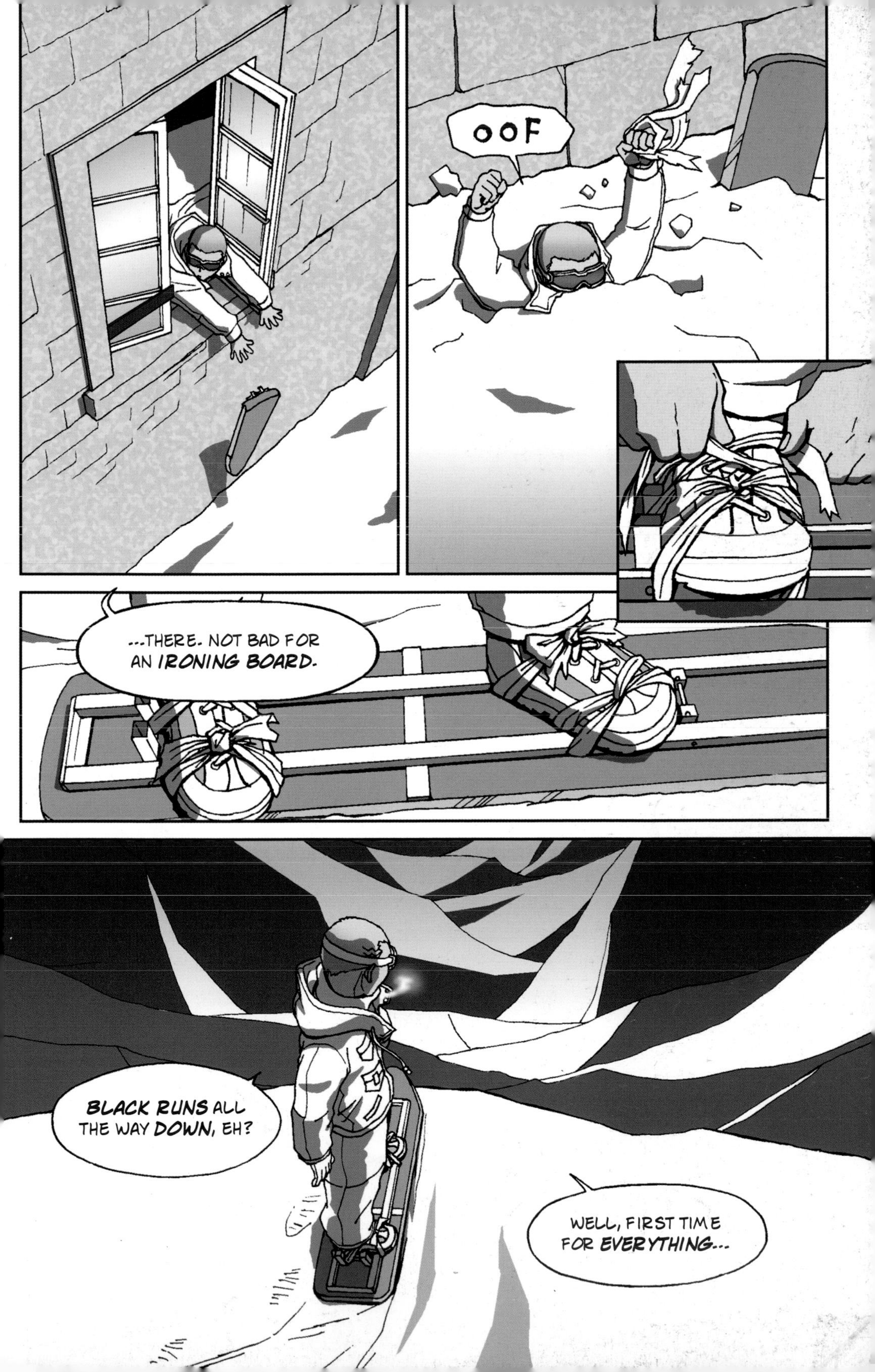
OOF
...THERE. NOT BAD FOR AN IRONING BOARD.
BLACK RUNS ALL THE WAY DOWN, EH?
WELL, FIRST TIME FOR EVERYTHING...

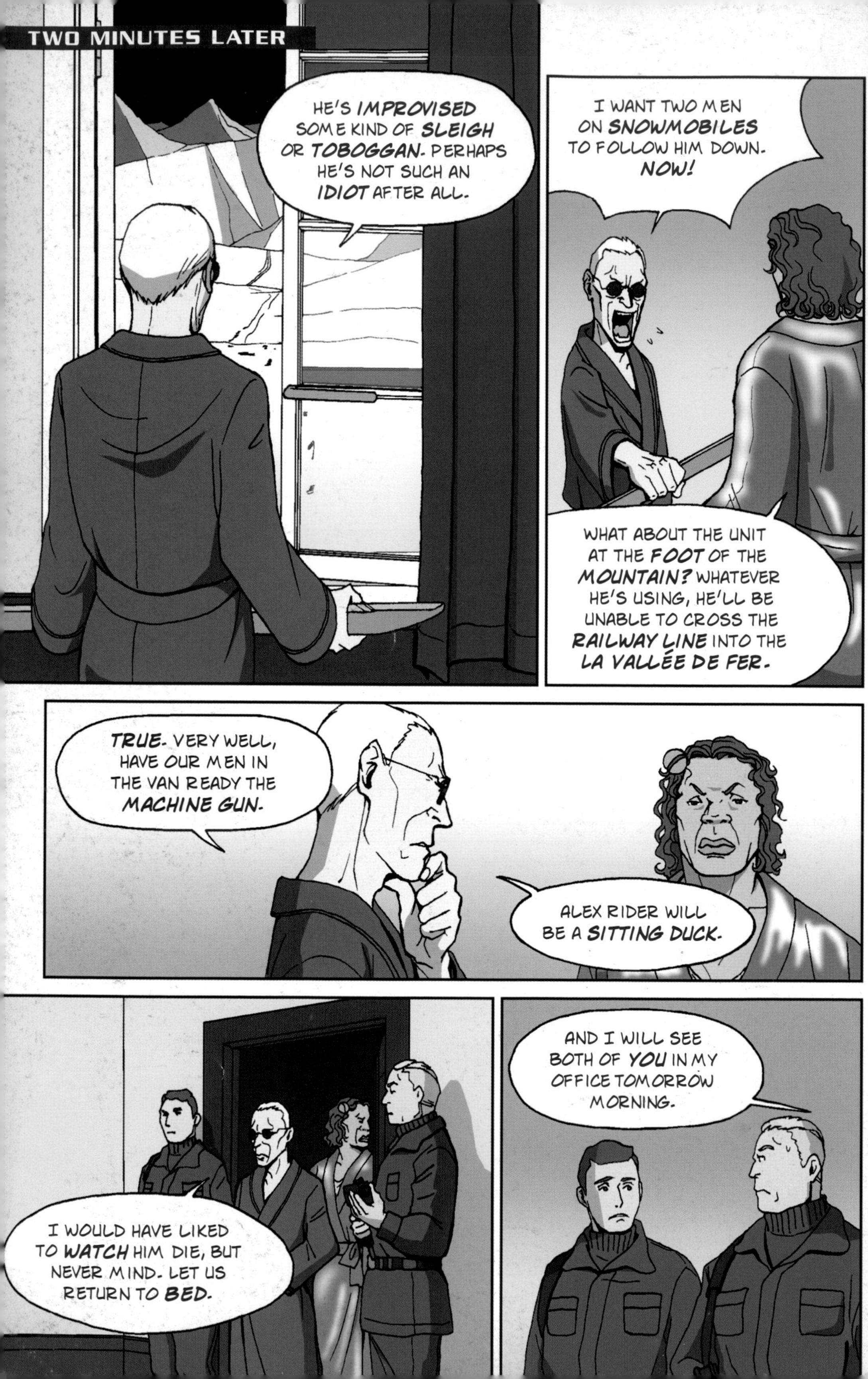
TWO MINUTES LATER
HE'S IMPROVISED SOME KIND OF SLEIGH OR TOBOGGAN. PERHAPS HE'S NOT SUCH AN IDIOT AFTER ALL.
I WANT TWO MEN ON SNOWMOBILES TO FOLLOW HIM DOWN. NOW!
WHAT ABOUT THE UNIT AT THE FOOT OF THE MOUNTAIN? WHATEVER HE'S USING, HE'LL BE UNABLE TO CROSS THE RAILWAY LINE INTO THE LA VALLÉE DE FER.
TRUE. VERY WELL, HAVE OUR MEN IN THE VAN READY THE MACHINE GUN.
ALEX RIDER WILL BE A SITTING DUCK.
I WOULD HAVE LIKED TO WATCH HIM DIE, BUT NEVER MIND. LET US RETURN TO BED.
AND I WILL SEE BOTH OF YOU IN MY OFFICE TOMORROW MORNING.

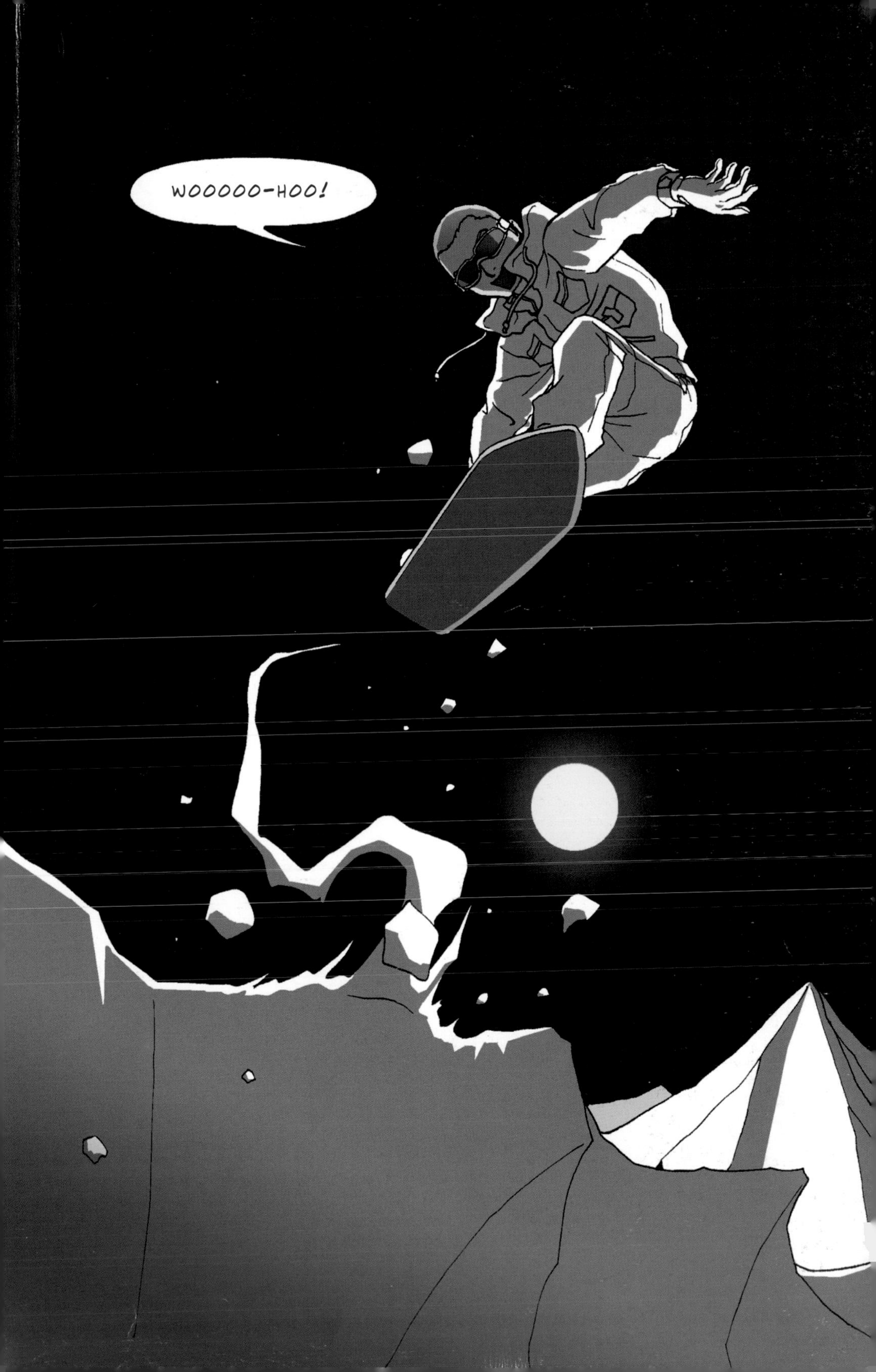
WOOOOO-HOO!

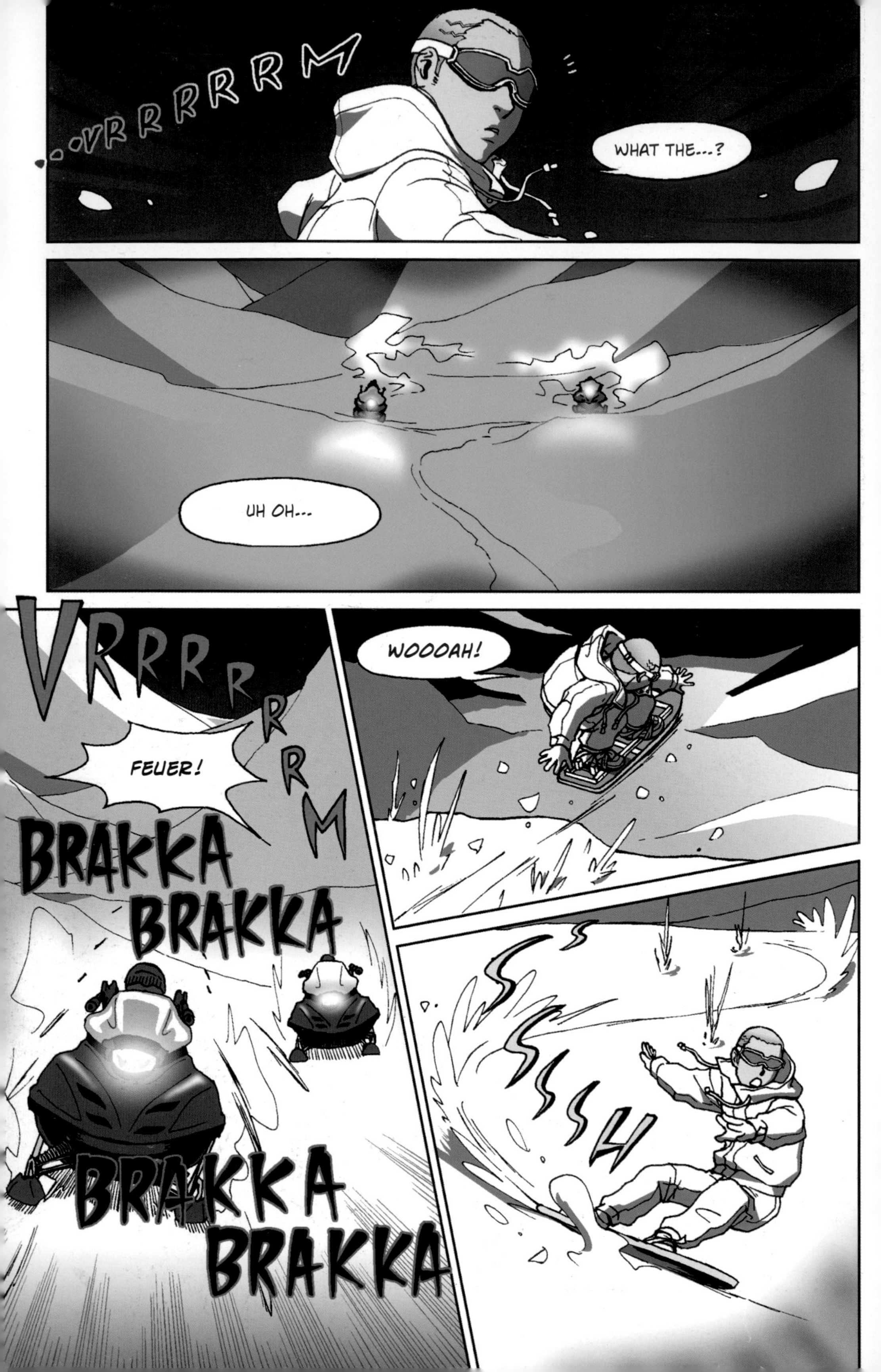

..VRRRRRRRM
WHAT THE...?
UH OH...
VRRRRRRRM
FEUER!
BRAKKA BRAKKA
BRAKKA BRAKKA
WOOOAH!
SSSSH

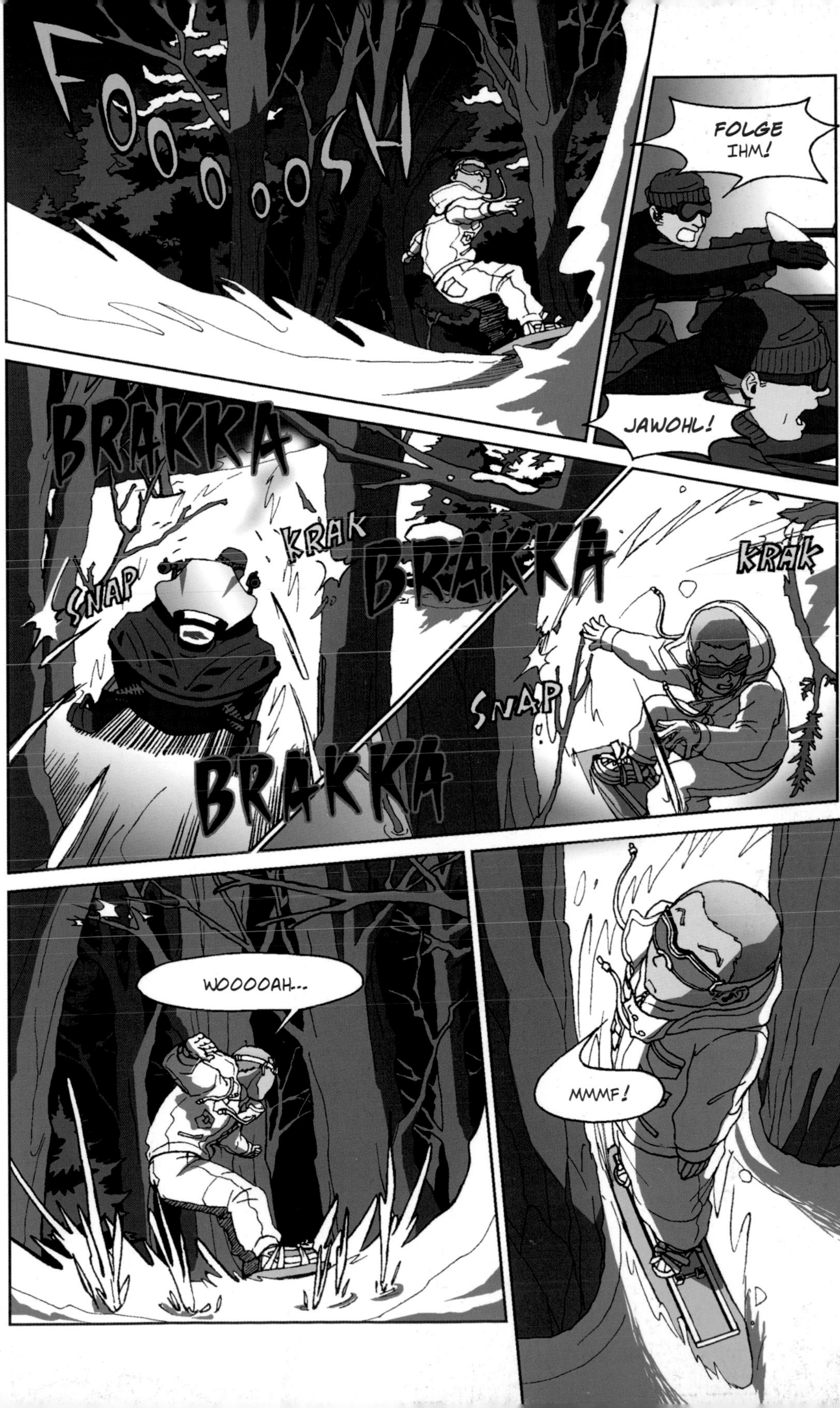
FOOOOOSH
FOLGE IHM!
JAWOHL!
BRAKKA
KRAK
SNAP
BRAKKA
BRAKKA
KRAK
SNAP
WOOOOAH...
MMMF!

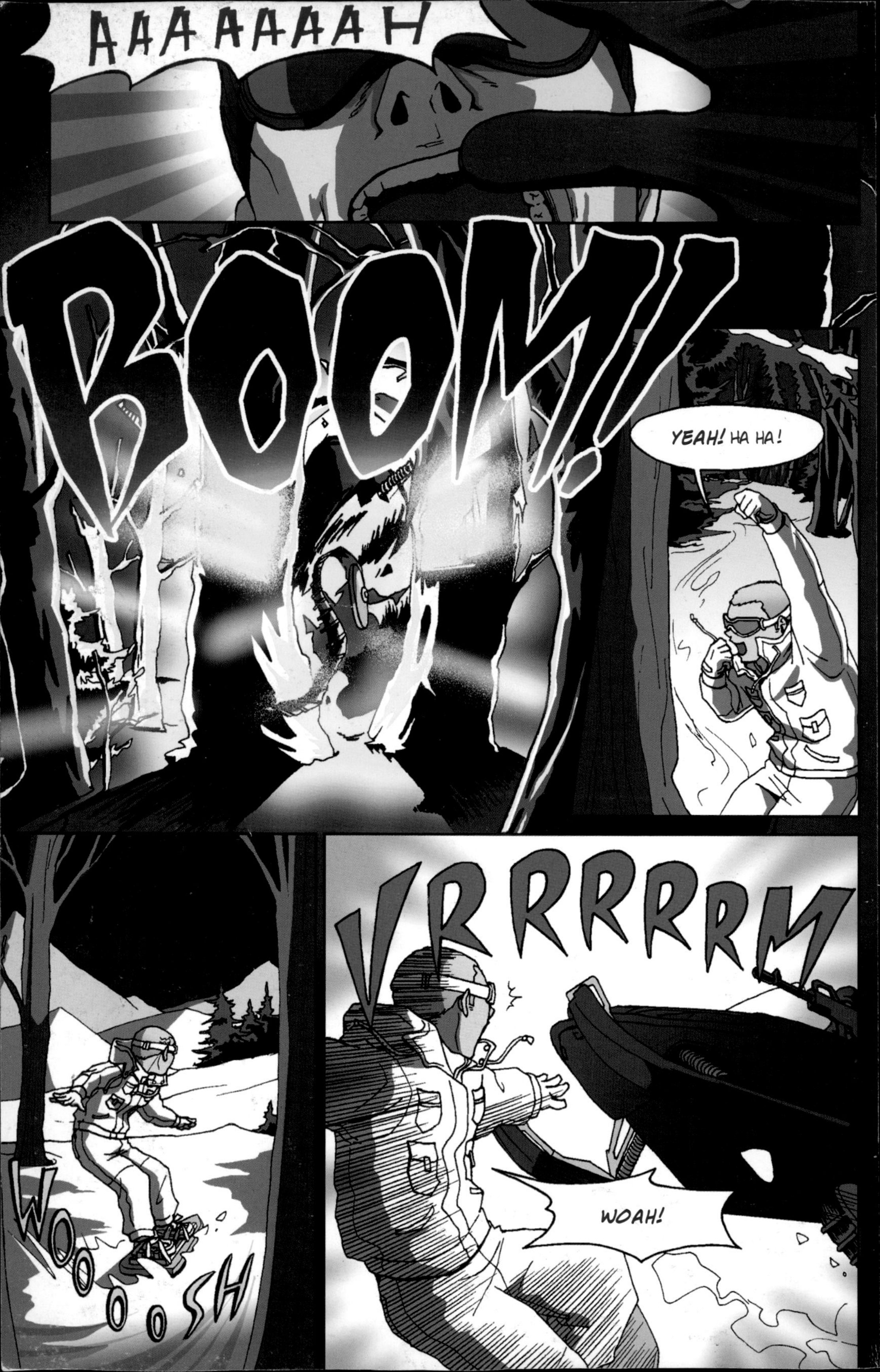
AAAAAAAH
BOOM!
YEAH! HA HA!
WOOOOSH
VRRRRRM
WOAH!

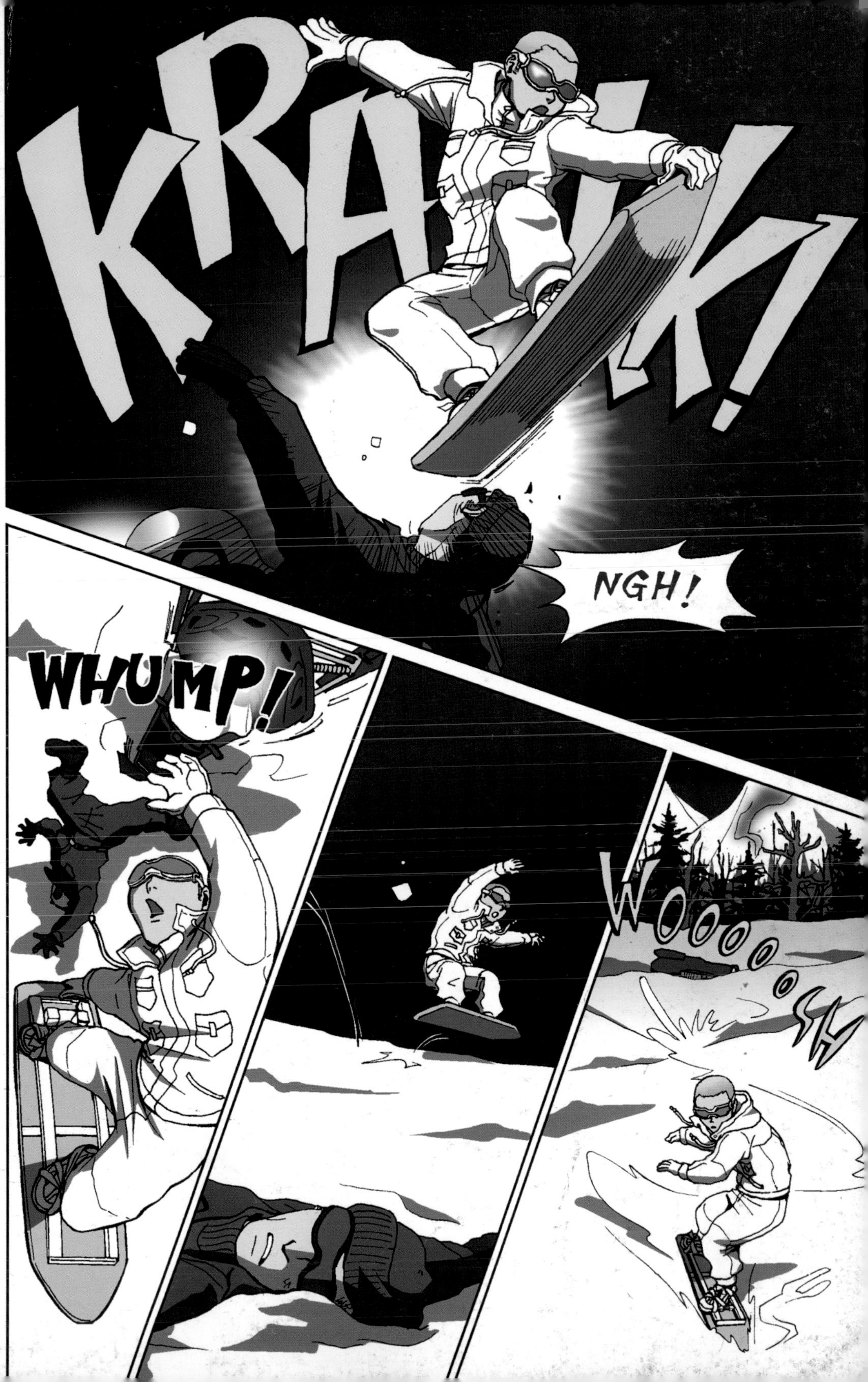
KRAKK!
NGH!
WHUMP!
WOOOOOSH

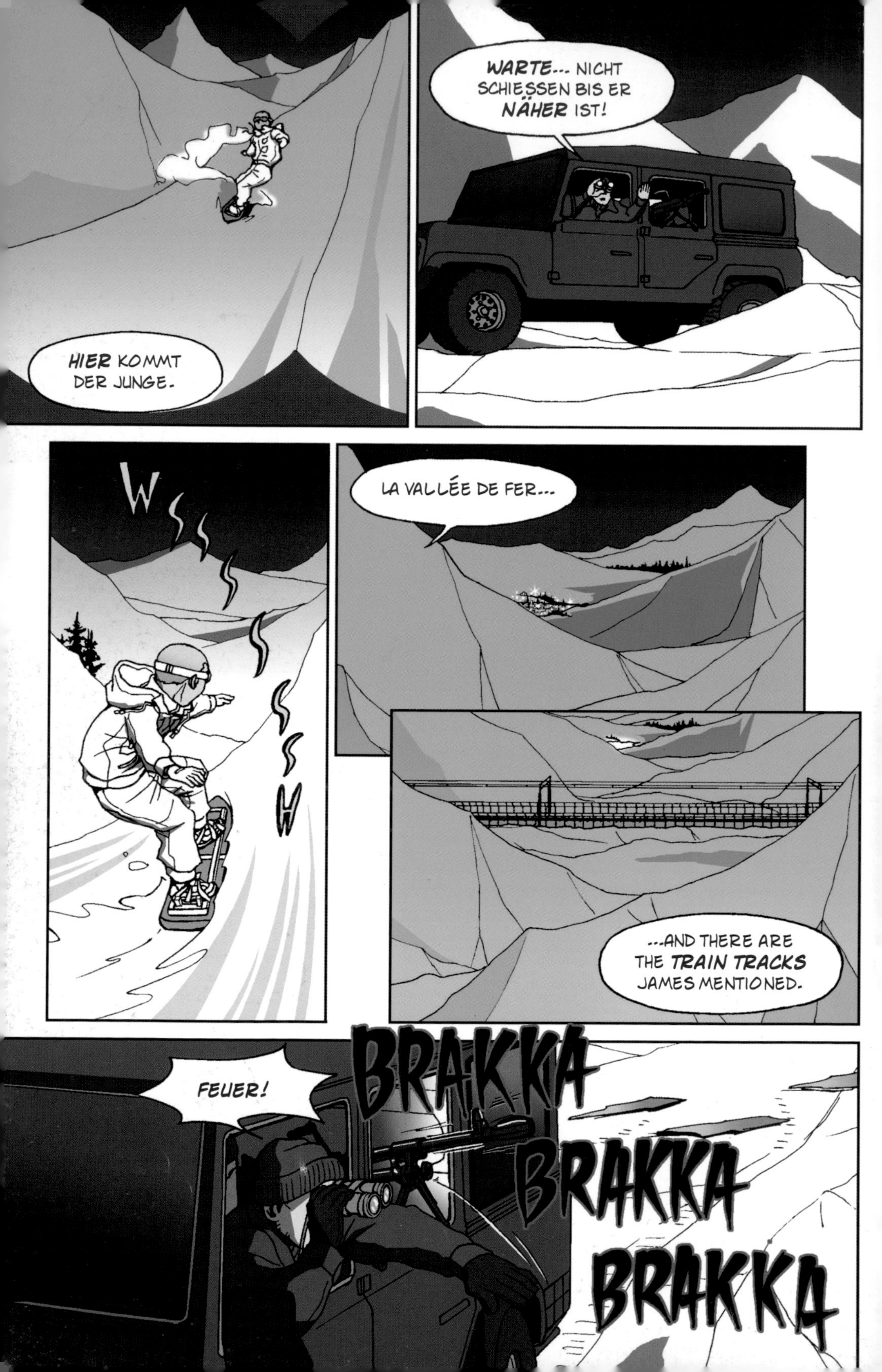
HIER KOMMT DER JUNGE.
WARTE... NICHT SCHIESSEN BIS ER NÄHER IST!
WSSSSSH
LA VALLÉE DE FER...
...AND THERE ARE THE TRAIN TRACKS JAMES MENTIONED.
FEUER!
BRAKKA
BRAKKA
BRAKKA

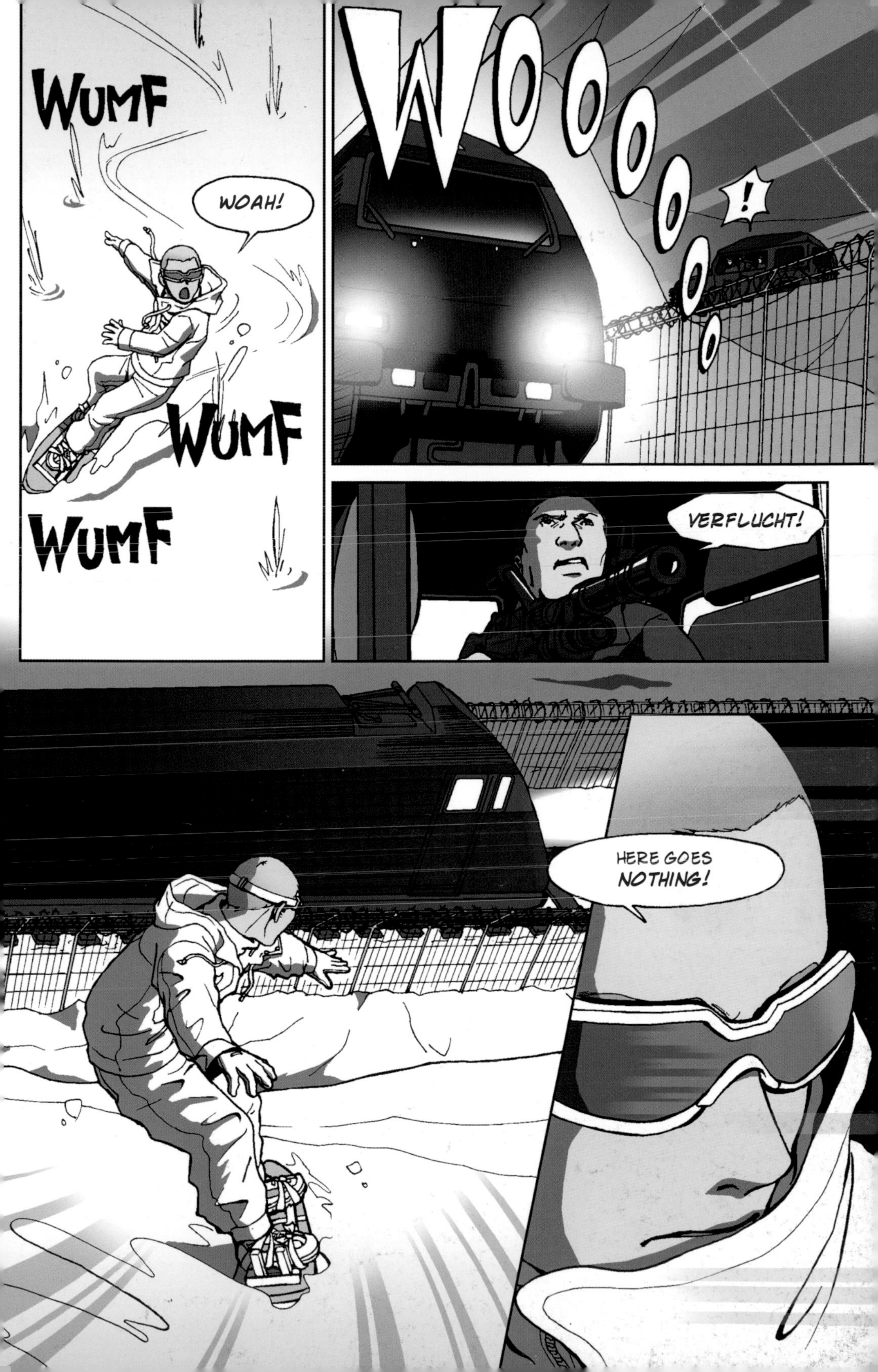
WUMF
WOAH!
WUMF
WUMF
WOOOOOOO
!
VERFLUCHT!
HERE GOES NOTHING!

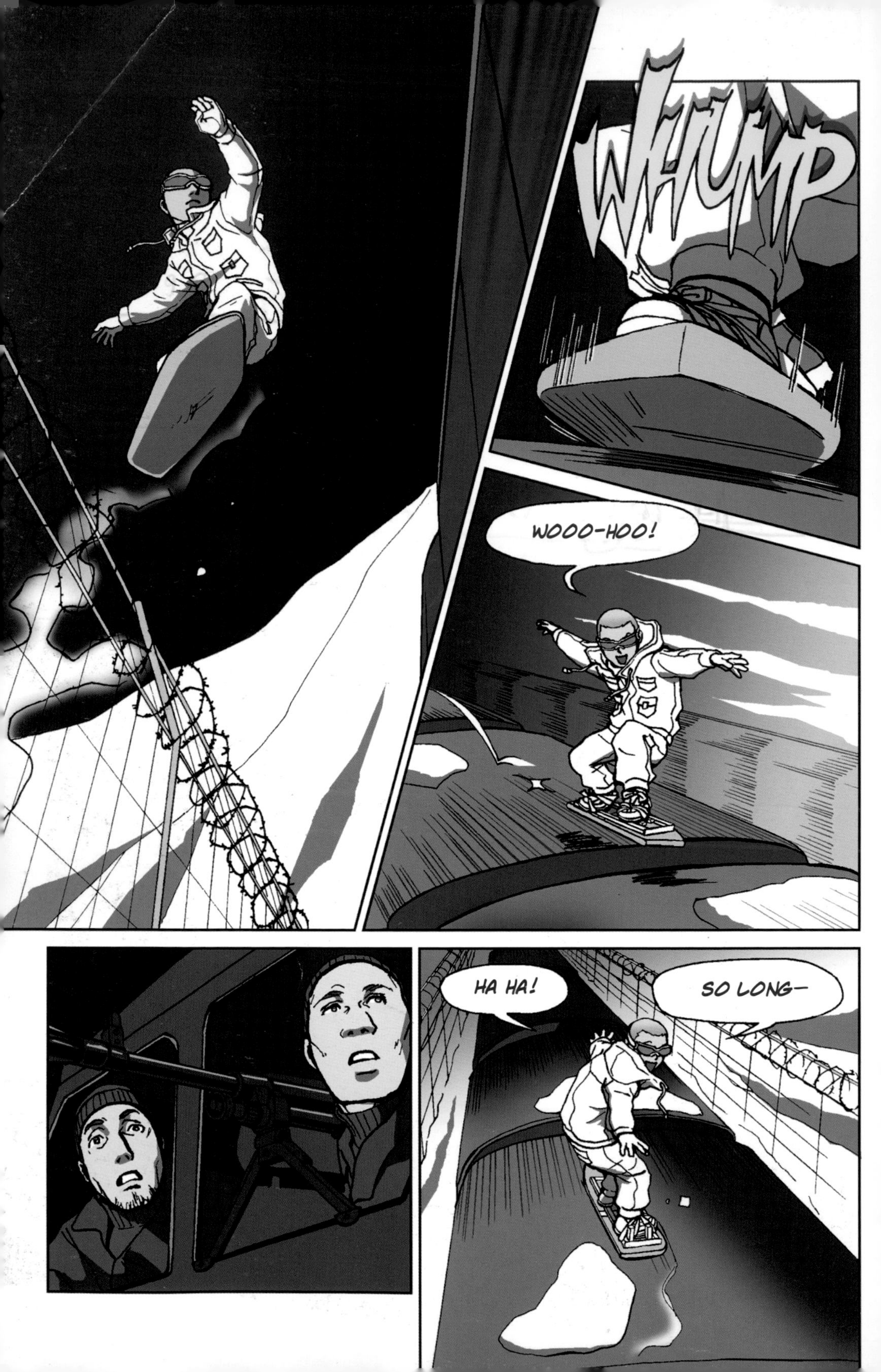
WHUMP
WOOO-HOO!
HA HA!
SO LONG—

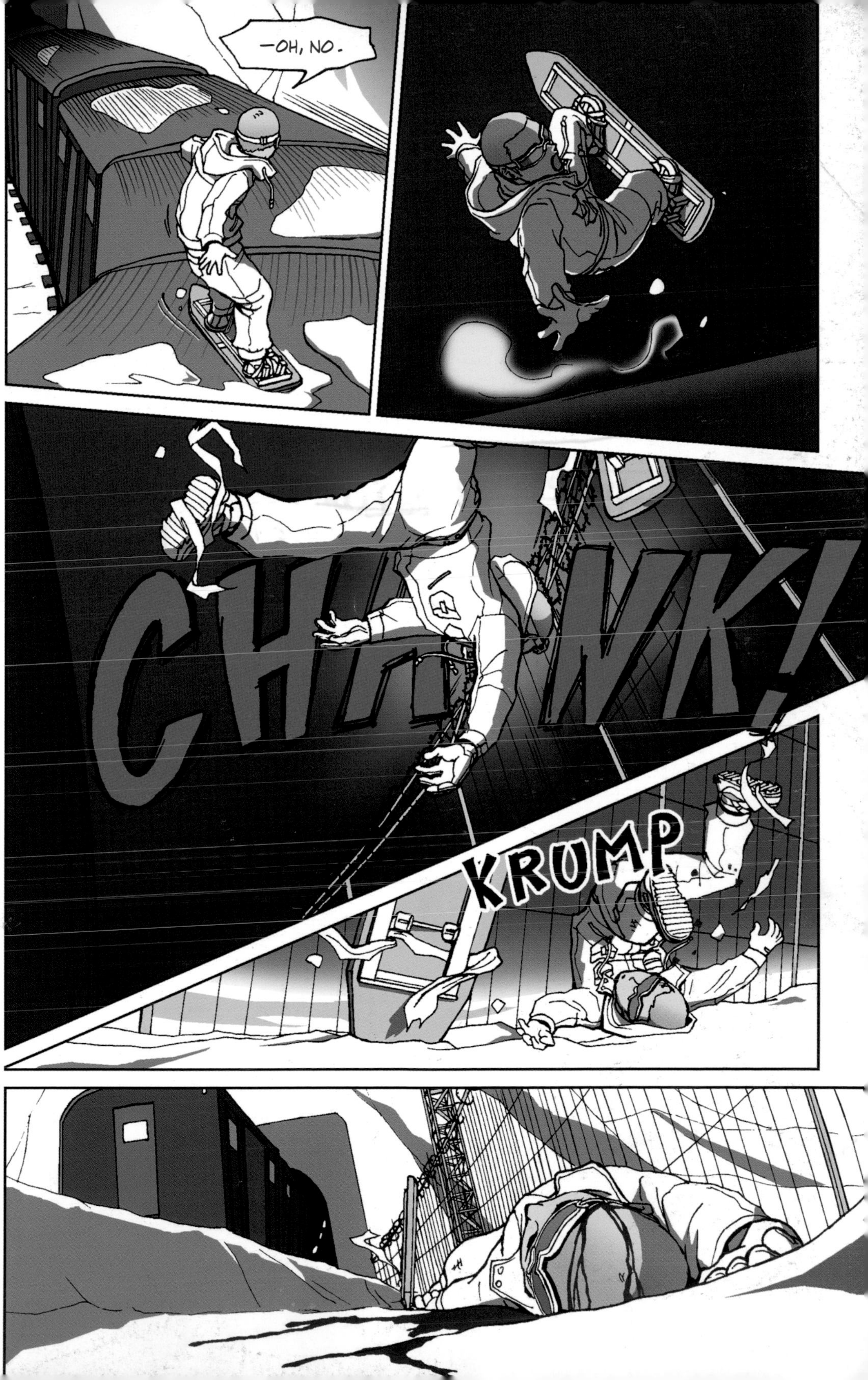
—OH, NO.
CHANK!
KRUMP

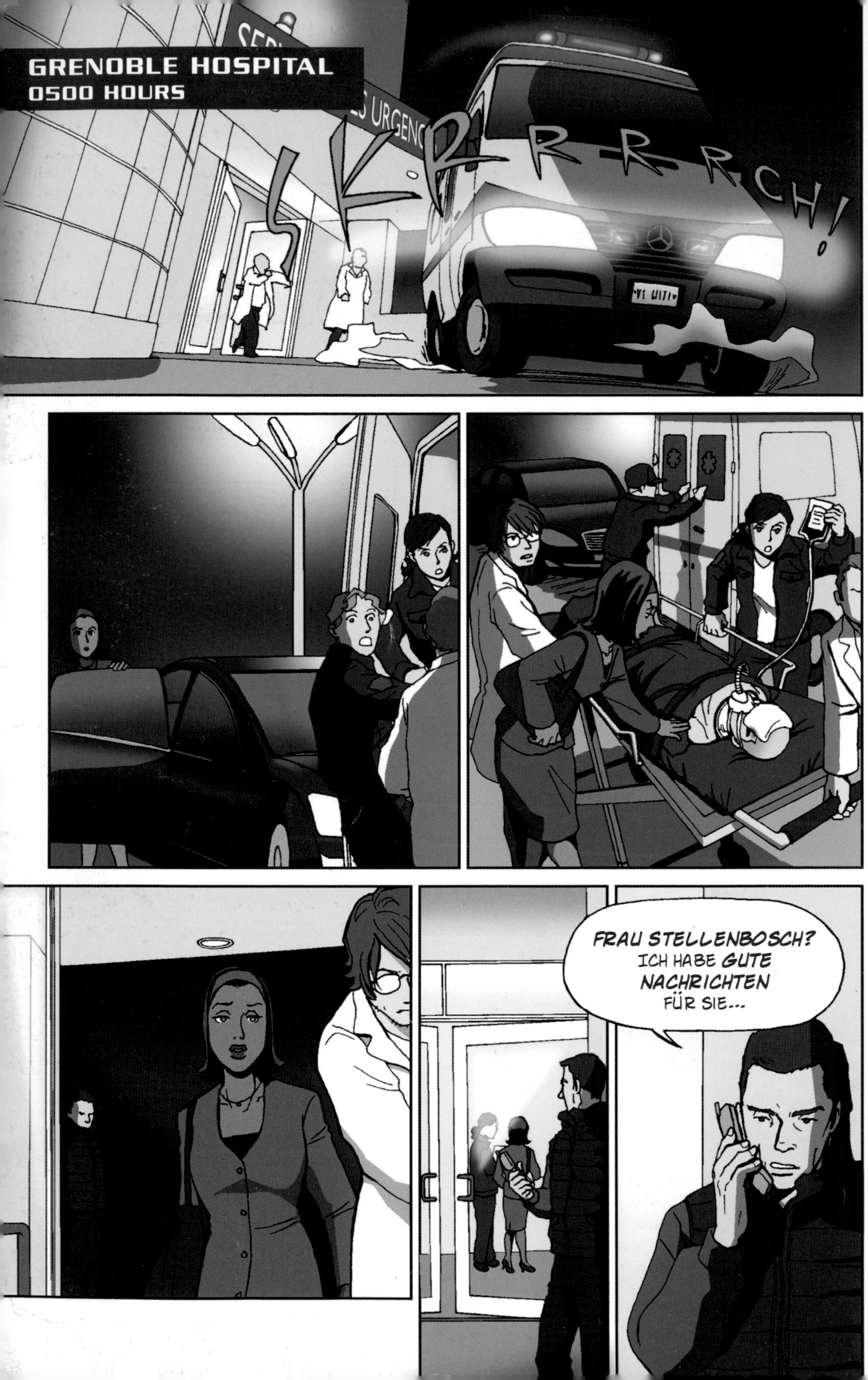
GRENOBLE HOSPITAL
0500 HOURS
SKRRRRRCH!
FRAU STELLENBOSCH? ICH HABE GUTE NACHRICHTEN FÜR SIE...

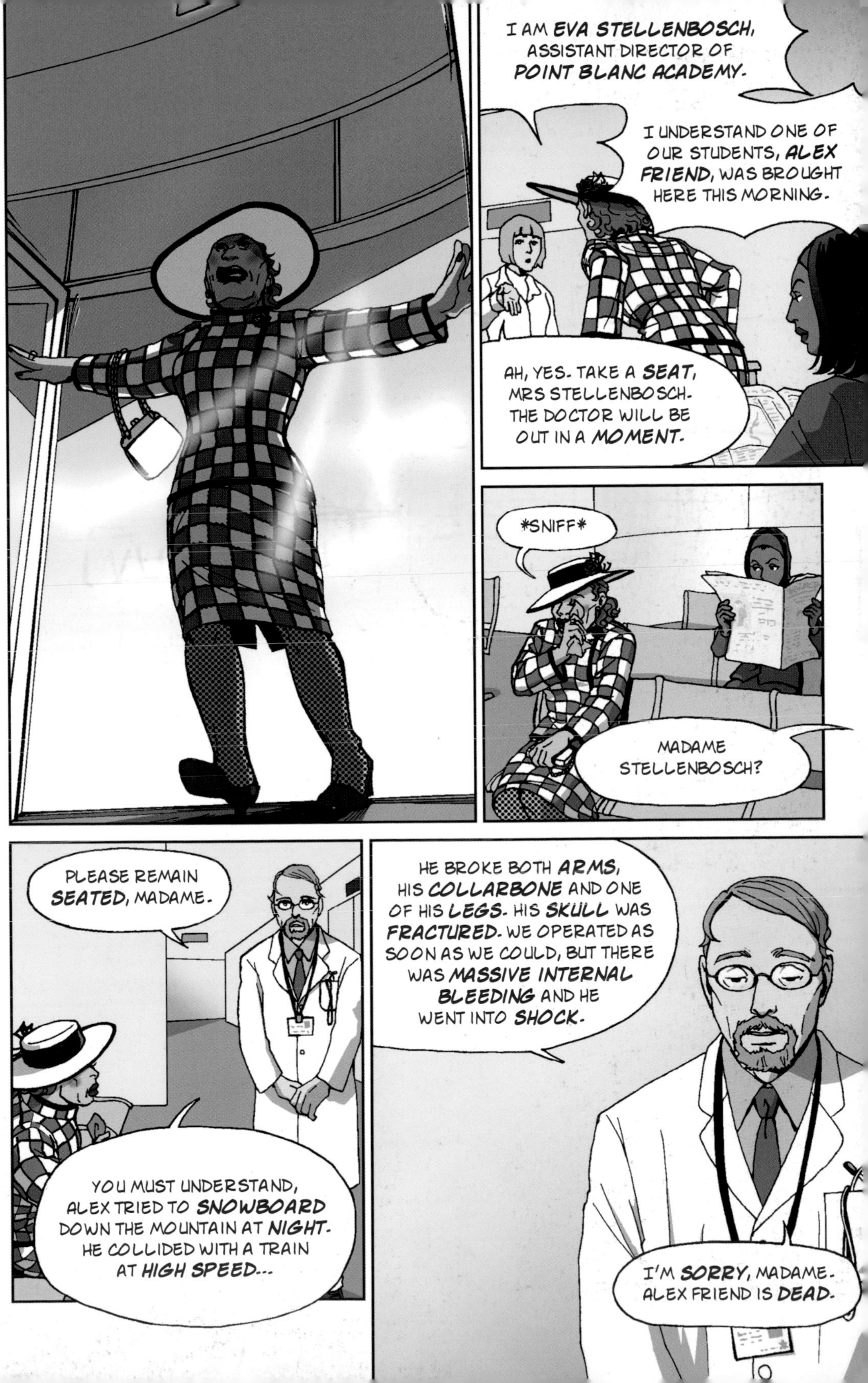
I AM EVA STELLENBOSCH, ASSISTANT DIRECTOR OF POINT BLANC ACADEMY.
I UNDERSTAND ONE OF OUR STUDENTS, ALEX FRIEND, WAS BROUGHT HERE THIS MORNING.
AH, YES. TAKE A SEAT, MRS STELLENBOSCH. THE DOCTOR WILL BE OUT IN A MOMENT.
SNIFF
MADAME STELLENBOSCH?
PLEASE REMAIN SEATED, MADAME.
YOU MUST UNDERSTAND, ALEX TRIED TO SNOWBOARD DOWN THE MOUNTAIN AT NIGHT. HE COLLIDED WITH A TRAIN AT HIGH SPEED...
HE BROKE BOTH ARMS, HIS COLLARBONE AND ONE OF HIS LEGS. HIS SKULL WAS FRACTURED. WE OPERATED AS SOON AS WE COULD, BUT THERE WAS MASSIVE INTERNAL BLEEDING AND HE WENT INTO SHOCK.
I'M SORRY, MADAME. ALEX FRIEND IS DEAD.

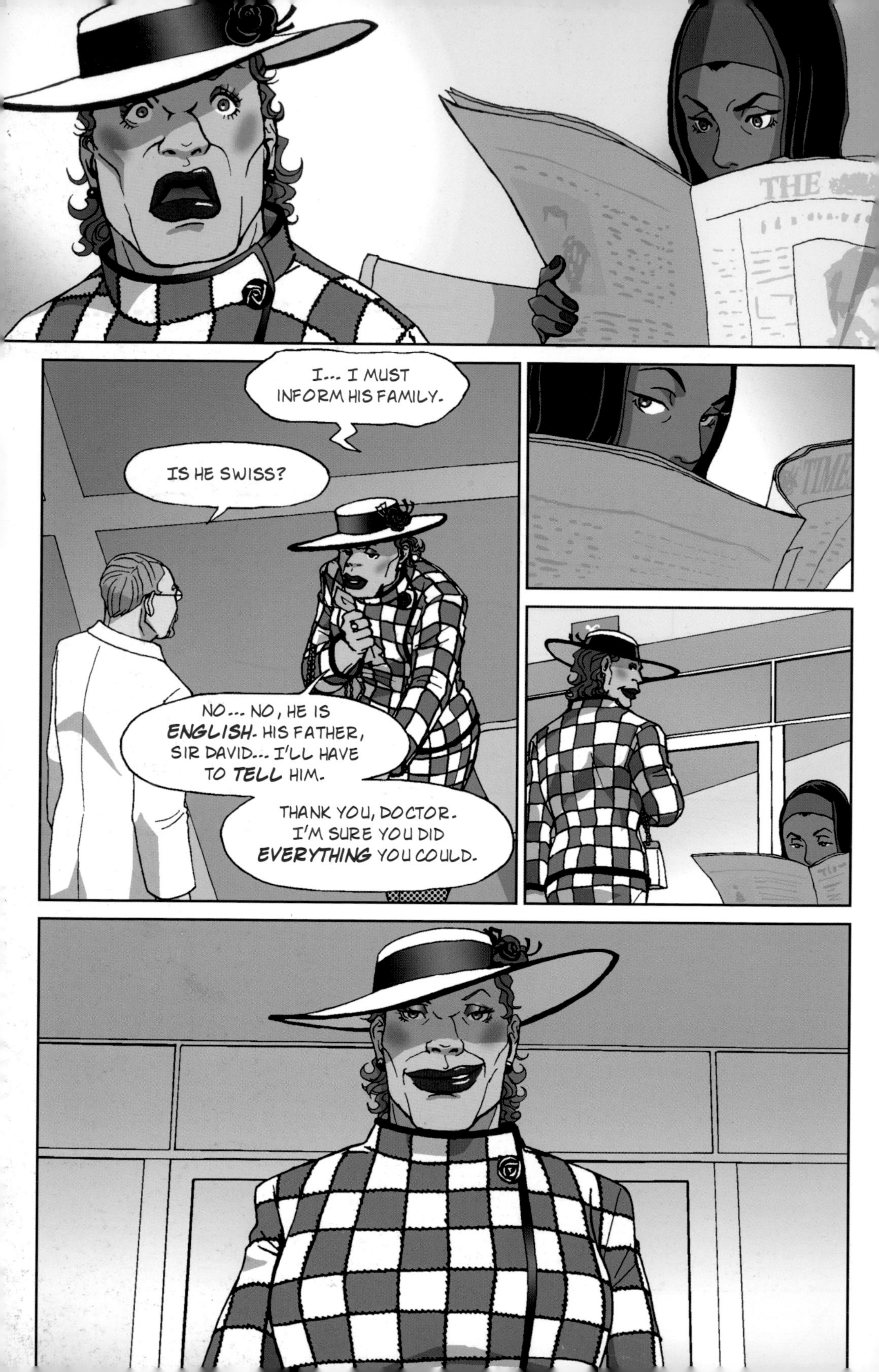

I... I MUST INFORM HIS FAMILY.
IS HE SWISS?
NO... NO, HE IS ENGLISH. HIS FATHER, SIR DAVID... I'LL HAVE TO TELL HIM.
THANK YOU, DOCTOR. I'M SURE YOU DID EVERYTHING YOU COULD.

SAINT-GEOIRS AIRPORT,
GRENOBLE

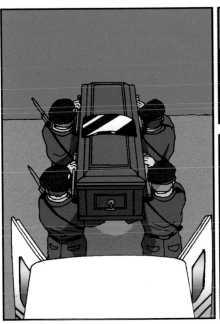

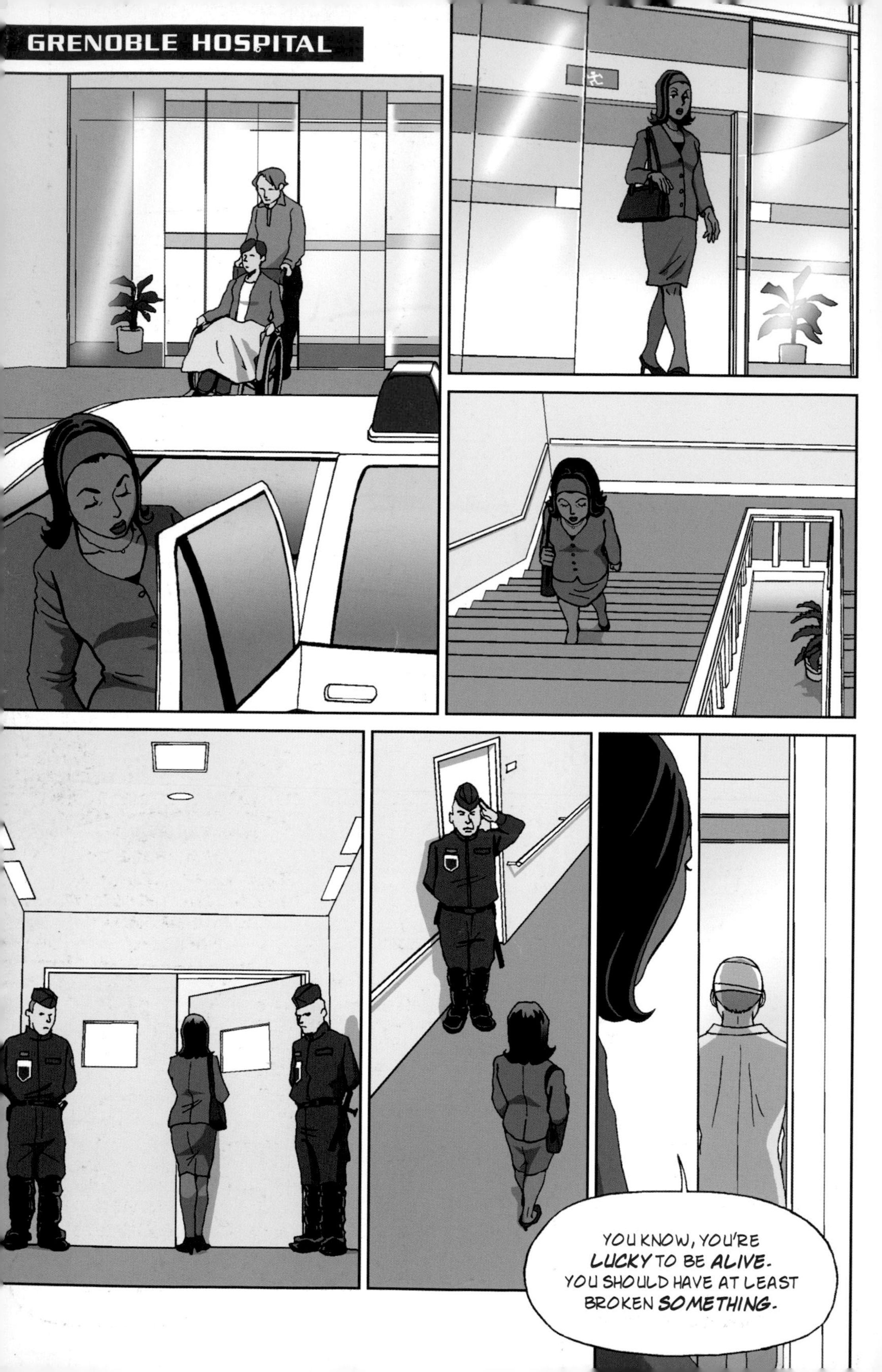
GRENOBLE HOSPITAL
YOU KNOW, YOU'RE LUCKY TO BE ALIVE. YOU SHOULD HAVE AT LEAST BROKEN SOMETHING.

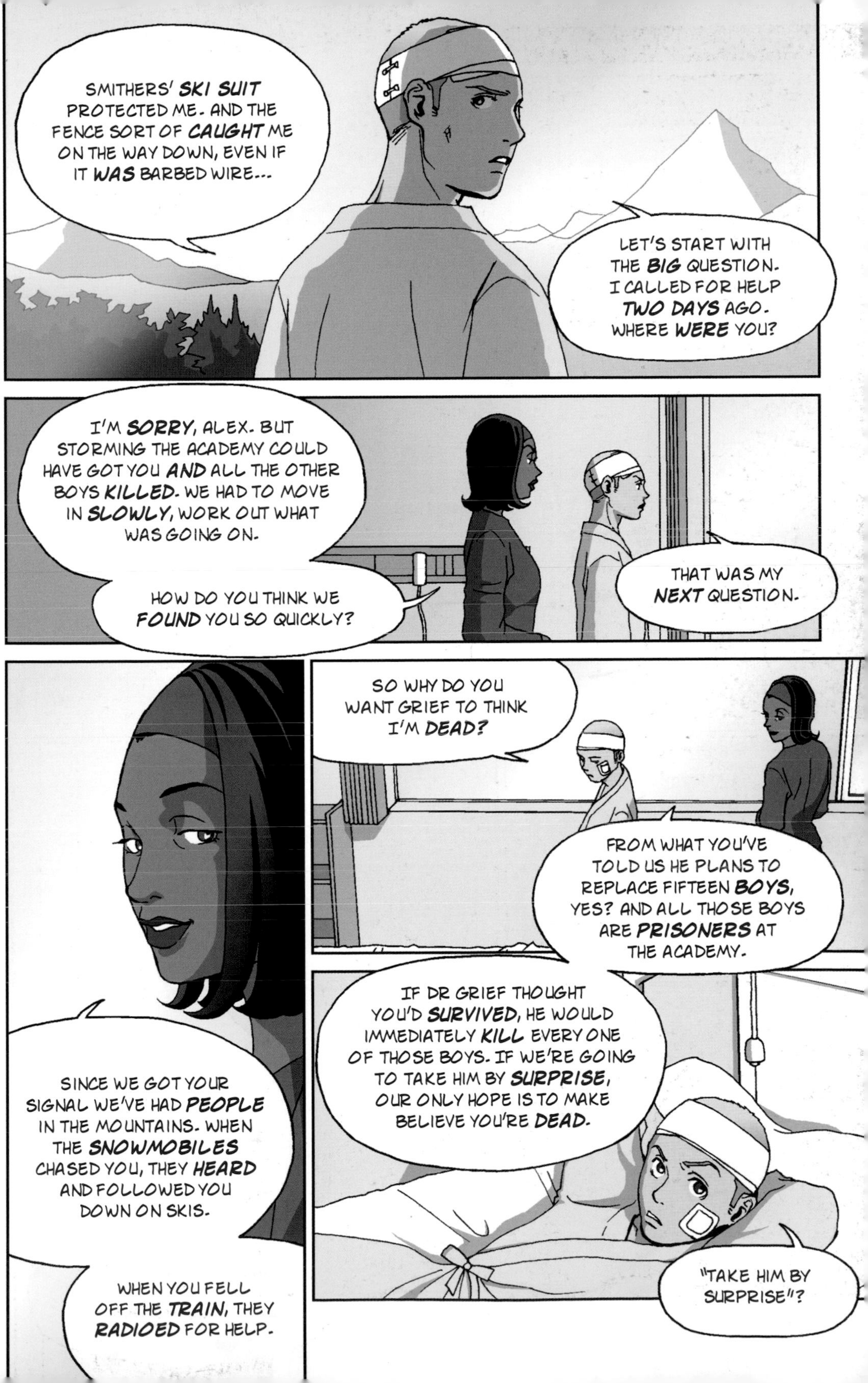
SMITHERS' SKI SUIT PROTECTED ME. AND THE FENCE SORT OF CAUGHT ME ON THE WAY DOWN, EVEN IF IT WAS BARBED WIRE...
LET'S START WITH THE BIG QUESTION. I CALLED FOR HELP TWO DAYS AGO. WHERE WERE YOU?
I'M SORRY, ALEX. BUT STORMING THE ACADEMY COULD HAVE GOT YOU AND ALL THE OTHER BOYS KILLED. WE HAD TO MOVE IN SLOWLY, WORK OUT WHAT WAS GOING ON.
HOW DO YOU THINK WE FOUND YOU SO QUICKLY?
THAT WAS MY NEXT QUESTION.
SINCE WE GOT YOUR SIGNAL WE'VE HAD PEOPLE IN THE MOUNTAINS. WHEN THE SNOWMOBILES CHASED YOU, THEY HEARD AND FOLLOWED YOU DOWN ON SKIS.
WHEN YOU FELL OFF THE TRAIN, THEY RADIOED FOR HELP.
SO WHY DO YOU WANT GRIEF TO THINK I'M DEAD?
FROM WHAT YOU'VE TOLD US HE PLANS TO REPLACE FIFTEEN BOYS, YES? AND ALL THOSE BOYS ARE PRISONERS AT THE ACADEMY.
IF DR GRIEF THOUGHT YOU'D SURVIVED, HE WOULD IMMEDIATELY KILL EVERY ONE OF THOSE BOYS. IF WE'RE GOING TO TAKE HIM BY SURPRISE, OUR ONLY HOPE IS TO MAKE BELIEVE YOU'RE DEAD.
"TAKE HIM BY SURPRISE"?

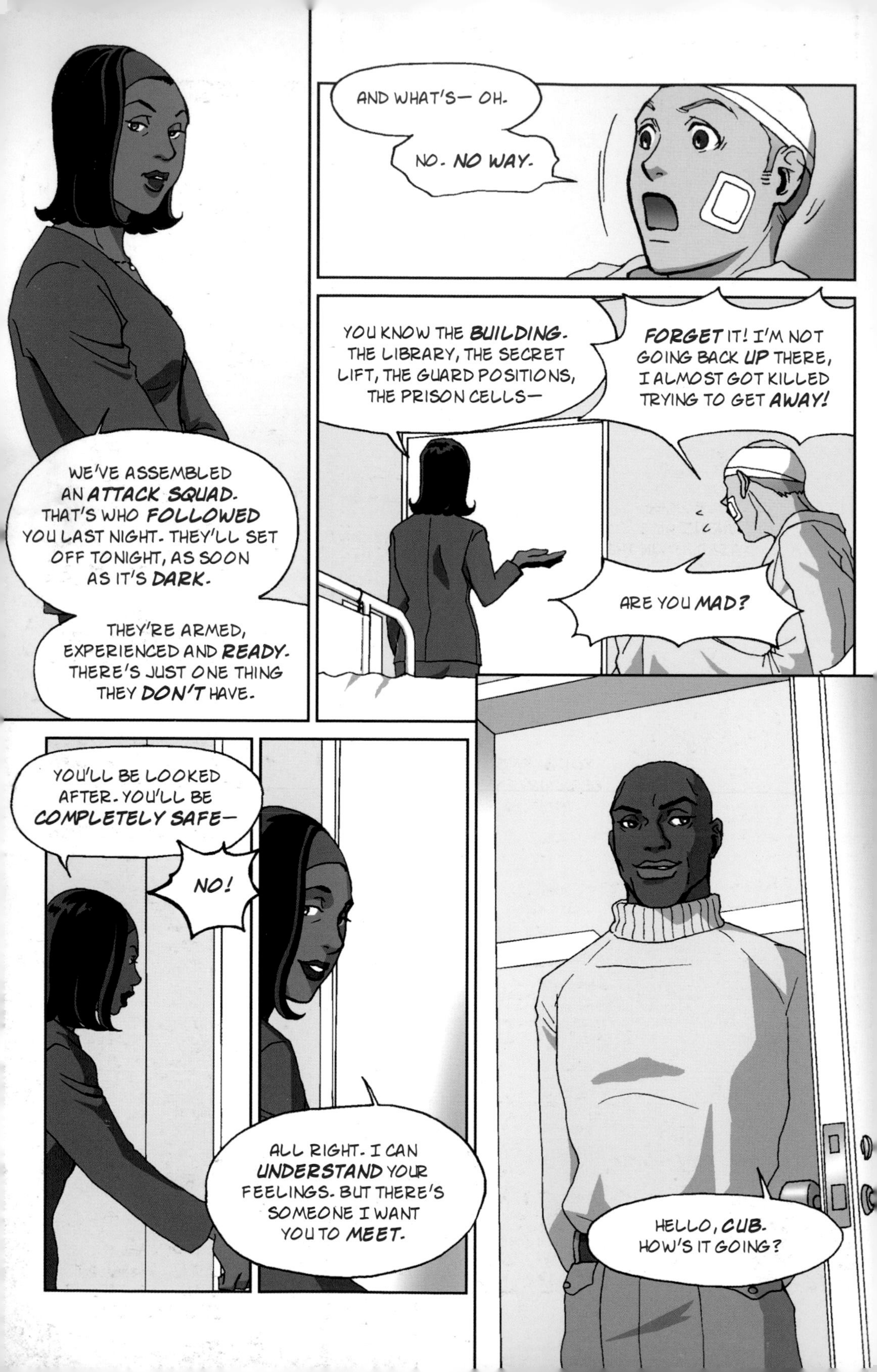
WE'VE ASSEMBLED AN ATTACK SQUAD. THAT'S WHO FOLLOWED YOU LAST NIGHT. THEY'LL SET OFF TONIGHT, AS SOON AS IT'S DARK.
THEY'RE ARMED, EXPERIENCED AND READY. THERE'S JUST ONE THING THEY DON'T HAVE.
AND WHAT'S— OH.
NO. NO WAY.
YOU KNOW THE BUILDING. THE LIBRARY, THE SECRET LIFT, THE GUARD POSITIONS, THE PRISON CELLS—
FORGET IT! I'M NOT GOING BACK UP THERE, I ALMOST GOT KILLED TRYING TO GET AWAY!
ARE YOU MAD?
YOU'LL BE LOOKED AFTER. YOU'LL BE COMPLETELY SAFE—
NO!
ALL RIGHT. I CAN UNDERSTAND YOUR FEELINGS. BUT THERE'S SOMEONE I WANT YOU TO MEET.
HELLO, CUB. HOW'S IT GOING?

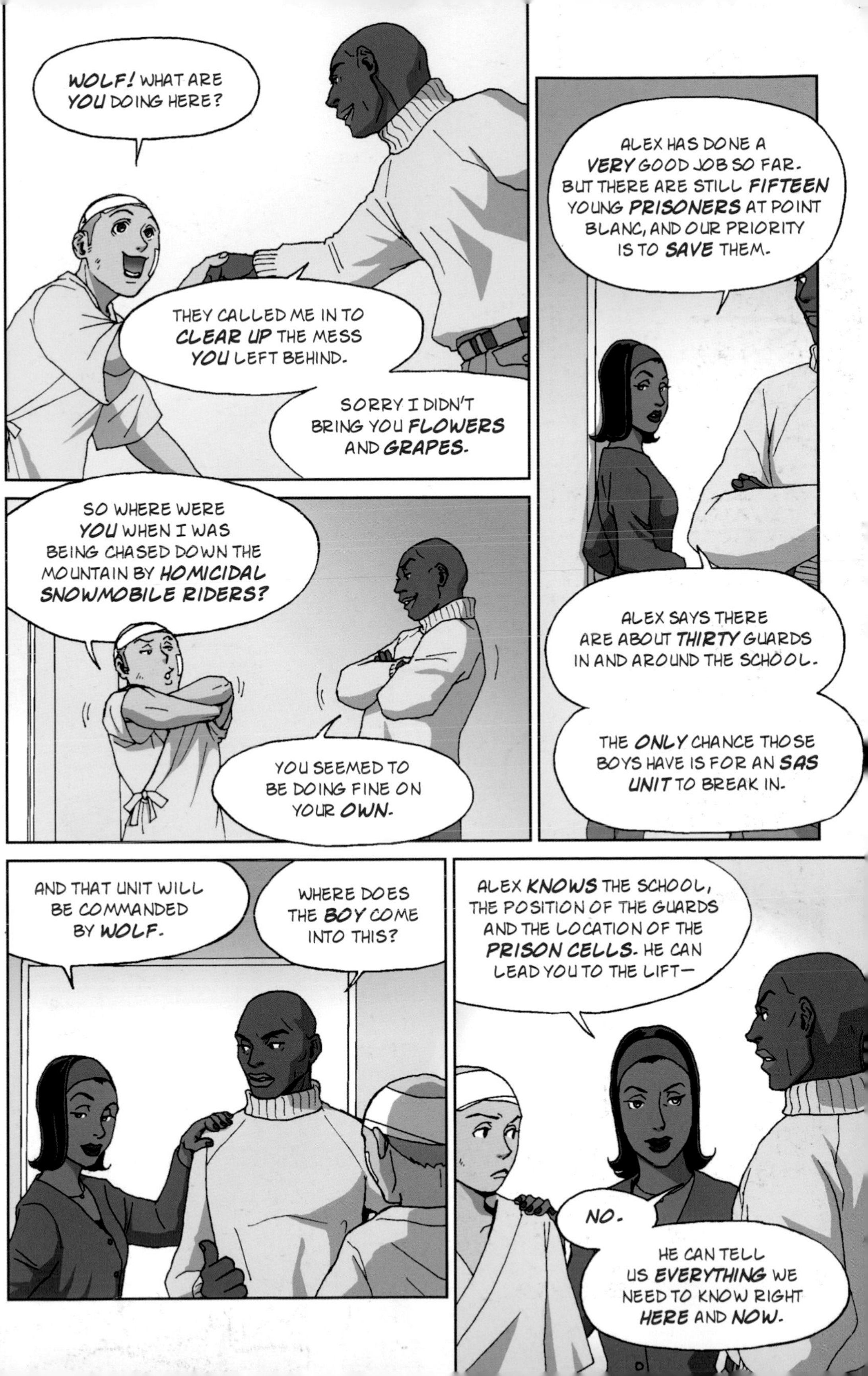
WOLF! WHAT ARE YOU DOING HERE?
THEY CALLED ME IN TO CLEAR UP THE MESS YOU LEFT BEHIND.
SORRY I DIDN'T BRING YOU FLOWERS AND GRAPES.
ALEX HAS DONE A VERY GOOD JOB SO FAR. BUT THERE ARE STILL FIFTEEN YOUNG PRISONERS AT POINT BLANC, AND OUR PRIORITY IS TO SAVE THEM.
SO WHERE WERE YOU WHEN I WAS BEING CHASED DOWN THE MOUNTAIN BY HOMICIDAL SNOWMOBILE RIDERS?
YOU SEEMED TO BE DOING FINE ON YOUR OWN.
ALEX SAYS THERE ARE ABOUT THIRTY GUARDS IN AND AROUND THE SCHOOL.
THE ONLY CHANCE THOSE BOYS HAVE IS FOR AN SAS UNIT TO BREAK IN.
AND THAT UNIT WILL BE COMMANDED BY WOLF.
WHERE DOES THE BOY COME INTO THIS?
ALEX KNOWS THE SCHOOL, THE POSITION OF THE GUARDS AND THE LOCATION OF THE PRISON CELLS. HE CAN LEAD YOU TO THE LIFT—
NO.
HE CAN TELL US EVERYTHING WE NEED TO KNOW RIGHT HERE AND NOW.

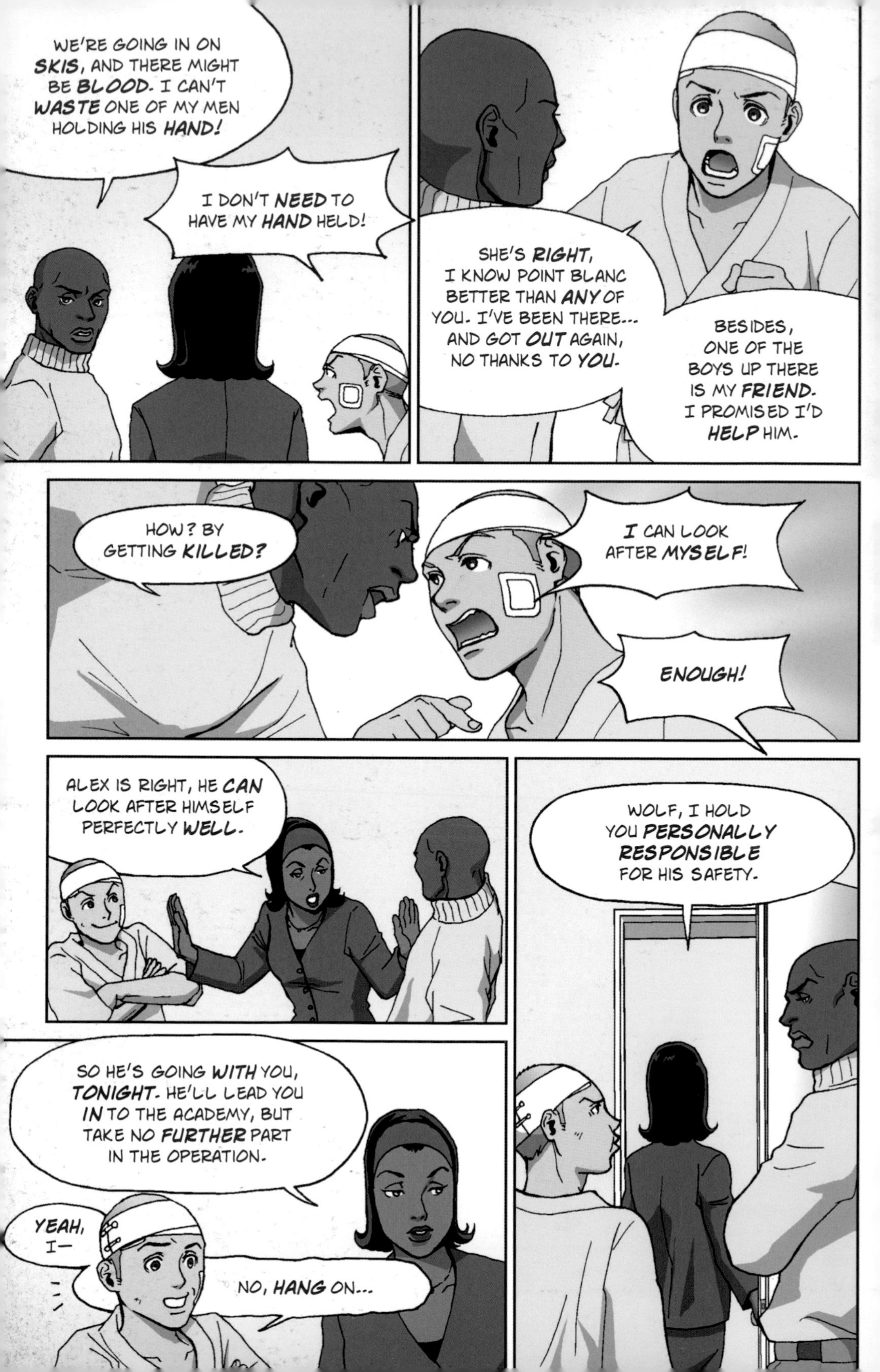
WE'RE GOING IN ON SKIS, AND THERE MIGHT BE BLOOD. I CAN'T WASTE ONE OF MY MEN HOLDING HIS HAND!
I DON'T NEED TO HAVE MY HAND HELD!
SHE'S RIGHT, I KNOW POINT BLANC BETTER THAN ANY OF YOU. I'VE BEEN THERE... AND GOT OUT AGAIN, NO THANKS TO YOU.
BESIDES, ONE OF THE BOYS UP THERE IS MY FRIEND. I PROMISED I'D HELP HIM.
HOW? BY GETTING KILLED?
I CAN LOOK AFTER MYSELF!
ENOUGH!
ALEX IS RIGHT, HE CAN LOOK AFTER HIMSELF PERFECTLY WELL.
SO HE'S GOING WITH YOU, TONIGHT. HE'LL LEAD YOU IN TO THE ACADEMY, BUT TAKE NO FURTHER PART IN THE OPERATION.
YEAH, I—
NO, HANG ON...
WOLF, I HOLD YOU PERSONALLY RESPONSIBLE FOR HIS SAFETY.

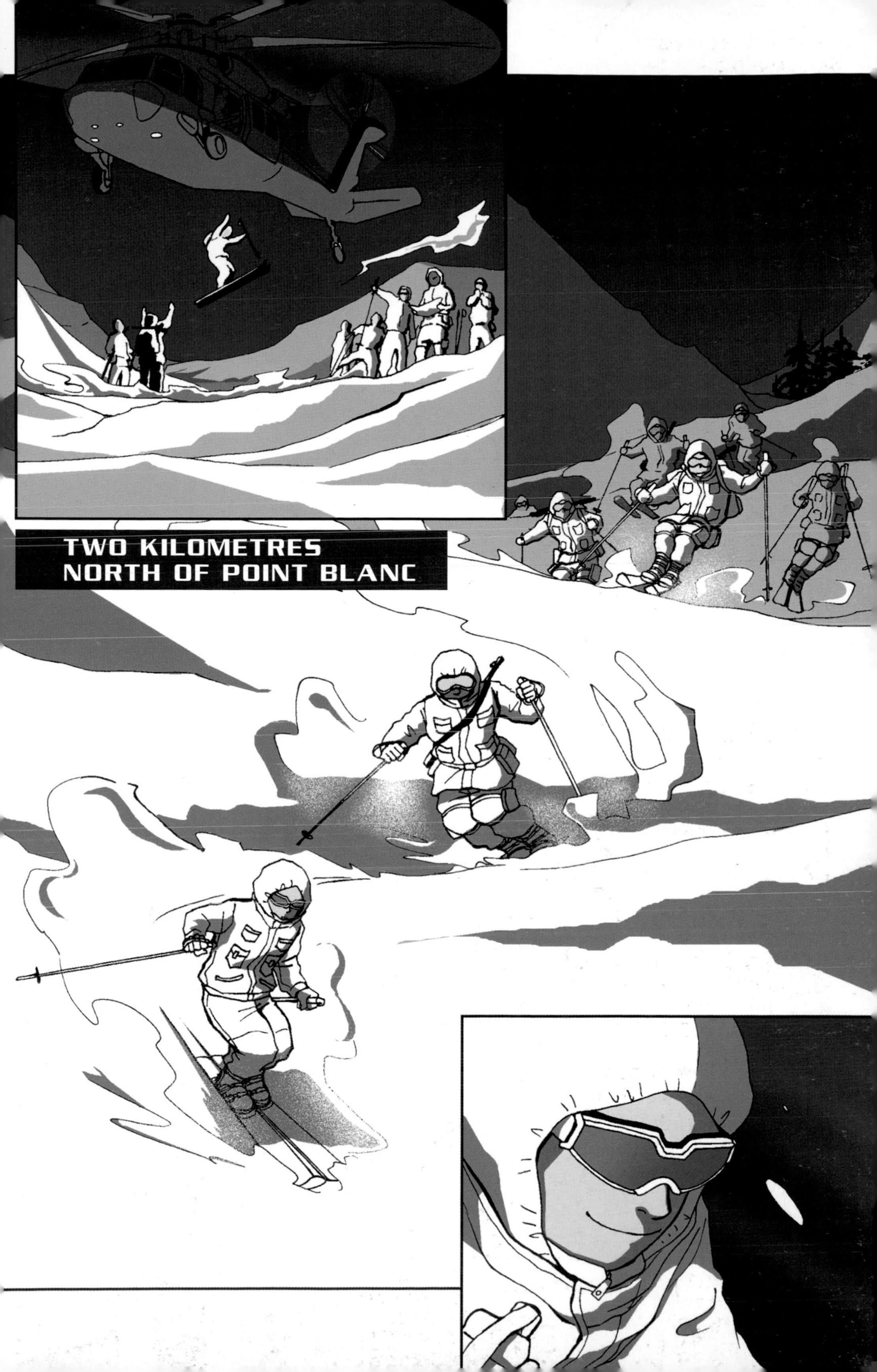
TWO KILOMETRES
NORTH OF POINT BLANC

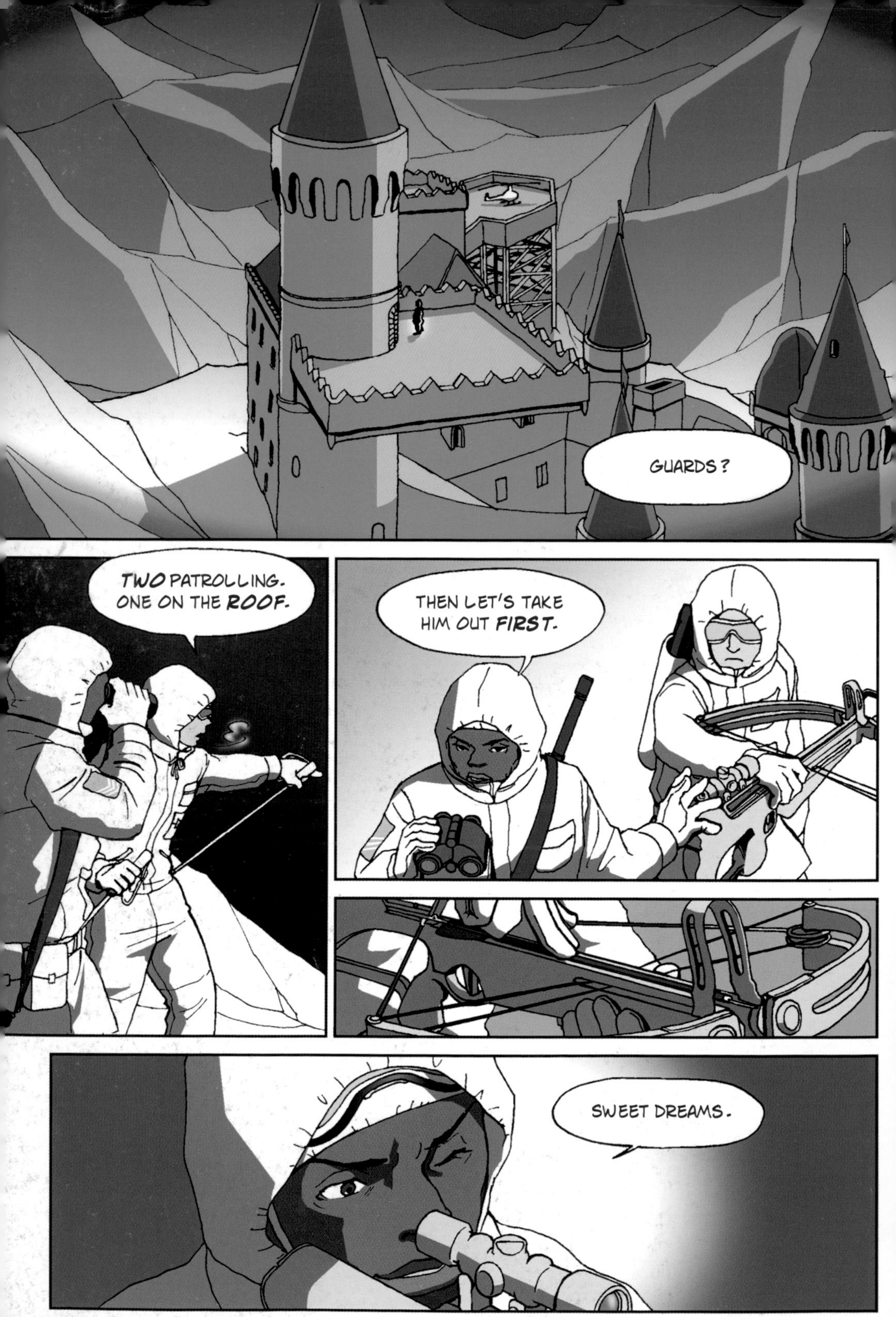
GUARDS?
TWO PATROLLING. ONE ON THE ROOF.
THEN LET'S TAKE HIM OUT FIRST.
SWEET DREAMS.

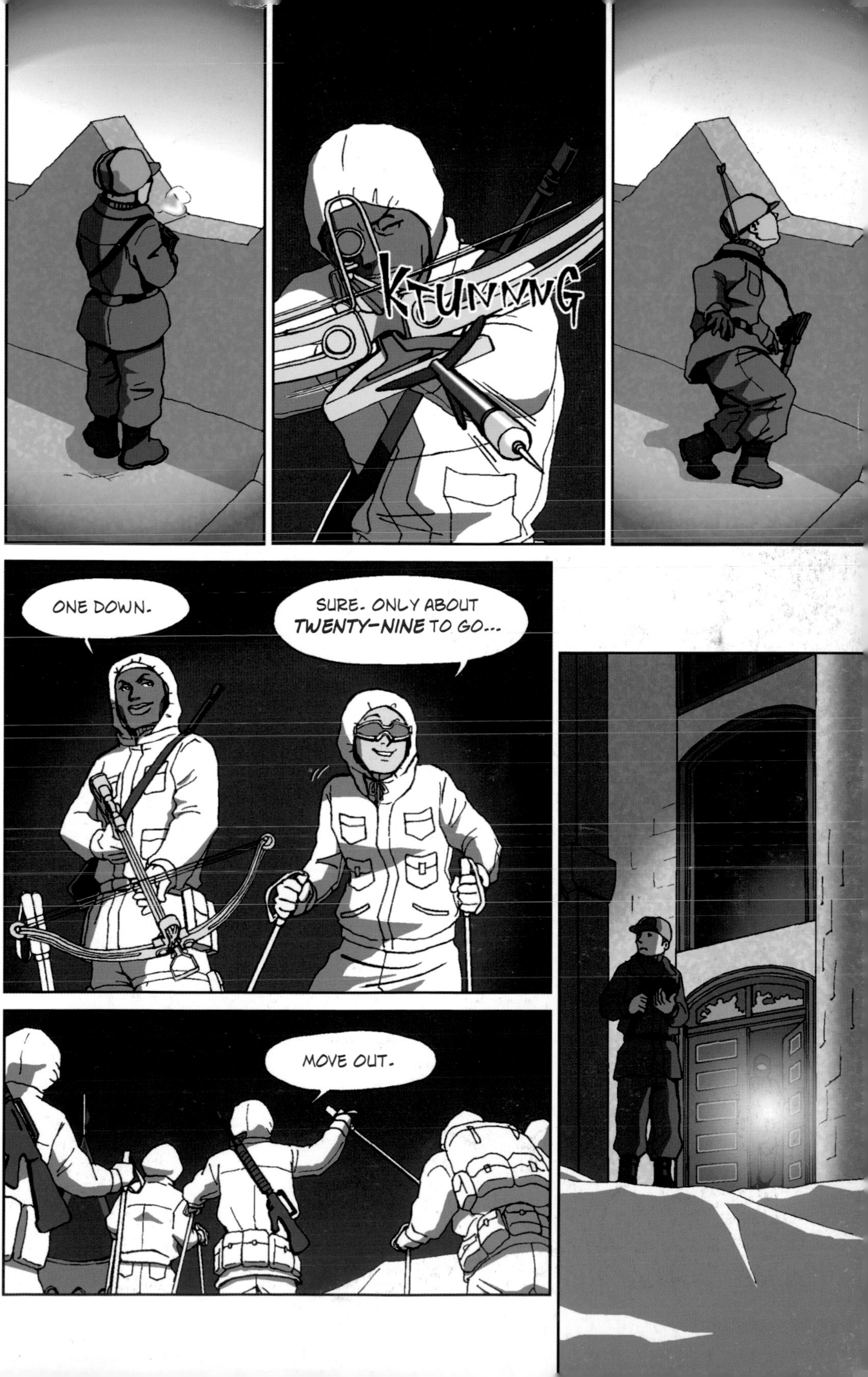
KTUNNNG
ONE DOWN.
SURE. ONLY ABOUT TWENTY-NINE TO GO...
MOVE OUT.

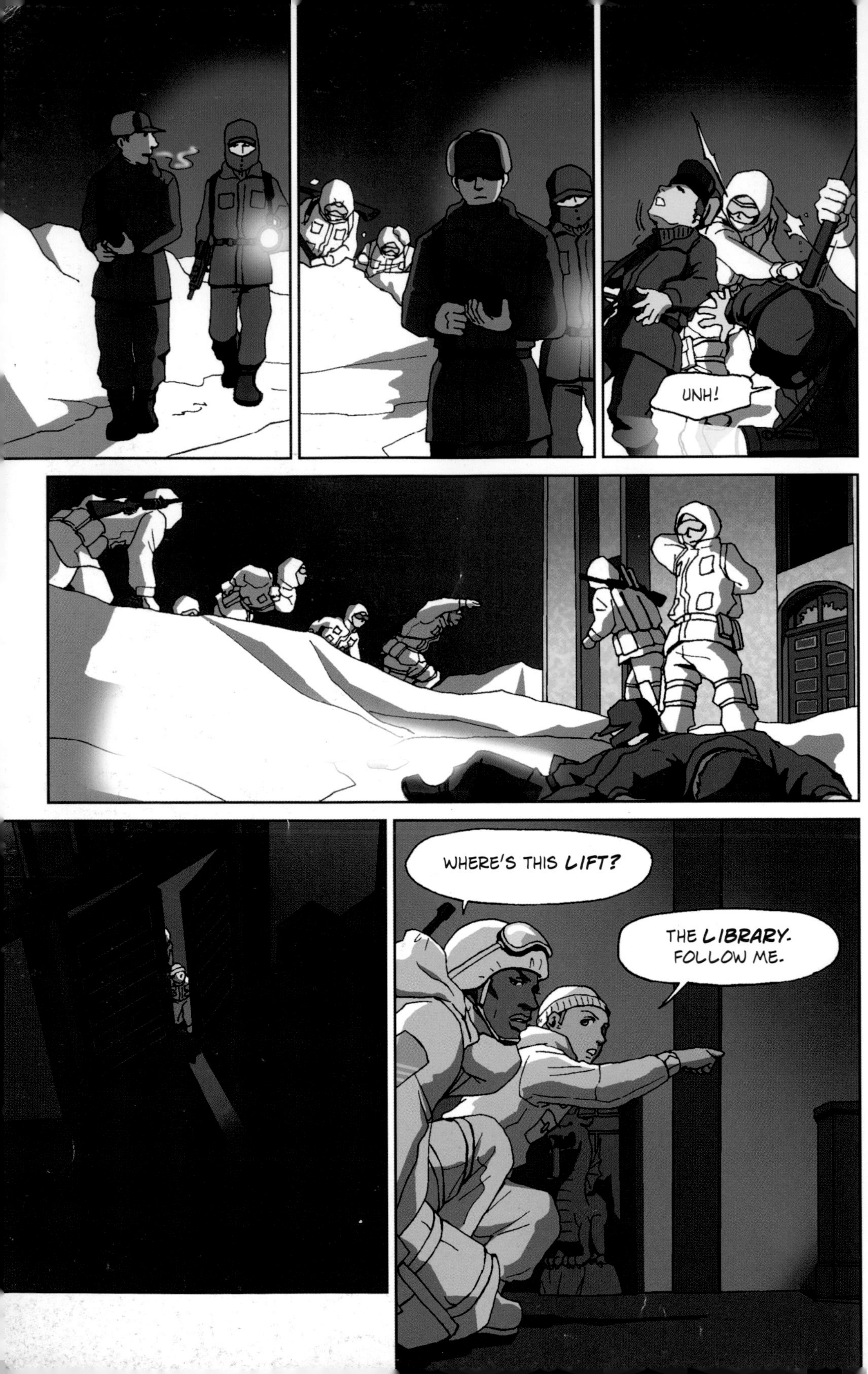
UNH!
WHERE'S THIS LIFT?
THE LIBRARY-
FOLLOW ME.

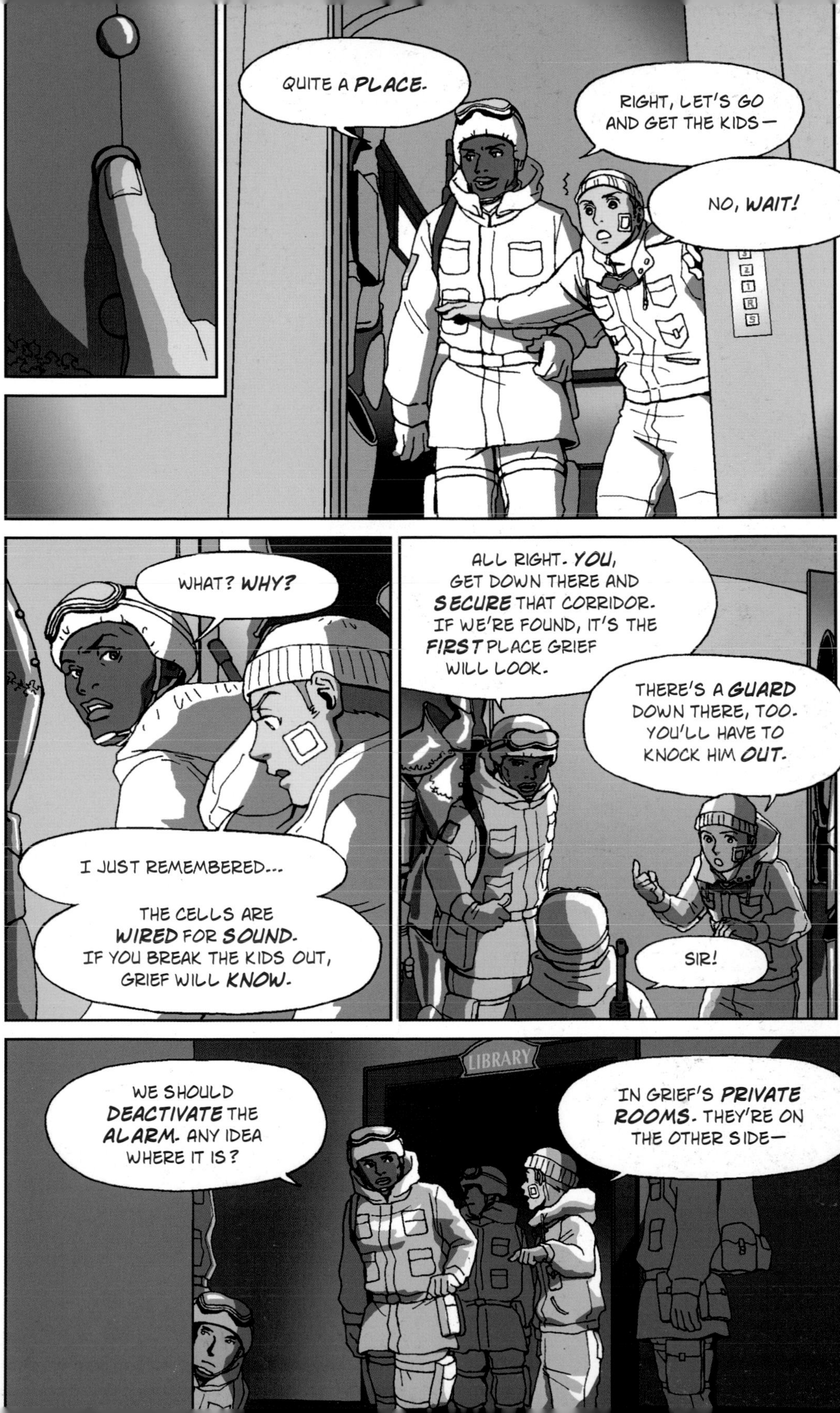
QUITE A PLACE.
RIGHT, LET'S GO AND GET THE KIDS—
NO, WAIT!
WHAT? WHY?
I JUST REMEMBERED...
THE CELLS ARE WIRED FOR SOUND. IF YOU BREAK THE KIDS OUT, GRIEF WILL KNOW.
ALL RIGHT. YOU, GET DOWN THERE AND SECURE THAT CORRIDOR. IF WE'RE FOUND, IT'S THE FIRST PLACE GRIEF WILL LOOK.
THERE'S A GUARD DOWN THERE, TOO. YOU'LL HAVE TO KNOCK HIM OUT.
SIR!
LIBRARY
WE SHOULD DEACTIVATE THE ALARM. ANY IDEA WHERE IT IS?
IN GRIEF'S PRIVATE ROOMS. THEY'RE ON THE OTHER SIDE—

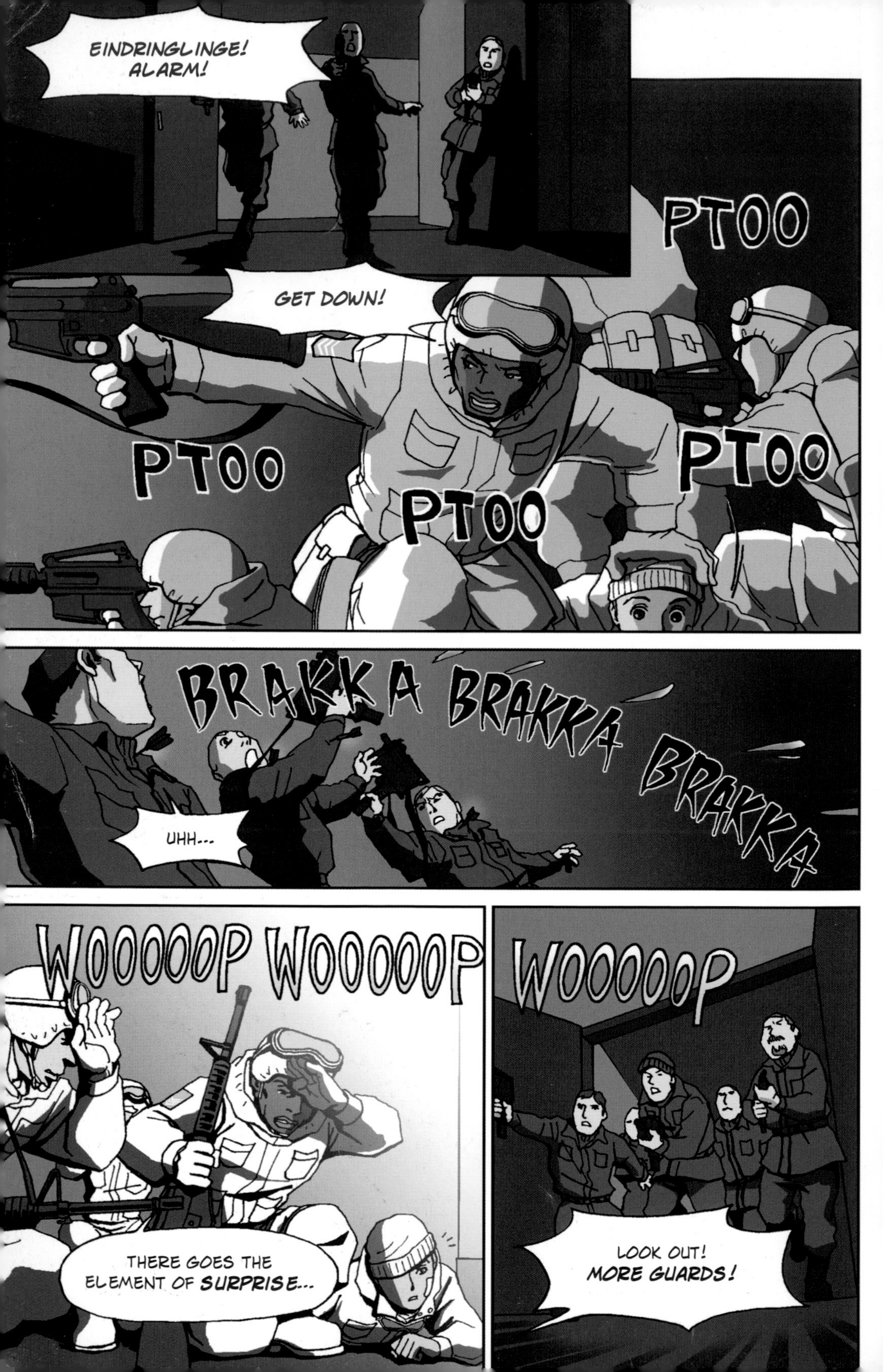
EINDRINGLINGE! ALARM!
PTOO
GET DOWN!
PTOO
PTOO
PTOO
BRAKKA BRAKKA BRAKKA
UHH...
WOOOOOP WOOOOOP
THERE GOES THE ELEMENT OF SURPRISE...
WOOOOOP
LOOK OUT! MORE GUARDS!

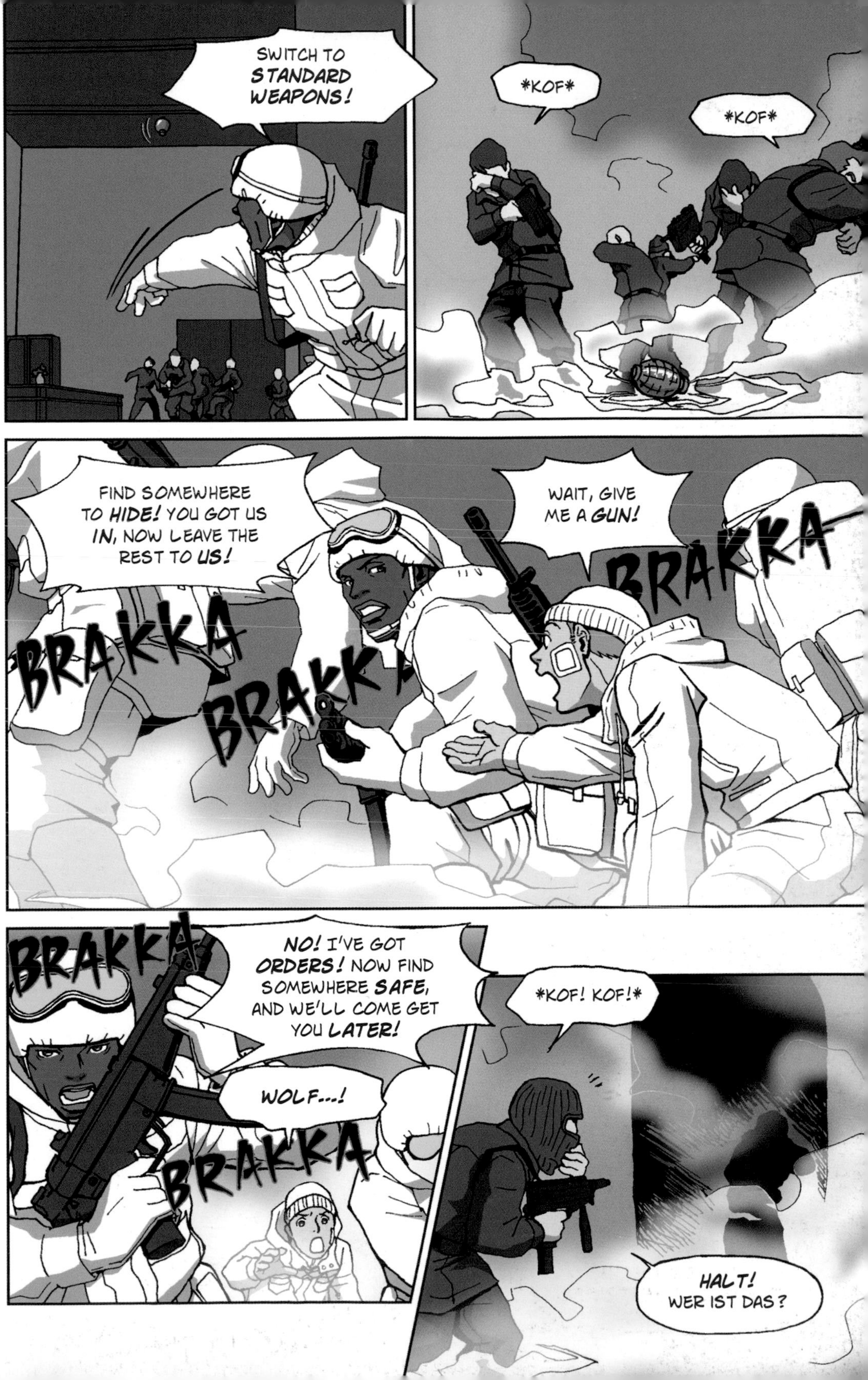
SWITCH TO STANDARD WEAPONS!
KOF
KOF
FIND SOMEWHERE TO HIDE! YOU GOT US IN, NOW LEAVE THE REST TO US!
WAIT, GIVE ME A GUN!
BRAKKA
BRAKKA
BRAKKA
BRAKKA
NO! I'VE GOT ORDERS! NOW FIND SOMEWHERE SAFE, AND WE'LL COME GET YOU LATER!
WOLF...!
BRAKKA
KOF! KOF!
HALT! WER IST DAS?

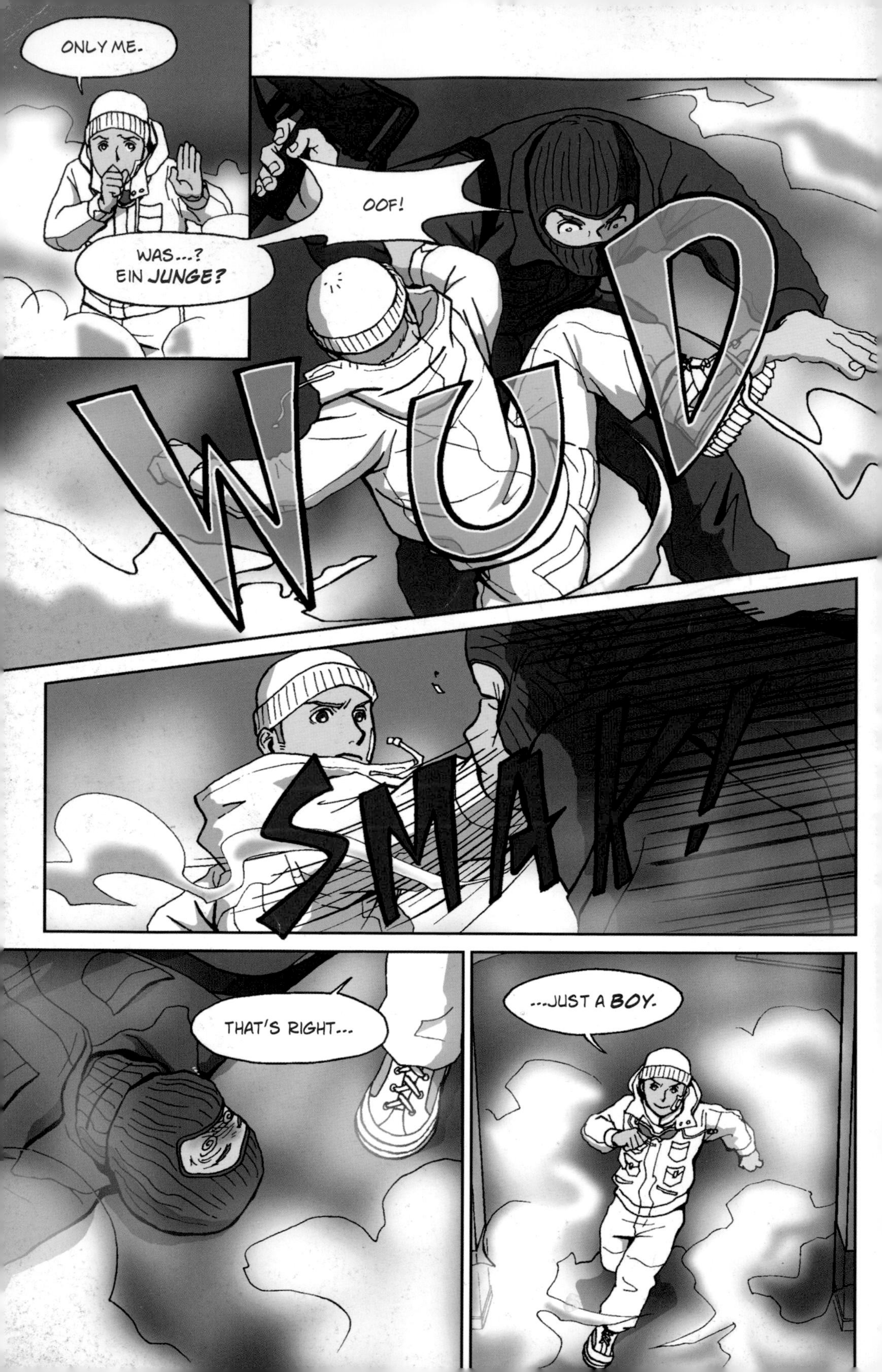
ONLY ME.
WAS...? EIN JUNGE?
OOF!
WUD
SMAK!
THAT'S RIGHT...
...JUST A BOY.

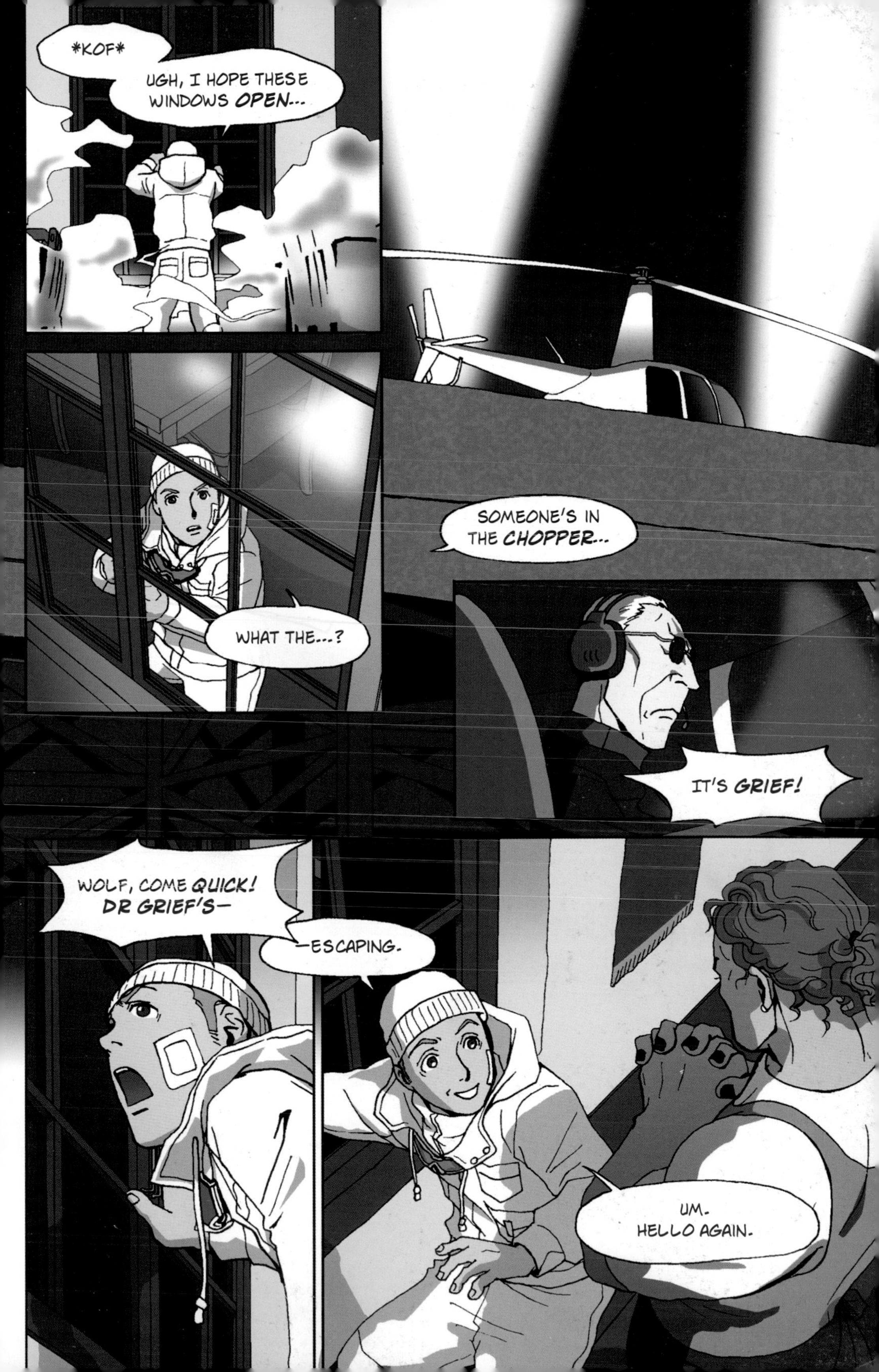
KOF
UGH, I HOPE THESE WINDOWS OPEN...
SOMEONE'S IN THE CHOPPER...
WHAT THE...?
IT'S GRIEF!
WOLF, COME QUICK! DR GRIEF'S—
—ESCAPING.
UM. HELLO AGAIN.

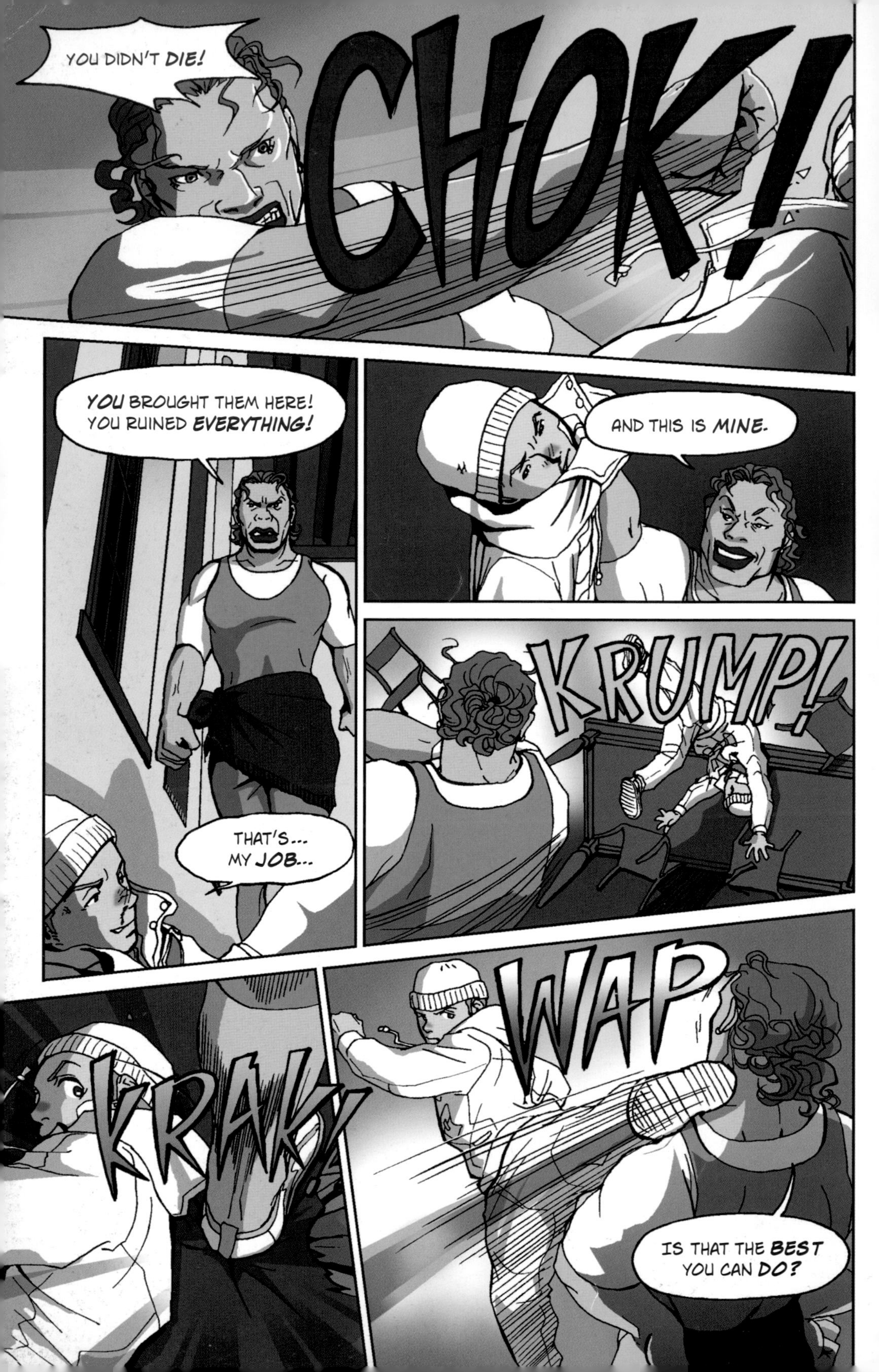
YOU DIDN'T DIE!
CHOK!
YOU BROUGHT THEM HERE! YOU RUINED EVERYTHING!
THAT'S... MY JOB...
AND THIS IS MINE.
KRUMP!
KRAK!
WAP
IS THAT THE BEST YOU CAN DO?

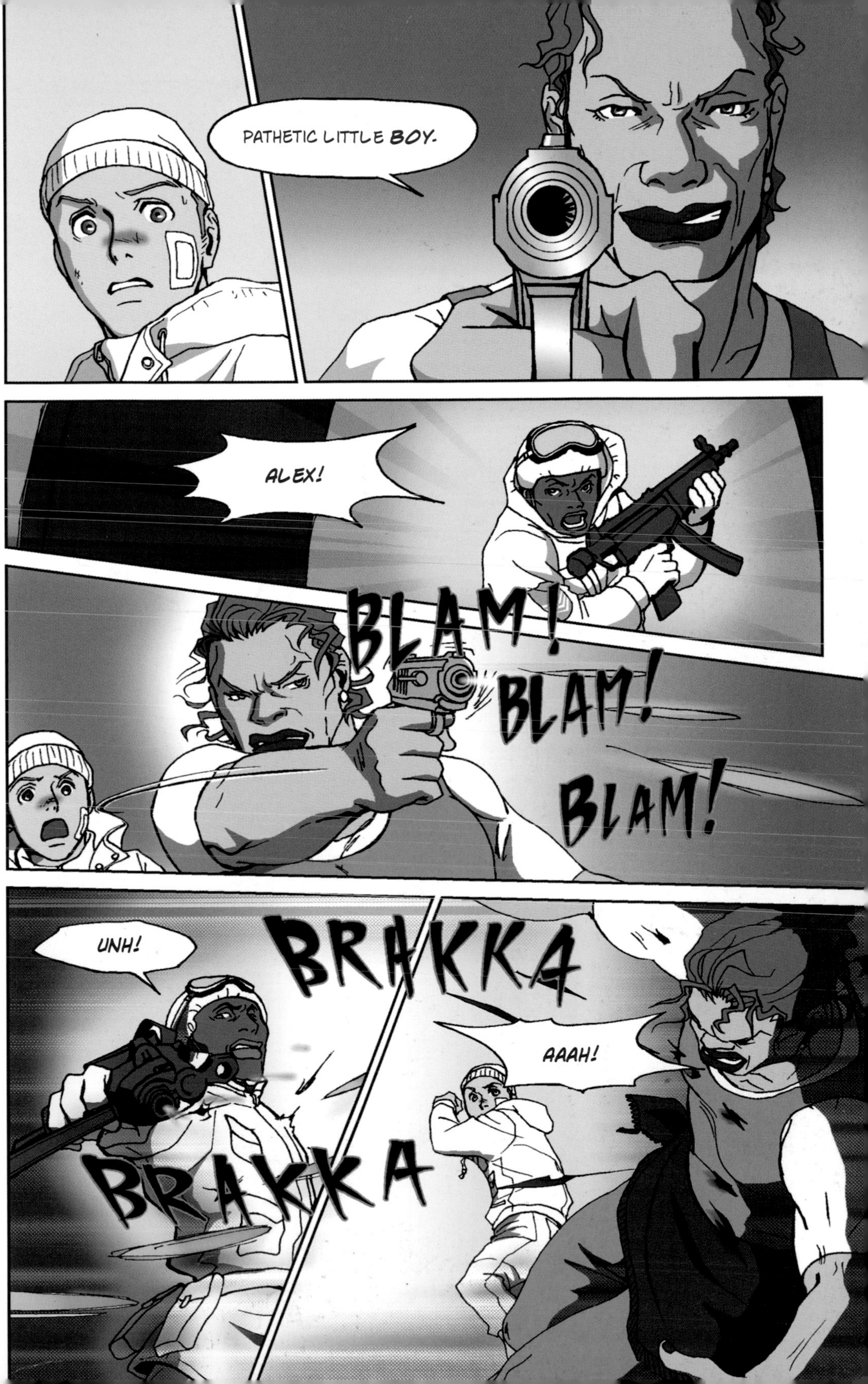
PATHETIC LITTLE BOY.
ALEX!
BLAM!
BLAM!
BLAM!
UNH!
BRAKKA
AAAH!
BRAKKA

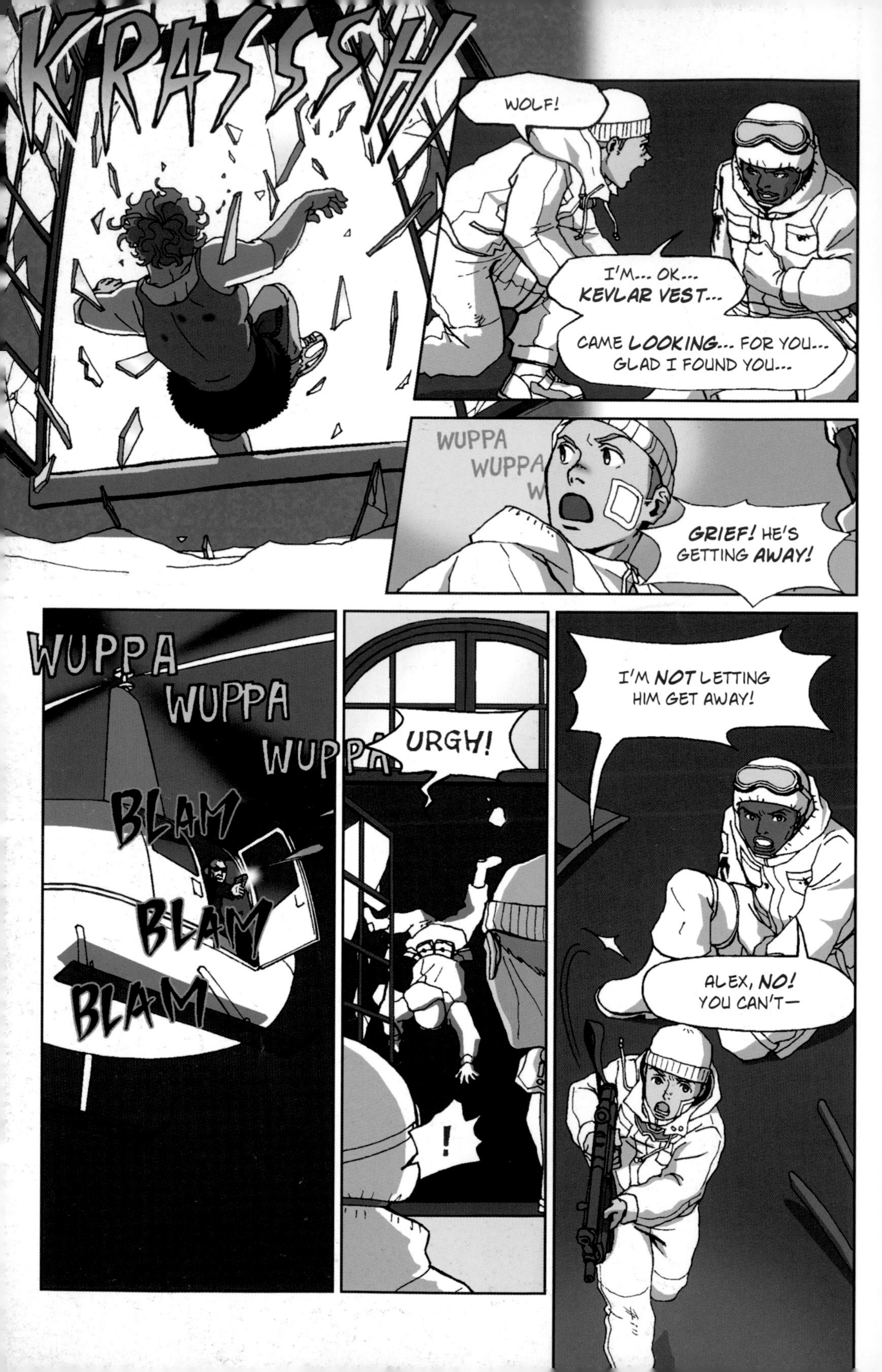
KRASSSH
WOLF!
I'M... OK... KEVLAR VEST...
CAME LOOKING... FOR YOU... GLAD I FOUND YOU...
WUPPA WUPPA
GRIEF! HE'S GETTING AWAY!
WUPPA WUPPA WUPPA
BLAM BLAM BLAM
URGH!
!
I'M NOT LETTING HIM GET AWAY!
ALEX, NO! YOU CAN'T—

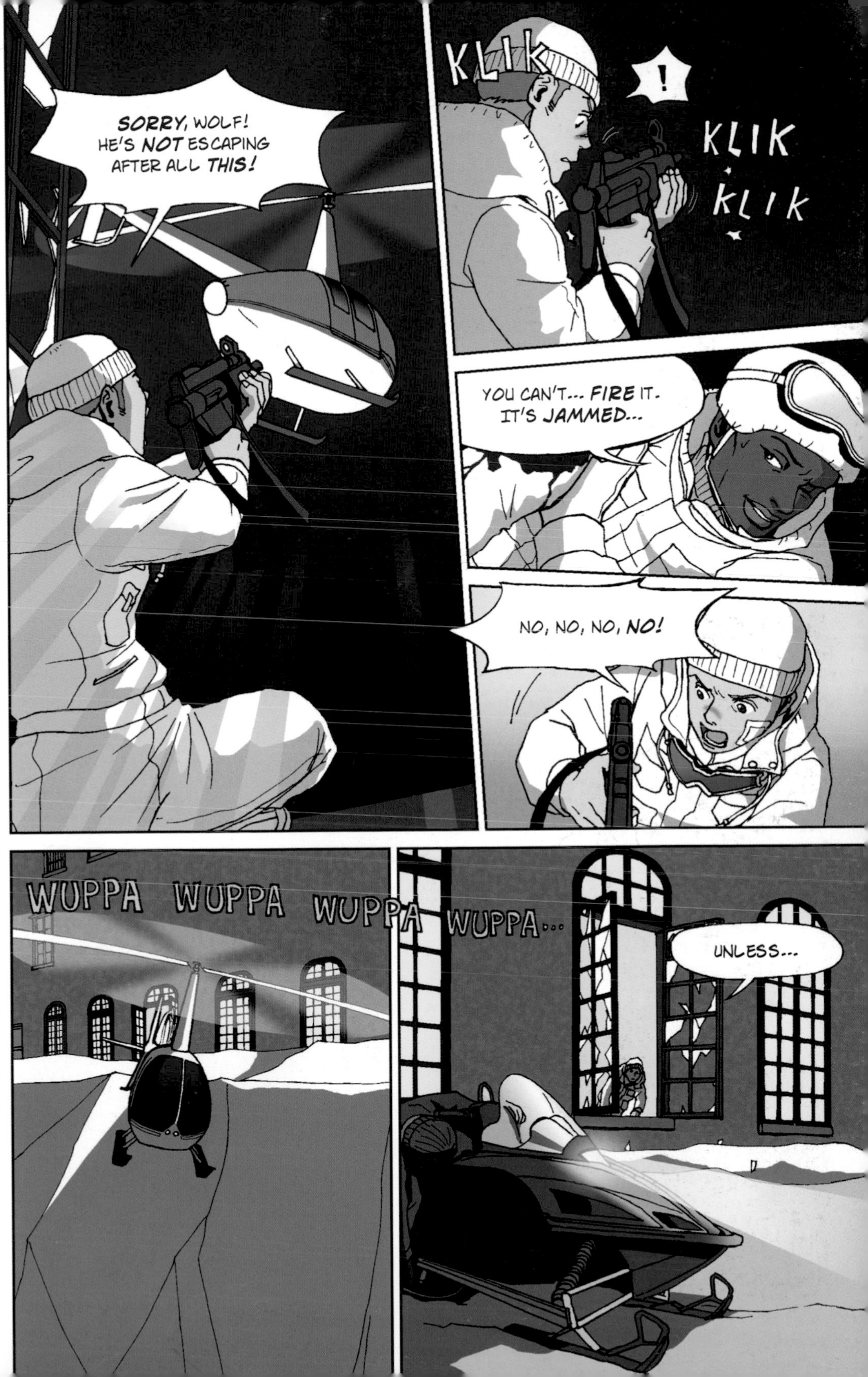
SORRY, WOLF! HE'S NOT ESCAPING AFTER ALL THIS!
KLIK
!
KLIK
KLIK
YOU CAN'T... FIRE IT. IT'S JAMMED...
NO, NO, NO, NO!
WUPPA WUPPA WUPPA WUPPA...
UNLESS...

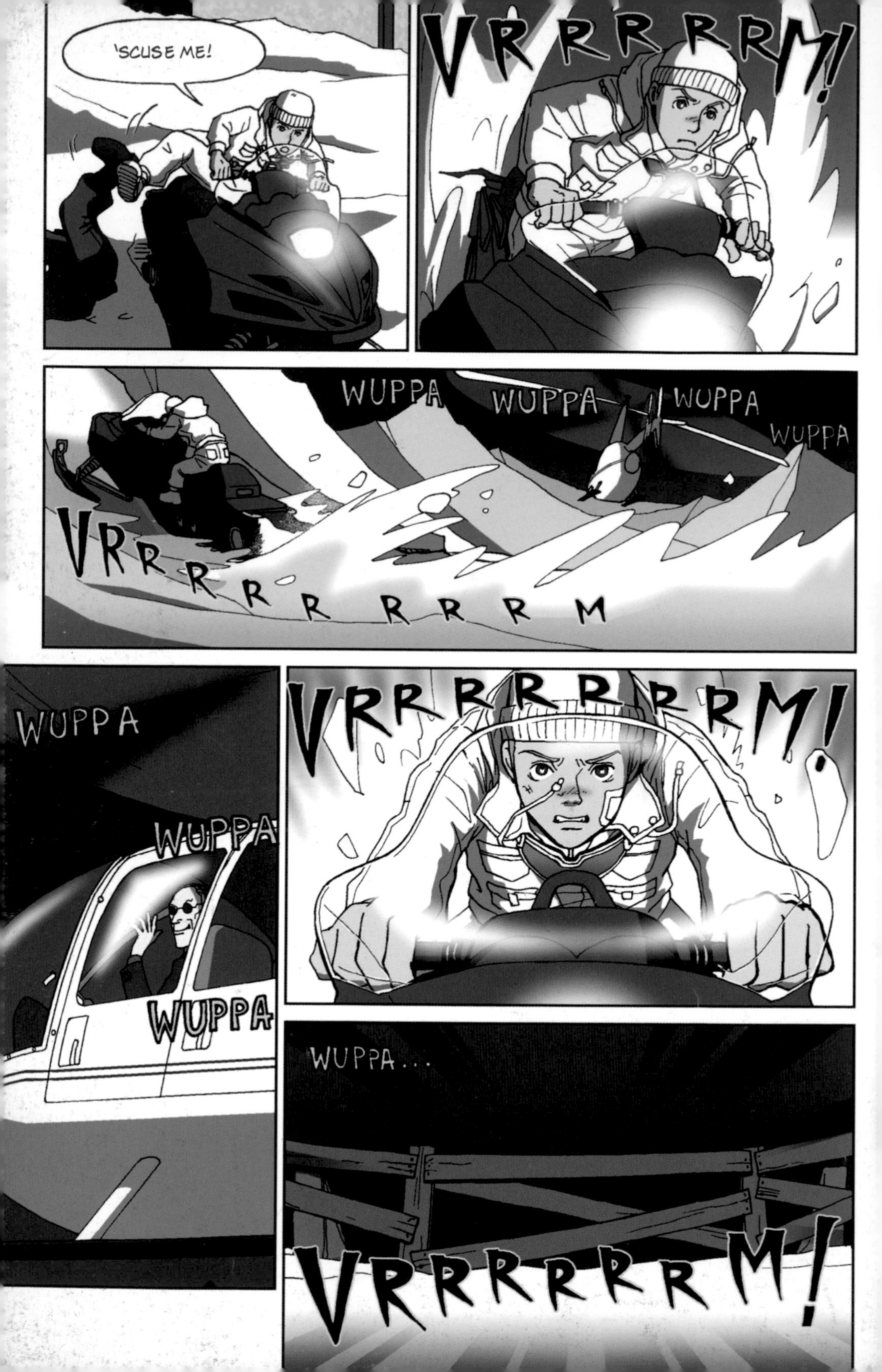
'SCUSE ME!
VRRRRRM!
WUPPA
WUPPA
WUPPA
WUPPA
VRRRRRRRRM
WUPPA
WUPPA
WUPPA
VRRRRRRRRM!
WUPPA...
VRRRRRRM!

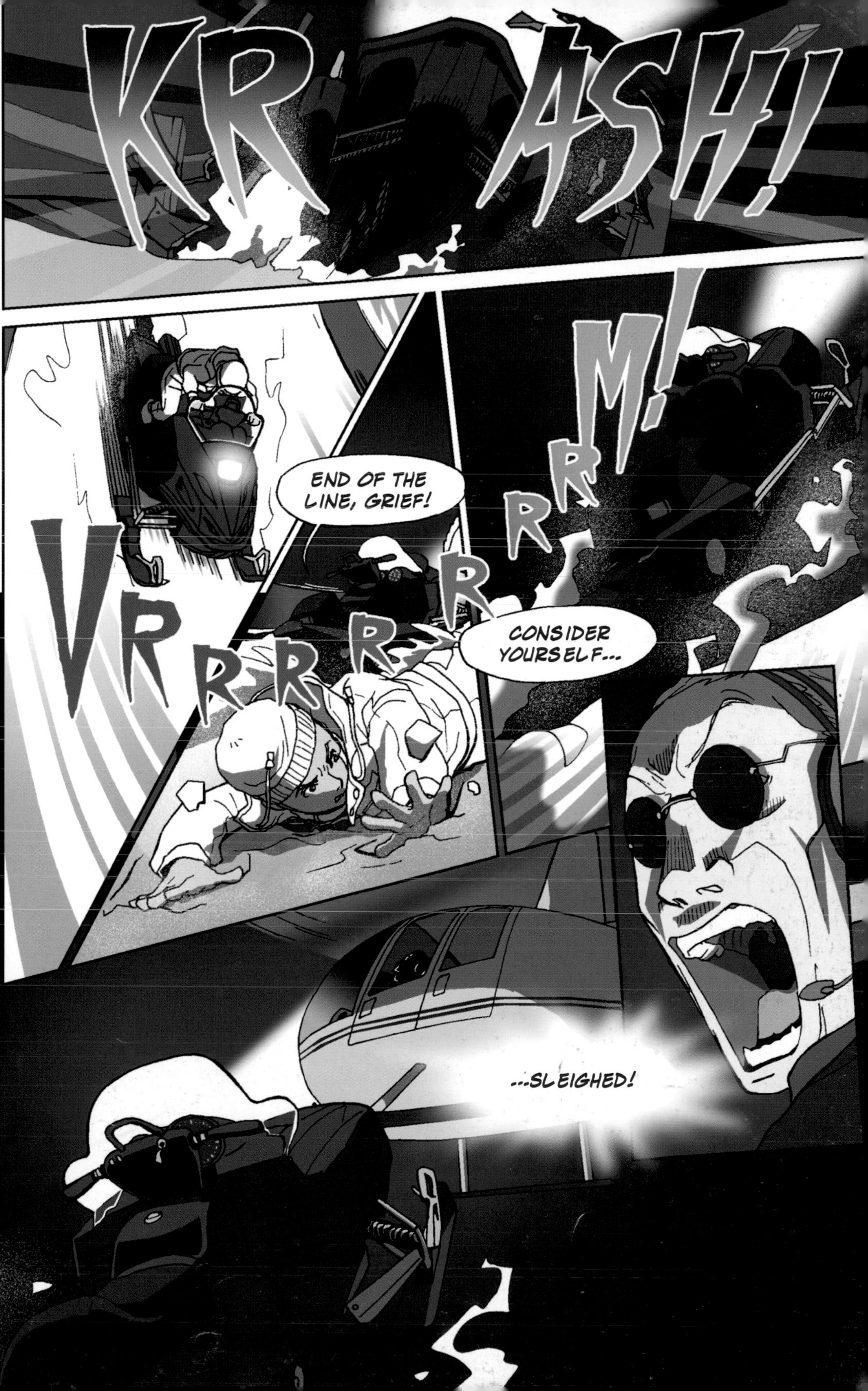
KRASH!
END OF THE LINE, GRIEF!
VRRRRRRRRM!
CONSIDER YOURSELF...
...SLEIGHED!

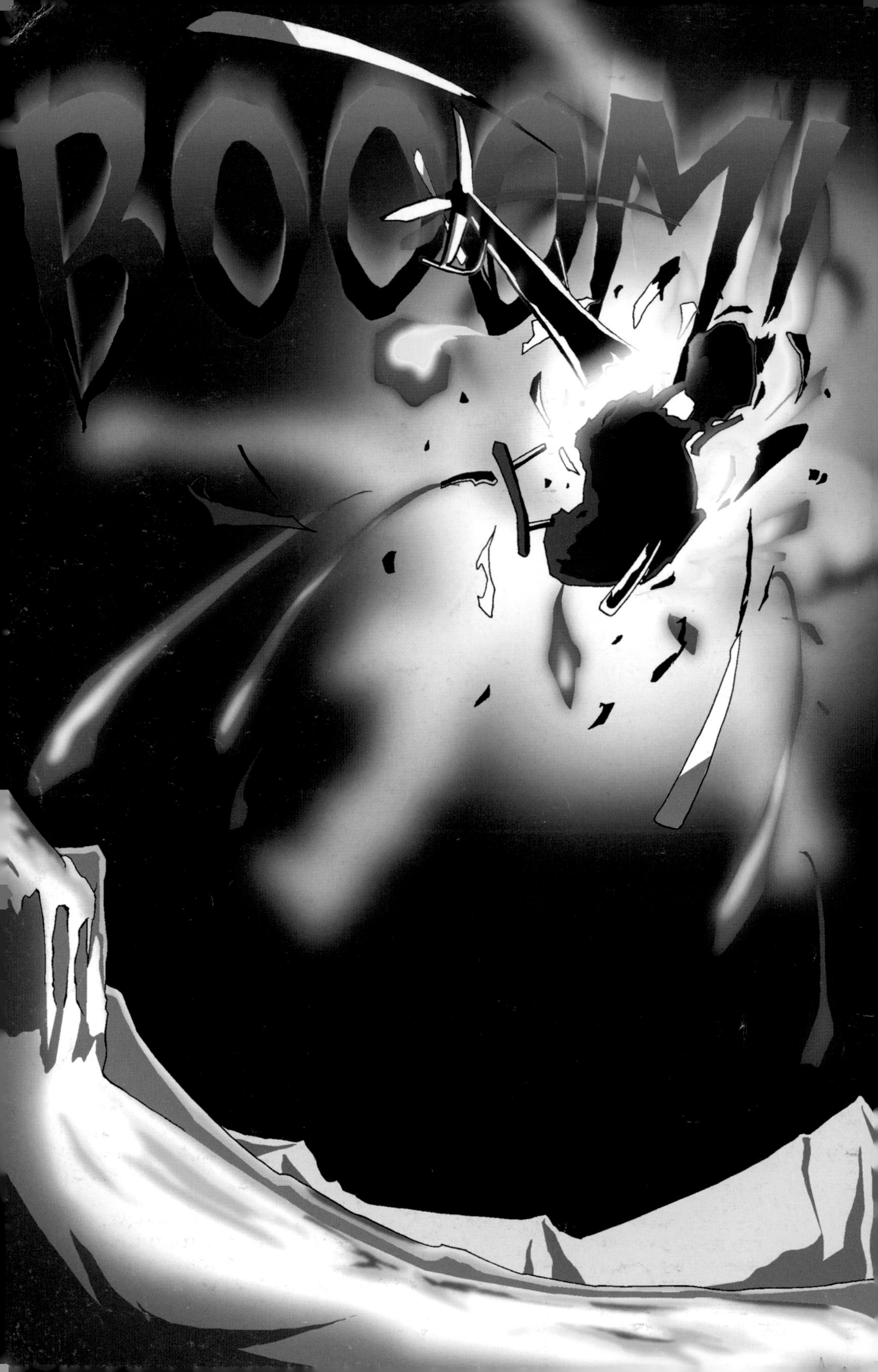
BOOOM!

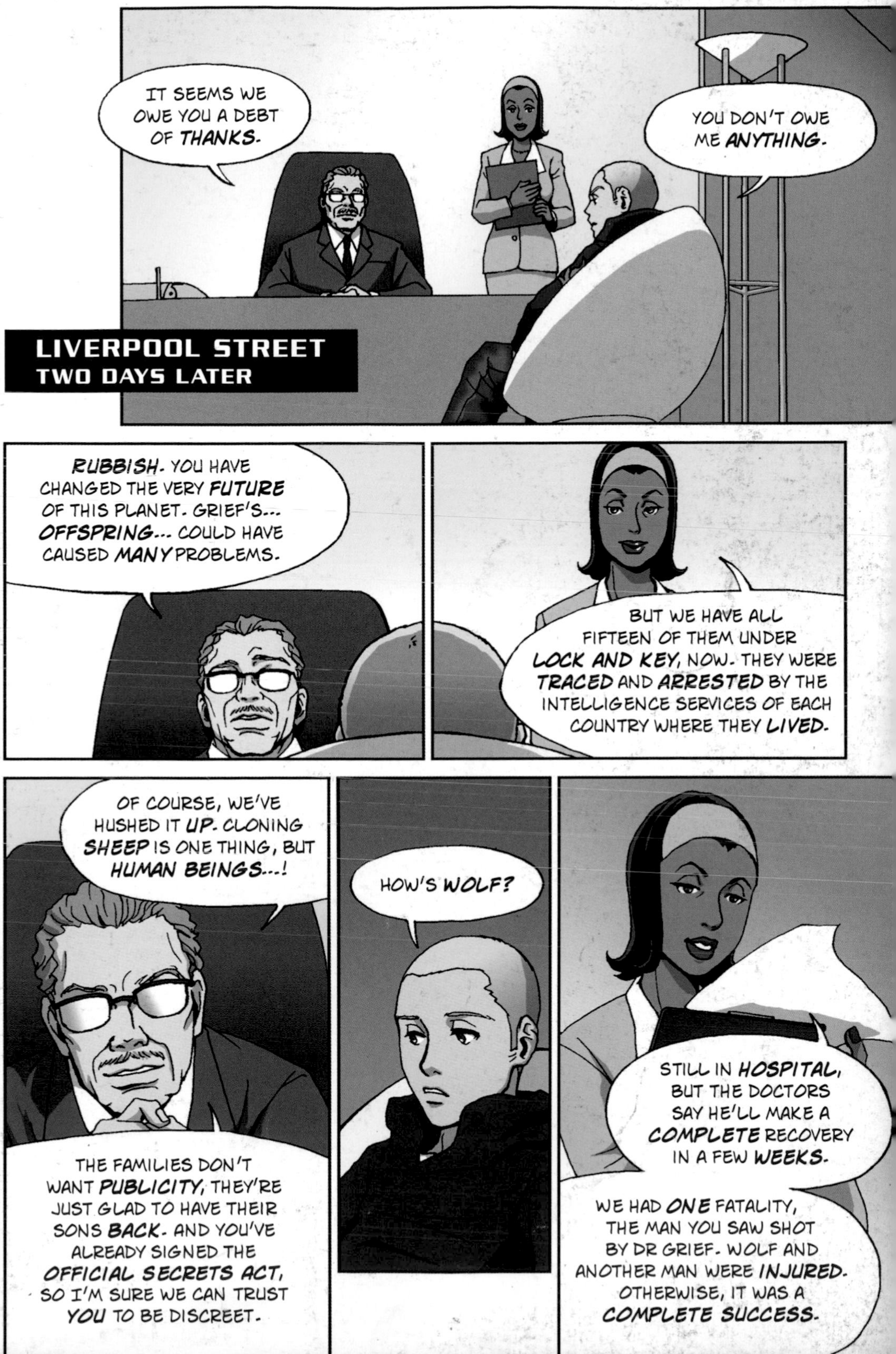
IT SEEMS WE OWE YOU A DEBT OF THANKS.
YOU DON'T OWE ME ANYTHING.
LIVERPOOL STREET
TWO DAYS LATER
RUBBISH. YOU HAVE CHANGED THE VERY FUTURE OF THIS PLANET. GRIEF'S... OFFSPRING... COULD HAVE CAUSED MANY PROBLEMS.
BUT WE HAVE ALL FIFTEEN OF THEM UNDER LOCK AND KEY, NOW. THEY WERE TRACED AND ARRESTED BY THE INTELLIGENCE SERVICES OF EACH COUNTRY WHERE THEY LIVED.
OF COURSE, WE'VE HUSHED IT UP. CLONING SHEEP IS ONE THING, BUT HUMAN BEINGS...!
THE FAMILIES DON'T WANT PUBLICITY, THEY'RE JUST GLAD TO HAVE THEIR SONS BACK. AND YOU'VE ALREADY SIGNED THE OFFICIAL SECRETS ACT, SO I'M SURE WE CAN TRUST YOU TO BE DISCREET.
HOW'S WOLF?
STILL IN HOSPITAL, BUT THE DOCTORS SAY HE'LL MAKE A COMPLETE RECOVERY IN A FEW WEEKS.
WE HAD ONE FATALITY, THE MAN YOU SAW SHOT BY DR GRIEF. WOLF AND ANOTHER MAN WERE INJURED. OTHERWISE, IT WAS A COMPLETE SUCCESS.

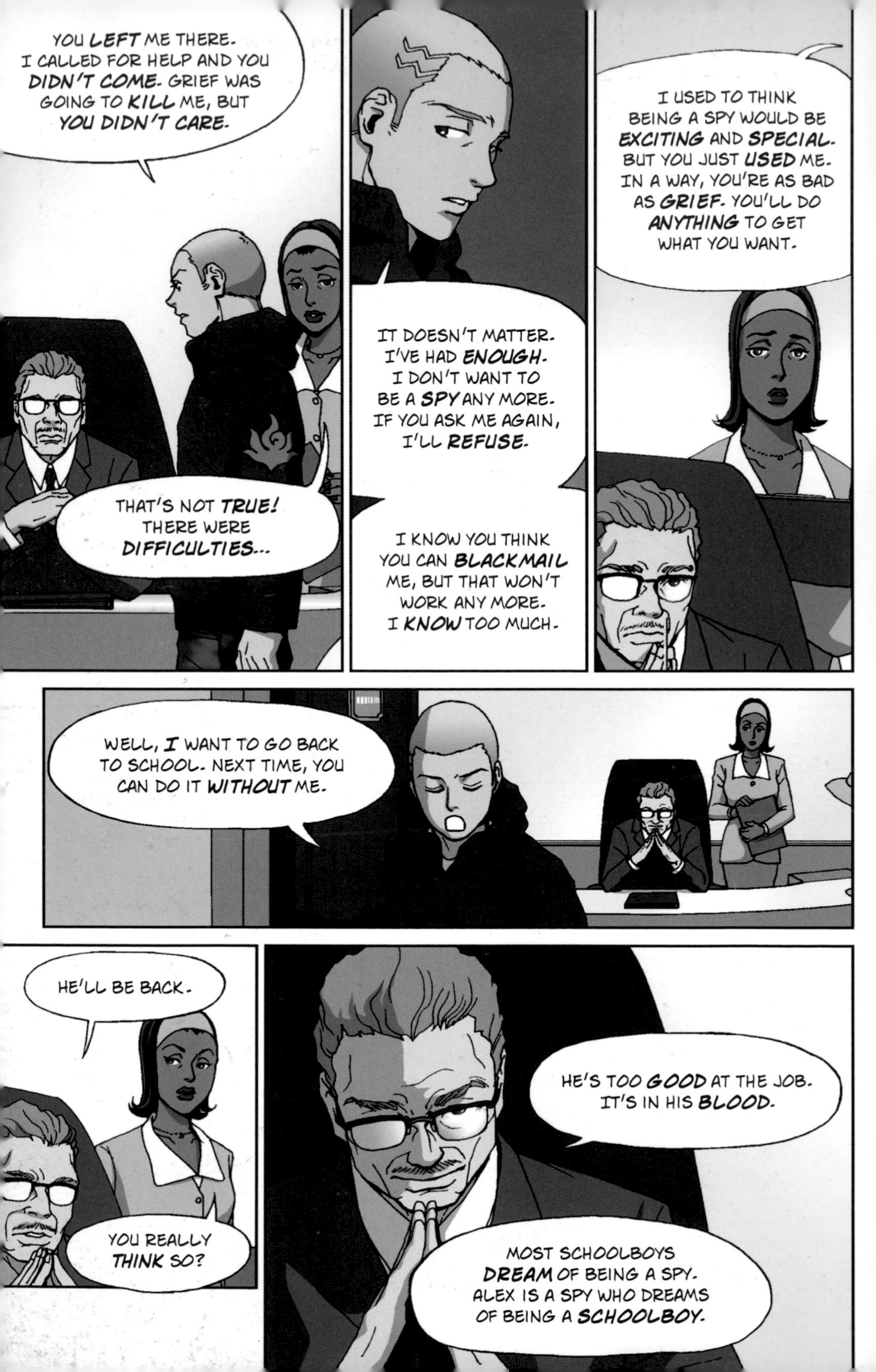
YOU LEFT ME THERE. I CALLED FOR HELP AND YOU DIDN'T COME. GRIEF WAS GOING TO KILL ME, BUT YOU DIDN'T CARE.
THAT'S NOT TRUE! THERE WERE DIFFICULTIES...
IT DOESN'T MATTER. I'VE HAD ENOUGH. I DON'T WANT TO BE A SPY ANY MORE. IF YOU ASK ME AGAIN, I'LL REFUSE.
I KNOW YOU THINK YOU CAN BLACKMAIL ME, BUT THAT WON'T WORK ANY MORE. I KNOW TOO MUCH.
I USED TO THINK BEING A SPY WOULD BE EXCITING AND SPECIAL. BUT YOU JUST USED ME. IN A WAY, YOU'RE AS BAD AS GRIEF. YOU'LL DO ANYTHING TO GET WHAT YOU WANT.
WELL, I WANT TO GO BACK TO SCHOOL. NEXT TIME, YOU CAN DO IT WITHOUT ME.
HE'LL BE BACK.
YOU REALLY THINK SO?
HE'S TOO GOOD AT THE JOB. IT'S IN HIS BLOOD.
MOST SCHOOLBOYS DREAM OF BEING A SPY. ALEX IS A SPY WHO DREAMS OF BEING A SCHOOLBOY.

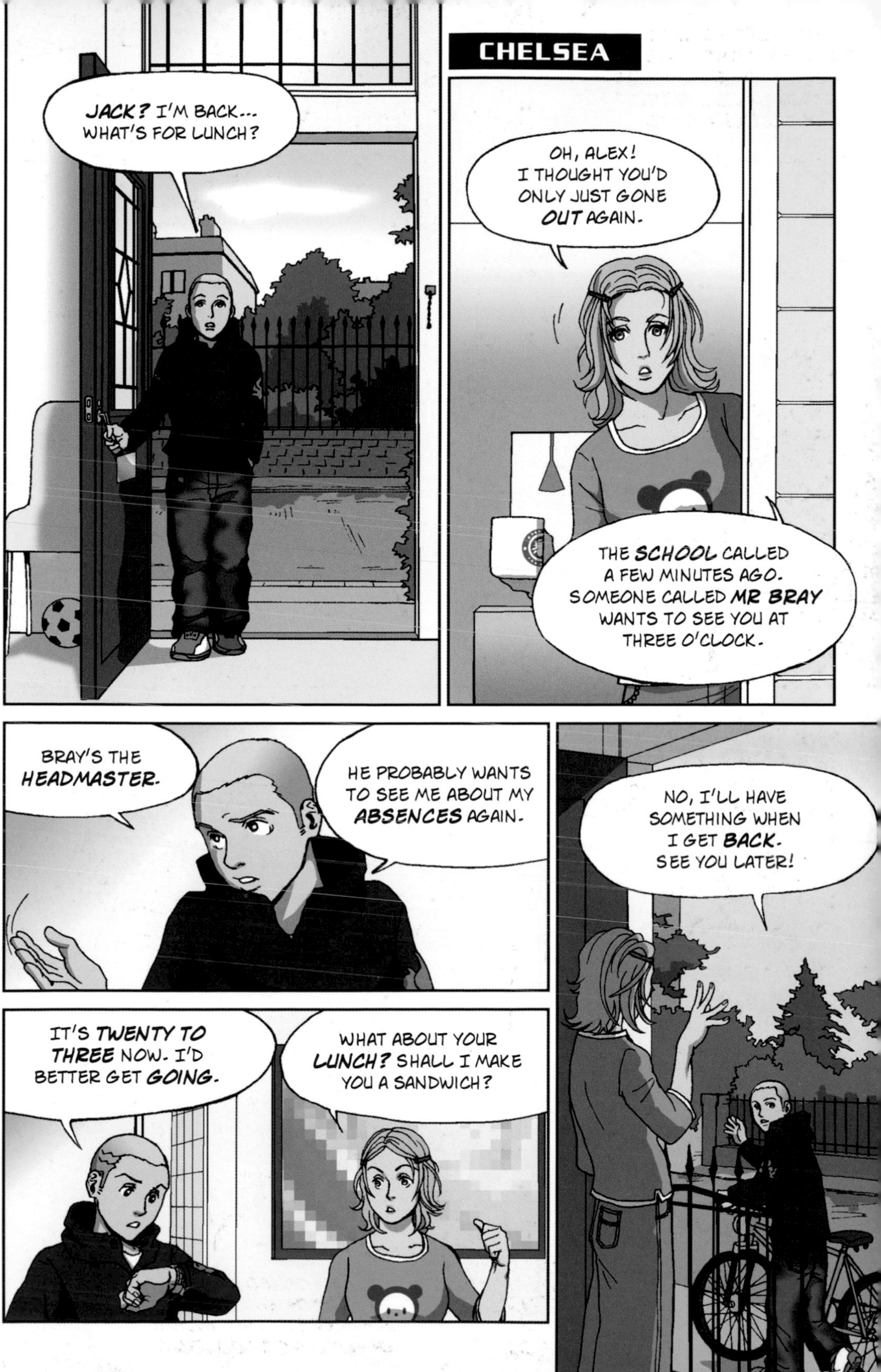
CHELSEA
JACK? I'M BACK... WHAT'S FOR LUNCH?
OH, ALEX! I THOUGHT YOU'D ONLY JUST GONE OUT AGAIN.
THE SCHOOL CALLED A FEW MINUTES AGO. SOMEONE CALLED MR BRAY WANTS TO SEE YOU AT THREE O'CLOCK.
BRAY'S THE HEADMASTER.
HE PROBABLY WANTS TO SEE ME ABOUT MY ABSENCES AGAIN.
IT'S TWENTY TO THREE NOW. I'D BETTER GET GOING.
WHAT ABOUT YOUR LUNCH? SHALL I MAKE YOU A SANDWICH?
NO, I'LL HAVE SOMETHING WHEN I GET BACK. SEE YOU LATER!

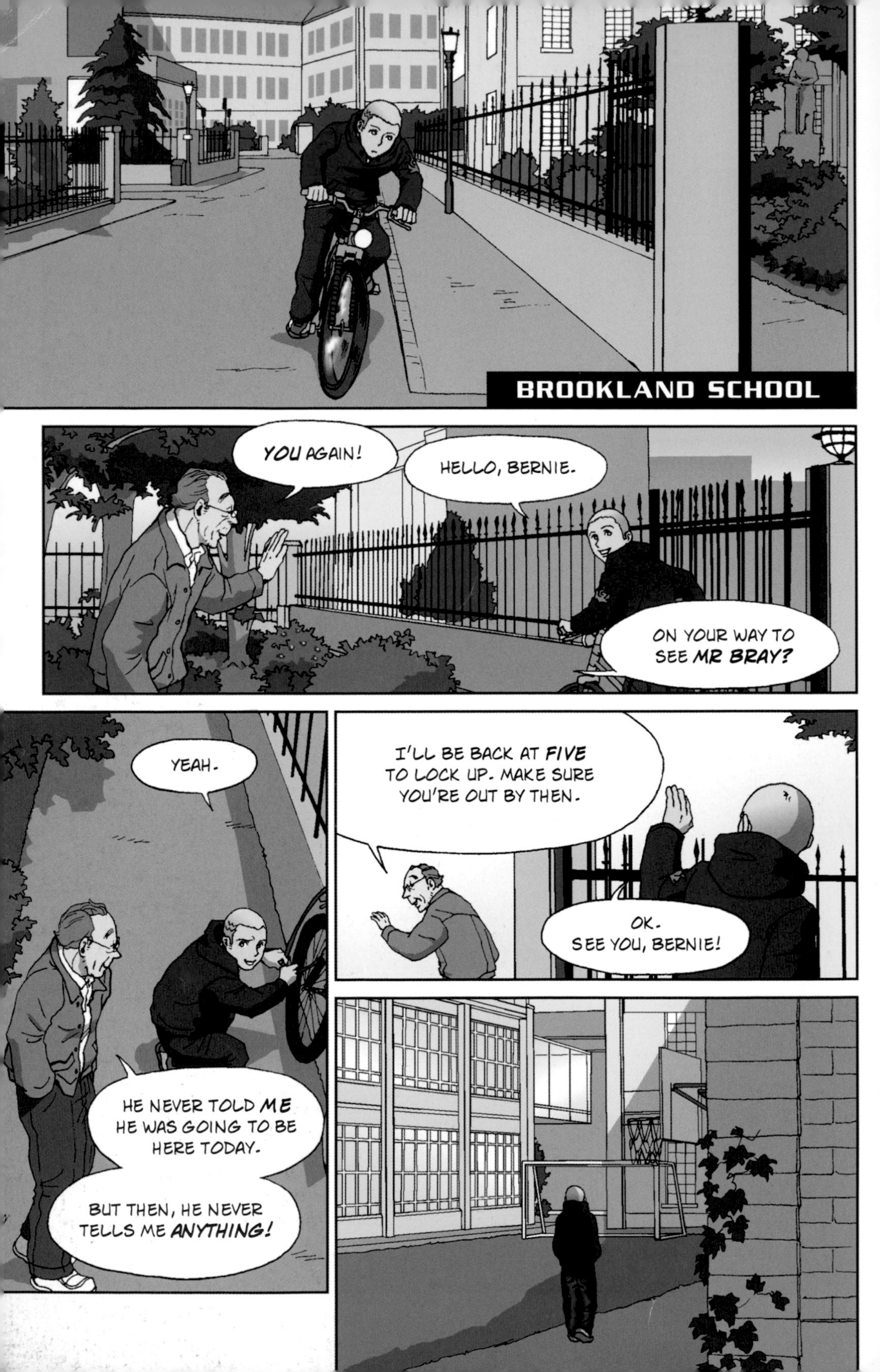
BROOKLAND SCHOOL
YOU AGAIN!
HELLO, BERNIE.
ON YOUR WAY TO SEE MR BRAY?
YEAH.
HE NEVER TOLD ME HE WAS GOING TO BE HERE TODAY.
BUT THEN, HE NEVER TELLS ME ANYTHING!
I'LL BE BACK AT FIVE TO LOCK UP. MAKE SURE YOU'RE OUT BY THEN.
OK. SEE YOU, BERNIE!

SCIENCE
BLOCK

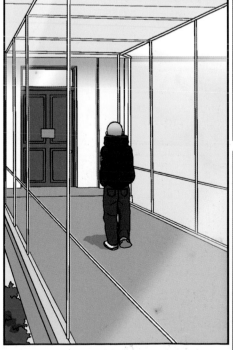

Mr. Bray
Headmaster

KNOCK KNOCK

COME IN!

YOU WANTED
TO SEE ME?

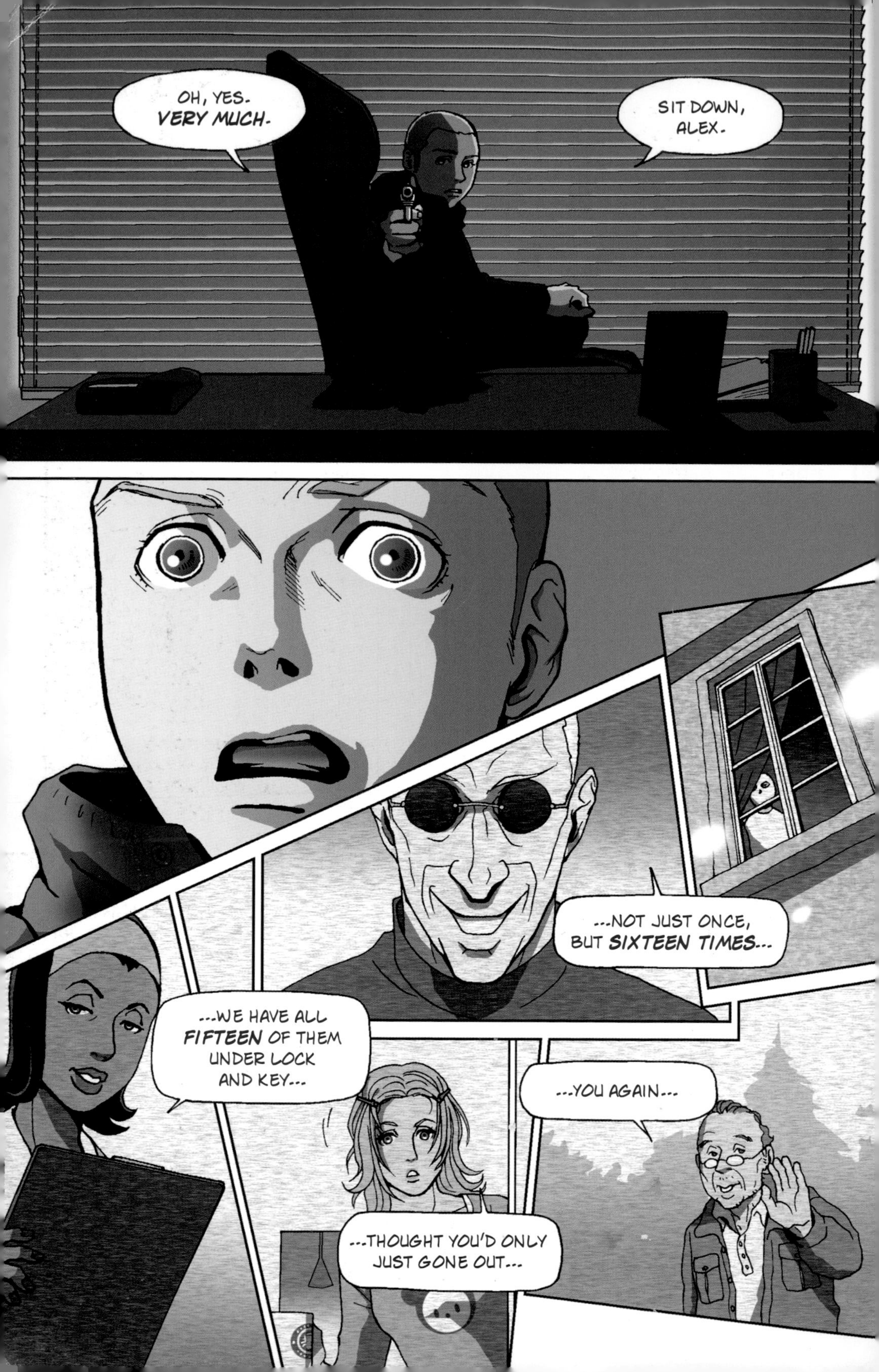
OH, YES. VERY MUCH.
SIT DOWN, ALEX.
...NOT JUST ONCE, BUT SIXTEEN TIMES...
...WE HAVE ALL FIFTEEN OF THEM UNDER LOCK AND KEY...
...YOU AGAIN...
...THOUGHT YOU'D ONLY JUST GONE OUT...

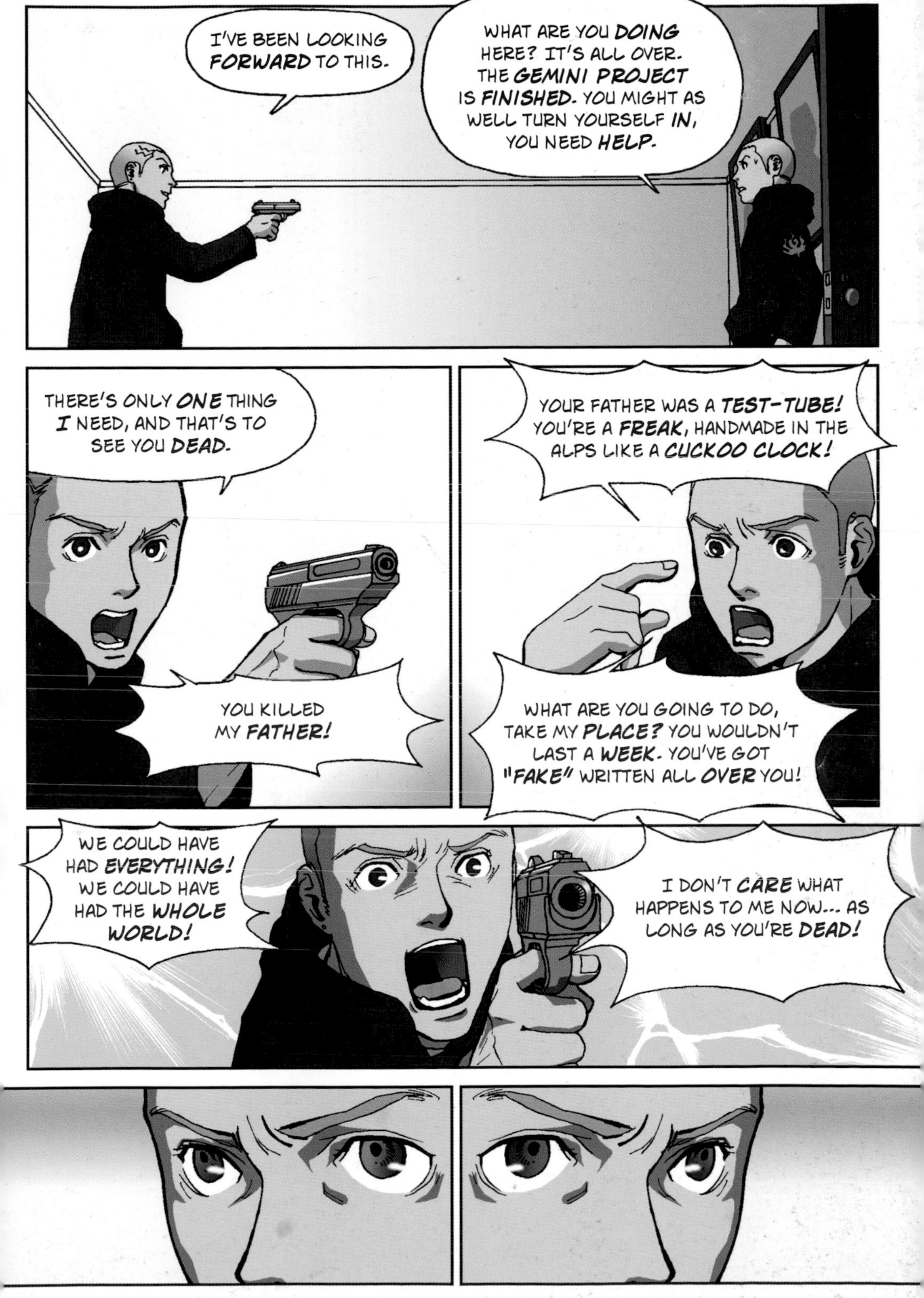
I'VE BEEN LOOKING FORWARD TO THIS.
WHAT ARE YOU DOING HERE? IT'S ALL OVER. THE GEMINI PROJECT IS FINISHED. YOU MIGHT AS WELL TURN YOURSELF IN, YOU NEED HELP.
THERE'S ONLY ONE THING I NEED, AND THAT'S TO SEE YOU DEAD.
YOU KILLED MY FATHER!
YOUR FATHER WAS A TEST-TUBE! YOU'RE A FREAK, HANDMADE IN THE ALPS LIKE A CUCKOO CLOCK!
WHAT ARE YOU GOING TO DO, TAKE MY PLACE? YOU WOULDN'T LAST A WEEK. YOU'VE GOT "FAKE" WRITTEN ALL OVER YOU!
WE COULD HAVE HAD EVERYTHING! WE COULD HAVE HAD THE WHOLE WORLD!
I DON'T CARE WHAT HAPPENS TO ME NOW... AS LONG AS YOU'RE DEAD!

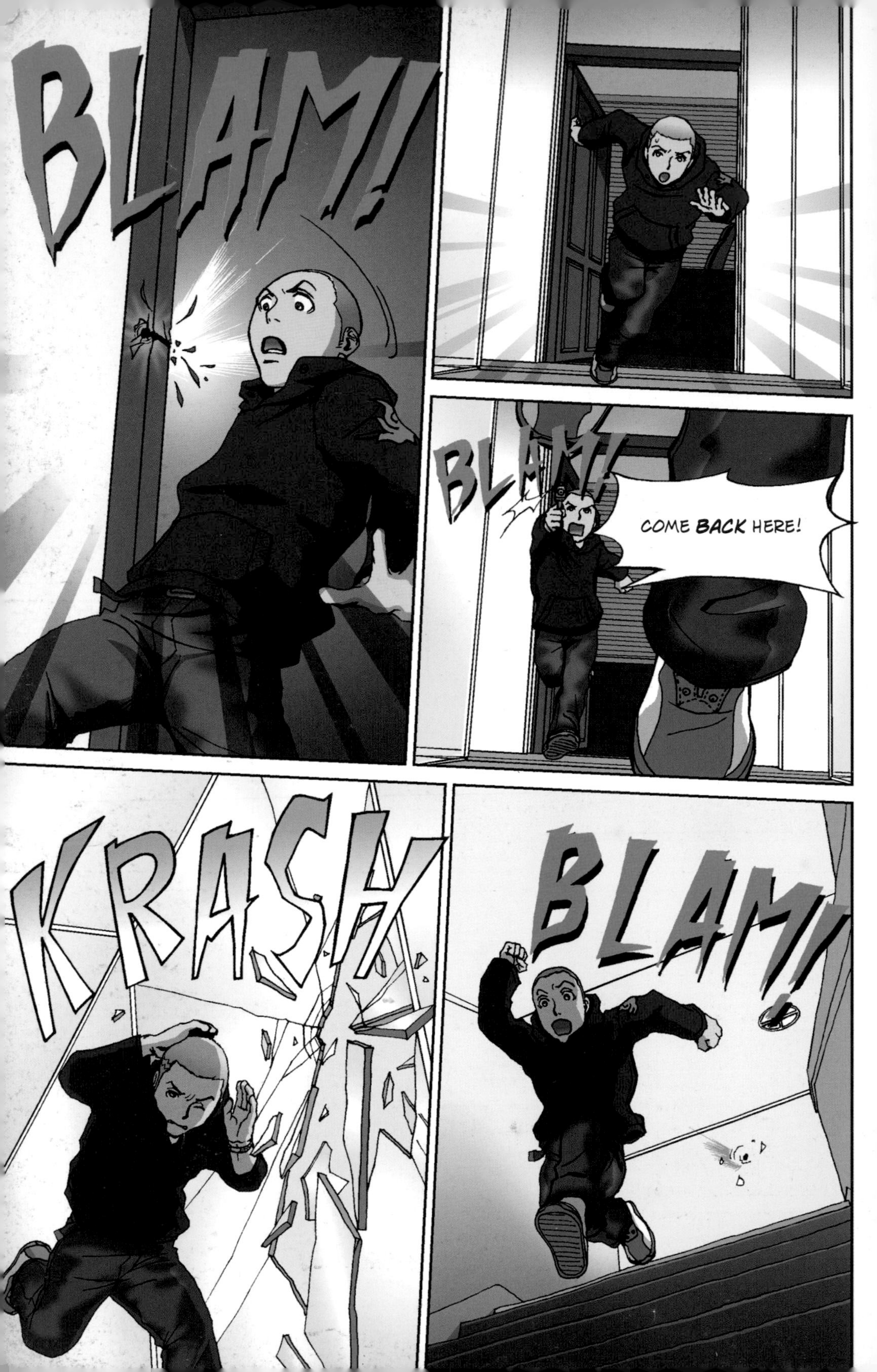
BLAM!
BLAM!
COME BACK HERE!
KRASH
BLAM!

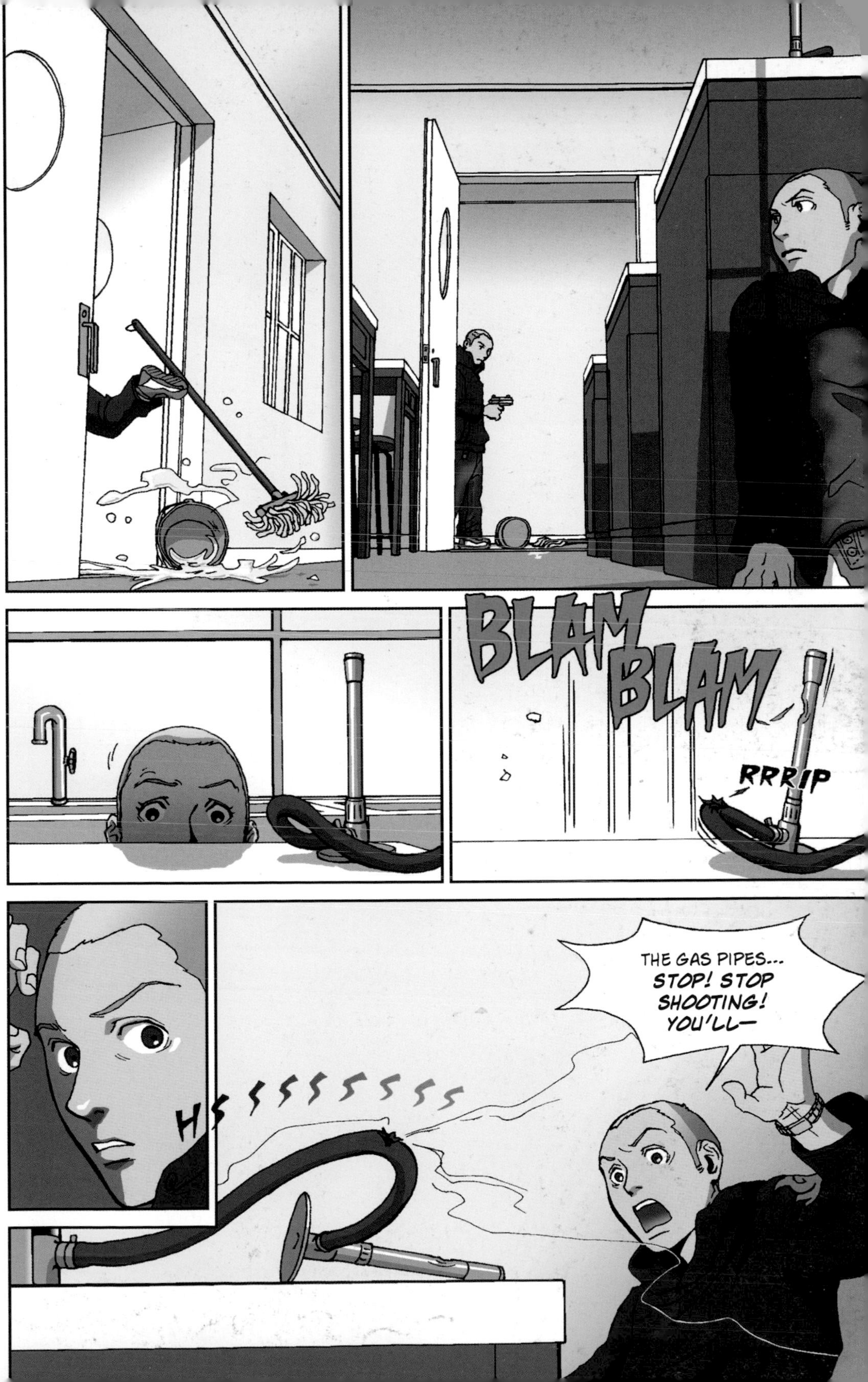
BLAM
BLAM
RRRIP
HSSSSSSSS
THE GAS PIPES...
STOP! STOP
SHOOTING!
YOU'LL—

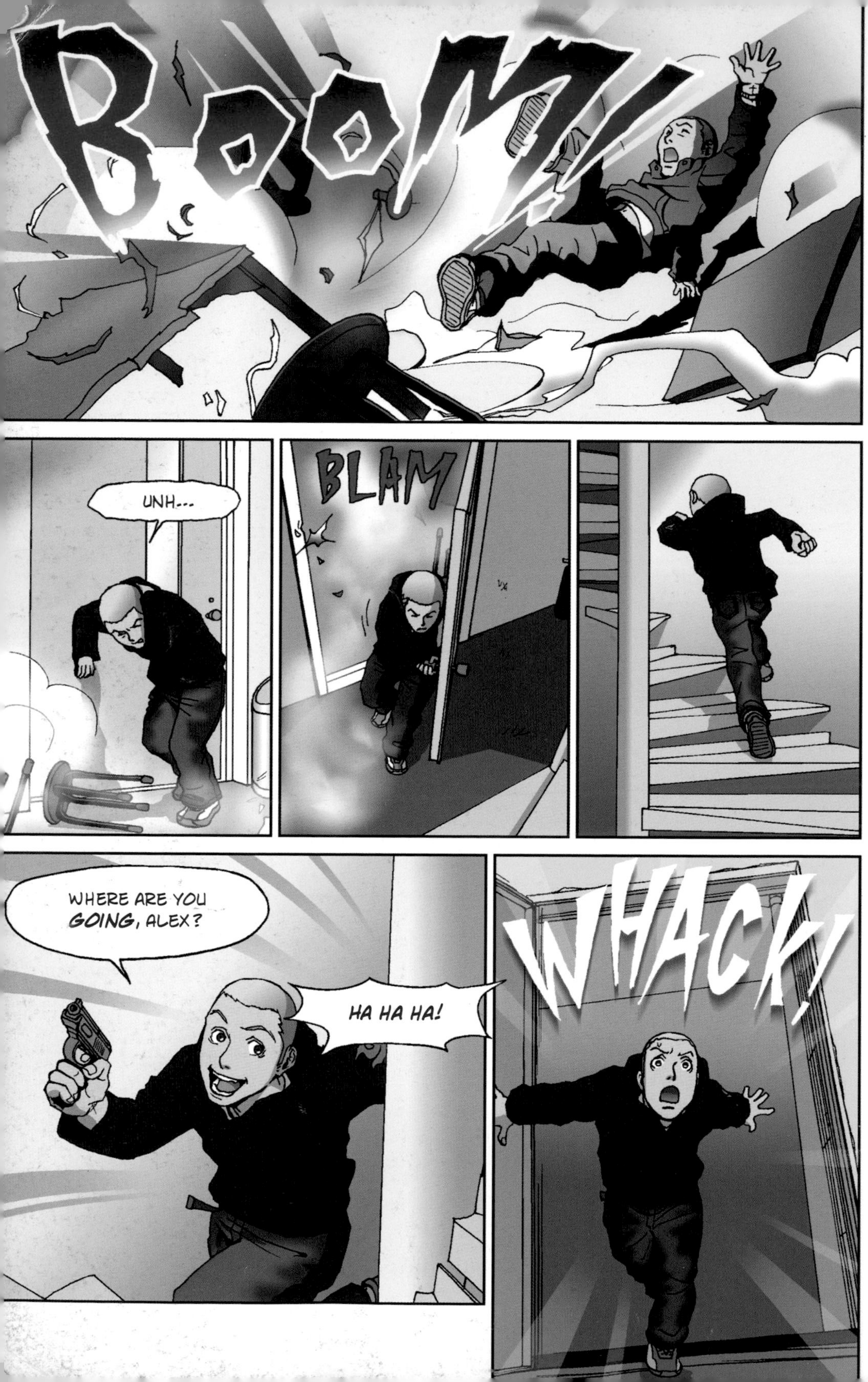
BOOM!
UNH...
BLAM
WHERE ARE YOU GOING, ALEX?
HA HA HA!
WHACK!

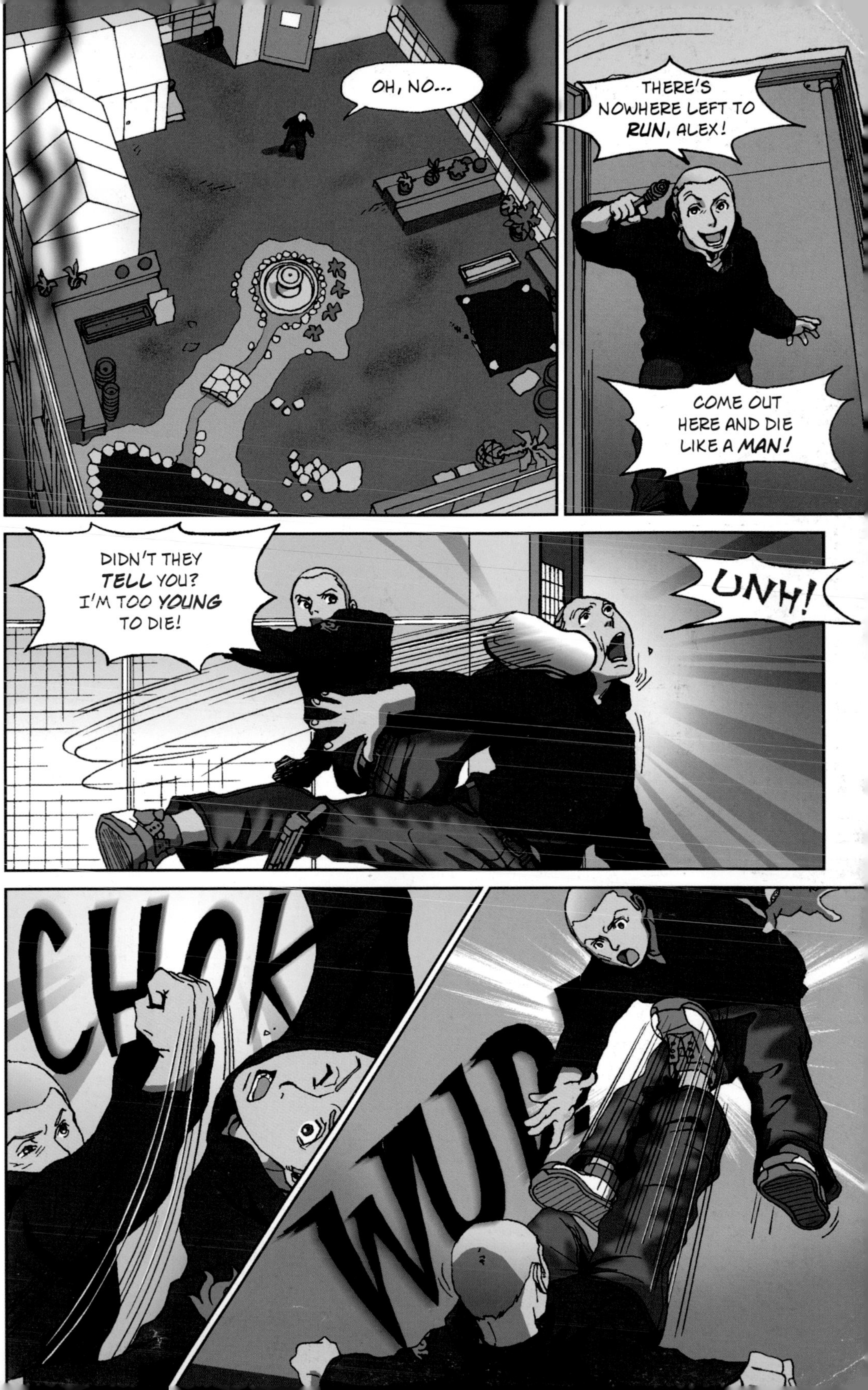
OH, NO...
THERE'S NOWHERE LEFT TO RUN, ALEX!
COME OUT HERE AND DIE LIKE A MAN!
DIDN'T THEY TELL YOU? I'M TOO YOUNG TO DIE!
UNH!
CHOK

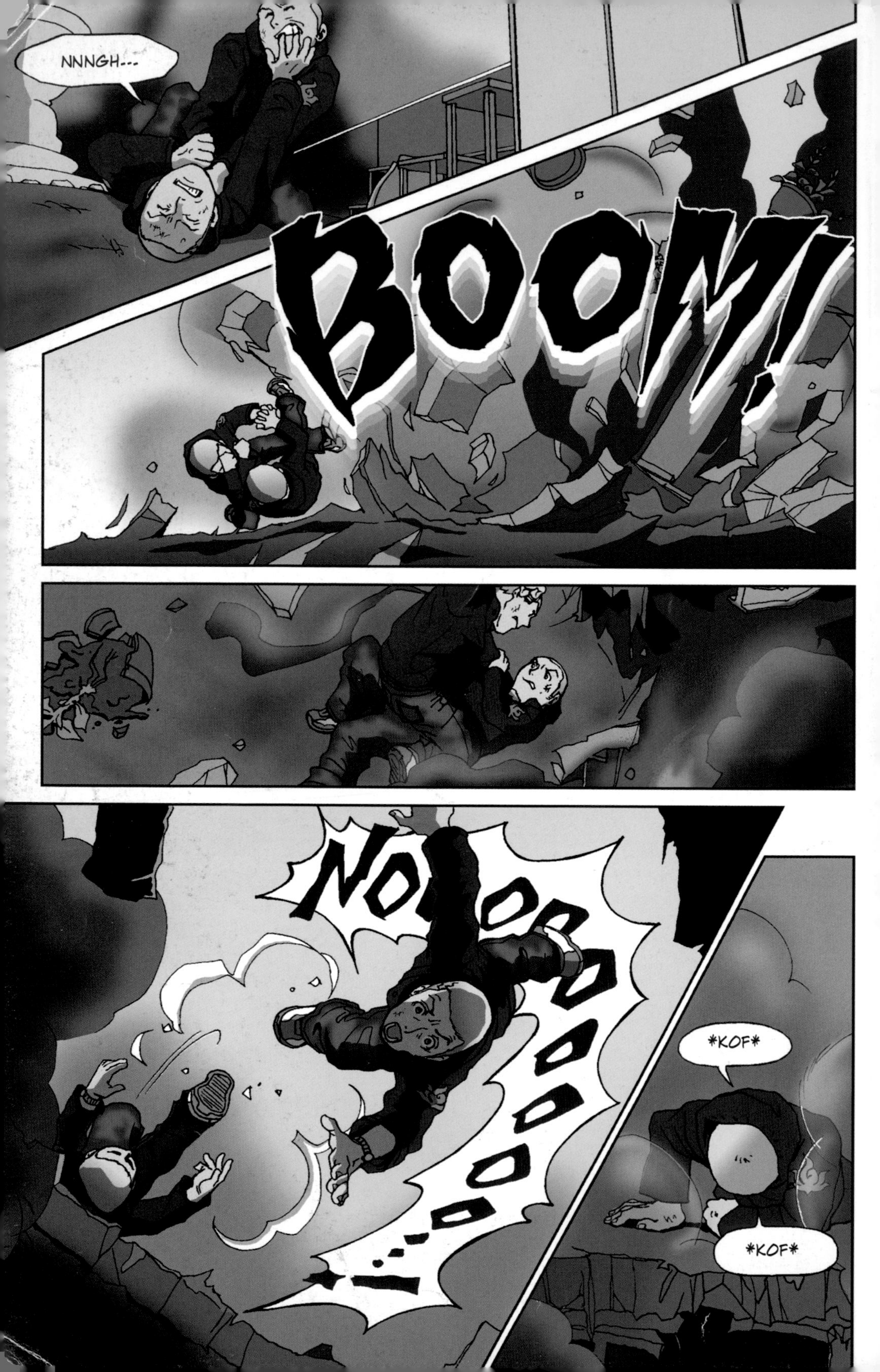
NNNGH...
BOOM!
NOOOOOOOOOOO...!
KOF
KOF

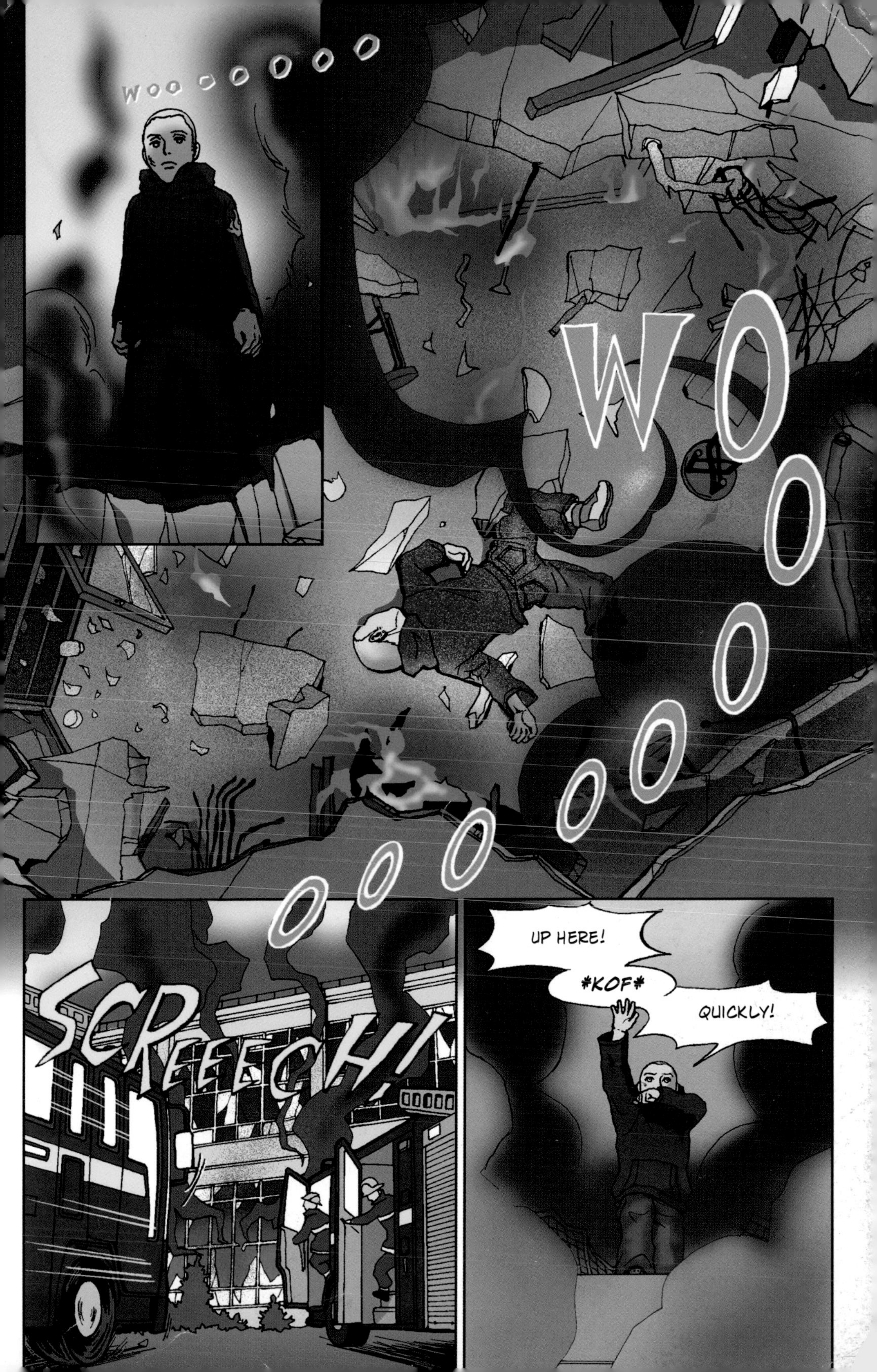
WOOOOOOOO
WOOOOOOOOOO
SCREEECH!
UP HERE!
KOF
QUICKLY!

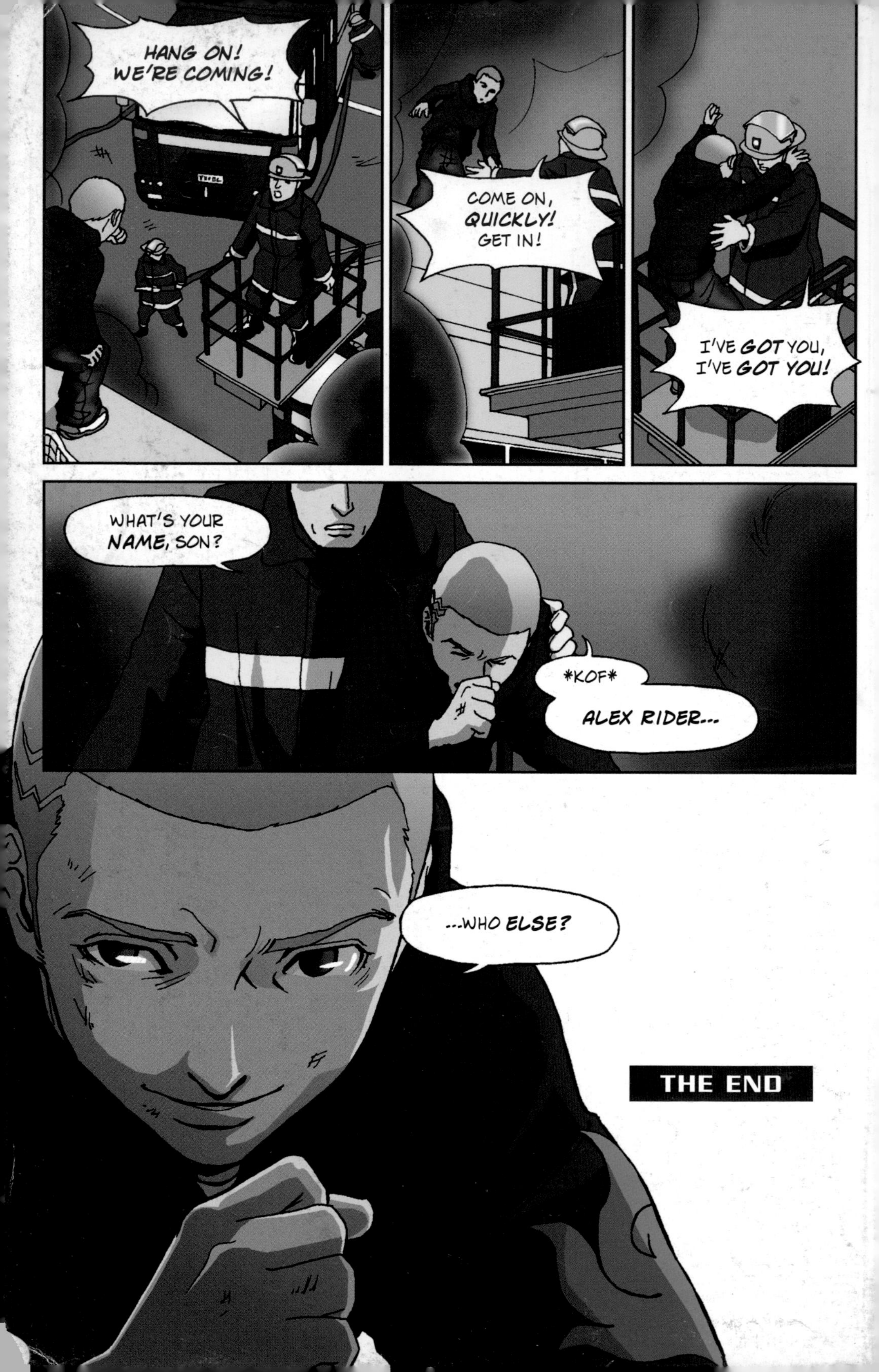
HANG ON! WE'RE COMING!
COME ON, QUICKLY! GET IN!
I'VE GOT YOU, I'VE GOT YOU!
WHAT'S YOUR NAME, SON?
KOF
ALEX RIDER...
...WHO ELSE?
THE END